ADVANCE PRAISE FOR

THE STOLEN LADY

"Like the masterpiece she writes about, Laura Morelli has created a work of art that is impossible to forget. *The Stolen Lady* is a wonderful homage to both art and the women in history who made art possible but whose stories have been forgotten. **A truly sublime novel."** —NATASHA LESTER, *New York Times* bestselling author of *The Paris Secret*

"A fascinating glimpse into the history and mystery behind the woman painted in the most iconic portrait to date—*Mona Lisa*—and the harrowing lengths to which the staff of the Louvre went to keep her out of Nazi hands during World War II." —ELIZA KNIGHT, *USA Today* bestselling author of the forthcoming *The Mayfair Bookshop*

"*The Stolen Lady* is **a beautifully written, must-read story** of the incredible journey of the *Mona Lisa* set amid two turbulent times in history. Laura Morelli offers a well-researched and richly told tale that captivated my attention from the first page." —MADELINE MARTIN, *New York Times* bestselling author of *The Last Bookshop in London*

"An unforgettable, page-turning tale of art history. With **exquisite historical details, surprising plot twists, and unforgettable characters who commit extraordinary acts of bravery** to create and protect art, *The Stolen Lady* entertains while giving readers a whole new perspective on the world's most famous painting." —STEPHANIE STOREY, bestselling author of *Oil and Marble* and *Raphael, Painter in Rome*

"Laura Morelli is second to none in her attention to detail in the realm of art history. I promise you that you'll never look at the *Mona Lisa* the same way again after reading this novel!" —ALYSSA PALOMBO, author of *The Most Beautiful Woman in Florence*

More Advance Praise for
The Stolen Lady

"A novel that has as many layers as a beautiful Renaissance paint-ing and is as enthralling. From sixteenth-century Florence in the grasp of perilous dynastic and artistic rivalries to World War II France where a handful of intrepid employees scramble to keep the Louvre's masterpieces out of Nazi hands, *The Stolen Lady* takes readers on a vicarious journey centered on art and courage, and how each can inspire the other. It's a lesson as timeless as *Mona Lisa*'s mysterious smile."

—Sophie Perinot, author of *Médicis Daughter*

"Two women, separated by centuries of time, struggle against ris-ing danger to protect not only treasures but secrets. The pace is cracking, the characters are intriguing, and the plot that con-nects them is clever. *The Stolen Lady* is a welcome addition to the historical fiction arena and a special delight for readers who love novels based on art history."

—Libbie Grant, author of *The Prophet's Wife*

"Morelli writes with a natural grace and love for the history of art that pulls readers into the spell of the painting's creation, the enigmatic woman who became Leonardo's most famous sub-ject, and the dangers that nearly destroyed her portrait. Moving seamlessly between Renaissance Italy and World War II France, this deeply researched, suspenseful, and breathtakingly romantic novel pulled me in from the first sentence and did not let me go until the last. Readers, clear your calendars—once you start reading, you won't be able to do anything else until you're done!"

—Melodie Winawer, author of *The Scribe of Siena* and *Anticipation*

"Laura Morelli paints another masterpiece with her gripping, powerful, and beautifully written tale of the most famous painting in the world. This is a page-turner of a book, whether you are savoring the origins of Da Vinci's *Mona Lisa* or cheering the heroic actions of the Louvre workers trying to prevent its theft by the Nazis in World War II. *The Stolen Lady* is a truly exceptional read."

—Crystal King, author of *The Chef's Secret*

"I was transported. Morelli perfectly ties the centuries together with the story of a work of art that lives on past the artist and his subject. You'll never look at the *Mona Lisa* the same way. A stunning accomplishment!"

—Jennifer Anton, author of *Under the Light of the Italian Moon*

THE
STOLEN
LADY

THE
STOLEN
LADY

*A Novel of World War II and
the Mona Lisa*

LAURA
MORELLI

WILLIAM MORROW

An Imprint of HarperCollinsPublishers

P.S.™ is a trademark of HarperCollins Publishers.

THE STOLEN LADY. Copyright © 2021 by Laura Morelli. All rights reserved. Printed in the United States of America. No part of this book may be used or reproduced in any manner whatsoever without written permission except in the case of brief quotations embodied in critical articles and reviews. For information, address HarperCollins Publishers, 195 Broadway, New York, NY 10007.

HarperCollins books may be purchased for educational, business, or sales promotional use. For information, please email the Special Markets Department at SPsales@harpercollins.com.

FIRST EDITION

Designed by Diahann Sturge

Mona Lisa portrait © agcreativelab/AdobeStock.com
Louvre image © 4kclips/Shutterstock, Inc.

Library of Congress Cataloging-in-Publication Data has been applied for.

ISBN 978-0-06-299359-5

21 22 23 24 25   LSC   10 9 8 7 6 5 4 3 2 1

For the memory of Lisa

CONTENTS

THE
STOLEN
LADY

Part 1
HIDDEN

LEONARDO

Florence, Italy
1472

My master tells me I'm no good at finishing what I start. It's become a problem.

Through the high, narrow windows of Master Verrocchio's workshop, I watch the summer evening sky turn its tawny shade of gold. Inside, the air is stifling and heavy with dust. The other apprentices have cleaned their brushes and arranged the day's sketches into neat stacks before leaving for the taverns, their stomachs rumbling and their tunics stained with paint. Master and I are the only ones left. I feel his beady eyes on me as a single drop of sweat licks the small of my back.

In the silence, I watch the flecked glow brighten the dim corners of the workshop. Suddenly, a magical crepuscular light pours through the window, illuminating the crumbling stucco walls as if gilding them. The light streaks across our panel in progress. I hold my wet fox hair brush in midair and survey our work.

Many weeks ago, Master Verrocchio completed the figure of the Virgin Mary and the magnificent, winged archangel who has swooped down from the heavens to kneel before her with a lily in his hand. I focus on the distant background, where I've outlined trees, mountains, and valleys receding into the distance. My master relies on the same tempera pigments his grandfather used, but I have begun to mix oil into my colors. I squint and consider the slick, wet haze behind the figures. Master has made Our Lady's arm too long, her hair disarrayed. But I don't say this aloud.

The monks are waiting, my master has said; he's said it more times than I can count. They've been waiting patiently for this promised altarpiece. Months have turned into a year.

My father is waiting, too. He's waiting for me to make something of myself. As usual, I have fallen short.

From across the studio, I feel Master Verrocchio's gaze burn into my back. I pretend to study the delicate flowers in the foreground—I painted them months ago—and judge whether I should add another layer of varnish over this flourishing enclosed garden, the *hortus conclusus* that symbolizes Our Lady's purity.

This is the last time I finish a painting for Master Verrocchio. I am nearly twenty years old now. Old enough to establish a workshop of my own. Young enough for my life to stretch before me, full of chances for the contraptions in my sketchbooks to become real. Armored carriages. Portable trebuchets that collapse with the turn of a lever. A flying machine with wings like a bat's. Beyond this workshop, beyond painting, perhaps even beyond Florence, opportunities lie yet untapped.

Suddenly, Master Verrocchio approaches me in the same way as the archangel, swooping in like a great bird of prey. Commanding. Full of important news. Just like Our Lady, for a moment I grasp the collar of my tunic and recoil. I cannot meet his eyes, so I set my gaze instead on the beautiful, serene face of Our Lady and wait for his words.

But my master says nothing. For a moment, the two of us stare at the panel. Then he peers over my shoulder at my patch of wet paint and frowns. A reaction to my work or force of habit? I will never know.

Hmm. My master grunts finally, then turns away.

Yes. It's better if I leave Florence.

Surely there is more to life than painting portraits of beautiful ladies. But I do not say this aloud, either.

In the end, we are all hiding something.

ANNE

Paris, France
1939

In the end, we are all hiding something, Anne Guichard thought as she tucked herself into the shadows and peered into the Louvre's Salon Carré. Perhaps she wasn't supposed to see what the men were doing. All the same, she was curious.

The sun had set hours ago, but Anne remained along with most of the museum staff, working through the night in a hushed frenzy. She had been fetching a box of carbon paper for her ancient typewriter when she heard the clamor in the Louvre's gallery of Italian Renaissance masterpieces. She paused in the corridor to see what it was.

Normally Anne walked through the Louvre's vast maze of galleries and offices when they were filled with filtered sunlight. It was eerie, she thought, to make her way through the museum's corridors at night. Once-crowded galleries now stood dark and emptied of their contents. Lone Greek and Roman statues cast looming shadows across the vacant galleries. In others, harsh beams from portable lights made colorful paintings appear little more than shiny black rectangles as curators darted about with clipboards and small bags of chalk.

From across the gallery, Anne recognized the elegant silhouette of the museum director, Jacques Jaujard. He stood by, hands on his hips, as two painting curators lowered some kind of case inside a wooden crate. Anne didn't dare enter the room. She was a lowly archivist's assistant and had no business there.

In every gallery, workers were busy removing paintings from the walls. They were packing smaller ones into crates and loading them onto creaky wheeled carts. Larger canvases were being pried from their frames and rolled into long, slim cylinders. Whispering curators, archivists, and their assistants followed with lists of inventories. As paintings came down from the walls, the curators traced rectangles where they had once hung. With nubs of white chalk, they scrawled artists' names, painting titles, and inventory numbers in the blank spaces.

In the space of a few days, as they went about the business of inventorying, Anne had seen priceless Old Master paintings, large sculptures, even ancient Egyptian antiquities, packed up as if they were little more than old furniture to gather dust in a warehouse. Anne struggled to grasp the scale of the museum's efforts to move its vast collection from the galleries to a safer location, to keep it from the hands of German officers who would have the audacity to claim these masterpieces for their own.

Anne watched a curator paint three red dots on the outside of the wooden crate. Then, two museum guards loaded the newly marked crate onto a small cart. The group filed out of the gallery and Monsieur Jaujard followed. The cart rattled into the corridor with its loose, squeaky wheel, then faded into the distance. Hushed voices and echoing footsteps fell away, then the gallery returned to its dark silence.

Anne pushed away from her hiding spot in the crook of the corridor and stepped into the empty gallery. Light came from a single electric bulb in a metal cage at the end of a long extension cord. Anne's eyes adjusted to the harsh beam. She stepped forward to the modest rectangle that a curator had traced onto the wall. All at once, she realized what had hung there only minutes before.

The *Mona Lisa*. *La Joconde*.

She really should return to the archives. Her boss, Lucie Mazauric, might wonder why she was taking so long to retrieve the carbon paper. But instead, Anne stood frozen before the empty space on the wall.

Anne had walked past the portrait of the Florentine lady so many times, she could see it as clearly in her mind as if it hung on the wall before her. She stared into the blank, chalk-lined rectangle as if the painting might reemerge if she waited long enough. All at once, she felt her breath catch in her chest. Anne thought of the thousands of visitors she'd seen walk through that gallery and stop to stare at Leonardo da Vinci's famous portrait of the woman with the enigmatic smile. She had seen their faces change when they came closer and looked into the mysterious dark eyes of the woman in the portrait as if they expected her to reach out to them, to span five hundred years of history with a single gaze, to change something deep inside them. That was the power of art, Anne thought.

Now, standing before the blank wall, Anne struggled to recall how this gallery looked on most days. The thousands of hushed conversations that rose together in layers of voices, rising to a great, echoing clamor. Parents whispering to their youngsters to lace their fingers behind their backs. *Touche pas*. The bump and tap of elbows and shoulders, as visitors passed behind one another's backs. The blur of bodies. The nervous pacing of the guards. *Touchez pas. Silence, s'il vous plaît*. The shifting layers of filtered light that brightened, diffused, then shadowed across the long opening hours. And now . . . a wooden crate with three red dots and a cart with a squeaking wheel.

In the gallery, the silence settled. Dust-filled. Heavy. Final. Anne no longer felt the portrait's presence; she felt its absence instead.

BELLINA

Florence, Italy
1479

I n the end, we are all hiding something. The thought swelled and pulsed inside Bellina's mind as she followed her master's family to the baptism.

Bellina struggled not to let her fingers go to her pocket, where a small treasure bumped against her thigh. It was a mere bauble, a tiny coral amulet of the type a grandma might fasten around a newborn's neck to protect it against a life of misfortune. The small piece had arrived among a pile of baptismal gifts celebrating the Gherardini's first child. Bellina had spotted it immediately when she answered the door the morning after the birth.

It was just a small thing, really. Now, it weighed heavily in the inner pocket of her linen shift. Amid a mounting collection of gifts—ceramic containers of beeswax, sweets made with almond paste and lemon, embroidered swaddling, two-pronged silver forks engraved with the parents' initials—they would never notice it was gone.

The house was full of small treasures passed down over generations, Bellina reasoned. Beautiful objects they tasked her with organizing, storing, bringing out, washing, dusting. Things she might long for but never dream of possessing herself. She never understood why the women of the house might leave their baubles stored in a box or cabinet. Bellina thought if she owned such things, she would wear them all the time.

At dawn, the family had left their musty rented house on a corner of the via Maggio, where water from the Boboli hill stagnated and drew mosquitoes. They made their way through the morning fog, toward the great octagonal baptistery alongside the cathedral of Santa Maria del Fiore. The bells at Santissima Annunziata clanged, calling the monks to their Terce prayers. Strangers called from their windows and nodded their congratulations as the family bustled through the streets with a dark-eyed newborn baby girl dressed in a green velvet cap and white linens. Ahead of her, Antonmaria Gherardini's nephew, Gherardo, wheeled and scampered from one side of the alley to the next, slapping his hands against the stones and soiling his finest hose while his mother screeched for him to stop it right now.

I haven't really stolen. It's more that I've . . . hidden the amulet. Maybe I'll return it. For an instant, Bellina's fingers went to the pocket sewn into the lining of her shift; she couldn't help it. *Surely, we are all hiding something.*

Bellina had never stolen anything from the family. But what servant hasn't thought to steal from her master? Sometimes, as she ran a feather duster over a carved wooden jewelry box or polished a bronze serving spoon, she wondered what it would be like to slip something into her pocket. Would anyone notice?

In all her thirteen years, Bellina had known nothing but the intimate details of the Gherardini household. She knew Lisa's mother preferred oil steeped with sprigs of oregano and only a small splash of water in her wine. Which powder to fetch when Signor Gherardini's throat burned after eating stewed tomatoes.

The timing of menses for all the women in the house. Which topics and situations might cause the cousins to squabble. She was the first to see the faces of Signor Gherardini's first two wives, one after another, go lifeless at the birthing chair.

Any time a mother and a newborn survived the ordeal of childbirth, she supposed it was cause for celebration. Bellina's own mother, a longtime servant in the house, had herself succumbed to the ravages of these travails. Bellina imagined that Signor Gherardini could have abandoned her easily on the steps of the Innocenti. Instead, he took pity on little Bellina and raised her in his household, neither a slave nor a full-fledged family member, but someone in between. They clothed her, fed her, offered her a cot piled with woolens. They treated her with kindness.

You have stolen from the person who's the closest thing you have to a father, some voice inside her mind scolded. But as the family had made its way toward the hulking tiled dome of Santa Maria del Fiore, Bellina pushed the thought away. It was precisely ownership of these small luxuries—the embroidered clothing, the jewelry, the little treasures—that separated Bellina from the rest of the family.

The hidden amulet bounced against Bellina's leg with each step as Signor Gherardini's little household—cousins, grandparents, and servants—bustled like a flock of geese down the street. The baby's exhausted mother had stayed behind, confined at home for the customary forty days. A light breeze wafted down the block as the wool dyers' warehouses appeared, sagging along the muddy banks of the Arno. They crossed the crowded Ponte Vecchio into the via Por Santa Maria. There, in the silk factories bordering the street, Bellina heard the relentless *clack-clack* of the wooden draw looms that heralded the dawn of a new workday.

To any of these strangers, Bellina realized, the Gherardini might have appeared as an upper-class Florentine family making its way to the baptistery. The baby's new aunts and uncles followed behind, bedecked in velvet brocades with silver threads, crimson-dyed gloves, and taffeta with floral patterns.

But as much as the city's impressive façades of coursed stones masked dingy interior courtyards, Bellina knew this family parade amounted to little more than a false veneer. Generations ago, the Gherardini had owned vast estates of olives, grapes, and wheat outside of Florence, and managed a network of tenant farmers. But over several generations, a series of misfortunes had dwindled their coffers. Beneath the voluminous, multilayered, and richly woven cloth that Bellina herself had mended dozens of times, the family wore ragged undergarments faded from washday. Their rented house sat on a damp corner with its sagging stairs, crumbling stucco, and a mostly empty root cellar. Still, they kept up appearances.

At last, the family arrived in the piazza before the hulking cathedral. The building's northern and southern flanks were a pleasing pattern of green and pink marble slabs, but its façade, unfinished, resembled little more than a mass of ugly red bricks. Bellina followed Signor Gherardini into the dark, cold air of the old baptistery. In the vast, domed building, the bustle of the streets fell away, leaving an overpowering silence. Flickering candlelight illuminated a high dome sparkling with gilded mosaics and geometric marble patterns on the walls. Father Bartolomeo, silver-haired and cheerful, smiled at the baby girl as he traded a few polite, echoing words with her father before leading the group to the center of the octagonal building. Bellina's eyes followed the complicated patterns on the floor until Father

Bartolomeo took his place and the family assembled around the great marble font.

Only now did the weight of this event dawn on Bellina. Signor Gherardini had explained that as of today, they would no longer treat Bellina as a child. After his daughter's baptism, they would charge Bellina with caring for her. At thirteen, she was old enough not only to sponsor the baby at the baptismal font, but to step into the role as confidante and protector. She had already had her first menses. She was a woman now. It was time for her to take on additional responsibility, and she should care for Lisa as if she were the baby's own mother.

A second priest, young and skinny, walked to a giant ledger propped on a podium and dipped his pen into an inkwell. In their native Tuscan, Father Bartolomeo addressed Signor Gherardini. "What name have you given this child?"

"Lisa," her father said.

Named for her nonna, Bellina realized, the dear old woman with eyes like plums who had died just a few years before.

"And what do you ask of God's Church for Lisa?"

Signor Gherardini answered, "The sacrament of baptism."

"Who will speak for the child?"

The baby's aunt carefully handed the swaddled, embroidered little package over to Bellina. The infant was fragrant and heavy in her arms. Bellina pulled the baby close to her body, careful to support her head, just as they had taught her. Then Bellina felt a hand at the small of her back, steering her toward the edge of the great baptismal font. Bellina looked into Lisa's eyes, dark plums just like her nonna's, as the old priest dipped his thumb in holy water and made a cross on the baby's forehead. Bellina marveled at the perfect features, at the delicate lips that seemed to spread, suddenly and magically, into a smile.

Now, Bellina felt Father Bartolomeo's eyes fall on her. She did her best to look responsible and pious like the new woman they expected her to be, but she felt as if his gaze might burn a hole in her pocket where she held the stolen coral amulet. Any minute, she thought, the old priest's searing gaze might cause her linen undergarments to burst into flames. Then, the amulet would fall from the bottom of her skirts and rattle on the marble tiles. Bellina would be left to burn there in the middle of the baptistery. She swallowed hard and clung to the baby's angelic expression.

But the priest turned his attention back to Lisa's father. "What should we record as the girl's dowry?"

Only the sound of water dripping filled the dark, cavernous space. Bellina watched the young priest skillfully drag the excess ink from his pen across the lip of the inkwell.

Finally, Lisa's father replied. "There is none."

For a long time afterward, there was only silence.

Bellina knew the Gherardini coffers were bare, but she wasn't expecting such a response. In the end, we are all hiding something, Bellina thought. But the absence of a dowry? Bellina supposed there was no hiding that at all.

Part 2

INTO THE FIRE

ANNE

Paris, France
1939

Anne,

As soon as you read this letter, I know you will want to come looking for me. But if you care anything about me at all, you won't. I can't explain more without putting both of us in danger and anyway, I hardly know where to begin.

Kiki knows nothing, so don't bother asking.

Just trust me.

—Marcel

Looking back, Anne believed the *Mona Lisa* had saved her. The first time she tried to explain it to Emile over a glass of wine at a sidewalk table, she conceded the idea sounded ridiculous. She had watched his mouth turn into a thin line, one side raised in a curious half-grin, as she recounted her first visit to the vast galleries of the Louvre as a schoolgirl. Anne remembered the echoing slaps of footsteps, the blur of filtered light and smocked gray uniforms, and the naïve chatter, as if she had been swept up in a gaggle of plain-looking geese.

But when the guide had clapped her hands and shushed the excited schoolgirls on their rare outing from the dreary classroom, Anne looked up to see the face of a lady with a mysterious smile and suddenly, the world came into sharp focus.

Did the girls know, the guide asked, that the *Mona Lisa* was a *real* woman, one who had lived and breathed and smiled at Leonardo da Vinci himself? That Lisa Gherardini, wife of a Florentine cloth merchant named Francesco del Giocondo, would become an icon, an embodiment of ideal beauty, a symbol of the Italian Renaissance itself? That the man who painted her would become one of the most famous names in history? That the painter captured not just a woman sitting, hands quietly folded, but an entire era in one portrait?

Anne had heard of *La Joconde,* of course, but now, standing before the picture, she squinted. Yes, the lady was smiling. But it was only the emergence, the suggestion of a grin that didn't yet reach the eyes. In fact, in Lisa's expression, Anne thought she saw instead something melancholy, perhaps even sad.

Anne was so wrapped up in the guide's explanation of Lisa Gherardini and her puzzling expression that for a few minutes, she forgot. She forgot her mother had chosen to spend her evenings at the dance hall rather than make dinner for her children. She forgot she couldn't be late to pick her younger brother up; with their mother absent, he was counting on her to be at the schoolyard gate. She forgot all the stories she had made up about a father—that he was a diplomat in a faraway country, that he had drowned in a shipwreck, that he was a spy. She forgot about the dozens of small things waiting for her at home: mittens to darn, pots to scrub, washing to hang.

Instead, that centuries-old Florentine lady had made Anne think about something more. Something bigger than herself. Of things that gave life mystery and meaning. A glimpse of the vast ocean of history and a world beyond her small one. Anne didn't know the first thing about art, but the Florentine lady had planted a seed in her heart, a spark of imagination that grew.

In the following years, Anne continued to read about art. She returned to wander the Louvre's galleries during the few hours a week the museum opened its doors free to the public. Each time, she lingered before the Florentine lady and attempted to decipher her secret smile.

When Anne graduated from *lycée,* she applied for a job.

AMIDST THE DEAFENING STACCATO of typewriter keys, Anne watched her fingers stamp out black letters on the thin layers of carbon paper in her roller.

OSIRIS. EGYPTIAN. OLD KINGDOM.
Accession number E 115.
RED 1

Clack. Clack. Clack. Ding. She pushed the return lever of the rattling Olivetti typewriter to start a new line.

Anne squinted beyond the harsh beam of the desk lamp toward the wall clock and wondered if it was time to go home. Normally, by this time, she would have left behind her job in the Louvre's archives hours ago. She might have stopped by the apartment to exchange her sober work clothes for her favorite red dress with its matching *cloche,* her cabernet-colored leather heels. She might have looped her hand through the crook of Emile's arm and made her way to their favorite neighborhood brasserie for a plate of steak-*frites,* or to a string concert in the Latin Quarter.

But now, for a few wavering clicks of the metal second hand around the clock dial, she realized Kiki wouldn't know whether or not she came home. Her brother, Marcel, was probably sleeping already, resting up for tomorrow's day of guarding works of art in this very museum, thanks to her own efforts to secure him a job. And Emile . . . ah. Emile wouldn't be waiting for her either, not since that terrible night he had told Anne he loved one of her closest friends, and in an instant, her lover, her best friend, and her dreams of settling down had disappeared. With a pang, Anne realized no one was waiting for her at all.

Anne took a deep breath and settled back in her metal chair. She might as well stay at work. She ran her fingers along the inventory of Egyptian antiquities that lay alongside her. To most people, these endless stacks of pages, with their dry recounting of accession numbers, dates, and provenance documentation, might appear the very essence of tedium. But for Anne, each brief entry told a story: the story of a one-of-a-kind creation that, through the centuries, had been coveted, preserved, collected. Even stolen.

Of all the fascinating tidbits of information, it amazed Anne to realize how many objects had come into the Louvre through nefarious means: precious antiquities pulled from tombs and loaded onto ships. An altarpiece looted from a church. Old Master paintings taken off walls and brought to France during the Napoleonic conquests.

Anne rubbed her cheeks and shifted in the hard chair. If she was going to work late into the night, she had to get her head straight. She was only a typist, yet accuracy was everything. If she missed even one line of text, it might mean the difference between a priceless object being returned to its rightful place, or going missing. She struggled to focus amidst the rattle of typewriter keys, the glare of dozens of desk lamps, and the voice inside that whispered she might never amount to anything but a reliable, lonely typist. That perhaps no one would be waiting for her ever again.

"Need a break?"

Lucie, the head archivist, stopped and gave Anne a look of grim sympathy. Had she read the silent desperation on Anne's face? For her part, Lucie was the picture of every Louvre staff person at that moment—filled with a strange mixture of hyper-industriousness and exhaustion. She'd tied her faded brown hair at the nape of her neck. Pale skin crinkled at the corners of her eyes. Still, her tight grin was filled with genuine concern.

Anne returned what she hoped was a grateful smile. "No time to be tired." She thumped her fingers on the stack of inventories still to type.

Lucie scanned the archives with a weary glance. Around them, newly constructed crates lined the corridors and buttressed the file cabinets. "Finish that entry and come with me. I want to show you something." Anne watched Lucie's trim silhouette disappear into the shadows.

The unease coiled in Anne's stomach. Whatever Lucie wanted to show her, she had a feeling it wasn't good. Good news had been in short supply this summer, ever since President Lebrun had advised the Louvre's senior staff to prepare for a German invasion. Every Louvre employee—even the lowliest archival assistant like herself—was corralled into the effort of inventorying and packing every last work of art in the museum.

In the galleries, Anne watched museum staff hurrying back and forth in worried silence as the clocks ticked past midnight. Everything from Egyptian mummies to oil paintings was being packed in custom-made wooden crates printed with "MN" for Musées Nationaux. It seemed wrong, Anne thought, to take down a priceless painting and pry it out of its frame. It was like watching a castle full of old nobles being forcefully evacuated: an injustice. Anne knew from her archival work that many of these works had been targeted before, but she felt her throat tighten at the thought that anyone would put these treasures in their crosshairs. With some thirteen kilometers' worth of galleries to pack, the task seemed impossible. Now, Anne understood why the Louvre had called staff back from holidays, recruited scores of volunteers, and why even a lowly assistant like herself was working long into the night.

In the darkened gallery exhibiting the Napoleonic crown jewels, Anne found Lucie with a stack of pages in the crook of her arm. When Lucie saw Anne approach, she gestured. "Not exactly what you signed up for when you took a job here."

"But I have always wanted to work here, ever since I was a girl,"

Anne responded truthfully. "Where else would I want to be?" She stopped short of admitting that busying herself long into the night kept her from facing the stark reality of an empty apartment and nowhere to go.

Lucie smiled, lighting up her eyes for a second before worry crept back in. "Yes. And hopefully there will be something for us to come back to."

"You really think the Germans would destroy it?"

Lucie pursed her lips and nodded. She peered into the glass cabinet displaying the crown of the empress Eugénie. "Or more likely take it for themselves. Anyway, we know what to do. It's our third time packing up."

Anne had heard the stories of how the Louvre had packed its treasures and moved them during the Great War. Trucks, train cars, and wagons had trundled the *Mona Lisa* and many more masterpieces to safety under the vaults of the medieval Jacobin church in Toulouse, nearly seven hundred kilometers to the south. And now here the Louvre staff were again, eyes wide open, knowing what might happen if they didn't act fast.

Anne approached an enormous window and looked down into one of the Louvre's inner courts. Sandbags nearly obscured the line of trucks forming there. Lucie followed her gaze. "Monsieur Jaujard has had trouble finding enough trucks," Lucie said. "He needed thirty, but last I heard, he only had managed contracts for twelve. He's chasing down five more now. We're going to need every truck we can find in this city."

"Where will you be taking them?" Anne asked as she watched wagons and trucks drawing up to the stately gravel courtyard in the dark.

Lucie hesitated. "Somewhere safe. Actually, multiple safe places."

Anne nodded. She could hardly imagine a place large enough, and safe enough, to hide the *Mona Lisa* and thousands of other treasures.

The women moved into a nearby corridor, busy with activity. Anne glimpsed marble among the piles of sandbags. Immediately, she recognized the pure white statue of the beautiful, ancient woman with the missing arms. "The *Venus de Milo*," she whispered, dismayed. "Surely she's not staying here!"

Lucie nodded grimly. "Michelangelo's *Slaves*, too. They're fragile. It's too risky to move them. Look. Here's what I wanted to show you." Lucie stopped. Along one wall, dozens of wooden crates stood in neat order. Lucie ran her fingers across the nearest crate. "You've already seen that keeping track of all these works is the most challenging part of this operation."

Anne looked at the number printed on the crate, realizing it matched the number on the stacks of paper next to her typewriter. "I've typed thousands of these in the past few hours. What does this mean?" Anne pointed to a green dot marked on the side of the crate.

"Triage," Lucie said. "A red dot means the contents of this crate are of the highest importance. A green dot means it's a little less valuable. Yellow means lower priority still."

Anne scanned the crates, her eyes taking in the simplicity of this color-coded system—and its vast scale. Through the galleries, many thousands of crates were being labeled and colored. The reality of it chilled Anne to the bone. She was glad she wasn't the one who had to make those choices. Egyptian, Greek, and Roman antiquities. Royal portraits. Michelangelo's sculptures. Even the entire contents of the Louvre library and archives. How

could anyone choose between saving one masterpiece over another?

"There is still much to do, and we must do it fast," Lucie said.
"Monsieur Jaujard has asked the archives to choose a few close
staff to go with us. The first person I thought of was you." Lucie
stopped and met Anne's gaze.

"Me?" Anne stood with her mouth open. "Go with you where?"

"With the treasures," she said, gesturing to the crates propped
against the wall.

Anne hesitated. "But I'm just a . . . a typist . . ."

"That may be," Lucie said, "but you're one of the most responsible people I've ever met." She gave Anne's arm a quick squeeze. "I
wanted to ask you first," she said. "We'll be on the road for . . .
Well, I don't know how long. And I can't say where we're heading.
I can only tell you we are going to a safe place in the countryside.
The Louvre will of course provide us with meals and a place to
sleep. And I'm going to need a lot of help."

Anne felt herself snap to attention. Typing accession numbers
was one thing; watching priceless works of art packed into crates
was another. But taking on the responsibility of their safety in the
unknown . . . It was overwhelming.

Lucie continued, "I wasn't sure about your family . . . situation.
Many of us have spouses. Children. It's not so easy to ask someone
to drop everything and leave Paris with a truckload of paintings.
My husband and I have arranged for our daughter, Frédérique,
to stay with relatives in the countryside. Of course, André and I
will go with the rest of the museum staff. With our positions, we
could hardly refuse."

The question of her family situation stopped Anne in her tracks.

Her mind flickered with Emile for a second, but she pushed the image away. Then it went to the rundown apartment she shared with her mother—when she deemed it worth her time to leave the dance hall—and her brother.

"Think about it . . . ," Lucie began. "But I must have your answer soon because—"

"I'll come," Anne interrupted.

Lucie's eyebrows rose. She hesitated, a long, silent pause. Anne watched her dark, expressive eyes flicker in the shadows. "I want you to be sure." She pressed her lips together. "I don't know how long we'll be away from Paris."

Anne thought back to her first encounter with the *Mona Lisa* all those years ago, then to the blank space on the wall where the famous portrait of the Florentine lady had stood only yesterday. One red dot on a crate, Lucie had said, meant the work of art was priceless. It was the first time Anne had seen three of them. Three red dots. Beyond value. Impossible to replace.

Anne turned to face Lucie. "I'm sure. And I'll bring my brother, too. How soon do we leave?"

She gave Anne a weary grin. "Go home and pack your things," she said. "The first trucks are leaving at dawn. I have a feeling the Germans will be here sooner rather than later."

HAD SHE SAID YES too quickly? It wasn't like Anne to make a rash decision. That was something Marcel would do.

Anne pushed her hands deep into her skirt pockets and walked northward across the shadowed Cour Napoléon. Anne had always felt a protective presence when strolling past the museum's stately façade, with its endless rows of pillars, its elegant archways, and most of all, its breathtaking scale. Yet as her feet crunched across the darkened gravel courtyard, it seemed the museum she loved had disappeared into packaging just like the *Mona Lisa* itself. Scaffolding masked the façades, supporting piles of sandbags. Workers were shouting, tossing up sandbags, throwing them down in puffs of dust swirling in the moonlight. It made her feel sick to think the sandbags were there to protect the building and its contents from destruction. She remembered the bitterness in Lucie's voice as she spoke of the past threats, and a little of it leaked into her own heart. Who would want to destroy something that celebrated the best of human creativity and achievement?

Paris always seemed vibrantly alive; no matter the hour, there was music and light coming from somewhere. Even in the middle of the night, there were vehicles and clusters of people in the streets. But not tonight. As she crossed a broad avenue toward the old Gare du Nord, Anne found the streets devoid of cars and pedestrians. A few lone shapes scurried along the sidewalks. On the main avenues, shop windows were shuttered.

Anne's apartment building was a narrow thing sandwiched among other cobbled-together façades lining a dingy street deep in the guts of the tenth *arrondissement*. She worked her key as quietly as possible through the lock, then slunk past the *gardienne*'s door. She didn't have the energy for old Madame Brodeur to come plunging into the hallway and berate her for the late hour. Anne tiptoed up the stairs toward the apartment that overlooked the street.

The apartment's familiar, dank smell embraced her as Anne pressed the door closed, careful not to wake her brother. The apartment stood dark and silent except for the creak of the floorboards. In the shadows, Anne made out the sagging shapes of their once-fancy, now tired-looking chairs handed down from past generations. Sometimes, Anne came home from work to find her mother sprawled across the sagging divan, floating in the abyss of absinthe home-distilled by a bartender friend, the butt of a hand-wrapped cigarette smoldering in the ceramic tray on a side table. But tonight, the room stood silent.

Anne groped her way to the tiny kitchen where the faucet dripped its relentless rhythm around the rust-stained drain. She turned the old tap to the right, but the leak persisted. Her eyes having adjusted to the darkness, she made her way down the hall-way to the small bedroom she shared with Marcel. How would he take the news that she was leaving Paris with the Louvre staff? Would he agree to come with her? She made out the shapes of the beds and the old lamp on the rickety table between them. When they were small, Anne and Marcel had lain in this dark room, whispering and fretting about their mother, who had entrusted Anne to take care of mischievous little Marcel while she flitted off to Montmartre.

Anne crossed the room and expected to see the familiar sight of the two narrow beds: hers neatly made in one corner, Marcel's rumpled in the other. But something was amiss. Her brother's bed was also neatly made. Anne paused for a minute, trying to process the sight. She ran her fingers across the tattered spread, as if Marcel were hiding under its smooth surface.

"Marcel," she said aloud. Silence.

"Marcel!" she called, hurrying back out into the *salon*. She flicked on the light and looked around. She pushed open the nar-row door to the toilet. No one.

Where was he this time? A few instances recently, he'd been evasive when she asked where he'd been late at night. Anne returned to the bedroom and switched on the lamp between their beds. Something white flashed on Marcel's pillow. Anne picked up a folded piece of paper with her name scrawled in her brother's careless handwriting.

Rushing from the apartment, Anne gripped the wrought-iron handrail as her feet slapped down the worn staircase. Standing in her doorway at the bottom of the stairs, Madame Brodeur stopped Anne in her tracks. The *gardienne*'s arms folded across the tattered gray housedress she wore like a uniform, her permanent scowl drawing deep, stark lines on either side of her mouth.

"You're heading out in the middle of the night, too, *mademoiselle*? Just like your brother?"

"Marcel," Anne said, breathlessly. "You've seen him?"

She nodded. "About two hours ago. Woke me up even before you did, making all that racket up and down the stairs, carrying his *sac marin* over his shoulder." She shook her head. "Looked like he might be up to no good."

Anne closed her eyes against Madame Brodeur's painful provocation. Marcel had packed his bag? She couldn't deny that she had pulled Marcel out of trouble more times than she could count. Anne didn't respond to the old *gardienne*. Instead, she pushed past her and headed back out into the street.

"But you seem like a responsible girl," Anne heard Madame Brodeur call behind her. "What's the matter with the rest of your family? You're not following them, are you? *Mademoiselle!*"

AS SHE WOUND her way uphill to Montmartre, Anne tried to calm her thudding heart. After all, this wouldn't be the first time that Marcel had disappeared.

Anne remembered being small—so small that she had to stand on tiptoe to turn a doorknob—and playing outside in the tiny scrap of garden behind the apartment block. She had turned her back for a moment to give her stuffed rabbit a sip of imaginary tea from the top of an acorn, and when she turned around, Marcel was gone. Even at that age, Anne had known that calling for Kiki wouldn't help. Looking back, it seemed ludicrous that two small children would call their mother by her stage name. Her real name, Anne learned much later, was Henriette, but Kiki was the only name they had ever heard her called and so it had seemed the most natural thing in the world. Anne had run toward the sidewalk, calling for Marcel until she spotted his waddling form headed for the street. His fat bare foot was outstretched over the road when she grabbed him, tugging him to her just as a car swept past in a rush of metal.

Ever since then, Anne had been running after Marcel, rescuing him from the brink. So many times, Anne had secured a job for him, only to have him walk out on it a few weeks later after another too-good-to-be-true scheme crossed his path. The disappearances, the late-night calls, a few brushes with the police when her brother spent time with the wrong people again . . .

Only weeks ago, Anne had secured a job for Marcel as a guard at the Louvre. She had stood before the old wooden desk of Georges Dupont, the oxlike head of museum security, while he peered over his glasses and listened to her promise that Marcel was responsible. Earnest. Trustworthy. She crossed her fingers behind her back and struggled to believe it herself. And now . . . Had he already abandoned the position she had put her reputation on the line to arrange for him?

Yet somehow, she had never stayed angry at him. His bright

smile and guileless, sky-blue eyes sparkled most when he was up to something. When Marcel wrapped her in his warm embrace and thanked her for looking out for him, she relented. They had been lifelong companions on an uncertain journey, Anne and Marcel against the world. Besides, he had a good heart, Anne reasoned. But she didn't know how many more of his disappearances she could bear.

This time felt different. He'd never left a note before. He'd never insisted that she not come after him.

Anne turned off the street and began climbing the steep stairs that led from the sidewalks of their neighborhood, up to the hill called Montmartre. Halfway up, she stopped to catch her breath. She turned to take in the familiar skyline of Paris. She expected to see the spires of Notre-Dame etched against the sky, but tonight, the Gothic church was only a hulking silhouette. Even the iconic Eiffel Tower had disappeared into the blackness so it couldn't be targeted from the air.

At the top of the stairs, Anne turned toward the streets where the once-venerable dance halls still welcomed customers. Montmartre might have appeared captivating at night, she thought, if it wasn't so closely connected with the tension that years of worrying over her mother had caused. Normally, there was laughter and accordion music in the streets. The shops lining the twisting, cobbled alleys would be garishly lit, their contents spilling onto the sidewalks to lure shoppers. But not tonight. The same pall that had fallen over the city had clutched Montmartre as well; the storefronts were dark, and many were battened with wooden and metal shutters. Only a few furtive figures darted across the streets.

The lights were still on at the cabaret where Anne's mother spent most of her time. Anne usually tried to avoid La Cloche, even when her mother chose to sleep there rather than in their worn apartment. The handful of remaining Montmartre dance halls had long ago lost their Belle Époque luster, the glamour and prestige of five decades wearing them down to gaudy caricatures of their former selves. They had survived a world war and a disastrous economic depression, but like an aging harlot who had lived to see the other side of relentless indignities, these establishments were weary. Worn down. Still brightly rouged. The same could be said of Kiki's colleagues, once-promising students of the city's prestigious ballet schools, now scraping together a living onstage and, sadly, in the backstage dressing rooms.

Anne slipped into the back door of the cabaret, steeling herself against the familiar stench, a nauseating mixture of waxy cosmetics, sweat, vomit, and sawdust. She found her mother draped over a narrow cot in one of the dressing rooms among rumpled sequined dresses, ripped stockings, and discarded cosmetic tins. Anne spotted a few gas masks lying among wooden stage props, dusty and forgotten, cluttered in the wings. They were a reminder that Anne had to get back to the Louvre as soon as possible. She had promised Lucie she would leave Paris with them as soon as the sun rose. She didn't know how long it would be before she saw her mother again. The thought was enough to rally some compassion.

"Kiki," she said, touching a frayed strap of her mother's cheap green gown. "*Maman*."

Kiki opened one bloodshot eye, then the other. Her words slurred thickly. "*Chérie*." She grasped Anne's outstretched hand and pulled herself to sitting. "What are you doing here?"

Progress, Anne thought. Sometimes when she visited the dance hall, Kiki didn't wake at all. She gripped Kiki's arm tightly.

"I need you to hear me," Anne said. "Can you listen? Please?"

Kiki said nothing, only reached for the butt of a half-smoked cigarette discarded on a nearby table. "Kiki," she tried again. "Listen to me. Marcel has gone."

"Gone?" hiccupped Kiki. Then she smirked. "No surprises there. Boy takes after his father." Kiki struck a match and lit the end of the short, ragged cigarette, then took a deep drag and squinted at her daughter. Among the garish costumes of the cabaret dressing room, Anne felt ridiculous in her neat white blouse tucked into her drab skirt and her worn, sensible leather shoes. "He left a note," Anne continued, pressing the folded paper into her mother's hand. "Did he come here to see you?"

"Marcel?" Kiki snorted. "That kid doesn't tell me anything." Kiki stood and pressed her hand into the small of her back, then rummaged around the detritus on her dressing table. "What time is it?"

"It should be light in a few hours," Anne said. "Do you have any idea where he might have gone?"

Kiki shrugged. "Maybe he's taken off with his new girlfriend. Jewish girl. Pretty."

A girlfriend? A pretty, Jewish girlfriend? "Marcel doesn't have a girlfriend," she said.

"Not that *you* know of." Kiki grinned affectionately at her daughter.

Anne shook her head. Marcel with a girlfriend? No, her mother was wrong about that, she was sure. Marcel told her everything. Didn't he? All at once, Anne realized he'd been eager to leave the museum on his lunch hours and he'd been staying out late more often.

Her mother seemed to read her mind. "I don't know why he

would tell you about her; you might crush all the fun. Anyway, you must be preoccupied with that *grand amour* of your own, *n'est-ce pas?*"

Anne grasped for words, but in the end, she only shook her head. How could she convey the weight of disappointment she had felt when Emile had walked away, when her mother seemed to pick up and discard men as easily as apples in the market? It was best not to mention it at all. She turned back to the subject of Marcel. "I'm afraid he might be involved in something dangerous. And just when we have to leave town . . ."

Her mother took another deep drag on the last half-inch of her cigarette butt, then stamped it out in the ashtray. "And just where are you going, *mon petit chou?*"

Anne sighed and sat on the edge of the cot where she had found her mother sleeping. "I'm not sure, actually." Anne recounted to her mother all that had happened at the Louvre in recent days, and the request for her to accompany the works of art—even the *Mona Lisa*—to a safer place. Her mother listened silently, squinting in the dust, then came to sit next to her daughter.

"*La Joconde!*" Kiki leaned back against the grubby pillows, draping her arms dramatically right and left. "An old broad like me."

Anne looked at her mother with a serious expression. "I don't know how long it will be before I come back." Anne suddenly felt a wave of unease flow over her. "Kiki, the Germans are coming," she said seriously. "People are leaving the city. You should get out of Paris, too. They say there will be air raids . . ."

Kiki only stared at her, then barked out a loud laugh. "Where would I go?"

"Come with me!" Anne said, but her mother's skeptical expression stopped her. Anne searched for an idea, but they had no relations outside the city. "I don't know. Somewhere the Germans won't find you."

"*Les allemands!*" Kiki laughed loudly again. "Let them come. They're some of my best customers." She shrugged. "Krauts, English. They all enjoy the shows. And they put food on our table." But Anne thought her mother looked like she subsisted on tobacco and absinthe alone. And if Kiki thought it was her own meager earnings rather than Anne's that put food on their table, well . . .

Anne sighed, beginning to feel the old wave of shame toward Kiki well up in her gut, but as she gazed down at the scrawny figure on the cot, all she could find in her heart was a kind of exhausted pity. She leaned down, brushed aside Kiki's greasy hair, and kissed her clammy, freckled forehead.

"I have to go, Kiki," Anne said. "I promised I would be back at the museum at dawn. Marcel was supposed to come with me. I don't know what to tell them now." She straightened and turned to leave, but Kiki's thin hand shot out, seizing Anne by her wrist.

There was light in Kiki's blue eyes as she gazed up at her, a clarity that Anne hadn't seen there in months. "Anne," she said.

Anne turned back, startled.

"*À la prochaine!*" she exclaimed, and Anne had the impression that her mother said that to all her departing clients, Germans and all. "Don't follow your brother, *ma petite*. Not this time." She gave Anne's hands a squeeze. "Let him go. You've spent your life chasing that boy. It's time you watched out for yourself."

ANNE RUSHED THROUGH the Tuileries Garden and into the yawning courtyard of the Louvre in time for a driver to sling her small suitcase—filled with a few changes of clothing and meager necessities—behind the passenger seat of a delivery truck advertising sewing machine repair on its side.

"Climb in." The driver gestured.

For a few moments, Anne hesitated. Her eyes scanned the uniformed guards standing in the Louvre courtyard, searching their faces. There it was again: the old, familiar feeling of wildly searching for her brother, who had weaseled his way from her view. This time, though, something felt different. Marcel was gone. *Really* gone. Beside her, the sewing machine repair truck engine roared to life. Reluctantly, Anne hoisted herself up into the threadbare passenger seat. In her mind, she cursed her brother.

"*Merci,*" she said aloud instead to the young man behind the wheel, taking in his sturdy forearms, dark curls, and elegant, even features.

"You just made it," he said, flashing a quick smile, then checking his side mirror and pulling out into the line of trucks in the convoy.

"Yes," said Anne, sinking into the seat. She turned to see the wide, enclosed truck bed loaded full of wooden crates, all marked with colored dots. Anne heard the suspension squeak as the vehicles rolled out of the great courtyard. She leaned out the window, looking back, hoping to catch one last glimpse of the museum's stately façades, one last view of the building she had come to feel was more like home than any other place in the world. But in the dawn light, all she saw was the mass of scaffolding and sandbags.

Her stomach flip-flopped. She was leaving Paris for the first time in her life.

"*Mon Dieu,*" she gasped. "Hard to believe that place is nearly empty."

The driver glanced at her briefly. "I've never been inside," he said.

"What?" Her eyes widened. "Never? You don't live in Paris?"

"I do," he said. "But I'm busy. I have a repair shop near the garment factories. We work on the machines used for upholstery and passementerie."

Anne smiled at his funny pronunciation of *passementerie*, a word that brought to mind fancy tassels and trims of homes much finer than Anne would ever dream to inhabit. "You are not French."

He shook his head. "Italian. Florentine, actually. My parents moved here when I was young. My father was a tailor back in Florence. But things got tough in Italy, and our cousin found work for him and my mother. They came here and started sewing in one of the garment factories of the Sentier. I was ten when we came to France."

"Then shame on you!" Anne said. "You've been here in Paris a long time—and in the neighborhood right behind the Louvre, no less. You should have visited the museum at least once."

"Too late now," he said, glancing again in his side mirror, watching the vast building recede into the distance behind them. "I'm Corrado."

"Anne," she said.

"*Piacere*. You work there? In the Louvre?" He scanned her briefly with his brown eyes before focusing back on the truck in front of them.

She nodded. "I'm an assistant in the archives, a typist, mostly." Anne shrugged. "I would have liked to be an artist myself some-day, but my family . . . I guess you could say I couldn't afford to be a painter. Took a job that paid the bills, and well, I just love being in the presence of these works of art."

Corrado smiled, and she noticed he had a handsome, tanned face and beautiful, straight teeth. Anne studied his profile as he navigated through traffic, passing Montparnasse and the old catacombs of Paris.

"You said you're a garment worker? Tailor?"

Corrado shook his head. "My parents and my brother are. Actually, my family's worked in the textile trade in Florence for, well, many, *many* generations. But I guess you could say I'm more of an entrepreneur. I repair those sewing and upholstery machines," he said. "You'd be surprised how complicated the ones are for making upholstery silks. Crazy contraptions. Anyway, I usually haul machines in the back of my truck," he said, gesturing. "I pick them up, bring them to my shop, and then deliver them back to the factories."

She nodded. "So, what are you doing driving *paintings* to . . . who knows where?"

"Chambord," he said, drawing out the "r" with a thick, pleasant Italian accent.

"Chambord," she repeated in her clipped Parisian. "The château? In the Loire Valley?" Anne had only seen pictures of the enormous white royal palace as she browsed the library shelves in the Louvre's archives.

Corrado nodded. "That's where we're headed. The museum director's office commissioned our delivery truck; sounds like they had trouble rounding up vehicles." He drummed his fingers on the truck's steering wheel. "I couldn't argue with a government contract, and in any case, I wanted to get out of Paris."

"I know that feeling," Anne said, glancing back one last time;

an image of Emile came into her memory and she pushed it away. The Louvre was in the distance now, and all she could see was a sea of sandbagged buildings. "You didn't have anything— anyone—keeping you here?"

Corrado shook his head. "My family left town a few weeks ago. Just locked the apartment and headed back to Florence. I guess they had some sense, after all. They knew the Germans would come. At first, I thought I would stay and keep an eye on things, but when the museum asked if they could requisition my truck, well . . . I wouldn't want anyone else driving this old girl." He patted the dashboard as if the truck were a beloved horse.

The convoy worked its way through the streets as the rising sun quickly brightened the ornate façades. Anne tried to ignore the fear that lanced through her heart. Were the Germans really coming to Paris? If they did, what would happen to Kiki and to Marcel, wherever he was?

"*Madonna*," Corrado said, making a clucking noise with his tongue as the truck slowed. "We're not the only ones heading south. Look."

Dozens of pedestrians had begun to fill the sidewalks. As the truck crept forward, the numbers of people increased until, eventually, it became surreal. There were few cars, but clusters of families and couples carrying homemade carts, piled haphazardly with all kinds of possessions—pots and clothes and chairs— made their way through the streets. Were people so desperate that they were leaving Paris on foot?

As the trucks squeezed their way through the crush of people and carts, Anne leaned out of her window, her eyes searching through the faces. With expressions of haggard resolve, families had bundled a few precious possessions in their arms and made their way slowly along the sidewalks, flowing into the street. Anne wondered if any of them had a plan, if they knew where they were going, or if they were all heading blindly into the unknown like she was, knowing in their hearts that anywhere might be safer than the city they loved. Refugees. Anne had never seen such a sight in all of her twenty-two years.

A tall, fair-headed young man, walking with his arm around a slim girl, caught her attention. Her heart leapt in her chest. Anne leaned out the window.

"Marcel!" she cried.

The young man turned, frowning, and she saw he had a full beard and a crooked nose. Not Marcel. She sat back in her seat and sighed.

"Someone you know?" Corrado asked.

"*Ouf!* From the back, that man looked . . . Well, for a minute I thought . . . *Bien*. I don't know where my brother is, except he said he was leaving." She leaned her elbow on the windowsill and looked again. "Only he told me not to come looking for him."

"Well, if he's leaving the city, that's good. He's doing the sensible thing," Corrado said.

Anne couldn't stop herself from barking out a laugh. "Marcel?" She shook her head. "I don't think he's done a sensible thing in his life. He's unruly. I've spent my life running after him, and now . . ." She let her voice trail off, disappearing into the rumble of the trucks.

"You've taken care of him," Corrado said.

"You could say that. He's two years younger than I am, but it seems not even a war can make him act like a grown-up." Anne sighed. "He was supposed to come with us. Our mother says he might have gone off with a new girl, but he never told me about her. When I saw that couple walking . . ." Anne's voice trailed off and she sank back in her seat, feeling the familiar sensation of worried defeat where Marcel was concerned.

"Young men do foolish things," Corrado said with a grin.

"You're telling me! I've always looked out for him." She stared out over the bleak ranks of refugees, more and more of their hunched figures illuminated as the sun began to flood the street with bright light.

"And you resent it," Corrado said.

Anne pressed her back against the seat. Was that true? She didn't know this Italian truck driver at all, yet he had just put his finger on something latent and raw deep inside her. Silence stretched between them as Anne's heart churned with anger and loss. How could Marcel have left her like this? She would never leave him. Never. Except now she had. A pang of guilt sliced through her chest, mixed with wondering if Corrado's assessment was accurate.

For a while, the two of them rode on in silence. Moving out of the city center, they saw the first signs indicating the direction of Orléans, and Anne's eyelids began to feel like lead weights. She couldn't remember the last time she had stayed awake all night. On and off, she fell into ragged bouts of sleep, but the rough rumble of the trucks jostled her awake.

At a certain point, Anne awoke to find them traveling through flat, neatly organized fields of gently swaying wheat and barley, large, undulating squares of green and gold in the landscape. She rubbed her face and looked at Corrado, only to see him look away quickly. Had he been watching her while she slept?

"So," Corrado said tactfully after she roused herself and rubbed her cheeks with her palms. "Why don't you tell me a little more about the art in my old truck?" He gestured with his thumb to the enclosed truck bed behind them.

Anne leaned back in her seat, trying to remember everything she'd seen loaded into the trucks. "Well, most everything is packed away," she said. "But I typed some of the inventories, so I know what's inside them. It's incredible to think that most of the Louvre has been packed into just a couple dozen trucks when normally, it fills a gigantic building. I can hardly believe it."

"It must have looked strange in there, once those galleries were emptied," said Corrado.

"It was *so* strange," Anne said, "to see the Louvre like a graveyard. I can hardly bear to think of all the priceless treasures loaded into these trucks, and what would happen if there was a collision or just enough of a jostle to cause damage. There are crown jewels, Egyptian antiquities thousands of years old . . . and so many beautiful paintings and sculptures."

"I saw one of them loaded onto one of the bigger trucks," Corrado said. "It looked odd—no arms, no head, just a body with wings. But *enormous*. It must have been twice the height of a man."

"The *Winged Victory of Samothrace*," Anne said. "It's been in the Louvre for many decades—and it's more than two thousand years old! That's why the head and arms have gone missing. It was carved from marble in the times of the ancient Greeks. I watched them wheel it down a specially made wooden ramp. It looked like it was flying down the staircase."

"Two thousand years old." Corrado shook his head. "Looked like it took that many years to make it."

"And one bomb—even a pothole—might destroy it."

"Don't worry," Corrado said. "We'll make sure she lands safely."

He smiled, but Anne's mood turned suddenly sorrowful. "It just seems wrong, having something as precious as the *Mona Lisa* packed into a wooden crate and shipped off in a truck like a bag of flour." Anne wrapped her arms around herself. They'd left the clamor of the city behind now, and the first groves of trees and fields opened before them. The crowds of refugees had thinned, but there were still small clusters of people marching along the roadside and the swaying wheat fields. "Everything about this is wrong," she said. "Do you really think the Germans are coming?"

"Without a doubt," Corrado said. "Have you been reading the newspapers? It is only a matter of time. We have to make sure we keep our heads down and stay out of trouble."

"I can do that," Anne said, looking out the window again and feeling a pang of fear for her brother and her mother. "I'm really not that brave."

Corrado took his eyes off the road again for a moment to consider her. "And yet, you agreed to come."

BELLINA

Florence, Italy
1495

B ellina wasn't that brave, yet somehow, she'd agreed to come.

"Meet us at the dyers' warehouse," Bellina's friend Dolce had whispered that morning at the washing well. "My brothers will be there. I'll wait for you."

It wasn't the first time Bellina had sneaked out of her master's house. In recent months, she'd been doing it more often. Bellina made her way to the river from their squalid street in the Oltrarno and mulled over the possible excuses she might offer if Lisa or her father asked where she had gone.

On one hand, Bellina felt sure Signor Gherardini wouldn't approve of her loitering around the old dyers' warehouses on the riverbank. And certainly not if he knew a group of *frateschi*, adherents of Brother Girolamo Savonarola, had begun to meet there. For months, Bellina, Dolce, and Dolce's brothers had joined ever-increasing crowds to hear the hooded, beak-nosed priest deliver passionate sermons in the church of San Marco. Meanwhile, in secret, neighborhood leaders—stirred to action by Savonarola's words—had gathered friends and guildsmen in their homes, artisan workshops, and tavern storerooms.

Bellina heard the flowing water long before she turned from

a narrow alley onto the broad expanse of the quayside bordering the Arno. The late-winter sun held the promise of spring, and Bellina turned her face to it. She squinted, and the dingy façades of the soap makers and wool combers facing the river suddenly blurred into brilliant gold, as vivid as newly dyed cloth. An awakening. Along the Ponte Vecchio, butchers were closing their stalls for the evening, tossing the scraps of the day's cuttings into the river and hanging bloody aprons on their hooks.

The longer Bellina had listened to Brother Savonarola spew fire from his pulpit, the more she felt as if someone had lifted a veil from her eyes. For the first time, she saw the sinful excesses around her. She saw the moral rot of ecclesiastics accused of lechery and gambling. For the first time, she saw the noble people's cravings for meat, their hunger for books, their coveting of painted pictures, of bronze sculptures, of small medals depicting their own likenesses.

And for the first time, Bellina's eyes were opened to the iniquities of Lisa's own house. All those faded dresses, the baubles passed down over generations, the painted pictures, the silver tableware. For so many years, she had wanted to possess even one of these luxuries for herself. Now, she saw she had been saved from the deadly sin of envy. And the family's preoccupation with worldly goods might doom them to eternal fire instead.

But as she walked toward the sun-spangled river, Bellina realized it was more than the exhortations of the strange priest that propelled her to the secret neighborhood meetings. If she was honest with herself, instead it was the promise of Dolce's brother Stefano that lured her to the riverbank. It was the possibility not only that she might turn Stefano's head but that he might *see* her at last.

Bellina had known Dolce and her brothers for years. As children, they had kicked a leather-covered ball of straw until Dolce's mother, a servant in a nearby house, said they were too old to play with boys. Every few weeks, Bellina met Dolce at the washing well, where they exchanged whispered secrets: intrigues inside their masters' houses, their shared envy for their mistresses' fine dresses and baubles. Some days, they dreamt of finding a husband or even a lover, someone strong and alluring, someone with the power to free them from a lifetime of selfless servitude.

But one day, Dolce began to talk of her brothers' involvement in a popular movement to rid Florence of the Medici family and their sinful excesses. Now, Dolce said, her brothers had turned their attention to galvanizing Savonarola's followers. Bellina should come hear what they had to say.

Bellina descended the ancient staircase toward the low-slung row of tanneries and dyers' warehouses perched on the muddy riverbank. From this precarious, often-flooded location, the workers of the cloth trades washed their refuse along the rushing waters toward Pisa and then the sea. Dyers toiled in the mud, their fingers, ears, and noses stained permanently midnight blue from the constant handling of the colors. She held her breath. The old scraps of fabric used in the dyeing process sent up such rankness of must and mold that even rag dealers refused them. Bellina sent a silent prayer of thanks that it was early in the year; during the heat of summer, the river's stench was overpowering.

"Bellina!" Dolce called in a loud whisper, waving her arm from the shadows of a willow tree. Stefano stood beside his sister, one leg crooked against the tree trunk, examining a scrap of paper in his hands as if the rest of the world had disappeared.

Bellina calculated that she and Stefano were the same age, yet at twenty-nine, she had matured into little more than a sober house servant. Dull as a mouse. Invisible. Long ago, she had accepted the cruel irony of her name. *Little Beauty.* A mockery. She never had captured a man's attention. At her age, Bellina figured, a husband was as out of reach for her as the lace collars and cuffs folded neatly inside Lisa's mother's drawer.

In the same time span, Stefano had transformed from an unruly neighbor kid into a brooding, skinny wool dyer who seemed to boil beneath the surface. Energy untapped. Bellina watched Stefano as he stood by the tree, studying the small piece of parchment he was unfolding, elegant fingers tinged with blue dye. At the top of his loosely tied linen shirt, his throat pulsed.

"What's that?" Bellina called.

At last, he acknowledged her. For a long few moments, Stefano's gaze raked over Bellina and lingered. His eyes were the color of the translucent amber gems in Lisa's jewelry box. Strange. Mesmerizing. She felt her cheeks turn hot.

"A list of Medici supporters in the city," he said. "Families in every quarter." He pushed away from the tree trunk and walked to her slowly. Was it her imagination or was he studying her as he spoke? Bellina nibbled her thumbnail. "Mark my words," Stefano continued. "Soon enough, our fortunes will turn."

Suddenly, there was a sharp whistle. They turned to see Bardo, Dolce's older brother, framed in the warehouse door, summoning them with a raised hand. Where Stefano was scrappy and brittle, his older brother Bardo was sturdy as a barrel in his worn leather apron and wooden clogs.

Dolce pulled Bellina by the sleeve and they stepped into the cool darkness of the warehouse, into the collective murmur of a gathering crowd. At once, Stefano vanished into the swarm of bodies. Bellina's eyes adjusted to the shadows as she wedged herself into the ragged group of faces both familiar and unfamiliar. Men and women, young and old. Blacksmiths, saddlemakers, tavern owners, shopkeepers. Domestic servants like Bellina herself. Dyers, weavers, combers, and others who supported the wealthy silk and wool traders of the city. Some stood. A few balanced on wobbling wooden chairs; others sat on the dirt floor. Around the group, the foul aroma of the wooden wool dyers' vats—some large enough to hold a carriage—filled the stagnant air. Rancid, mud-colored sludge rippled inside the nearest barrel. She pinned her nose.

Suddenly, Stefano clambered atop a stack of crates in one corner of the warehouse, his head and upper body now visible above the throng. "We are one of many!" he called to the crowd, without preamble. "Cells of *frateschi* are gathering in the dyers' warehouses, yes, but also in artisan workshops, in private homes. In enclosed gardens across the city." Murmurs and calls of approval filled the air. Dolce pressed two fingers to her lips and let out a shrill whistle in support of her brother.

"You already know that many among the poor have dedicated themselves to our cause," Stefano continued. His hair was lank and uncombed from the edges of his cap, his woolen gown wrinkled and threadbare in spots. Yet to Bellina, watching Stefano rise above the crowd was like watching a bright star emerge where there had been only darkness.

"Now, there are more wealthy than ever among us," he said. Bellina felt the room fall still, the ragged crowd focused on Stefano's passionate words. "It's true. Rich, powerful. But, my friends, as much as we want the lords of our city to turn away from wickedness and repent exploiting the poor, we cannot let their lust, their obsession with things of this world cloud our vision, our purpose. We must stay strong. And above all," he continued, "if ever there was a time to throw the trappings of your own envy to the dung heap, it is now."

At that moment, a streak of golden light filtered through the warehouse door, falling on Stefano's slender frame above the crowd. Suddenly, his voice boomed. "Who among you will open your flesh with the whip this very night? Who among you will deny yourself the marriage bed?" Another round of whistles filled the warehouse. "Who will deny the lust in their hearts?"

Bellina watched Stefano's amber-colored eyes reflect the golden light. It was like watching the dawn. Like watching the birth of a terrible, avenging angel.

WHACK!

Bellina wielded the leather strap, letting it crack across her bare flesh. The sting shot across her back and radiated through her limbs. Her jaw clenched tight as Stefano's words filled her. *Who will live our Lord's example? Whipped and beaten in the streets? Who will deny the lust that most excites the human heart?*

Whack!

At first, Bellina had been surprised she could cause herself such physical pain. But as Stefano's words echoed in her head, this cracking open of her flesh seemed a small act. The least she could do. In the end, insufficient. That was because she had gotten it all wrong.

About the time Bellina had convinced herself she believed more in Stefano's internal fire than in Brother Savonarola's, incredibly, the priest's predictions came true. He wasn't an imposter, like some said. Instead, he was a prophet.

Bellina had stood sweating in the crowd when Brother Savonarola claimed he had seen a flaming cross in the sky. A divine warning, he had cried until his eyes strained against their sockets. Unless the Florentines repented of their evil ways, unless every person committed themselves to self-denial, their city would fall under siege. A holy punishment. At the time, it had seemed impossible to imagine, but to Bellina's amazement, he'd been right.

She'd seen it with her own eyes: The ugly, red-bearded king of France reining his warhorse through the city gates with an embroidered canopy over his head, held aloft by four knights with feathered plumes sprouting from their helmets. Strange archers, crossbowmen, and foot soldiers breaking down doors, ransacking bakeries, setting fires in the squares. Lisa's wide-eyed father tucking his women into the root cellar and his last remaining valuables into a locked cabinet. For eleven days, there were no rules. Florence was filled with terrifying stillness and smoke. Breathless.

When Bellina and Dolce finally met at the near-deserted washing well on the twelfth day, they learned the Medici had fled the city with the clothes on their backs and a few scattered baubles tucked into their pockets.

Whack!

Bellina got down on her hands and knees like a dog, her breasts swaying free from their stays, tingling in the cold air. She breathed heavily through the nearly unbearable sting of the leather strap across freshly opened flesh. Yes, their lustful hearts must be denied. She calculated the days until the next meeting at the warehouse, the next time she would see Stefano, the flaming center of her mind. She felt a new, inner hysteria rise, and then slapped it down with another lash.

After a few moments, the pain faded, leaving a throb to remain until the next strike. Surely they were guilty of coveting worldly things in this very house? Lisa's family had been evil for amassing their small wonders, and Bellina had proven herself evil by coveting them. By believing they would bring her some sense of worthiness, some illusion of deserving. But no. She didn't deserve any of it.

The worst part had been finding Lisa's father sobbing by the hearth, mourning the loss of his few remaining tenant farms. The French soldiers had burned and looted their way through the countryside beyond the city walls, he told her. With a single torch, they had wiped out generations of grapevines, wheat fields, and olive trees. Signor Gherardini was helpless; he could only watch his meager fortune dwindle.

Yes, Stefano may be only a pawn, but surely he was right. They were being punished. It was the Florentines' own iniquities, their own pride, their own luxuries that brought such misfortune. It was time for self-sacrifice, for self-examination. Bellina knew she wasn't the only one opening her flesh on this night. In houses across the city, people were knotting ropes before makeshift home shrines.

Bellina set down the leather strap and lay prostrate in front of a small wooden crucifix flickering in the candlelight. Her mind swirled, trying to reconcile her self-denial with her incessant longings. In her head, she knew she must deny herself earthly pleasures in exchange for eternal salvation. And if she proved herself to Stefano, would he see her as worthy? As desirable? As deserving of something more than a lifetime of lonely servitude inside Lisa's house? But it was precisely those carnal desires that drew her back to the riverbank.

She crawled back to where the leather strap lay on the bare floor and picked it up again.

BELLINA WAS TRYING to sneak back into the house from the latest meeting at the riverbank when Lisa spotted her.

"There you are, Bellina! Where have you been?"

Still glowing with the fire of the *frateschi* and—if she was honest with herself—Stefano's bewitching presence, Bellina had hurried through the narrow alleys toward the Gherardini's sagging, rented house. The sun had already sunk below the glowing rim of the riverbank. Bellina had lifted the hem of her skirts and side-stepped the puddles near the public latrines. She had stayed out too late; they would be calling her name through the house. Bellina had slipped quietly through the back door near the bread ovens, hoping she could escape notice, but it was too late.

Since those days of French terror, the crowds around San Marco and in the dyers' warehouse had swelled. The austere Savonarola had filled the void left when the Medici fled. Now, the streets of Florence overflowed with *frateschi*. Unless they abandoned their luxuries and sinful acts, another French siege might be the least of their worries, Stefano had said. Instead, the people of Florence would be dragged into the bowels of Hell.

"I was worried. It's not safe to be in the streets by yourself." Lisa ran into the dim courtyard of the damp, old wool trader's house, divided into a warren of rented rooms years ago. She tugged at her skirts, exposing her bare feet on the worn tiles. Bellina had scrubbed that floor on her hands and knees, but the dirt of generations was embedded in its pitted surfaces. Nearing sixteen years old, Bellina's mistress was in the flush of budding womanhood, her eyes dark and sparkling, olive skin flawless, shimmering black hair falling in waves to her waist.

"I . . ." Bellina's voice trailed off. How stupid of me, she thought, not to have prepared an excuse.

But Lisa didn't let her finish. "But . . . I have news!" Lisa cried, jumping up and down and grasping Bellina's hands forcefully. Her eyes and face glowed as if she might burst from joy. "I'm to be married!"

"Married!" Bellina gasped. "Already!"

"Can you believe it?" she cried. "The matchmaker's just left. You missed the whole thing! Where were you?"

Lisa's father appeared in the shadows, a lanky, clean-shaven old man. Antonmaria Gherardini smiled and placed his hands on Lisa's shoulders. "I couldn't have imagined a better match for my girl," he said.

"Then you must tell me every detail, *polpetta* . . . ," Bellina said, mirroring her mistress's glowing face and squeezing her hands in return. "Who is it?"

"Francesco del Giocondo!" Lisa exclaimed.

"Giocondo . . . ," Bellina began. The name sounded familiar.

"Of the Silk Guild," Lisa chattered on. "His family owns a fine home near San Lorenzo. There are lands in the countryside near Montughi, horses, many hectares of olives and grapes, and . . ." Bellina watched heat rise to Lisa's face as she stole a shy look at her father. "He's not so bad to look at."

"Giocondo of the silk and wool trading enterprises," Signor Gherardini said, brushing a lock of hair from his daughter's face.

A Medici supplier—and no doubt, supporter. Bellina felt the welts on her back flare.

"And there's just one little boy to care for," Lisa continued. "Bartolomeo. Poor thing's mother has gone to God."

It seemed like yesterday Bellina had peered into baby Lisa's dark eyes for the first time, all those years ago in the echoing shadows of the baptistery. And just like that, Lisa was to be married. Bellina made herself smile. "I wish you a lifetime of joy, then, *polpetta*."

Lisa stared back, incredulous. "But . . . silly thing. You're coming with me!"

"You know I wouldn't send my Lisa anywhere without you, Bellina," Signor Gherardini said.

For a moment, Bellina felt as if she'd been slapped. She was going with Lisa? Across the river to San Lorenzo? The truth dawned like a rush of winter air through the hearth. In an instant, she understood the family's expectations of her. She was to dedicate herself to Lisa, to be responsible for her life as if it were her own, to move to a household of strangers who might lust for everything Bellina now loathed. The future had caught up with her sooner than she thought: Bellina would never seek a life for herself outside of Lisa's house. For a moment, she was afraid she might vomit up the morning's bread right there on the worn tiles.

"You remember how I placed my baby girl in your arms when she was only days old. Who better to serve her as she takes on the duties as a wife and mother?" He sighed with pride. "One of our city's most important households, no less."

Bellina dipped her head. "Yes, sir." The ramifications of Signor Gherardini's decision pooled into the crevices of Bellina's mind like the swell of the river on the bank. Of course they assumed she would follow her mistress. It was silly to think she might aspire to a husband and a house for herself at twenty-nine years of age, that she might aspire to a purpose beyond the walls of Lisa's house. They knew nothing of her pursuits at the riverbank and would never understand.

For a moment, Bellina heard Stefano's voice in her mind, saw his flashing amber eyes reflecting the sunset. Her body trembled; her impure thoughts had to be refused. Punished.

No.

She was destined to spend her days dressing Lisa, hanging laundry, swaddling babies, and growing old by the light of a window with her embroidery. Lisa's father had only ever shown Bellina kindness. Charity. The magnanimity of his heart. But in that moment, she hated him.

How had Lisa's father managed such a union? Had Signor Gherardini raised a dowry in the years since Lisa's birth? Glancing around the damp, crumbling courtyard, Bellina could hardly imagine it.

Lisa's father seemed to read her mind. "I had the fortune to meet Francesco del Giocondo and his brothers during one of my family business arbitrations; seems another brother who runs their silk trading office in Portugal owes them money. Anyway, I found an opportunity to mention that my daughter is of marriageable age and notable beauty. We put together a modest bride price by conveying to Francesco del Giocondo our estate at San Silvestro in Chianti—one of our last remaining and, in my view, our best. But at least our Gherardini name, our legacy, counted for something."

"And surely her virtue counted for more, Signor," Bellina said.

"That goes without saying." Her father smiled, affectionately running his knuckle along his daughter's jawline. "You'll go on caring for Lisa as always," Lisa's father continued. "Before long, God willing, she'll have children to look after. You've been a good and loyal servant, Bellina. Francesco del Giocondo and his family will welcome you into their household. It's written in our contract." He broke a smile, but it quickly disappeared. Did he realize he hadn't asked her first, before writing her name in the marriage contract? "As much as Lisa, you will represent our Gherardini name. You'll be held to the same standard as my daughter."

"Of course she will, *papà*!" Lisa took Bellina's hands again. "You know Bellina is the most trustworthy person in the world, and she will take great care of me. Bellina! Isn't it perfect?"

Bellina forced a grin. "It's perfect," she said. "*Perfetto.*"

LEONARDO

Milan, Italy
1497

My fresco is perfect, the monks tell me. *Perfetto.*
But I know it's not.

How to render the very face of treachery? The question has plagued me for longer than I care to admit.

The northern wall of the monastery refectory has some color, at last. For months, it has stood as a blank surface of white plaster, hundreds of charcoal marks sketched, rubbed out, and sketched again. The composition is set now, a symmetrical arrangement of Christ surrounded by his disciples at the table. A Last Supper to end them all. I have worked out the faces of the figures. All but one.

"The prior is getting impatient."

Ludovico Sforza, Duke of Milan. My patron. My friend.

The stocky, dark-haired duke paces, hands clenched at the small of his back. At the refectory doors, his guards stand idle in their ridiculous-looking armor, fingering carefully engraved sword hilts. They must be bored, standing all day by the doors and watching me pace back and forth, making small adjustments with my charcoal. Now, they watch me climb down from the tottering ladder and take a few steps back from the fresco in progress.

"Yes, my lord." I scratch my beard, knowing well enough that it's Ludovico who's become impatient with my slow pace, not that silly prior. My eyes flit back to the figures taking shape on the wall. Judas Iscariot. That traitor. He is the only one I haven't worked out in my mind.

A long table, just like the ones in this very refectory, stretches across the wall in the foreground. The apostles assemble around the Christ, composed into invisible triangles that please the eye. An old trick. While the Dominican friars of Santa Maria delle Grazie spoon watery stew into their mouths, they will consider this new Last Supper on the refectory wall. For generations to come, it will be an exercise in spiritual contemplation.

But things have not gone well. I take a deep breath, inhaling the familiar aroma of wet plaster and pigments, a smell so much a part of me I think it must emanate from my pores when I sweat.

Under normal circumstances, Ludovico invites me to eat with him among the monks, or he comes to watch me paint. It calms him, he tells me, to watch me lay pigments on the wall. A slow, painstaking process. I feel for him. The man has just lost his wife, Beatrice, only twenty-one, and his newborn baby, too. Both suddenly gone to God. Black silks hang still over the windows of the Castello Sforzesco. Who am I to begrudge him the simple distraction of watching paint dry?

But Ludovico doesn't care about how to make the face of Judas. That is my job. And besides, the duke is preoccupied with other things.

The French are coming. At least that's what the friars say.

I'm surprised the French haven't already arrived at the gates of Milan with their muscular, black steeds, their flags flapping royal blue and gold, and their shining metal helmets. But it seems they have gone to my home city of Florence instead.

"Leo."

Ludovico, duke of Milan, comes to stand behind me. I hear his gruff voice utter my nickname; it echoes in the vast space. Then there is the familiar jangle of emblems that decorate the front of his blue silk gown.

For a moment, I grasp the rungs of the old ladder with my paint-stained hands. "My lord," I say, turning to face him. Once, I stood in trembling awe of Ludovico Sforza Il Moro, this powerful man, even though he stands a full hand shorter than I. But now, I feel only compassion. No, pity. He regards me shrewdly, chest out, a prized rooster even now. But up close, I see that his beard, usually thick and oiled, has become scraggly. Unkempt. His eyes are sunken, shot through with red veins, ringed in shadows. The unfortunate events of the last year have taken their toll.

As long as I have stayed in Milan—some fifteen years since I managed to escape Florence—Ludovico has been my sponsor, yes. But he also has become a friend and confidant, or rather, I have become his. And it seems I have become something of a marker of his status. But now, he is mostly impatient with me.

"The brothers and the prior," he says. "They have been forgiving until now. What do you need to finish the work?"

For the length of a silent pause, I consider telling him the truth. That my new, experimental pigments refuse to bind to the plaster. That the entire thing is peeling and blistering. That I want to tear it off the wall with my bare hands and leave Milan before the French arrive at the gates. That none of it matters anyway if the red-haired French king takes Ludovico Sforza as his prisoner.

"It's the Judas, my lord," I say instead. "You have seen my sketches. I am still working out how to render the face."

I know he is right. I must finish, but not to satisfy the prior, the monks, or even His Lordship. I must leave because it's no longer safe to be here in Milan. And meanwhile, my father has written me a letter. I can come home, he tells me. There are new opportunities in Florence.

But I hesitate. My father and I have rarely seen eye to eye in all my forty-five years. And Florence may be more dangerous than Milan, in the end. The French are at least as interested in its treasures as in those of Milan. Plus, there is a fanatical priest who has somehow taken control of my native city. Girolamo Savonarola. A passionate man. Perhaps demented. And—no surprise to me— the Florentines are deranged enough to believe him, to follow him. My old Medici patrons have been lucky enough to flee to Rome with little more than their lives. Savonarola spews fire from the pulpit of San Marco. People throw garbage at noble families who wear fine clothes in the streets. Behind closed doors, women lash their backs with knotted ropes. How long can that last?

And yet, for now, I do not have a better prospect.

All the same, I am in no hurry to leave Milan. I feel guilty. Ludovico has kept me employed in all sorts of artistic endeavors. I have painted portraits of two mistresses and began another of his young wife before she succumbed to the ravages of childbirth. I have decorated rooms, orchestrated marriage ceremonies, painted murals in the towers of the Castello Sforzesco, not to mention the untold number of designs for hydraulic and scientific projects. I have even designed a gigantic metal and clay horse in honor of Ludovico's father.

But the clock ticks loudly. My time here is soon finished. There is no longer any doubt.

Surely His Lordship senses I am ready to go, for he has presented me with gifts to lure me to stay. My favorite: a tract of vines along the outskirts of this very monastery. After a season, the vines have turned lush and heavy with fruit, the promise of good wine to come.

As much as I would like to stay here in His Lordship's good graces, I see as clearly as anyone that his days are numbered. Returning to Florence makes as much sense as any other solution. There, at least, I might decide my next step, find my next patron. To make a big change, something must push and something else pull; at least that's what Salaì, my valet, tells me. Sometimes, the boy utters something intelligent beyond his years.

"Choose one of the monks as your model for the Judas and be done with it," Ludovico proclaims, a grin on his face.

"Even better, the prior," I say. "If only he could keep still and his mouth shut long enough for me to paint him."

Ludovico spits out a laugh as though it has escaped him before he knows he will laugh at all. "Perfect!" he exclaims. "Put the old dotard in the painting. His pride will grant us all merciful silence for a long time. Do it for me if for no one else."

I nod. The duke is my friend and patron. If he wants a minor devil to represent a major disciple, then who am I to deny him? "Judas he is," I say, and climb the ladder with a stick of red chalk.

The duke, still chuckling, turns away. His guards spring to life. At the doors, he turns once more to face me. Suddenly, his face darkens and his smile disappears.

"Finish it." His voice echoes in the vast space. He knows my time is up, too. Then the ringing metal of his emblems grows fainter as he departs.

My rickety ladder scrapes across plaster as I climb back down. I step back and contemplate the ghastly purple, the raw orange, the garish, failed colors of my fresco.

A disaster.

But it's time to let it go. I will gather Salaì and all the other precious things I've collected in Milan. Yes. I will finish the Judas and then consider my next step. I may even return to Florence, after all these years.

BELLINA

Florence, Italy
1497

S tefano wanted to see her. That was what Dolce had whispered at the washing well. But Bellina couldn't imagine what he would say—or how she might explain herself.

The last time Bellina had encountered Stefano in the streets nearly two years before, she had ducked behind the wheel of Lisa's wedding carriage so he wouldn't see her.

The marriage procession had proven miserable, at least as far as Bellina was concerned. She knew Lisa's new husband, Francesco del Giocondo, had made a fortune in the silk and wool trade, but Bellina had failed to predict such a public spectacle. Bellina attempted to hide behind Lisa's gangly cousin, Gherardo, whom Francesco had agreed to employ as an apprentice in his silk workshops as part of the marriage contract.

As the wedding carriage creaked through the wealthier streets, well-wishers whistled and called their congratulations from their windowsills of coursed stone. In the poorer sections and squares, people threw garbage, and an old woman screamed that wedding processions were no longer lawful in Florence. Was this true? Bellina wondered. Turning into Francesco's neighborhood of San

Lorenzo, they passed the church where past rulers of the Medici family were laid to rest inside elaborate chapels.

A few steps away, they reached the bright yellow, arched doorway of Francesco's fine home on the via della Stufa. Bellina praised Heaven that Stefano hadn't seen her following behind this abhorrent parade of worldly excess.

Still, Stefano had known where to find her.

Ever since Lisa's marriage, Bellina had avoided the dyers' warehouses; in fact, she had hardly left the house at all. She was ashamed to imagine what the *frateschi* would think of her now, serving one of the most unabashedly wealthy families of Florence. The thought of marching to the dyers' warehouses from a house filled with fine silk frocks, brightly painted ceramic dishes, gilded coffered ceilings, and chests inlaid with walnut seemed impossible to fathom. And she was ashamed and afraid of what her friends might think of her. So, she had stayed away.

Soon enough, the flow of wedding gifts had turned into baptismal presents as Lisa gave birth to a son, Piero, and a daughter, Piera, in quick succession. They shuttled the babies to the baptistery, then put them in the hands of wet nurses as Francesco looped sparkling gemstones on silken cords around Lisa's neck. Other small treasures arrived in packages each time Bellina answered the bell at the door: brass and silver basins, goblets of blown glass, leather boxes filled with tassels of gilded threads and cords, gilded scissors with an engraved sharpener, hollow ostrich eggs, and strands of black amber from the Baltic Sea. Each time Lisa unwrapped a package, Bellina shuddered at the same time that she was struck with wonder.

During the day, Bellina threw herself into the relentless work of infants, doing her best to ignore the glaring displays of sinful excess around her. She listened to the gleeful singing and friendly advice of Alessandro the cook, who warned her to keep the children quiet and to steer clear of Francesco's mother. She coddled Francesco's four-year-old son, Bartolomeo, whose young mother had died in childbirth. The poor thing, Bellina thought. Two more hungry mouths have usurped him. Bellina found the little boy's wide brown eyes and angelic smile impossible to resist. She slipped him small pastries from the kitchen when no one was looking and taught him the same hand-clapping games and songs she had once taught Lisa and her siblings years ago in that run-down house across the river.

At night, in her stark, third-floor servant's bedchamber, Bellina washed her face in the basin, stored her plain tunic in the wooden cabinet, and lie face down on the cold tiles. In the quiet, her mind swirled with images of Lisa's new velvet cloaks and ornate salt-cellars, with desperate prayers intoned before Savonarola's pulpit, with her self-inflicted lashings. She struggled to push away her darkest yearnings. The old, serpentlike curl of temptation. Her lustful heart. Instead, she forced herself to focus her prayers on Lisa and her growing family. Surely Lisa's father had been right; dreaming of anything more than working at Lisa's side was absurd.

But then, one morning over the scrubbing board, Dolce had whispered that Stefano wanted to see her. And as much as Bellina dreaded what he might think, she couldn't deny the temptation to see him, a pull as inexorable as a wave dragging her into a vast sea. Now, Bellina made her way through San Lorenzo and past the cathedral. As she passed the Orsanmichele, she felt the frowning eyes of its sculpted saints staring down from their niches in its old façade. Wriggling away from their stony judgment, she ducked behind a cart stacked high with tanned hides as it rattled across the cobblestones. Heading into the Por Santa Maria near Francesco's silk workshops, Bellina heard the relentless clacking of hundreds of wooden looms, the constant labor of teams of men and women.

Above all, Bellina realized, it was Francesco who had taken some getting used to. Where Lisa's father had been kind and gentle, her husband was brash and broad-chested, swaggering through the house like a rooster. When he arrived home after a day in his textile workshops, the atmosphere of the house shifted. Lisa became suddenly coy; Francesco's mother caught even more wind in her sails, and the servants—including Bellina—retreated to the shadows.

Francesco's mother, who spent her days with her rosary or embroidery needle, emerged only to fawn over her son as if he were a prized horse. When Lisa appeared, having spent hours at her mirror preparing for his return, Bellina watched Francesco's eyes light up with delight. But then he took his meal and retreated to a ground-floor room where he received business associates. There, by the light of a dozen candles, he pored over the thick ledgers chronicling the processing of silkworm cocoons, the dyeing and reeling of finished thread, the preparation of gilt-silver strips, the exchange of coinage between Antwerp and Lyon. Francesco clicked and clicked the beads of the abacus until well into the night. Only then did he retire to his bedchamber to lie with his young wife.

Bellina knew Francesco was a staunch supporter of the Medici, but she did not know how far his influence reached. Francesco's wealth and the silk trade were precisely what she, Stefano, and the *frateschi* had stood against. She did not want to see Lisa dragged to Hell by the goods and wealth of her new family, but how could she say such a thing to her bright-eyed mistress, who was living a life beyond her imagining and swelled with hope for the future?

AT THE RIVERBANK, Bellina tucked herself behind the trunk of the draping willow tree and watched people file out of the dyers' warehouse. She recognized a few faces, but since the last time Bellina had attended a meeting, the crowd had swelled larger than any she had ever seen.

When at last the crowd dispersed, Bellina made her way to the door. In the dim light of the warehouse, she recognized Stefano's familiar silhouette hunched over the ashes of a small fire. The embers struggled in the dank, uncirculated air.

"Stefano," she said. "Dolce told me that—" But when he turned and set his piercing eyes on her, her voice left her.

"You are living with Giocondo," Stefano said bluntly from across the room.

Bellina swallowed and stared at the dirt-stained hem of her dress. "I can explain," she began, as he stepped slowly toward her. "Lisa's father made me follow her when she wed Francesco and tend her for . . ."

She wished he would take his eyes off her so she could catch her breath and gather her courage. But suddenly, Stefano was right beside her. He reached for Bellina's hand, and she did gasp for air then. His touch, a warm, rough palm, was overpowering. He smelled of unwashed hair, of the moldy riverbank, of the fire's charred remains.

"I know," he said. His eyes, as unusual and arresting as the engraved amber gems that filled the leather boxes in Lisa's bedchamber, studied her face. Bellina felt a warm rush flow through her veins. She saw his nostrils flare. "It's a sign; I'm sure of it."

"A sign?" Bellina wavered.

"You have been placed in the home of a wealthy merchant. A known adherent of the Medici."

Bellina's thoughts flew to Lisa and her babies, and to little Bartolomeo with his angelic face. She didn't wish to bring harm to any of them.

"The Medici made Francesco a rich man," Stefano continued, meeting her gaze in a look that went on long enough for Bellina to swallow what felt like a cold stone in her throat.

"They are not doing anything against us," she said, comforting herself that this may be a lie only in part. Lisa cared little for politics, but Francesco's opinions might be very different. She looked into Stefano's eyes, conflicted. "I promise . . . ," she said. "Everything that's been said here I've held in the strictest of confidence. I've told no one, not even Lisa . . ."

Stefano nodded. "You misunderstand. I'm not questioning your sympathies. You can help us—perhaps better than anyone."

"Me?"

"You may be in the perfect position to help our cause. We are sending bands of followers—young boys—to the finest homes to demand luxuries for a great bonfire in the Piazza della Signoria. Servants are organizing in noble households across the city. I'm sure Francesco del Giocondo has collected a few vanities that might burn on the pyre."

Then he leaned in so close that Bellina's senses filled with him—a powerful mixture of smoldering embers and perspiration. For a moment, Bellina thought he might kiss her. A hot wave of panic mixed with desire flushed through her.

"I don't know what to say." Her voice wavered.

Then she felt the rough stubble of his chin against her ear and he only whispered.

"Say yes."

"FRANCESCO, YOU SHOULD have a painter make a portrait of your wife."

Bellina watched Francesco's sister-in-law, Iacopa, lean over the dinner table, green and gold beads sparkling in her elaborate cap and braids. "It's the least you can do," she teased him. "Lisa's already given you *two* living children. And anyway, any husband worth his weight is doing his wife the honor of having her likeness painted. Look at the Strozzi and Rucellai. Am I right, *caro*?" She tugged her husband's silk sleeve.

Bellina set down a basket of unsalted bread and backed away from the table. Every Sunday, the midday meal brought Francesco's brothers and their families to the house. Bellina was now accustomed to the routine of joining the other servants in the dining room shadows, their sole focus serving the extended family and at the same time making themselves invisible. Pressing herself against the wall, Bellina observed Lisa quietly twirling a long noodle around a two-pronged silver fork. Francesco sat opposite, ripping a piece of coarse bread between his fingers and dredging it into the duck drippings. Francesco's mother sat to his right; his two brothers and their wives filled the rest of the table. On the other side of the swinging kitchen door, Bellina could hear the wet nurse babbling a quiet tune to Lisa and Francesco's babies.

Francesco's brother ignored his wife's proposal of a portrait. "I made a deal with that Flemish wool broker," he interrupted. "I raised the price by ten percent, and they still agreed."

"We might charge more after the shearing season causes a shortage in the fall," the older brother said. "That worked *perfectly* with the French last season. They won't know the difference."

The younger brother nodded. "They are already short on supplies, and their flocks were reduced by disease, so I had them at a disadvantage. There was nothing they could do but agree to a higher price."

Francesco's mother sniffed loudly and frowned at her youngest son. "Should have gone up considerably more than ten percent, then." She set a merciless glare on him, and for a moment, Bellina pitied him. "Or were you feeling sympathy?" she asked.

Francesco reached over to pat his mother's hand, but the old woman pulled away as if scorched. He tried again. "My brother did well, and with the bulk the Flemish buy, he's made a tidy profit. Besides"—Francesco gave his brother a significant look— "they will order from us again, for we have not abused their trust, and likely before prices recover. We can get more then."

The old woman patted her lips with a linen cloth, though the pasta and rich stewed duck on her plate went untouched. "Well, in the meantime, we have other problems. Some of the baptismal gifts have gone missing."

Francesco held a forkful of noodles suspended in the air between the plate and his mouth. "Missing."

Bellina felt herself freeze, but she couldn't stop her hand from reaching for the small pocket she'd sewn into the hem of her *camicia*. There, she felt the handmade lace cuffs and rubbed together a pair of pearls, hard and round as pebbles. She had been keeping them there for weeks, ever since she'd seen Stefano. If everything went as planned, they would burn on the pyre. But Bellina felt these cursed objects might burn a hole in her conscience instead.

Suddenly, Bellina saw Lisa's gaze flash toward her; her heart felt as though it had stopped. Did she suspect? No. Though Bellina felt she knew Lisa's heart, the opposite was not true. Bellina felt sure Lisa knew nothing of her time spent with the *frateschi,* nothing of the rocky landscape of her own mind. Bellina noticed that several goblets stood empty. She took the ewer of wine and stared into the deep, gem-colored liquid that smelled of earth and dark fruits. She refilled each goblet, careful to still her shaking hands. She avoided making eye contact with anyone at the table.

Francesco's mother continued, lowering her voice. "It can only be the fault of one of those new wet nurses you insist on keeping in the house. I told you from the start that bringing women from outside the city was a bad idea. We cannot trust them. Poor judgment, in my opinion," she said, looking pointedly at her sons. "But no one asked me."

"But we need them," Francesco's middle brother said, stabbing a piece of meat from a platter in the middle of the table.

Iacopa interjected again. "I for one lock my bedchamber doors at night. You never know when one of your servants might steal a knife from the kitchen and kill you in your sleep."

Francesco's mother gasped and placed a hand over her heart. Bellina set the ewer down roughly and returned to the kitchen to fetch dessert as the young scullery maids cleared empty plates, gathering around the family like bees to a flower.

"Well, Mother, you don't have to worry," Francesco said, licking his fingertips. "Piera is nearly weaned, and we will send them back to the country. We're bringing in new help to assist with the chores."

Iacopa reached for Lisa's hand, a beatific smile on her face. "That's kind of you, Francesco." She glanced at her brother-in-law as Bellina began setting out dessert plates. "You see?" Lisa's sister-in-law whispered loudly enough for everyone at the table to hear. "You have a good husband. We'll get him to have a portrait made of you yet. Have you heard," Iacopa continued, "about this . . ." She turned to her husband, a question in her eyes. "What was the name of those people? The nasty little boys."

"*Fanciulli*," Giuliano answered around a deep drink of his wine.

"Yes, them. I hear they're going from door to door asking for tributes—paintings, jewels, dresses, silver. Whatever valuables people have."

"No, not a tribute," he corrected his wife, wagging a finger in a gesture Bellina thought he must repeat frequently. "That monk or priest or whoever he is . . ."

"Girolamo Savonarola," Francesco said.

"Yes, Savonarola. He wants to make a display of destroying luxury and wealth at the Carnival. They're trying to scare us, but it's for his own self-aggrandizement."

Lisa said, "But he seems to have earned the loyalty of those who feel they have no voice."

Iacopa looked indignant. "Well, I for one am not surrendering my dresses or jewelry to them or anyone else. Have they come here?" She leaned over her husband to ask the question directly to Lisa.

Lisa shook her head. "No. Not yet."

Bellina cleared her throat. "Master Francesco." She curtsied deeply, heat rising in her cheeks. Bellina had been invisible, but now all eyes were on her. "Seeing that I am the one who usually answers the door . . . If the *fanciulli* come here, what shall I do?"

Francesco spooned a dollop of ricotta with cinnamon onto his plate and turned to her. He looked as though he'd forgotten she was there. "Just"—his hand waved in the air—"just give them some cheap baubles and send them on their way."

"Yes, sir." Bellina stared at the tiles and backed away from the table, returning to the shadows of the unseen.

"BELLINA," LISA SAID quietly as she closed the bedchamber door.

"What is it, *polpetta*?" Bellina said, loosening Lisa's long, thick braid. She already had the bed warmer nestled deeply within the blankets of Lisa and Francesco's bed.

"All this talk of new uprisings and *fanciulli* has made me nervous. What if they come here? Do you think they would try to harm us? Or maybe conspire with the servants? I don't want to give up all the beautiful gifts I've received. I shouldn't have to hand them over just because some naughty little boy knocks on the door." Her eyes were wide with uncertainty; for a moment, Bellina saw Lisa as the same five-year-old whose fears she had calmed as she tucked her into bed.

On the table next to the looking glass, Bellina had lined up the metal tweezers she used to keep Lisa's brows free of hair. She poured a small vial of Lisa's favorite skin treatment, a concoction of snail water and donkey milk distilled in the sun for several days, to calm and moisturize reddened skin. "Don't worry yourself, *cara*," Bellina said, but her voice wavered.

"I have an idea," Lisa said. "You have to help me. Let's gather everything I've received as a gift since the wedding. Bring it all here. I have a hiding place no one knows about."

"A hiding place!" Bellina exclaimed. For a moment it was

impossible to breathe. Bellina held back the tearful confession that threatened to burst from her as the lace cuffs—as ethereal as a spider's web—and the tiny earrings suddenly weighed heavily inside her dress pocket.

"Yes. Look. I don't want to keep secrets from my husband, but . . . I know I can trust you. Go get the plates and gilded leather boxes from the drawers in the *salone* and bring them here."

Bellina dashed from the room, keen to be on her mistress's errand and having a goal to replace the guilty ache that consumed her.

When she returned, carrying a fragile-looking pair of ceramic plates with a man and woman in profile, she saw Lisa struggling to press the upper half of her body deep inside a wooden cabinet. Bellina had been in the cabinet many times for linens, hairbrushes, and various concoctions for body and hair in ceramic, glass, and metal containers. Lisa pulled the back of the cabinet free, revealing a false back and a deep, hidden cavity. Bellina gasped.

Lisa stood up, pressing her hand to the small of her back. "We can fit some things in here."

IN THE PIAZZA DELLA SIGNORIA, a great bonfire rushed to life.

Bellina's feet slipped as she walked on cobblestones slick with the detritus of Carnival celebrations. She pulled her threadbare cloak around her thin shoulders, holding it tight at the throat against the onslaught. Young men and women, bodies writhing. Earsplitting, cacophonous tunes on wooden flutes. Disreputable women draping themselves over balconies, calling to the men passing below. The reach of an arm, the press of bodies against her back. On any normal day, Bellina thought, you would never experience such salaciousness, but Carnival had its own rules—or none at all.

Perhaps she should turn around and return home, Bellina thought. She could simply pick apart the stitches of the pocket she'd sewn inside her shift and remove the tiny treasures. She could even hide them inside the secret cabinet compartment that Lisa had shown her. No one would ever know. In this great crowd of people, Stefano would never know if she was there or not.

But somehow, Bellina felt herself pushed along with the crowds headed toward the square. And as the tall, skinny tower of the Signoria came into view, she heard the crackle of the great bonfire. Bellina felt herself launched into the square, borne by a great wave of people. A great wooden pyramid had been constructed, and the fire had already reached the height of two men, its flames inching higher, sending black plumes into the sky.

As the flowing crowd deposited Bellina into the Piazza della Signoria, she saw there must have been thousands there, gathered around the flames. Artisans, launderers, seamstresses, bakers. Even a few richly dressed nobles. All of them watching the symbols of the wealthy burn with enraptured eyes. On the other side of the fire, Girolamo Savonarola, dressed in a simple cassock and leather sandals, stood atop a flight of steps, lifted his arms, and blessed the crowd. She stared at him in wonder. If Stefano had a fire in his eyes, the priest held the sun itself within his soul.

Two men pushed their way past Bellina. They held a large painting between them. They swung it backward once and tossed the painting into the air, bright colors illuminated as it fell onto the pyre and ignited. The crowd cheered and stomped their feet. More young men arrived; this time the crowd parted for them. A silk gown caught even before it left the hands of the man throwing it into the flames. It created an arc of fire as it billowed up and vanished in a cascade of sparks while it danced over the flames.

Bellina gasped at the next item. A book. Painstakingly copied by hand, the value was immeasurable. The contents mattered not, the leather-bound volume, itself a rarity, a treasure beyond imagining. Bellina had never learned to read or write; Lisa's father would have considered it a waste to provide such education for a servant. But her heart clenched when the heavy pages caught, and the binding turned and blackened.

Some people brought items of their own, handed over reluctantly, but mostly Bellina recognized the young men and boys that Stefano had corralled to bring the spoils of the wealthy who were not there to defend them. One by one and in pairs, the *fanciulli* threw more of the collected items into the blaze. Each item thrown into the flames elicited a cheer from the crowd.

Bellina moved closer to the fire, close enough to feel the heat on her cheeks, scorching the very air she breathed.

Only then did she see Stefano.

He stood at the edge of the fire, observing the boys throwing the treasures onto the pyre with a look that seemed to Bellina like desire, perhaps even passion. She felt the old, uncomfortable mixture of attraction and hypervigilance rise to the surface. Bellina reached into her pocket, fingering the precious spoils she'd plundered from the girl she'd raised as her own daughter.

Compared to the paintings, furniture, silken gowns, chessboards, playing cards, shoes, and treasures that fed the frenzy, these simple baubles seemed insignificant to the point of meaninglessness. What did it matter if these small trinkets were added to such an all-consuming blaze? She tightened her fist around her small hoard. For a moment, she considered turning around and

walking home. Surely, she could slip the items back into the cabinet. No one would be the wiser. And Lisa would never suspect her.

But all at once, she felt Stefano's eyes on her. Bellina watched a
wide grin stretch across his face, and then he nodded to her from
across the flames. It was too late to turn back; he had seen her,
acknowledged her presence. His eyes seemed alight in the reflec-
tion of the tongues of flame, as if the bonfire were somehow inside
him. She held her breath.

Bellina pulled the lace and pearls from her pocket and slowly
opened her fist like a child caught stealing treats. The pearls
gleamed in the reflected firelight. It seemed to Bellina that her
hand moved of its own accord. Bellina tossed the stolen treasures
into the flames. The pearls simply vanished, but for a moment
suspended in time, she watched one of the lace cuffs float in the
swirls of smoke, seeming to skip and dance, licked by flames before they consumed it. The cheers from the mob consummated
her sacrifice.

But when she looked up to judge Stefano's reaction, she saw he
was no longer watching her at all. Instead, he had moved into the
crowd, directing the *fanciulli*, urging them to add more luxuries
to the flames until the bonfire rose above the roofs and threatened
to burn Heaven itself. Then the crowd swallowed him and he
disappeared from view.

Such was the reward for her theft, for her act of resistance.

Bellina felt bile rise into her throat and she struggled to swallow down the truth.

She had betrayed Lisa.

No. She had betrayed herself.

She had sold her soul for a smile.

LEONARDO

Milan, Italy
1498

"They burned that crazy priest after all."

I scan my father's letter again, fold the parchment, and set it on the bench beside me. The days have turned warmer. I watch Salaì, my young pupil, walk through the neat rows cleared between my grapevines outside the monastery walls. Some have already sprouted small clusters of young blooms that, God willing, will hang heavy with grapes. Salaì stops to rest a delicate spray of flowers in his palm. With a sudden pang, I realize we may not be here to observe the harvest.

"Not surprising." Salaì peers at me over a row of neatly pruned vines. "It's about time the Florentines came to their senses, don't you think, Master?"

I can't help but smile at the boy's innocent reaction, his appraisal of my city's people, his clipped Milanese accent.

In Florence, they will eat him alive.

I unfold the parchment again and peruse my father's neat handwriting, perfected over years of working as a notary to our city's bankers and merchants. "Father says they built a gallows and a great pyre in the Piazza della Signoria."

"Is that the same place where your city's people burned all their worldly goods last year?" Salaì asks.

I run my finger over the smooth edges of the wax seal imprinted with the lily, our city's beloved *giglio*. "One and the same. And now, a gallows erected for a madman," I mumble to myself. Through the years, I've witnessed many acts of Florentine justice. I've seen men burned at the stake and hung from the high windows of the Bargello prison. I was present in the Duomo—just one among thousands—when those conspirators attacked Lorenzo and Giuliano de Medici with their daggers during High Mass.

"But I don't understand," Salaì says. "Now that Brother Savonarola is dead, does that mean the Medici will return to your city?"

"Ah." How to explain the complexities of Florentine politics to a Milanese boy who's never so much as set foot in Tuscany? How to convey the dozens of factions—people who dine together in the evenings and would slit one another's throats at breakfast? I've been away for so long that I imagine I won't be able to name all the groups that have formed, especially in the wake of Savonarola's destruction. "It's not so simple, my friend."

"Well, all the same, anyone might have predicted an execution," Salaì says, turning his beautiful green eyes on me. "You've said yourself that in Florence, people's attentions are short. And anywhere, people love a spectacle."

I watch the sun set over the vineyard wall and contemplate my home city. They once called Savonarola a holy man, though from the beginning, some claimed he was an imposter, a criminal. And once the priest confessed he had invented his wild visions, what choice did His Holiness have? He defrocked and excommunicated him. No longer under the pope's protection, Savonarola could only be called a heretic. Perhaps even a lunatic.

Here in Milan, the chaos of Florence has seemed far away. But now, with my father's letter in hand, I imagine the pillory in the Piazza della Signoria as if it stood before me. In my mind's eye, I see the swelling crowds. I hear the cries and chants, the drums. I watch the bodies of the condemned priest and his two companions dance and dangle from the rope, the struggle of the spirit for a last inhale of life.

And then, the flames. Fire creates distortions, illusions. Fire turns hanged men into martyrs. Still, there are those who see Girolamo Savonarola as holy. They say that after the fire, women wailed and Savonarola's followers rushed to pick up pieces of bone, scraps of cloth, and bits of charred flesh to carry home as relics.

Ridiculous.

Why would I want to return to a city of people so easily misled? But returning home is exactly what my father's asked me to do.

"Surely things have calmed down, now that this . . . this fire . . . is over?" Salaì asks.

I pick up the letter again and wave it in the air. "My father is saying that with the rise of a new city government, there will be new opportunities for people like me. The chaos of Carnival will resume. Rich ladies will stroll the streets in silk capes and pearl-studded hair. The wool and silk traders will emerge from their homes. They will flaunt their wealth as never before. No one will stop them. No. Indeed, they will be received as princes. And, my father reminds me, wealthy men will want portraits of their wives."

"Then I can't wait to see it," Salaì says. This time, he smiles.

I sigh. Am I ready to return to all that? To my city, to new patrons, to new opportunities? It's not that I'm afraid of the French invasions. I'm not afraid of false prophets or starting anew, or even of the unknown. The truth is that I dread looking my father in the eye.

"You should consider your father's offer," Salaì says, as if he could read my mind.

I nod. "Perhaps you are right. You haven't changed your mind about coming with me?"

For a moment, Salaì's face darkens. I am not sure he's telling me the truth of how he feels about leaving his birthplace and heading with me into the unknown. "They say Florence is the most wondrous city, Master. And anyway, where else would I want to be except by your side?"

I spit out a small laugh.

"Then together we go, son. Into the fire."

BELLINA

Florence, Italy
1498

I n the privacy of her tiny bedchamber, Bellina pulled a fistful of
charred remains—a few tiny human bones—from her pocket
and laid them on the rickety table. They rattled like dice against
the rough wood. Bellina turned a bone over and looked at it by
the flickering light of a single candle. She thought it might be a
piece of a finger, but she wasn't sure.

At first, Bellina had watched the proceedings, spellbound
and appalled, unable to look away. She hadn't even turned her
head when the body of Girolamo Savonarola—a man who had
seemed immortal—twitched and danced wildly at the end of the
rope then fell still at last. She kept watching while laborers piled
bundles of wood under the feet of the hanged men. The flames
had caught quickly, greedily consuming the logs. The blaze was
twice the size of the one Savonarola had ordered at last year's Carnival, and the bodies caught quickly in their white robes. At last,
Bellina watched the squeaking, tugging ropes give way, and the
bodies simply dropped into the fiery abyss.

How quickly people had followed Savonarola. And how quickly
they had brought him down.

Hours later, Bellina had stood before the smoldering remains of the great pyre where Girolamo Savonarola and his companions had gasped their last breaths. She recognized the faces of a few *frateschi* picking through the still-hot ashes, looking for any trace of the priest to take with them, as if his charred remains might confer some miraculous power. At the time, it had seemed natural to rush forward and pick up these relics, to gather any last shard of Savonarola and place it in the hidden pockets of her skirt. Why had she stuffed these rattling bones there? Had she still been under the illusion that Brother Savonarola was a prophet?

Now, Bellina realized, it seemed a silly thing to do. Had she been misled by that priest, like so many had said? Ever since she had thrown Lisa's stolen baptismal gifts into the fire a year before, Bellina wondered if she had been naïve and stupid to follow the *frateschi*. Would the crowds still gather at the dyers' warehouse? What would they do now, with their once-magnetic leader turned to ashes and a few shards of relics? Had her efforts, her beliefs, her piety mattered at all? Was she a true believer or just desperate for Stefano's attention?

In the end, it didn't matter since Stefano had disappeared and no one—not even his sister, Dolce—knew where he had gone.

Bellina collected the small bones, pushing them deep into the woolen mattress filling. Suddenly, her fingers found another small, hard object in the stuffing. She pulled it out. The old coral amulet on a silk cord, the one Bellina had snitched from Lisa's father's house all those years ago. It had been meant for Lisa's protection; instead, Bellina had become Lisa's protector. The talisman had ended up in Bellina's pocket and later in her mattress stuffing. She had forgotten about it. She turned the hard, red pendant over in her fingers and pressed it back into the mattress. Now, she was relieved that, in one of her disillusioned fits of ardor, it hadn't ended up as a burnt offering at the altar of Gi-rolamo Savonarola.

Within the thick walls of Lisa and Francesco's house, no one spoke of the fallen preacher anymore. There was no more discus-sion of those pesky bands of boys who might take their treasures. In the evenings, Bellina and Lisa took turns rocking little Piera back and forth, singing her rhymes and brushing her hair back from her hot forehead. The little girl had turned sickly. For days, she lay pallid and listless. Then her cheeks colored again and they resumed the rhythm of their days.

Madre sent Bellina with handwritten messages to their friends' fine homes and to Francesco's silk workshops near the Ponte Vecchio, where teams of women operated complicated, clacking, groaning draw looms that produced long *braccia* of colored silks, damasks, satins, and brocades; where workshop managers oversaw the weaving, storage, and sale of the colorful fabrics. Bardo, Ste-fano and Dolce's older brother, returned to his work as an overseer in Francesco's silk weaving workshop, observing the women laying one bright color alongside another into the loom until a shimmer-ing length of silk took shape in the pile. Lisa's cousin Gherardo, who had grown from an exasperatingly disobedient boy into a hand-some youth with coarse hairs beginning to sprout from his chin, was learning how to appraise metallic threads of gold and silver. He was learning the order of textile boxes and sacks, the coordination of mule carts en route to Lyon, Antwerp, and Lisbon. Francesco clicked the abacus late into the night, as textile production ramped back up to a level not seen since the days of the Medici.

Everything, it seemed, had returned to the way things were before—and for what? The Medici were long gone—and now, so was Girolamo Savonarola. There was a new regime in Florence.

Did any of it matter? Lisa and her mother-in-law dressed in ever finer layers of velvets and beaded brocades. New friends—the women of the Taddei, Doni, Strozzi, and other families whose fortunes turned on the squirm and twitch of hundreds of thousands of silkworms—pulled Lisa into their fold. Bellina dutifully followed Lisa to great courtyards filled with sculpture and orange trees, where Lisa and her mother-in-law fawned over the possessions of others.

The squares no longer stood empty, echoing with the aftereffects of the fire, the shouting. Now, they filled once again with brightly dressed people. With brocaded bags held together with twisted silk cords, velvet capes the color of jewels, and high wooden clogs that lifted them from the filth of the streets. The wool traders emerged from their homes made of fine, coursed stone to flaunt their wealth as never before. No one stopped them. Indeed, they were welcomed as princes. Everyone, Bellina thought, seemed to have returned to their sinful ways. Would they all go to Hell? Or was it just an illusion?

Bellina felt stupid. For how should she have imagined anything for herself beyond the walls of Lisa's house? She belonged to Lisa. Their lives were as intertwined as the tautly woven silk threads in Francesco's textile workshops—Lisa a bright thread, Bellina a dull one. Lisa and Bellina were the warp and weft of a fabric bonded so tightly together that neither could imagine a life without the other.

For his part, Francesco seemed oblivious to everything except one. There was only talk of finding an artist to paint a portrait of his Lisa—a token of his esteem for his wife and an object of pride that his important friends and associates might admire. He spoke as if it were the only thing that really mattered.

Part 3

WARP AND WEFT

ANNE

Chambord, France
1939

"A nne. Wake up. We're here."

A gentle hand on her shoulder. Anne raised her head, still heavy and fuzzy with the weight of sleep. Sharp corners of light at the edges of her eyelids. She focused; Corrado grinned at her.

"I don't believe it," Anne said. "Finally."

A journey that should have taken a few hours had taken five days. Five days of slow, relentless movement, stopping only to camp on the ground or sleep in the trucks, had left every bone in her body aching. Five days of trading stories with Corrado made her feel she had known him forever. She had told him about her work in the archives, how the Louvre had become like home. She described her routines with Marcel and Kiki, her life without a father. How she had shielded and rescued Marcel from countless bad decisions; how he, in turn, had taught her how to cheat at card games, how to light a fire without a match, and how to drive a car.

In turn, Corrado had told Anne about his childhood in Florence, his parents' multigenerational legacy of working in Florentine textile production, and their decision to make new opportunities for the family by moving to the garment factories in the Sentier district of Paris. He was so easy to talk to, this friendly Italian sewing machine repairman. It seemed odd to realize that less than a week ago, they were strangers.

Anne stepped down from the truck, working the knots from her neck and shoulders. As her eyes adjusted to the bright openness of the sky and field, she looked ahead. A gasp tore loose from her chest.

The château of Chambord towered above the surrounding flat, green fields, more like a gigantic cake than a building, its round towers reaching for the sky. The castle's perfect symmetry made it seem as if it had been lifted from the pages of a fairy tale and set down larger than life. Anne realized her jaw was hanging open. She had grown up in the shadow of Notre-Dame cathedral and had spent countless hours inside the Louvre, but nothing could rival the splendid grandeur before her eyes.

Corrado opened the door of the truck, got out, and stretched his arms above his head. "*Madonna mia!*" he exclaimed, his voice filled with laughter, and Anne could think of no better expression to describe the sight. She laughed, too.

Anne stepped toward the entrance, feeling her knees crack in protest after days of being squashed into the cramped cab. She heard Lucie's voice.

"*Venez!*" she called. "The head of the depot is going to show us where to unload everything. We need to have our inventories ready to take notes. They're sending the drivers straight back to Paris tomorrow for another load."

The drivers were returning to Paris? Already?

"*Oui, madame,*" Anne said, then turned around to face Corrado, who stood watching her closely. For five days, the two of them had only had each other for company. Now, abruptly, their long hours of conversation had come to an end. Of course they had. They had arrived at their destination. Anne felt a wave of emotion, something like embarrassment, wash over her.

Corrado clapped his hands together. "We made it. And the *Mona Lisa* made it, too."

"*Merci,*" she sputtered, "for . . . safe passage here. I guess I'll see you later."

"See you," said Corrado, and she left him standing there next to the truck, hands in his pockets. She felt his brown eyes sear marks into her back as he watched her walk away.

MONSIEUR SCHOMMER, an elegant man with graying wisps of hair at his temples and a tight bow tie, was not so enchanted with the château of Chambord.

"This building presents special challenges," Schommer announced, his voice echoing through a cavernous, vaulted entryway that smelled of mothballs. Anne followed Lucie, joining several dozen Louvre guards, curators, conservationists, archivists, and their assistants, all exhausted after the trip from Paris. They resolutely gathered around Monsieur Schommer to hear their instructions.

"For a start," Schommer continued, "as beautiful as the château is, it's not as well-maintained as we could have hoped." Anne watched beads of sweat collect on Monsieur Schommer's brow. The air inside the château was stifling, even as the sun had sunk low in the sky and evening approached. "There's damp everywhere." He sighed. "We have to locate the driest rooms for storage."

Surely the Louvre administrators had known what they were

doing when they chose Chambord as the location for their primary depot? Now, Anne wasn't so sure.

"Looks like if you lit a match, the whole thing might go up in smoke." Anne wheeled around to see a portly man with bright blue eyes and a white mustache in the shape of bicycle handlebars. He wore a faded, shabby uniform and the short-billed cap of the Louvre guards.

Monsieur Schommer hesitated, then said, "It's a fair point, Pierre. Monsieur Jaujard and the other authorities are already aware of the fire risk. That's one reason many of the works will be here at Chambord temporarily and then sent out to other depots in the Loire Valley. But Chambord is our best option for now. It's far enough from Paris and is one of the few buildings in the government's possession remotely equipped to store the contents of the Musées Nationaux. We also have things coming to us from the Château of Compiègne and other collections. We have to find space for everything."

"If you can get them past that ridiculous staircase," Pierre whispered loudly behind them and then huffed a laugh, sending a murmur through the staff.

Anne stared. Pierre's assessment was right. A giant, complicated staircase with interlocking spirals rose before them, its elegant shape swooping and diving against the backdrop of the vaulted wall. It was only a staircase, Anne realized, but it was perhaps the most complex assemblage of curved banisters, shadowy recesses, and irregular treads she had ever seen. Anne couldn't help taking a step forward to admire it.

"The staircase," Monsieur Schommer said, "you may know, was likely designed by Leonardo da Vinci."

"Leonardo da Vinci was here? In the Loire Valley?" one of the conservators' assistants asked.

Schommer nodded. "François I lured Leonardo here from Florence in the last years of the artist's life; the king became Leonardo's primary patron. This innovative, double-helix staircase even appears in the pages of Leonardo da Vinci's notebooks. We believe he may have been responsible not only for the staircase but also for an ingenious system of air circulation in the castle." Monsieur Schommer stepped toward one of the dark doorways. "The doors are low, *messieurs-dames*. Mind your heads," he said, swatting a cobweb. "Many of our crates will not fit through the openings. Follow me."

Anne filed into the next room behind Lucie and the others. Pierre, the white-haired guard, limped alongside them, and Anne wondered what kind of injury had caused such a lasting impediment.

Among the crowd, Anne suddenly caught sight of Georges Dupont, the head of museum security and the man who had hired her brother. She ducked behind Lucie. What excuse could she possibly offer if he asked where Marcel was? Why hadn't he come with them on this important trip? Anne had put her reputation on the line to secure that job for Marcel. Now, she didn't know what to say. She tried to stay out of Monsieur Dupont's line of vision as they moved from one splendid room to another, listening to Monsieur Schommer drone on about the joys and challenges of Chambord. High, arched windows let in beams of golden evening light.

At last, the staff moved back outside, where the drivers, more guards, and the rest of the staff were moving back and forth in exhausted rotation. Anne searched for Corrado, and she found him unloading crates from the back of his own delivery truck. Lucie stood among a group of senior curators huddled around the back of a second truck.

Immediately, Anne recognized the special crate with the three red dots. The *Mona Lisa*.

"*La Joconde*," Anne whispered to Lucie. "Where will she go?"

"Schommer has promised Monsieur Jaujard that it will stay at his bedside. He won't let the crate out of his sight."

Anne nodded, but then she heard a loud huff beside her. Pierre stood alongside them, propping a small crate against his crooked leg. "Have they not noted the fact that this gigantic building is standing in the middle of an empty field? An easy target from the air, if you ask me." The women followed his gaze to the cloudless sky and then Pierre lifted the crate and hobbled toward the château's main entrance. Anne and Lucie exchanged a stifled laugh, but Anne hesitated.

"You think he's right?" Anne whispered. "Surely Monsieur Jaujard . . . Monsieur Schommer . . . wouldn't put us—everything—in danger like that?"

For the first time, Anne noted deep furrows between Lucie's eyebrows. "They've worked hard to find the safest place. And it's still safer than Paris, I can promise you that." Lucie hesitated. "You're not regretting your decision to come, are you?"

Anne stared into the truck bed, where dozens of color-coded crates awaited. "No. Of course not."

For the next couple of hours, until the sky turned the color of the deep sea, Lucie, Anne, and a few other staff worked to organize seemingly endless boxes full of files and archival materials. Late in the evening, a curator brought them *pain au jambon*, which Anne gratefully accepted.

In a large dining room, Anne and Lucie arranged and rearranged the boxes of archival records, discussing how they might
best keep things straight, and how they might track everything
that came through the door. They decided on a naming system
for the vast galleries within the château that might serve as storage spaces for everything from Egyptian mummies to priceless
oil paintings.

When it became too dark to work, two museum guards entered the room, announcing they would show everyone to their
sleeping quarters. They led Lucie and some higher-ranking staff
members to bedrooms throughout the château. Down the hallway from Lucie's room, Anne and a few other female assistants
were brought to an enormous, vaulted hall—a room as big as
her entire apartment building, she guessed—where narrow cots
in neat rows stood on the marble floor. She recognized a few of
the other typists and curatorial assistants moving tiredly among
the cots. Anne spied her old, worn suitcase clustered along with
others in one corner of the room. She wondered if Corrado had
brought it up for her.

She stopped the guard who had shown her to the room. "Where
are the drivers sleeping?"

"They've been sent into town to find lodging. Not enough
room here for everyone. *Bonne nuit, mademoiselle.*" He turned
and disappeared into a dark corridor.

Anne sat down hard on the cot and looked up at the vast,
dark ceiling, feeling suddenly alone in the enormous room. Two
of the other typists had thought to bring flashlights. The angle
of the feeble beams cast looming shadows on the walls as Anne
scrambled under the thin, musty blanket. Her body felt wretched
and wrung out, desperate for sleep, but all around her, there were

unfamiliar sounds. Creaks, shuffles, coughs, whispered prayers. Anne couldn't stop herself from listening for the drone of engines, unable to forget what the guard had said about the château being an easy target from the air. Would the Germans find them? Were they looking for the *Mona Lisa* and the other works, even now?

As her mind quieted in the darkness, her thoughts turned to her brother. Marcel. Where was he tonight? Anne's thoughts waffled from paralyzing fear to blistering anger toward her brother. Maybe he was dead, she thought, but she refused to accept that. Why hadn't he just told her where he was?

"*Messieurs-dames!*" The women heard a guard's voice echoing down the hallway. "Come! There is news on the wireless!"

Anne bolted up and made her way to the door. Museum staff, some finishing the last cigarette of the night and many already in their nightclothes, had assembled in the hallway. Wrapping the thin blanket around her shoulders, Anne followed them down to a large gallery on the main floor.

"The Huns have come," one of the curators whispered as they descended Leonardo da Vinci's great double-helix staircase. Was that true? Anne felt a shiver reach to the small of her back.

The staff shuffled into the great hall to find Pierre, the white-haired guard, crouching beside a sturdy wireless, fiddling with the knobs as static blared through the speakers. Others gathered around him; Anne spotted a disheveled Monsieur Schommer, and Professor Jacqueline Bouchot-Saupique, who had given lectures back at the École du Louvre in what felt to Anne like a lifetime ago.

Pierre straightened up as a clear voice came across the airwaves. "Listen," he whispered. "Monsieur le Premier Ministre is about to give a speech."

The crackling voice of Edouard Daladier came through the

machine. "Today, the ultimatum that our country issued to Germany has expired." The prime minister's voice sounded strange and scratchy through the old machine. "Germany has failed to withdraw its troops from Poland and continues to advance on France. Thus, a state of war now exists between our two nations."

Around the dusty little radio, everyone fell still. Anne registered fear in every pair of eyes. Even though they had prepared for this outcome, they had hoped that war could be averted. But now, their worst imaginings had come true, and they had left Paris with the museum's treasures just in time. Had she made the right choice to come, too? Anne wished there was a way to know.

ANNE SAT BACK on the seat of the borrowed bicycle, letting it wheel easily down a slope that led away from the château of Chambord and into a nearby village. In the distance, the few houses and winding streets sat neatly on a patterned blanket of green and gold fields dotted with farms.

"It's beautiful," said Antoinette, another young typist who worked in the antiquities department. Antoinette had blond hair and freckles over her nose, accentuating her large brown eyes. Monsieur Schommer had sent the two women into town to buy food and to inquire about additional sleeping space for the guards. They rode side by side, except when they had to fall into single file to navigate around the occasional automobile, mule cart, or cluster of people on foot. Even though the streams of Parisian refugees lay many kilometers behind them, Anne saw that here, too, people were leaving their homes. The news that Germany and France were at war seemed to have stirred everyone to move into the streets.

"It's not Paris, that's for certain," Anne said.

"Just be glad you're not there right now," Antoinette said, but Anne only felt a pang in her gut for her mother and Marcel.

"This town is hardly a dot on the map," Anne said. "I can't think how we'll ever find room for everyone who still needs somewhere to sleep."

"Look," Antoinette said. "There's the *gendarmerie*. They'll be able to direct us." Anne felt her stomach tighten. What could the police do?

Anne followed Antoinette from the bright sunlight into the station's cool, drab interior. A bored-looking officer greeted them. Antoinette batted her eyelashes and asked about places to stay while Anne turned to a desk where a swarthy officer with gray streaks in his hair was busy writing in a ledger. When Anne approached, he looked up.

"*Bonjour,*" Anne said nervously. She hadn't always had good encounters with the police, especially not when she'd come to rescue Marcel from the cells at their local precinct. But this policeman seemed relaxed. He sat back in his chair and surveyed her blankly.

"I'd like to report someone missing," Anne said.

"You and everyone else," he said tiredly. He opened another notebook and picked up his pen. "Tell me what happened."

"It's my brother, Marcel Guichard," Anne said. "I came home one evening—the evening of August twenty-eighth, just before leaving Paris—and he wasn't home." She took the letter out of her pocket. She'd been keeping the letter there ever since she found it on Marcel's bed. Without a word, she laid it on the officer's desk.

The officer unfolded the page and skimmed it, his eyes remaining somber. "You live in Paris." He closed his notebook.

"Yes. Please," Anne begged. "I'm worried that my brother might be in some kind of trouble."

"You can file a missing persons report," he said, studying her. "But have you looked outside on the streets, *mademoiselle*? So many thousands of people disappearing right and left . . . Do you imagine that we'd be able to locate one young man from Paris? Our departments are overflowing with missing persons reports all over France."

Anne felt her heart sink. "But you'll try."

Something in her face must have provoked sympathy because the officer reached into a file drawer and produced a form to complete. He pushed the page and a pen across the desk. "I'll send it to my colleagues in Paris."

Anne slunk off to a worn wooden chair against the wall to complete the report. At the station door, she found Antoinette still flirting with the young *gendarme*. Anne stepped out into the bright, narrow street and took a deep breath. How could a tired officer in a small-town *gendarmerie* miles away from Paris find her wayward brother? Especially now, with so many people fleeing with little more than the clothes on their backs? The officer was only pitying her. It was futile.

"There," said Antoinette, coming out of the station, her face bright. "All sorted. They gave me the addresses of a dozen residents with rooms to let. They even came up with a few extra bicycles. We'll have plenty of room for everyone." She paused. "Anne. Are you all right?"

"I'm fine."

AT A PORTABLE field typewriter set up near the window of an ornately decorated corridor, Anne worked slowly, trying not to miss any detail. *Engraved coral amulet on a silk cord,* she typed. *Italian

Renaissance, perhaps Florentine, circa 1450. She added a crate number next to the description in the ledger. She wondered how many conflicts that amulet had seen in the centuries since it was made, and if any of them could be worse than this. Did its original owner believe it might protect her from evil? she wondered. How many times had someone swiped this lovely, tempting bauble, and hidden it inside their clothing or under their mattress?

"This is not working." Monsieur Schommer entered the corridor with his mouth stretched in a grim line.

Anne glanced up from her typewriter, but her fingers continued to drum and click on the keys.

"What's not working?" Lucie said from her place at a table where she was poring over a row of crates standing stacked against the wall, calling out their contents to Anne at her typewriter. The number of crates was overwhelming and ever-changing. Some had already been taken to different châteaux and other locations around France, but there seemed to be a never-ending stream of them that needed to be counted, tracked, accounted for. Anne was beginning to think that keeping an accurate record was going to be impossible. One error, and some of the most unique and irreplaceable art in the world might go missing.

"We've opened the crate . . . with the three red dots," Monsieur Schommer said, starting to pace back and forth.

The *Mona Lisa.* Anne's fingers stopped and the clatter of the typewriter fell silent.

Schommer continued. "The dampness is already beginning to show. If the painting is damaged, there's nothing we can do to repair it in this place. I've written to Monsieur Jaujard to ask that we move her. As soon as possible."

Lucie's jaw dropped. "Where in the world would we take it now?"

Monsieur Schommer ran his hand over his thinning hair. "Maybe to Blois, Louvigny, or Chèreperrine—even to a vault at the Banque de France if we have to." Anne noted his haggard face, his eyes ringed in gray.

Lucie nodded. "If we have to redo the inventories, then of course we'll do whatever it takes." She looked around at the room, calculating the massive scale of the job to track the ever-shifting movement of the crates. "But for now," she said, "we break for lunch."

Anne was grateful to hear those words. She finished the page and stopped. It had already been a long day. She got up from her place at the rickety old table, turned around, and almost walked straight into Corrado.

He winked at her. "*Ciao, bella.*"

"*Bonjour!*" she gasped, delighted. "Haven't seen you in weeks. How was the ride from Paris?"

"The sculptures arrived here safely, and my old delivery truck is holding up well. But I'm spending a few days here now. They tell me I have something important to do—another mystery."

Anne smiled, surprised by how glad she was to hear that Corrado would be staying.

"Seeing as it's a nice day, they've laid out food on the lawns instead of in this dusty old castle," he said. "We should make the most of it before the winter comes."

Anne followed Corrado outside onto one of the rolling green lawns bordered by towering stone walls. Anne wondered if, centuries ago, the château's residents had gazed up at those walls and felt they were safe against any kind of threat. That, of course, was long before bombers took to the sky and started dropping destruction from the air.

Anne sat on a worn blanket spread in the shade of a great tree and watched Corrado from a distance as he filled his plate. He was a sturdy, lean man, with a kind of lively energy and internal spark whose charm was impossible to resist.

Corrado came to sit next to Anne, his plate nearly overflowing. She laughed and pulled her wool sweater closely around her.

"What? I have to keep myself going," he said defensively. "Why were you working in that musty old hallway?" he asked. Then he held a hard roll up to his nose and sniffed deeply. He made a disgusted face but took a bite anyway. "I thought you and Lucie had already set up in the dining room."

"We started out there," Anne said, "but then someone told Lucie the table had been used to conduct autopsies in the eighteenth century. She was pretty quick to move us out of there."

"Autopsies! And to think we've eaten off that table." He glanced down at his roll again with a new level of disgust. "I'm glad you're telling me this at a picnic." It felt good to laugh, Anne thought, even about autopsies.

"You brought us more treasures," Anne said, gesturing to the newly arrived convoy parked in the gravel drive before the château.

"Yes. You'll be glad to know I actually went inside the Louvre. Unfortunately, now it's nearly empty." He grinned. "Driving along like this with all this priceless art, I feel like Vincenzo Peruggia."

"Vincenzo Peruggia . . ." said Anne.

"Never heard the name? I would have thought the mention of it would have you spitting mad," said Corrado.

"Who's that?"

"A thief!" Corrado said dramatically. "An *Italian* art thief. He stole the *Mona Lisa* in 1911."

"Ah, yes. Of course!" Anne said. "The famous story of the man who walked out of the employee entrance of the Louvre with the *Mona Lisa* concealed in a smock. I have heard it; as well as the fact that he was caught and imprisoned. Not a very successful heist. Anyway, you know more about art than you let on, *signore*," Anne teased.

"Well, I do live in Paris," said Corrado. "I must know something about the Louvre. You told me that." He winked at her. "Anyway, maybe Monsieur Peruggia had a good idea. Many Italians say the picture should come back to Italy. Leonardo da Vinci was Italian, after all. Not French. Italians say the French stole it—along with many other Italian paintings now in your great museum, *mademoiselle*."

Anne paused, sitting with Corrado's assessment. On the one hand, his argument held some merit; some works of art had come to the Louvre after conquests and colonial campaigns of the past.

But then, turning back to Corrado's grinning face, she couldn't help but tease him back. "You're only half right," she said. "In the case of the *Mona Lisa,* perhaps you haven't heard that Leonardo da Vinci himself brought the portrait to France? So, your argument doesn't hold up, and plus, the story didn't end well for Monsieur Peruggia. And it won't end well for you either, unless you make sure the *Mona Lisa* goes back to the Louvre safely," she said.

He nodded, seeming to accept that she might outwit any of his artistic arguments. Instead, he changed the subject.

"Tell me . . . How is the search for your brother going?" Corrado asked. "Did the police turn up anything?" He set down his empty plate on the blanket. At that moment, she saw Monsieur

Dupont cross the lawn with a plate of food. She turned her back and pulled her hat down lower over her forehead as he passed by their blanket.

"Not yet," Anne said, remembering how ridiculous the local *gendarme* had made her feel.

"He's a grown man," Corrado said. "I'm sure he can take care of himself."

"Marcel?" Anne shook her head. "I don't think so. That's been my job." She paused and pushed down the rush of emotion that formed in her throat.

"Maybe you should give him the benefit of the doubt," said Corrado gently. His eyes were velvet soft, the color of a milk chocolate bar. "He might be doing something important."

Anne nodded, appreciating that Corrado was trying to say something nice. "I just wish I could find a way to make sure he's safe."

"We all wish that for our families in this time," Corrado said. Anne watched an uncharacteristic darkness descend over his face.

"I'm sorry," she said. "You must be worried about your own family."

Corrado nodded. "They thought it was prudent to leave Paris, but I worry about them in Florence, too. We have our own problems in Italy."

"You think it's safer to be in Paris than in Italy right now?"

"Perhaps, but I don't know how much longer it can last," Corrado said grimly. "There are blackouts every night. People are leaving Paris in a flood, and there are shortages of everything. Shops are closed." He sighed. "If you could see it . . . The whole street in the Sentier where my parents worked has been boarded up."

"And my mother refuses to leave," Anne said. She swallowed

hard, thinking of her drunken mother lounging in the dance hall. "I hope Marcel at least had the sense to get out of Paris. My family is crazy, Corrado."

They spied Lucie walking toward them, holding a plate with an apple and a knife. Lucie sat down beside Anne and passed a pale hand over her eyes. She dredged up a smile. "Nice to see you again, Corrado."

"*Madame,*" said Corrado. "Is everything all right?"

Lucie heaved a sigh. "I thought so. But just when we've started to get organized . . . We've finally got the archives put in good order. But now, Monsieur Schommer wants to move some things. We started to unpack some of the works to see how they survived the journey, but now, we need to repack and double-check our inventories to make sure everything's accounted for. He's worried about the *Mona Lisa,*" she said. "We need to move it, but the logistics seem impossible. Monsieur Schommer wants us to take it to Louvigny. He wants you to drive the truck with the painting, Corrado. You're one of our most proven drivers. That's why he's wanted you to stay at Chambord, I think."

Corrado's cheeks grew pink. "*Merci.*"

"Unfortunately, other paintings need to go, too," Lucie said. "Only . . ." She rubbed her eyes. "It's complicated. We've managed to secure a few more vehicles, but the drivers have returned to Paris, so we don't have a way to use them. And none of the other guards knows how to drive, so we're stuck."

Anne looked up from her plate. "I know how to drive."

LEONARDO

Milan, Italy
1499

I know how to drive a mule train." I run my hand down the length of the pack animal's neck until it calms under my touch. When the beast exhales, I yank the leather saddle strap tight. An old trick.

"I still think you should ride in the carriage, Master Leo. And anyway, I told you we should have left town last night." Salaì looks at me with those big, pitiful eyes that inspired me to pull the urchin off the streets of Milan years ago.

"Nonsense," I say, but my eyes cannot help but scan the narrow alley for any sign of my friend Luca Pacioli. I would hate to leave him behind. We Florentines must stick together in times like these. In Florence, a brilliant mathematician like Luca will soon have patrons beating down his door.

"If Pacioli doesn't show soon, we should go ahead, Master Leo. It's too dangerous to stay here," Salaì insists, his eyes shifting nervously in the alley.

The predawn air lays a chilled, moist mantle over the cobbles. The Milanese are just stirring, the morning brick ovens of the *panifici* not yet lit, the vendor wagons still quiet in their stalls.

Above our heads, an old woman slaps open the wooden shutters of her high window.

I see no sign of the French soldiers who have entered the city overnight. But suddenly, a shadow approaches.

"Master Leonardo! There you are."

Pacioli emerges finally, bearing the weight of two wicker baskets laden with provisions for our journey. He struggles under the load and piles them onto the cart.

I leave Milan with so much more than I arrived with, more than fifteen years ago now. It's taken six trunks to pack my painting supports, pigments, brushes, cases, and palettes. The four larger ones have my silk gowns, velvet shoes, and the latest Milanese hats. A man is how he dresses these days and nowhere is that statement more important than in Florence.

"His Lordship has already fled the city," Pacioli says, fear in his voice. That can only mean one thing, I think. Overnight, Milan has fallen to the French soldiers. They will overrun the city now that the defenses are broken. "And now the French are looking for *you*, my friend."

"For me?" I stand, incredulous. "Why?"

"I told him we should have left before sunset yesterday," Salaì whispers loudly. Salaì has never learned to curb his tongue; on that count, he remains the same incorrigible street child I found stealing purses. Yet I am irresistibly drawn to my dream of what he may someday become. He is my project, my challenge.

"They have seen your fresco in the monks' refectory at Santa Maria delle Grazie," Pacioli says. "The prior told me the king wanted to bring your *Last Supper* back to France with him. He was disappointed when the monks explained it couldn't be lifted from the wall!"

For a fleeting moment, I consider the idea of staying in Milan, of presenting myself before the French king, who seems already to be an admirer of my work. He might be a worthy patron. But Salaì and Pacioli . . . Well, it would be mutiny.

I look in both directions but see no sign of armored men, neither French nor Milanese. In the end, I admit that my Lord Duke Ludovico Sforza made himself an easy target for the French king. His claim of direct inheritance was problematic from the start; it took poisoning his own nephew to clear his way to the ducal seat, and his brute-force regime could last only so long. Anyway, perhaps what they say is true; the French king's own bloodline to Milan is stronger than Ludovico's. Ludovico has no friends powerful enough to come to his rescue now; he has fled just in time. I cross myself and say a prayer for his safe passage out of Milan—and ours.

Salaì is already astride his mule, which steps sideways under the load. Luca mounts his own mule, taking the reins of a fourth beast who bears the burden of several more leather cases.

The mules lean into their collars. The wagon groans under the weight of the trunks. I climb onto my own mule and press my heels into its bulging side. We step through the narrow alley toward the Porta Ticinese at the city's southern edge.

I have already transferred money into my bank account at Santa Maria Nuova in advance of our return to Florence. And meanwhile, my father writes to tell me he has secured lodging for me with the Servites at Santissima Annunziata. They have promised me an altarpiece commission as soon as we arrive.

But still. I am in no hurry to return to Florence. First, we will sidestep to Mantua and perhaps Venice, which must be full of wealthy patrons. I must remember not to smile too much, lest I appear too eager. It makes patrons suspicious. I will break the news of our detour to Salaì and Pacioli once we are underway. They may protest, but what can they do? I am the one who will pay our way home. I turn my head to the men behind me.

"Keep your heads down and follow me."

ANNE

Louvigny, France
1939

How did you avoid getting arrested?" In the passenger seat of a rusty Renault moving truck, Pierre raised his eyebrows so high, they disappeared under the brim of his uniform hat.

From behind the wheel of the squeaking truck, Anne stole him a quick glance before putting her eyes back on the road. The Renault, heavy with crates, swayed and bounced through potholes as Anne watched the back of Corrado's smaller delivery truck with its sewing machine repair logo. She gripped the wheel until her knuckles turned white.

"I could never have gotten away with it," Anne said, smiling at the memory of the day her brother had taught her to drive. "The window shattered, and the shopkeeper witnessed the whole thing. I'd driven straight into it!" she said. "But Marcel somehow convinced the man it was the other driver's fault." She shook her head. "Marcel's like that—the type of person you always want to trust, even if you know you shouldn't."

"What did he do—the shop owner?"

"If you can believe it, we walked out of there with a bag of sweets. Then he went storming off after the other driver."

"And this is the young man who got a job guarding priceless masterpieces?" Pierre teased.

"Mmm," Anne said, then bit her lip. Pierre was right. It seemed ludicrous to think that Marcel was qualified to protect the precious contents of the Louvre. What was she thinking?

"He didn't want to come with you on this adventure?" Pierre asked.

Anne hesitated at first, but in spite of his churlish demeanor, Pierre seemed harmless enough. "I wanted him to, but it seems my brother left Paris just before we did; I have no idea where he is," she said. "And to be honest, I've been hiding from Monsieur Dupont." There. It was out in the open now. She felt only relief to have unburdened herself.

"Monsieur Dupont!" The bushy eyebrows flew up again, then Pierre chuckled. "You have nothing to fear, my dear, though I realize he appears intimidating on the outside. A big man. He and I go back a long way," he said. "Served in the Great War together. He was connected with resistance groups down south where he came from," Pierre said. "He led a group that was spying on a German airfield, and he even organized a few escape routes for British soldiers."

"In the war . . . ," Anne said. "Is that how you were injured?" She glanced momentarily at Pierre's leg, stretched out straight in the passenger seat.

"Yes, at the Somme," he began, but he paused when Corrado's delivery truck suddenly slowed to a crawl. Anne touched the brakes. Despite Corrado's skill, the truck jostled a little as one wheel skimmed the edge of a pothole. Anne and Pierre flinched in unison.

"It'll be all right," Pierre said, gesturing to the truck in front. "You saw the contraption they made."

Anne nodded. The curators had strapped the crate with the *Mona Lisa* on a custom-made stretcher with elastic suspension, as if it were a high-risk medical patient in an ambulance instead of a priceless masterpiece being transported to another secret location. "Plus," Anne said, "Monsieur Schommer is with it."

"I hope he can breathe in there," Pierre said. "That truck is airtight, and it's been a long drive from Chambord already. But we must be almost there."

"Good," Anne said, tugging on the gear shift as Corrado sped up ahead of her. "Two hundred kilometers feels halfway around the world when you're transporting the *Mona Lisa*."

Overnight, the air had covered the wheat fields with a layer of frost. The line of trucks trundled onward through the barren landscape. Lone farmhouses stood empty and quiet. A vast landscape of fallow fields stretched out before them. A few times, they heard the whir of airplane engines, but when they looked into the sky, clouds obscured their view. Were German troops watching them? Would they be attacked from above?

At long last, a quiet, centuries-old manor home loomed at the end of a long gravel lane. At first sight, Anne could see that the Château of Louvigny was a gem of French Renaissance architecture, with narrow, shuttered windows on two stories, a steeply pitched roof, and a skinny, octagonal tower with a tall spire. She felt her heart lift at the sight. The castle's owners, they'd been told, had readily seen the value of the museum's mission. They agreed to find alternate accommodations and let the Louvre staff hide the masterpieces there. In spite of its impressive façade with imposing rows of windows, compared to Chambord, the old Château of Louvigny seemed a small thing. The building was nestled between groves of stark trees and formal gardens, now neglected. Anne steered the truck to a halt in the gravel drive alongside Corrado's.

Pierre shimmied down from the passenger seat before Anne could turn off the engine. Just as eager to see how the *Mona Lisa* had survived the trip, Anne scrambled out behind him. They heard the rumble of several other trucks crunching through the gravel behind them.

Corrado was already unlocking the back doors of the truck. "Monsieur Schommer!" he called, slapping on the back door with a flat hand, but gently, as if not to wake the sleeping *Mona Lisa*. "I'm opening the doors. Watch out."

There was no response. Corrado glanced at Anne, his eyes worried. "Monsieur!" he called. Silence.

"*Dieu!*" Pierre cried. "Open it."

Corrado yanked the doors open, and all of them peered into the dark truck bed. The crate with the three red dots still rested safely on the ambulance stretcher, rocking ever so gently in its suspension; but Monsieur Schommer sat with his back to the wall, sweat pouring down his cheeks, his face a horrible shade of green. He raised his head with an effort and stared vaguely at Corrado.

"Monsieur!" Corrado cried. "Are you all right?"

"Let him get some air," said Pierre. He leaned into the truck, gripping the old man's arm. "Don't worry, Monsieur. You'll feel better in a minute."

Anne hurried to assist him, taking Monsieur Schommer's other arm and helping him down out of the truck. The depot head—normally rigid in his bowler hat and bow tie—could barely stand, but they guided him gently to the ground, where Corrado thrust Schommer's head between his knees.

"Pierre, please," Anne said. "Bring him some water." She watched the old guard limp back to the truck for his metal canteen.

"Poor thing," said Anne, fanning Monsieur Schommer with her hands.

After a few moments, to Anne's relief, Monsieur Schommer lifted his head. His cheeks were growing pinker. "Well," he said. "That was an adventure."

"Why didn't you just bang on the side of the truck?" cried Corrado. "I would have stopped."

Monsieur Schommer waved his hand irritably. "We can't expose her to this freezing air," he said.

"But you could have *died*," Anne said. At once, she realized they were all risking their own safety to hide these masterpieces.

Monsieur Schommer shrugged. "It's the *Mona Lisa*," he said. "She'll be here long after I'm gone. At least if we have anything to do with it."

Throughout the morning, more trucks filled with works of art arrived. Anne's work was tedious. She stood at the door with her stack of inventories and a clipboard, checking and double-checking again. The smallest mistake meant that a priceless masterpiece might go missing. A small group of Louvre staff surveyed the various rooms to gauge the best ones to store the crates. By midday, they had all the hearths in the old château stoked with wood and burning. There was no central heat; one step away from the fireplace and Anne's fingers went numb.

Once the trucks were emptied, Anne walked into one of the large, formal salons to find Corrado and Pierre wheeling the crate with the three red dots across the floor. Monsieur Schommer fluttered in their wake.

"Can I help?" asked Anne.

"Open that wardrobe for us," Monsieur Schommer said.

Anne hurried over to the stately, ebony-inlaid cabinet in the corner of the room and pulled it open. Moving as gently as if the crate contained a sleeping child, Pierre and Corrado lifted it into the armoire and closed the doors.

Pierre breathed out audibly. "There. Safe at last."

Monsieur Schommer removed his hat and ran his hands over his hair. Anne noticed that the normally elegant man remained haggard, his suit wrinkled and his hair out of place. Anne glanced at Corrado, who was smacking his hands clean, looking satisfied with his work. When he caught her eye, she realized she was smiling without meaning to. He winked at her, and something that felt like champagne bubbled up through her veins.

"Now. Let's get something to eat. Then we head back to Chambord," Monsieur Schommer said.

Corrado's eyes widened.

"You and I have our work cut out for us." Schommer pulled at Corrado's sleeve. "There are still many things to be taken to other locations—and you're my best driver."

"Of course . . ." Corrado wouldn't look at Anne. "But in the front seat this time, Monsieur," he said, wagging a scolding finger at Schommer.

Schommer continued. "Anne and Pierre, you will stay here to help the depot heads and the other curators."

A winter wind suddenly howled against the château doors, and the flames in the hearth shuddered. Anne steeled herself against the rush of cold that swirled in through cracks in the tall windows.

The group stepped back outside as several more trucks crunched to a stop in the gravel drive before the castle's front door. Behind them, the castle loomed, casting a great shadow across the gravel and the grounds beyond. Anne and Corrado watched the curators and other staff slamming doors and opening the backs of their trucks to unload more crates. Corrado looked at her with his large brown eyes, but he seemed to struggle to find anything to say.

Anne, too, fought for words, any words other than what she wanted to say: that she desperately wanted him to stay. After a few long, empty moments, Anne said, "What do I do now?"

Corrado shrugged. "Do as Monsieur Schommer, I guess. That portrait of the lady in the cabinet? Protect her with your life."

For a long time afterward, Anne stood alone in the castle drive. She watched the dust kicked up by truck tires resettle and listened to the rustle of leaves that had fallen from the tall hardwoods. She hugged herself, trying to generate the smallest bit of warmth against the bitter winds that whipped across the fields.

BELLINA

Florence, Italy
1499

J ust as she had promised Signor Gherardini in the baptistery
some twenty years earlier, Bellina had come to accept that she
was to spend her days caring for Lisa. To protect her with her life.
It might have been a bitter potion to swallow if she didn't believe
she was undeserving of anything else.

But then, to her utter astonishment, Stefano was back. And he
wanted to see her.

Bellina could hardly believe her ears when Dolce had brought
news of her brother to the washing well. A whole year had
passed since Girolamo Savonarola's execution and Stefano's un-
explained disappearance. Bellina had avoided the dyers' workshops and had even avoided the washing well at the times she
knew Dolce would be present. Still, they found Bellina.

What did Stefano want with her after all this time?

Bellina pushed her way through the crowded San Lorenzo market toward the riverbank. Around the food stalls, women bustled in
search of supplies for the midday meal. Bellina cut through a butchers' alley, where hairy ham hocks swung from metal hooks, and
dried peppers and buds of garlic hung from the rafters on braided
cords. The smell of ripe, salty cheese made her mouth water.

She began to cross the Ponte Vecchio, but at the center of the bridge, she hesitated. She placed her palms on the railing and let the breeze rustle her linen shift. It wasn't too late to turn around and return to Lisa's house, she thought. It was her desperation for Stefano to see her, to pull her from her invisible existence, that had driven her to take Lisa's baptismal gifts. It was Stefano's words that had prompted her to steal from the one person who had been true to her for life. And for what? The praise and approval of a man who barely paid her attention? Who asked her to steal and then disappeared? She could leave him there, waiting, wondering what had happened to her just as she had wondered where he had gone all these months.

After all, Dolce's message at the washing well couldn't have come at a worse time, Bellina thought. In Lisa's house, Piera struggled to hold on to her small life. Over months, the baby girl's cheeks had turned pink, lifting their hopes. Then there was a new pallor and spike of fever, then silent days when Bellina begged the child to cry or make a sound, to wail the sickness out of her. Hope surged when the girl's dark eyes seemed alert and interested in the world; it plummeted again when she fell blurry-eyed and silent. Bellina had become attached to little Piera. Piera's big brother Piero, a year older, was as boisterous as his sister was quiet, and followed his older brother Bartolomeo from one room to the next. Francesco delighted in his two sons, calling them into his ground-floor offices and pulling them onto his lap to kiss their pudgy fingers and tousle their hair. In those times, Bellina pulled little Piera close to her, humming an old tune to the feverish little slip of a girl by the light of the window.

Meanwhile, in the final weeks of her newest pregnancy, Lisa sweated and lumbered around her bedchamber, tossing, turning, and fanning herself. She complained of pains in her legs, her back, her abdomen. Her throat burned and her ankles swelled. Bellina brought her tea infused with mint and instructed Lisa to chew on fresh basil leaves from the courtyard herb garden. Still, she suffered.

Now, Bellina realized as she hesitated at the top of the bridge, those little ones had saved her from lonely hours reliving how Savonarola had burned, how the *frateschi* had scattered, and how Stefano had vanished as if by some kind of sorcery. Her days were little more than repeated, soon forgotten moments of sweeping, of washing, of scolding and praising; of the wiping of mouths, noses, and bottoms. The relentless rhythm of the children's needs, their games, their tears, their hunger, their endless questions—all of it had kept Bellina from retreating into the tormented silence of her own mind.

Then one day at the washing well, Dolce had whispered in Bellina's ear, and for a moment, the old, strange mixture of thrill and trepidation filled her. Stefano was back in Florence. He'd fled the night Savonarola was dragged to the square, Dolce told her. He'd stayed hidden all these months. But now, he'd sent word through the remaining *frateschi* that he wanted to see Bellina. He *needed* to see her. That's what Dolce had said. In an instant, the old feeling of nervous desperation for his approval welled in her chest.

Bellina hesitated again at the top of the bridge. Then her eyes followed the flow of the river toward the dyers' warehouses along its banks. She considered their hulking forms from this high vantage point. She saw several tanners' apprentices soaked with river water, hanging skins on their wooden drying racks. Was Stefano down there, waiting for her? She felt his presence like a prickling in the small of her back; she continued across the bridge.

The old warehouse, where the dyeing vats once stood rancid and the river rats listened to the secrets of the *frateschi,* was no longer abandoned. A new owner had begun to clear the site for an enterprise to supply the renewed demand for luxurious textiles. For a moment, Bellina was disoriented.

Beyond the last warehouse in the row, a small grove of fruit trees stood forgotten and overgrown. Bellina picked her way through the brambles, her dress catching on twigs and thorns. She pulled her skirts free, wincing at the sound of rips as she pressed through the tangled vines. In the middle of the grove, a clearing parted the brush. There, she saw Stefano's familiar, lean silhouette and she thought her heart might leap into her throat. Bellina could barely breathe as she stepped through the brush that grew along the riverside. He sat on an overturned wooden bucket, his knees splayed wide, whittling. The weeks of trying to keep Piera alive, the endless harsh glances from Francesco's mother, the anxiety around the luxuries piling up inside Lisa's house . . . In an instant, all of it seemed to vanish from her mind.

"Bellina." Stefano stood and walked toward her. For a moment, his palms opened, but he stopped short of touching her.

Bellina hesitated. "I . . . I didn't know what happened to you."

Up close, Bellina saw that Stefano had grown skinny and haggard in his months of self-exile. He was a more subdued version of the man who had stirred bands of *fanciulli* to strip noble houses of their most valued possessions. Now, the fire in his eyes seemed to smolder under layers of ashes and soot.

But he didn't tell her where he had gone. "You are still living with Francesco del Giocondo," he said instead.

She struggled for an answer. "Yes," she breathed.

He nodded, stepping closer. He smelled of perspiration and

unwashed clothes. Something like iron. Like blood. "They have profited from the new . . . order."

Now, her mind rifled through the stacks of gilded, ceramic plates in the dining room, the silk shoes in Lisa's wardrobe; the brass dishes, leather bags, and velvet capes scattered in the cabinets throughout the house. Bellina hedged. "I don't know much about Francesco's business," she said. "My job is to serve and protect Lisa. But I won't . . . I can't . . . *steal* from them anymore." Her heart pounded in her ears and her throat was so dry it burned.

Stefano's face wavered. He seemed to want to reveal something but stopped himself. Then he reached out and she felt his rough palm brush her cheek. For a long second, the thrumming heartbeat in her ears vanished.

"No," Stefano said finally. "One more silk dress on the pyre won't make a difference at this point. You have a bigger role for us."

"Me?" Bellina's eyes widened.

He nodded. "From inside Giocondo's house? Yes. Servants are good at making themselves invisible. You can be an important source of information for us, the very thing we need. Perhaps you know there is a new plan to bring the Medici back to the city."

He watched her closely, perhaps assessing whether she would tell the truth, but she only shook her head. "I know nothing."

"It seems they have gained powerful allies in Rome. And here, well . . . there are still many who would profit from their return. Your own master, for example."

"You . . ." Bellina desperately searched his face for something to indicate that he wasn't, *couldn't be* serious. "You want me to spy." She slipped from his hands, stepping backward toward the thicket. Was that his reason for calling her to the riverbank? To coerce her into spying on her mistress's household?

He began to pace around the remains of a campfire. "We can do more with the information you bring us than a hundred women could do outside such a house."

"You want me to come here"—Bellina's voice shook—"and report to you what Francesco's family and friends are doing."

He shook his head. "Not to me. You remember Bardo? My older brother? He'll be your contact. He's secured a foreman's position in one of Francesco del Giocondo's silk workshops so that he may have a better view of—"

"Where are you going?" Would he vanish once again?

"I am well known as an adherent of Savonarola," he said. "Now my role will be less . . . visible."

"While I remain. And spy on Lisa's family." She searched his eyes.

"It's not like that, Bellina." He grabbed her shoulders, and suddenly, the fire in his eyes was there again, burning brighter than ever. Why was it she'd never seen this side of him, this ability to manipulate his followers like senseless marionettes on strings? How had she been so gullible?

"It's just," he said, "I have spent many months in discernment. I will be taking the habit of the Servites. I intend to replace the holy men who perished at Savonarola's side. I'm entering the novitiate at Santissima Annunziata."

Bellina's voice left her then. Stefano, as though suddenly impassioned, seized her face in his palms. He hesitated for a second, then pressed his lips to hers. It was the kiss Bellina had dreamt of, the passion for the cause, for Savonarola, for the *frateschi*, now focused only on her. Her entire being filled with his teeth, the tang of his mouth. Here finally was passion and lust and affection and desire. For a moment, Bellina felt as if she stood on the edge of a precipice, then let herself fall into an abyss, feeling the long, silent suspension of gravity, the hanging in midair. Bottomless. For an instant, she surrendered to the delusion that it was real.

But Bellina knew that kiss wasn't for her. How could she not have seen that he had been manipulating her—all of them—for so long? She thought of Lisa and little Piera, and suddenly, all she wanted to do was slip away from his warm, double-edged tongue and go home.

She fought to get her hands on his chest. She pushed him with all the strength a lifetime of menial labor could manage. Stefano stumbled backward. He protested, his hands tight on her arms as she struggled.

Then Bellina got one arm loose from his grip and slapped him. It was a hard slap from calloused hands, and she swung her entire body into the blow. His face registered shock.

Bellina tore through the brambles, heedless of their thorns, tearing a pathway from Stefano to the street beyond. Free of the cloying vines, she ran again, fled from her past and her delusions, leaving them like a ripped, bramble-cut dress, like rags on a warehouse floor. Bellina hobbled home as a drizzling rain began. In the San Lorenzo market, the fruit sellers were closing early, battening the wooden enclosures of their stalls against the rain. She could still taste the briny flavor of Stefano's mouth, his musk in her hair.

"YOU WANT THE BLUE THREADS, *polpetta*?" Bellina stood at the cabinet in Lisa's bedchamber and rifled through a basket of bright embroidery threads. "The yellow is pretty, too. What do you think?" She turned to look at Lisa's back, a silhouette at the window. She sat still. Silent.

Bellina had done everything she could think of to cheer Lisa, but little Piera's death had sucked the life out of her mistress as well. For months, Lisa had not changed out of her black mourning dress. In fact, Lisa refused to do much of anything at all. Lisa handed her new baby girl, Camilla—born soon after little Piera was placed in the family tomb—to the new wet nurse, then sat blankly with an untouched embroidery ring on her lap.

Bellina had held Lisa close to her bosom and stroked her thick black hair, whispering words that had little meaning in themselves. Bellina had sung to her in a fierce whisper, the same song she had sung when small Lisa skinned her knee or suffered some disappointment. But now, Lisa only gave short, vague answers when asked a direct question. Otherwise, she sat by the window, empty and silent, as if she could not see beyond its frame. Bellina couldn't be sure yet, but she suspected Lisa might be pregnant again.

Now, all Bellina could think was that perhaps she should have pulled that coral amulet from the stuffing of her mattress and put it around Piera's neck. Perhaps she should return it to Lisa and confess everything she'd ever done.

Bellina stood at the cabinet and ran her fingers across a stack of embroidered silks that were a specialty of Francesco's workshop in Por Santa Maria. Her fingers ran across the bumpy stitches and the slick, iridescent silk. It was just the sort of thing Stefano would have had her toss into the blaze, Bellina thought, sighing. *If Stefano was a fool, then I am twice the fool he was. Savonarola deceived both of us.* Bellina cursed herself for being so naïve. She thought of that one fiery kiss and felt repulsed, then sad.

Bellina comforted herself with the realization that Savonarola's rhetoric had ensorcelled not only her but many people across the city. Rather than revering Savonarola as a saint, now they vilified him. As the streaks on her back had healed into long, ragged scars, some were saying they believed he had cast some devilish spell upon them. Perhaps they were right.

Sometimes during her errands, Bellina walked across the square where the arcaded façade of Santissima Annunziata came into view. With a pang, Bellina wondered if Stefano was just on the other side of the high, thick wall of the monastery where he'd entered as a novice. She imagined him prostrate in a bare monk's cell and she hated herself for feeling his pull, even from the other side of the wall. She turned the fiery kiss over and over in her mind, and then thought of a hundred better things she might have said to him, if only she had the chance to relive it. Did he regret his decision to come here? Did he agonize over the kiss like she did? Did he remember her at all?

But she had to push it from her mind. Lisa needed her attention and care now. Lisa's father had given Bellina a home and a purpose. Was it in her to spy on Lisa's household? The things she'd done in the name of the *frateschi* and their mission still ached. Perhaps those betrayals would forever tear at her this way, as though she'd carved a hole in her soul. *I am the lady's maid to a worthy and noble woman. I am the caretaker of her children and her confidante. I owe her my care and attention now, in her time of distress and need. It was wrong for me to aspire to anything more than what I have.* That wasn't such a bad thing to be, Bellina thought.

While Bellina's position was humble, Lisa's need was real. By Lisa's side, Bellina at least was valued. It was enough. There was no need to chase mysteries and politics. Betrayals were not nearly so romantic and exciting as she had once thought. No. This was a finer life, a finer calling than anything Stefano could offer her.

Lisa depended upon her, giving her something to hold and cherish. She was a lady's maid, a good and dutiful servant. Such was enough to last a lifetime. Wasn't it?

"I think I'm being punished," Lisa said suddenly. It came out little more than a whisper; for a moment, Bellina thought she may not have heard it correctly.

Bellina moved to the window and put her hand on Lisa's shoulder, then laid her cheek on the top of Lisa's head. Together, they peered out at the drab stone wall across the street.

"MASTER LEONARDO HAS returned to Florence. Did you know his father is Ser Piero da Vinci? The notary."

Francesco hardly seemed to notice that Lisa wasn't listening. Her eyes vacant and dark, Lisa adjusted the silk sash that ran across her husband's shoulder and down his back. Bellina's mistress was in trouble. What could she do to pull her out of the darkness? Bellina turned the problem over in her head while she busied herself at Lisa's dressing table. The blackness of grief, Stefano's request for her to spy on her masters . . . All of it had created a dark, suffocating cloud over Bellina's head. She had tried everything she could to coax Lisa out of the abyss, but nothing had worked.

Around her, the household buzzed with the news that Francesco was leaving his textile workshops in the hands of his brother and its overseers, after his colleagues in the silk guild had elected him to serve a term on the council of the Dodici Buonomini. There, Alessandro the cook had told Bellina, Francesco would advise the Signoria and its other elected councils. Aside from receiving a government salary for his service, he would be provided with a crimson, ermine-lined cape, a group of livery servants, and a place at a special table in the Palazzo Vecchio complete with delicious meals and jesters to entertain him and his colleagues while they ate.

"Seems Master Leonardo's father has secured him an altarpiece commission for the Servites at Santissima Annunziata," Francesco continued, in an upbeat tone as he fastened the button in the loop on the front of his cloak.

"Mmm," Lisa said in distracted acknowledgment, brushing stray bits of ermine fur from the wool.

As Bellina rearranged small ceramic pots of face creams and oils on Lisa's dressing table, she observed her mistress. Her face had transformed since the day they had placed Piera's little gray, lifeless body into the family tomb at Santa Maria Novella and closed it with a marble slab. Lisa tried to brush off the sadness, but Bellina knew Lisa too well to miss the gray circles that had appeared around her eyes. The tight fist of grief had gripped her heart and wouldn't let go.

"Seems he made a name for himself up there in Milan, at least before the French came and everything went to Hell," Francesco continued. "I heard he made a colossal horse, but those frog eaters are already using it for target practice. Ha!" Francesco turned and wagged a finger toward Lisa. "Mark my words. It won't be long before Soderini gives Master Leonardo a civic commission in Florence. Don't you think, *cara*?"

Lisa only shrugged. She no longer had an opinion about anything.

Even though Bellina had decided not to spy on Lisa's household, the truth was that she had been paying attention to everything Francesco said. She knew Francesco had business dealings with the Servites. For the brothers of Santissima Annunziata, Francesco's workshops provided finely made altar cloths and Francesco himself handled exchanges of florins to other currencies far beyond Tuscany.

From the wardrobe, Bellina carefully picked up Francesco's new crimson velvet hat and placed it on the end of the bed. Francesco, now fully bedecked in his official costume of the Twelve, smiled at her. "Thank you, Bellina."

Without a further word, Bellina knew she was being dismissed. She nodded and was headed for the hallway when she heard Francesco say quietly, "I am eager to hear what the other eleven will say when I arrive. The rumor is that Piero de Medici is planning a return."

Bellina stopped and lingered by the doorway. She might not be a spy, but all the same, servants were good at making themselves invisible.

LEONARDO

Florence, Italy
1500

I f you knew what was good for you, you would abandon those contraptions of yours and focus on painting."

Many things in Florence have changed since I've been away, but my father is not one of them.

I struggle for a response. The silence stretches between us. Thick. Uncomfortable. My father paces back and forth, nearly wearing a path in the stone pavement of the monastery cloister where the monks of Santissima Annunziata—thanks to the old man's efforts—have agreed to house me.

I finger the stack of drawings on the worktable where I am unpacking my brushes and pigments. A young novice named Stefano, with eyes like fire, has been assigned to haul my crates from the mule wagon to the room I will use as a workshop. In an adjacent bedchamber, Salaì is unloading my cases, shaking out my velvet and silk cloaks, and hanging them to air at the window.

"I am nearly fifty years old, *papà*," I say finally. "I should think I am grown enough to make a few decisions of my own. I survived for years in Milan without you, you know."

I could go on, but I don't see the point. We've had the same conversation for years. Even though I am the oldest of some twelve

children over a mistress plus four wives, the fact that I am my
father's firstborn yet only illegitimate son matters more than anything else. He expects much of me for someone who has never
fully accepted me as his own. But no good will come of stating
this aloud.

"Ha!" he spits in response then shakes his head so hard that
his now-sagging jowls waggle like those of an old dog. His face
has turned lined and gnarled during my years away. Nearly all his
teeth are gone. But some things never change. "You don't know
the first thing about what we've endured in this place since you
left."

Salaì emerges from the next room with a swath of purple silk
one of the ladies at Ludovico's court presented to me years ago.
He spreads it carefully over a table, a bit of welcome color to en-
liven the otherwise drab cells the monks have assigned to me. "If
you mean that ugly business with Savonarola, I'm well informed,"
I say, "but it's in the past now. And Milan has not exactly been a
Garden of Eden."

"You've had it easy up there!" He sets his dark, narrow-set eyes
on me. I am a man of peace, but my father loves to argue, to
blame, to accuse. He has made a career of arguing finer points in
contracts and agreements among the Florentine rich. There is no
use weighing the relative merits of Florence or Milan with him.
Another long silence.

"I knew it was a mistake to come here," I say finally. I pick
up my things and make a show of repacking my brushes in my
satchel. I will not relive the years I spent disappointing him, those
years I carry like a cross.

"Leonardo." Suddenly the old man springs to action and grasps
my forearms with his bony hands. "*Dai*, stop. I only have your

interests at heart. These machines, these crazy contraptions—you waste your time. They will be gone and forgotten before they are ever made or used. And you will be forgotten along with them."

The sting of rejection—it always comes alongside any compliment. I meet his dark gaze. "You will see, *papà*. They will make me."

I prepare for a protracted argument, but instead, the old man only sighs. "Take the painting commission, *figlio*. And any others that come in. All I'm asking," he says, resuming his pacing, "is that you direct your energies to where they will be practical. You have spent years pursuing these inventions and these men of power. I know you love the life at court, but that will get you nowhere, and maybe even get you killed. You're lucky to have made it here from Milan in one piece."

"I can build a machine that will win a war, and then I might make a bigger difference than leaving behind a dusty altarpiece inside some monastery where no one will ever see it," I say, gesturing around my secluded monastery rooms with a dismissive hand.

But my father continues. "You cannot direct the tides of history from your drawing board. Wars are not won by an underwater boat or a flying machine or a bulletproof wagon." I must admit, he argues well. He is well suited to his job as notary and business advisor for the most learned men in the city of Florence. It's the reason the Servites have hired him to negotiate their business dealings.

I let the energy in the room settle. Then I pull my signed agreement with the Servite brothers from my trunk and place it on the worktable.

"Well, I have already accepted the monks' commission, as you can see. You drew the contract yourself."

He nods. "That is a start. But you must still do the work. They did not want to hire you at first. They say you are easily distracted, that you cannot concentrate on one task at a time." He pauses. "If you fail to maintain an acceptable pace toward completion, they can terminate the contract and leave the balance unpaid."

My reputation? This is a surprise to me, that people talk about me like that. But then, this is Florence. It has been more than three decades since a jealous assistant slipped an accusation in the letterbox of the Signoria. It's why I left Florence to begin with. But perhaps some things never change.

"They know nothing about me." I bristle.

My father looks at me suspiciously. "They know all they need to just by looking at the way you dress."

"What's that supposed to mean?"

"The monks feel your wardrobe is not suitable inside the walls of a monastery," he says.

These friars . . . The Servites founded this establishment some three hundred years ago, when a group of prosperous cloth merchants exchanged their comfortable existence for a life of poverty and penance. Here in their mother church, they wear sandals made of wood tied to their feet with leather straps, robes of wool or horsehair tied with raw, hempen ropes. They shovel mealy, bland gruel into their mouths with wooden spoons. I steal a glance into the back room, where Salaì is arranging my hand-sewn, buckled blue velvet shoes from Milan, my violet cape with the sweeping collar, and the lilac hat.

"Is that all?" I say to my father.

He nods and puts his hand on the door latch. "If you show you can finish something, then I might convince other wealthy patrons to commission you, too. This should be the time in your

life where you plant yourself and focus on the practicalities of
your work."

Father has had the last word. He has given me his mind on
things, secured my cooperation, insulted my personal choices,
and now he can go on his way. Nothing I said was ever going to
be heard. He hasn't changed. "Also, plenty of men in this city will
pay you to paint their wives," he adds.

Another painting of a lady. Father's plan for me begins to sur-
round me like a noose. Paintings of ladies from now till the end.
The world is so much larger than that. My last portraits were of
Ludovico Sforza's women. And look how that turned out.

"I'm working with Francesco del Giocondo, the silk trader," he
says. "Now that the . . . environment . . . is more favorable to the
cloth guilds, I'll bet he'd be open to discussing a commission for
a portrait of his wife."

Part 4

PORTRAIT OF A LADY

ANNE

Louvigny and Paris, France
1940

Through the dark winter months at Louvigny, Anne spent many hours reading up on Leonardo da Vinci. The dusty volumes in the castle's library yielded some surprises; she hadn't realized that the Italian Renaissance master was responsible for so many ingenious inventions across France. By the harsh light of a desk lamp, Anne read about Leonardo da Vinci's tenure at the court of the French king, François I. She learned more about Master Leonardo's elaborate double-helix staircase and his innovative air duct system at Chambord. In Lyon, he had presented the French king with a walking mechanical lion. He had designed a hunting lodge, an assault chariot, and a revolving bridge. Louis's predecessor Charles VIII, who believed he was the rightful ruler of the kingdom of Naples, had set off with his legions to take it. On their way, they had laid siege to cities across Italy, including Leonardo's own native Florence. A cruel irony.

During the long, quiet days, the Louvigny depot director and the handful of curators required little of Anne and her inventories. Only Pierre became a faithful fixture, an unlikely companion where she might have found only loneliness. The two of them sat near the cabinet that hid the *Mona Lisa*, sharing books, newspapers, bits of information. Together, they speculated about what might have become of her brother, but Pierre knew no more than she did. Anne had come to appreciate Pierre's gentle heart, thinly veiled behind a crotchety exterior. She relied on him for news, for wisdom, for opinions, and now and then for a bad joke. Anne had never known what it was like to have a father; Pierre's peculiar brand of grumpy protection warmed her heart.

At last, signs of spring had come creeping to the edges of the lonely château: a blush of green along a footpath, the musty smell of rain-soaked moss, a pale blossom pushing through the frost that crunched under her feet. She hadn't seen Corrado since he'd driven Monsieur Schommer back to Chambord months ago. And her letters to Kiki and Marcel went unanswered. Some days, the silence of the château grew deafening. Anne's walks in the meadows and grounds were her only solace. Without Pierre to offer a piece of fatherly wisdom, a humorous observation, or a far-fetched story about his younger days in Moselle, Anne thought, the winter would have been a vast, dark landscape of loneliness.

But just about the time Anne began to believe the war was far away, they learned their worst fears had come true: the Germans were on French soil at last. They had marched right through Belgium and across the Ardennes. "Monsieur Jaujard has sent us an urgent telegram. The art left behind in the Louvre is no longer safe," the depot director had told them. "There's no choice. We must go back for it before the Germans arrive."

A return home to Paris. Anne knew it was dangerous. But maybe, if she was lucky, she might find Kiki and Marcel.

ANNE STAMPED ON THE BRAKE so hard she fell forward against the steering wheel, accidentally adding the blare of her own horn to the cacophony surrounding her. From the street, an old man tugging a worn cart behind him gestured furiously at her.

"Sorry. Sorry!" Anne gasped, her heart thumping with the knowledge that she'd nearly killed him.

In the passenger seat, Pierre shook his head. "It's not your fault, *chérie*," he said. "He stepped out in front of you."

Anne swallowed hard. "If it's this difficult to get into Paris, how am I going to drive out with all those paintings in the back?"

"It'll be all right," Pierre said, but it didn't sound like he believed his own words. His knuckles were white where he clutched the brim of the Louvre guard cap perched on his lap.

"Protecting the *Mona Lisa* was easy compared to this," Anne said, but it wasn't entirely true. As much as Anne looked forward to returning to Paris with a small group of museum staff, she had to admit she felt a pang of regret as she left behind the treasures, especially the one in the ebony-inlaid cabinet in the castle's salon. But a return to Paris . . . Anne had jumped at the chance—even to drive a big, lumbering truck—even with German soldiers on the city's threshold.

But now, trundling into the outskirts of Paris, Anne felt only trepidation.

"The Panzers are already in Picardie." Pierre seemed to read her mind. The old guard's eyes gleamed with fire, and Anne glimpsed a younger Pierre—one who had thrown himself into battle against the same enemy in the Great War little more than twenty years ago. "The city is unprotected."

Unprotected. Anne felt fear lance through her like an arrow in her chest. As much as she longed to find them at home, Anne prayed that Kiki and Marcel had found a way to leave the city. And if they were still there, could she convince them to return with her to the relative safety of the countryside? Some Louvre staff had begun to write letters, luring their family members to join them in the country, where they might find safety. Could Anne convince them to come?

Anne tugged on the gear shift and edged the truck forward, trying to avoid a knot of pedestrians that suddenly spilled into her lane. She checked the small mirror mounted to the driver's door. She caught sight of the face of the antiquities curator, Christiane Desroches-Noblecourt, driving her own ramshackle Citroën behind them, making her way as if swimming upstream. The curator's tires had already worn paper-thin the first time she had reached Chambord. Corrado had been horrified when he told Anne. He couldn't believe she'd made it there safely. And now, Christiane had driven her car all the way back to Paris again.

As they crept closer, Anne realized no one was traveling into the city except their little convoy. Everyone else was leaving.

When the familiar silhouette of the Eiffel Tower and the steeped roofline of the Louvre came into view, Anne had to push back the lump in her throat. But as they crept into the Louvre's Cour Napoléon at last, she found the building's façades still masked by sandbags and wooden scaffolding. The grand windows stood dark and vacant, like the eyes of a great, empty skull. The near-empty building was a hollow shell of the Louvre she loved.

Inside, Anne followed a small crowd of curators as they wandered through the vast, empty galleries. Glass cabinets stood dusty and vacant. Hooks, pegs, chalk outlines, and the scrawled names of pictures stood lonely on each wall. Every so often, they passed a gallery with monumental sculptures of ancient Greece or Egypt; a few of Michelangelo's famous *Slaves;* the *Venus de Milo;* or other works considered too fragile to move just a few months ago. Now, they had to risk it and find places for them outside Paris.

Anne followed the group into a series of vast second-floor galleries. She sucked in her breath to see the gigantic Napoleonic canvases painted by Jacques-Louis David still hanging on the walls. This gallery had always been one of Anne's favorites. She liked to come here on her lunch hour and sit on one of the benches, marveling at David's re-creation of the coronation of Napoleon. Some canvases, if they were laid flat, might take up more square meters than a house.

In the David gallery, she recognized the museum's director. Jacques Jaujard was a trim, elegant figure usually dressed in a fashionable suit, but now Anne saw he looked disheveled, with deep lines sketched along the sides of his mouth and dark hollows under his eyes. With haggard resolve, he shook each curator's hand and welcomed them back to Paris.

"We had hoped we could leave them here since they are so enormous, but that won't be possible," Jaujard was saying to a small group clustered around him.

"How will we move them?" one of the curators asked.

"That's what we're here to figure out. We only know that the Germans will want them. Hitler sees himself as the new Napoleon," Jaujard said bitterly. "They will be looking for these."

"We can't possibly move everything in one convoy," another curator said, dismay dragging at her voice.

One of the paintings curators clucked. "Some things will still have to stay behind; there is no choice. A terrible decision to make, but we have to save what we can. There might be looting even if the Germans don't take everything."

"If only we could get more trucks," Pierre murmured.

"We're short on everything," the curator said. "Trucks, fuel, people . . . We have to do what we can with what we have."

"Where are we taking them?" Anne asked.

Monsieur Jaujard sucked sharply on his cigarette. "We've secured a new depot near Toulouse. It's isolated and should be safe, but it's going to be a difficult drive. The terrain is mountainous, and the roads are not good."

Anne glanced over her shoulder out the window. She couldn't see her apartment building from here, but it felt close enough to touch. "How long do we have?" she asked.

"Long enough to go home and rearrange your bags," he said. "The trucks are leaving again as soon as everything is packed."

Anne made her way down a darkened back stairwell toward the staff entrance. At the door to the museum security office, she lingered. A young man in a guard's uniform sat in Monsieur Dupont's place, his feet on the wide desk, idly twirling a pen between his palms. When he spotted her standing at the door, he quickly removed his feet. "Mademoiselle?"

Anne introduced herself and explained she was looking for Marcel Guichard. "Haven't seen him in months," the young man said, shaking his head. "Not since the trucks left for the depots."

The man must have read the solemn desperation in Anne's expression because he stood. "Let's have a look," he said, and Anne leaned against the doorjamb, watching the young guard rifle through an ancient filing cabinet. After a few long minutes, he retrieved a folder and opened it on the desk. "Says here he was transferred." Anne stared down at the single word hastily scrawled across the top page of Marcel's employment dossier.

"Transferred!" Anne said. "To where?"

The young man shook his head. "How could we keep track of anyone these days? Look outside, mademoiselle. Anyway, only Monsieur Dupont would have known that."

Monsieur Dupont. Anne thought of all the days she had spent avoiding an encounter with the man. She had feared he would judge her for recommending her brother as a guard, when he might have been the only one who could tell her where Marcel was. But now, Anne didn't know where Monsieur Dupont was either.

ANNE TOOK THE STAIRS two at a time.

"Marcel! Kiki!" she cried, her voice echoing up the tall, dingy stairwell. Compared with everything else she was facing, the old *gardienne*'s wrath was the least of her worries. Anne's worn suitcase banged her knees as she climbed.

Her hands were shaking as she thrust the key into the lock, she wrenched it open and strode into her little apartment.

Silence. Flecks of dust hung in the filtered light and then disappeared into the shadows.

After more than nine months of château living, Anne could see the apartment through new eyes. She realized with a pang how sad the little place was. In the narrow kitchen, the sink was filled with greenish water, a thin line of oily scum staining the metal. The dining table was covered with a layer of dust. Anne stepped forward, and something rattled on the floor at her feet. An empty wine bottle.

Anne stepped into the room she shared with Marcel. It was exactly as she'd left it, both beds neatly made. Her heart plummeted.

As far as she could tell, he hadn't returned home since that strange night he'd simply walked out the door with a packed bag. For a gut-wrenching moment, Anne feared the apartment had simply been abandoned.

But then, in her mother's room, she found the bed was left rumpled and unmade. A dirty glass sat on the bedside table. A dingy gown had slipped from the back of the chair onto the floor. In the bathroom, her mother's face powder had made tracks across the porcelain sink. Anne made her way through the clutter to the window, where the clothesline was strung above the alley. A lacy *culotte* hung within her reach; she touched it and found it stiff and brittle. She brought it in from the line and draped it over the chair. Anne hovered in her mother's room, wondering if she should stay and wait for her to come back. She must be carousing at the dance hall or somewhere else, but Kiki would probably come home.

Maybe Kiki and Marcel were both safe and well, and if she waited for them—if she cleared away the bottles and washed the dishes, pulled things out of the cold box and started dinner, the way she had done as long as she could remember—they'd come through the door and she could wrap them both safely in her arms at last. She could tell them about everything she had seen and done in the last weeks; how she had even traveled to safety alongside the *Mona Lisa*. Would they understand? But it wasn't safe for anyone to be in Paris right now.

Anne closed her eyes, thinking of the great Napoleonic paintings, the giant rolls of canvas tucked away carefully in the truck that she was supposed to drive across the country in just a few hours. One curator had said that despite two more trucks expected to arrive the next day, and the fact that Lucie had acquired her driver's permit while Anne had been at Louvigny, they needed every driver they had. If she wasn't back at the Louvre soon, Anne knew that some of those artworks would be doomed.

"*Dieu*, look who's back." A raspy voice interrupted her thoughts, and Anne realized she had left the apartment door gaping open.

As much as her life, her city, and the world had changed in the past months, Madame Brodeur appeared unchanged: a gray apparition in the same ragged housecoat, the same tobacco-stained snarl. She took a deep drag on her rumpled cigarette and squinted at Anne.

"Madame!" said Anne, strangely relieved to see the old, familiar fixture of Madame Brodeur's stout frame. "My mother and Marcel . . . Have you seen them?"

"*Oui,*" snorted Madame Brodeur. "At least, I've seen your *maman*. Heard her, too. Singing those ridiculous tunes, stumbling up the stairs at all hours, waking everybody on the block . . ."

"And Marcel?" Anne interrupted.

Madame Brodeur sucked on the cigarette again, forming a wrinkled circle around the butt until a long trail of ash threatened to fall to dust at her feet. "Not since you left. But then, he doesn't have his nanny to drag him out of trouble anymore, does he?" Her wrinkled mouth stretched into a mean, thin line.

Anne supposed she should be glad Marcel wasn't in Paris, under the circumstances, but she wished she could have taken him with her to the provincial depots. Transferred? What did that mean? Anne's heart plummeted to realize that now, he could be anywhere.

"It's just your mother and me left in the building now," said

Madame Brodeur. "Ha! The two of us old hags. Who would have thought? I'd throw her out for disturbing the other boarders if anybody were left here. Well, I wish your mother would leave, too, like those Jews upstairs. Strange people." She shook her head. "You staying here now, mademoiselle?"

Anne surveyed the sad apartment. What could she do? Try to convince Kiki to leave Paris? She'd never been able to persuade her mother to do anything once her mind was set, and Kiki had made it clear she'd never leave the city. Madame Brodeur examined her with her hard, beady eyes.

"No," Anne breathed. "I have—responsibilities." She paused. "Everyone is leaving the city, Madame. You should leave Paris, too, while you still can."

"I was born here, girl." The old woman turned and made her way down the stairs, clutching the iron handrail. When Madame reached the bottom of the staircase, Anne heard the *gardienne*'s door close and the lock turn loudly.

They'd be missing her at the Louvre, and she needed to repack her bag. But first, she pulled a sheet of paper and a pen out of her nightstand and wrote a hurried note to her mother on the dusty surface. Anne had never thought they could justify the expense of a telephone for the apartment. A few of their neighbors had one, but to Anne, it had seemed a luxury. Now, she wished they had splurged. At least she could try to reach the dance hall or the neighboring bar in Montmartre for news of her mother.

As soon as she laid the letter on her mother's pillow, a shrill sound pierced through the apartment, making Anne jump. It was the distinctive ring of a telephone coming from the apartment upstairs. Anne had been used to hearing the sound, but now, the once familiar chime sounded foreboding and hollow. She stood in the middle of the empty room as the phone just rang and rang.

HURRYING THROUGH THE STREETS toward the Louvre, Anne was astonished to find there were still many pedestrians moving among the sandbagged sidewalks. As sunbeams streaked through the intersections of the grand façades, Anne searched the faces of men, women, and children making their way through the streets. So many people with expressions of worry, fear, determination. She was still hopeful that she might see her brother's face among them. The steady stream of southward-bound families continued. But she recognized no one.

When she arrived in the Cour Napoléon, she heard the rumble of diesel engines already running. Workers were slamming doors on the last of the trucks; as she watched, a few wooden crates were thrust into a truck and tied down. Anne recognized Lucie among a clutch of curators surrounding Christiane Desroches-Noblecourt's old Citroën. On the back seat, small crates were stacked to the ceiling.

"The streets were so full," Anne gasped.

"It's all right; you're here now," said Lucie, searching the convoy, "but you'll have to see who has room. An extra driver came up from Chambord just in time, so you're off the hook for driving. But we have to get out of the city *now*. Find a truck and get in."

The urgency in Lucie's tone sent a cold rush through Anne's veins. It left her disoriented, gazing around wildly for a truck with space for her and her meager suitcase.

"You again, *signorina*?"

A familiar voice. She turned, and in spite of herself, she felt her jaw fall. "Corrado!"

He flashed a row of straight, white teeth. The trials of recent months had stolen some of the roundness from his face since she'd last seen him, but the glimmer in his eyes was still the same. Anne had to stop herself from hugging him. Instead, she settled for gripping his hand in both of hers. "I'm so glad to see you."

"So am I," he said, "but you need to let go of my hand now, because they've packed my delivery truck again. We're getting out of this city before the Germans come. You can ride with me if you want."

He yanked on the driver's door handle and stepped up into the truck. Anne huffed in disbelief. They had assigned him the most arduous task of all—driving a large flatbed truck loaded with the giant Napoleonic paintings, now hidden under a series of canvas tarps. Anne ran to the passenger side, wrenched open the door, and scrambled up into the cab. Slamming it shut behind her, she only turned and said, "*On y va!*"

The truck growled forward, Lucie's car right behind, following the rest of the convoy out of the Louvre courtyard and into the streets. People rushed along the sidewalks, eyes wide and possessions clutched haphazardly in their arms. A stream of vehicles crept through the streets. The trucks weaved among the chaos, determinedly seeking a route out of the city. It was déjà vu, the two of them once again moving out of Paris and heading south with treasures of inestimable value.

Anne was relieved that Corrado was driving instead of her. He sat in terse silence, his lips pressed together in concentration as he fought to guide the heavy truck as quickly as he dared. A bump in the wrong place could damage something priceless. When they reached Montparnasse cemetery and the southern ring of the city, Anne let out a breath she hadn't realized she'd been holding.

"How long do you think we'll be driving this time?" she asked Corrado. It was three times farther to the countryside around Toulouse than to Chambord.

He gave her a quick smile and a shrug. "Under normal circumstances, a day's drive," he said. "But now? Better not to ask."

A long, shrill noise ripped through the air, drowning his words. The rising wail made every hair on Anne's body stand bolt upright. She grabbed Corrado's arm. "What is that?" she cried, feeling the muscles in his arm tense and twitch.

"An air raid alert." Genuine fear filled Corrado's voice for the first time since Anne had met him. "We need to get out of here right now." Corrado revved the engine, and a few pedestrians moved out of the way of the truck. He pressed forward, his dark eyes scanning the crowds. Corrado pressed the gas pedal as much as he could without running over anyone.

As the wail of the siren continued, screams filled the air around them. Pedestrians scattered, mothers snatching for their children, diving into the recesses and alleys of the surrounding buildings in reckless terror. Horns blared as desperate cars sought a way out, and then Anne heard the first shell explode. It was a sharp noise, a distant crack, as if the very air was blown to pieces. She looked up and saw a white cloud burst across the sky. Anne screamed.

"It's all right!" Corrado gasped. "It's all right!"

But it wasn't all right. There was another crack, and another, and another, and then Anne saw the first bomb plummet to the ground. A spray of dirt flew into the air, opening a great crater in the earth as white smoke curled from the explosion. The truck shook with the force of it. Clapping her hands over her ears did nothing to keep out the sound. Then she heard the whine and drone of planes passing high above, and clouds of white smoke filled the sky.

"Kiki!" Anne gasped, terrified. She twisted in her seat, staring back toward the center of the city. There was a huge black cloud over it; for a horrible instant, it looked like a swarm of demons had come to devour the city she loved. It took Anne a minute to realize that they were pigeons, terrified by the sound of the blasts.

"*Maman,*" she sobbed. "She's somewhere in this city. My God! She's going to be killed."

"Look, Anne," Corrado said. "They're firing around the outskirts. She'll be all right." Anne knew he was only trying to soothe her.

There was a terrible crack somewhere near them, and the ground shook again; this time she felt the truck window vibrate. Her senses were overcome with smoke and metal. She screamed and covered her head with her arms, curling herself up in the passenger seat, unable to watch for a moment longer. She felt Corrado's protective palm on her head, and then the truck accelerated with a breathtaking jolt into the darkness.

LEONARDO

Florence, Italy
1501

A portrait of a lady? I could do one in my sleep.

I drag a nub of red chalk across the parchment. A swish of hair across the cheek. The swell of a lower lip. The hint of an eyelash. A few hatch marks.

On the other side of the monastery wall, I hear the market vendors singing their wares— one extols the virtues of tomatoes, the other aged pecorino. I hear wooden shutters slapping closed against the blistering sun, turning the interiors into darkness. How many times have I walked through the market and captured the likeness of a girl picking cabbages, only to turn her into a Madonna months, even years later? How many times have I turned Salaì into a John the Baptist?

Beside my sketches is a stack of pages. There is an urgent letter from Isabella, marchioness of Mantua. It is her likeness that filled my sketchbooks in the weeks that followed our departure from Milan, that idyllic period when she was kind enough to accommodate all of us in her home. And ever since we left, she has done nothing but hound me for a painted portrait.

But it's my own letters in progress that fill my mind, that send it spinning in a hundred directions. Offers of service to powerful patrons far beyond Florence's city walls.

"I couldn't find any artichokes." Luca, followed by Salaì, comes through the door and lays his sack of onions on the table.

I abandon my image of the Mantuan noble lady in red chalk and turn the page of my sketchbook. Ahead, there are many more sketches. Pages and pages. Collapsible bridges. All manner of war machines. Canals. Defensive foundations outside the walls. A new tower for the Olivetan monks at San Miniato. A design for a villa at Angelo del Tovaglia for Isabella's husband, Francesco Gonzaga, lord of Mantua. Fortifications. Tunnels filled with explosive devices. Beyond this city, there are men who will pay for this work.

Instinctively, I slap a blank page over my letters. It is better if they don't see them, if I don't tell them we may leave Florence again unless I have a solid offer.

"What's that?" Luca asks, already suspicious. He gestures to the pages on my worktable.

"Nothing," I say. "Letters. An invitation. Maybe." Luca joins me at the worktable. Salaì abandons his own drawing and lingers in the doorway.

If they knew I'd written to powerful men beyond Florence, they might be angry, all of them. My little Salaì, who has already told me that my flitting about is exhausting him. The monks. And especially my father.

But in my defense, I've made an appearance in the sanctuary each day to appease the old prior of Santissima Annunziata. We take measurements. We consider my drawing. We discuss colors. We look at the faded frescoes in the old side chapels. We speak of biblical sources, the placement of a hand, the fall of drapery, the luminescence of a saint's halo. My notebooks are full of hands, faces, halos. The carpenters have built the wooden armature above the altar to my specifications.

And yet, I can tell the monks are not pleased with me. They whisper behind their hands in the choir stalls. The prior calls me aside for a conference. I have stopped joining them for meals, making excuses for other engagements.

"Well?" I feel Salaì's and Luca's eyes on me.

I sigh. They will figure it out eventually. "I've written to several men—the duke of Ferrara, the duke of Mantua, the lord of Romagna—for an engagement as a military engineer."

"Cesare Borgia?" Luca sits quietly digesting the news.

Salaì, on the other hand . . . "Borgia?" The boy pushes away from the doorjamb and comes at me as if he will take me by the shoulders and shake some sense into me. "No, Master Leo! This is a bad idea."

"Salaì. Keep your voice down. This is a monastery."

"Borgia!" he exclaims again, ignoring my plea for silence. Salaì's face flushes red, and he begins to pace while Luca stays seated, hunched over as if he's admitted defeat. "You would bring us into the inner circle of the Prince of Darkness, Master? Have you not heard the stories? He will slit our throats faster than any French!"

"I realize now it's a mistake for me to stay here in Florence, son," I say with as much finality as possible. "Besides, Borgia is the pope's own child. If he looks favorably on my offer, he'd be in a position to give me even more important commissions."

"But, Master Leo," Luca says, finally speaking up. "You have done excellent work here. That small Madonna has already won you favor with the French king." He is arguing for his own self-interest, I think. He wants to stay in Florence.

I stand. "I am soon fifty years old, gentlemen. I will not spend my remaining years painting portraits of ladies. Beyond this city, there are opportunities to make a difference in the world before my time runs out. But it will only work if I can get into the good graces of a powerful man again." For a moment, I feel a pang of sorrow for my longtime patron Ludovico Sforza, who I understand has been betrayed, captured, and taken to France in chains.

"But . . . What of your other commissions?" Luca asks.

I drum my fingers on the table, thinking of our commission at the church at San Salvatore dell'Osservanza, where Luca has used his mathematical skills to help me design a new foundation and waterworks that might prevent it from sliding down the mountainside with the next flood. I think of my plans submitted to the Signoria of Florence for linking the Arno with a system of canals.

Luca begins to see Salaì's point of view. "Things are finally peaceful again here, Master Leo, now that Soderini is in charge of the Florentine government. The violence seems behind us. Why would you leave now?"

I shrug. "I am not afraid, Salaì. Could any engagement be more dangerous than working for His Lordship in Milan?"

But he only clucks and turns to the window. He pushes open the shutter, takes a breath of fresh air, and then tugs at the roots of his hair.

"I'm staying." Salaì's voice comes out little more than a whisper at the windowsill.

"Don't be ridiculous, Salaì."

But he only turns his face toward me, and I see his resolve. "You must make your own decision, of course, Master. But I must also make mine. And if you leave Florence, you go alone. I have already made up my mind. I'm staying."

ANNE

Chambord, France
1940

In the luster of a summer afternoon, the old château of Chambord appeared as magnificent as Anne remembered, its symmetrical, round towers surrounded by a complex garden design of clipped hedgerows.

This time, though, the château was no longer a safe haven. Instead, it lay firmly in the Nazis' crosshairs. Anne's heart throbbed. Pierre had been right in his assessment all those months ago. Even those powerful walls couldn't keep them safe from bombs dropped from the air. And Chambord was an easy target: a giant, white castle in the middle of an open field. The now-familiar château could no longer be a refuge; it was only an interim stop, and there was no rest for the weary now.

The Louvre staff hurried back and forth, moving crates into the dusty trucks. Everyone was exhausted and frayed from the harrowing hours on the road from Paris, waiting for more explosives to be dropped from the sky. Anne shook her head to keep herself alert; she hadn't been able to rid her mind of the blasts. It had sounded as though the whole world was ending around her, with the constant thunder of explosives punctuated by petrified screams. Somehow the truck had rumbled on, and Corrado's murmured reassurances went on, too, until the terrible sound of the battle had at last faded into the distance.

Anne struggled to keep her mind focused on the ragged inventory pages pinned to her clipboard as she moved among the trucks. If she couldn't keep her mother and brother safe, if she couldn't bring them with her, then she should at least do everything in her control to safeguard the works of art in her care.

A new truck came to a halt in the gravel drive, with Christiane's Citroën pulling up alongside. Anne wondered how Christiane had found the courage to keep driving through the deadly onslaught in her ramshackle car. Lucie stepped out of another truck, and Anne couldn't help it; a huge smile broke across her face. She wrapped Lucie in a wordless hug of relief.

"There are more trucks coming from other depots," Lucie said, returning Anne's tight embrace. "They've had to empty Louvigny with the Germans so close. They pulled the *Mona Lisa* out of her cabinet."

"*Mesdames!*" The voice belonged to Monsieur Schommer, who strode out of the castle into the sunlight. "Are you all right? We've gotten the news from Paris on the wireless. My God."

Corrado stepped in. "Everyone is here."

"Good," Monsieur Schommer said. "We need to get the crates away from this place as soon as possible. I'm sure I don't need to explain why."

Another woman approached, and Anne recognized Professor Jacqueline Bouchot-Saupique, a tired and worried version of the drawings curator, whose bright cheeks and high forehead made her resemble one of the eighteenth-century nobles in the drawings collection. "The last of the crates are being loaded up now at Louvigny," she told Monsieur Schommer. "One of the trucks broke down, and the roads were terrible. Everyone is fleeing in panic."

"*La Joconde?*" asked Lucie.

"The Lady is safe," Jacqueline said, "at least for now. We've put her back on the stretcher in that truck again, but this time we convinced Monsieur Schommer not to ride along."

"Good idea," Corrado said. "We nearly had to give him the kiss of life last time—and I'm not kissing *him*."

A ripple of laughter moved through the crowd. Anne flashed a grateful smile. She wondered how Corrado was able to lift everyone's spirits at a moment like this.

Monsieur Schommer reappeared. "Everything here is loaded. Our plan is to reach Loc-Dieu before midnight."

"I know a shortcut," Corrado volunteered. "We came through there from Italy one time."

"*Très bien,*" Monsieur Schommer said. "You will lead the way, then, Corrado. Anne, you will drive the next truck in line. Then Christiane and the others. I'll take up the rear."

ANNE GRIPPED THE STEERING WHEEL, keeping in close step behind the truck with the giant paintings secured in place under tarps. This time, packing up again seemed like performing a well-known yet poorly rehearsed stage show. Lucie and Anne scratching checkmarks on tattered inventory pages as the guards and curators shuttled back and forth with marked crates. Drivers shifting boxes, tying ropes, slamming doors. Shifting again. Crossing out and marking again. Everyone proficient, no one fully prepared.

The group had started out with new resolve, eager to traverse the some six hundred kilometers south to the new depot, far from Paris and the Loire Valley. Far from the Germans. Anne squared her shoulders and leaned forward in the driver's seat. Truck fumes filled the air with each uphill climb, and Anne watched the ropes and gently flapping tarps for any sign of loosening. They had tapped Corrado for the most important job—leading the group through the winding, mountainous passages and carrying their most precarious cargo.

As each kilometer crept by, Pierre and two other guards did their best to keep the atmosphere in Anne's truck light. They jabbed one another over petty arguments they'd had in the châteaux; they argued over the results of past card games and poked fun at themselves, three old Parisian men being driven across France by a young woman. They had never needed driving skills, they said. And now look at them—they were the butt of their own jokes.

But underneath the levity lay a relentless, pervasive tension. As the hours progressed, the men grew increasingly quiet as Anne steadied the errant steering wheel and stared into the two golden fingers of light cast by the headlights. Each kilometer ticked by at an excruciating pace. When darkness fell at last, they had barely crossed into the Poitou region. They bumped over a rutted country road, and with every rattle of the truck, Anne's jaw clenched tighter. She drove as smoothly as she could but couldn't avoid a dip in the road that made something rattle in the back. She thought of the priceless treasures among her cargo, impossible to replace, and she resolved to be more careful.

"I hope he knows where he's going." Pierre gestured toward the huge painting-laden truck at the front. In the back seat, the other men grumbled in agreement.

The headlights illuminated a crossroads, and Corrado brought the truck to a stop. One by one, the other cars and trucks came to a halt. Anne braked hard.

"Whose idea was it to trust an Italian to get us where we are going?" one man in the back exclaimed. A rumble of laughter and an exhausted sigh filled the back seat.

After a few moments, Anne watched as the drivers cut their engines and turned off the vehicles' lights. Then car doors began opening and slamming.

"He's lost! I told you," the man in the back insisted.

One by one, curators, guards, and staff got out of the trucks. Stretched. Chatted. Gestured to the convoy. Cupped their hands around their mouths, lit cigarettes, and puffed rings of smoke. Stumbled into the tree line to relieve themselves.

Anne pulled up the emergency brake and cut the engine. She looked to the front of the convoy for Corrado.

She saw him emerge from the driver's door, hands in his hair. His eyes were wide, cheeks pale as lines of stress appeared around his eyes and mouth. Anne watched him shove his hands deep into his pockets as he walked out onto the crossroads and stared right, then left.

After a few moments, another figure moved through the muddy street to Corrado. Anne gasped. Monsieur Dupont. She recognized his broad silhouette, the purposeful, intimidating stride that only the head of a museum security department might have earned.

From this distance, she couldn't hear his words, but they made Corrado take a step back. He shook his head, eyes to the ground, and mumbled something that made Monsieur Dupont launch into an angry tirade. Gesturing, his yelling faintly audible through the thick glass of the windscreen, he ended by throwing up his hands and storming off. Corrado stood still for a few moments before walking back to the truck, defeat written loudly on his face.

Anne saw the curators and Monsieur Schommer climbing into the flatbed to check the straps on the gigantic Napoleonic paintings. Three guards with flashlights pored over a tattered road map.

Anne rolled down her window. "Corrado!" she called, but she stopped when he turned his face to her, full of shame. Her heart went out to him, transporting the most precious cargo of his life—and getting everyone lost.

Monsieur Schommer went down the line of vehicles, shouting, "We're turning the convoy around!" Anne watched Corrado drag himself back up into the truck's driver's seat. Monsieur Dupont handed him the map and yelled some directions. Anne wanted to rush over and question Monsieur Dupont about her brother's whereabouts, but he had climbed in his truck, and the convoy was already moving. She had to follow to keep her place in the line.

Turning the convoy about-face was an exercise in advanced driving skill. The lane was narrow, with barely enough room for one truck to maneuver at a time; it seemed to take an eternity to get all the vehicles turned around. Eventually, Monsieur Dupont's truck was in the front, with the *Mona Lisa*'s truck right behind it. The sight of it made Anne feel sick. She wondered if the five-hundred-year-old painting had been damaged by its long, bumpy journey over these country roads.

Inside Anne's truck, the old guards continued to mumble their disapproval of the whole situation and especially of Corrado, the Italian who had gotten them into this predicament. After a while, the men fell silent, but as Anne watched the twin headlights of the truck streak through the darkness, her mind revisited the look of dumb shame on Corrado's face.

It was nearly midnight when the convoy rolled into Châteauroux. In the stark beam of her flashlight, Anne ran her finger down the tattered map; they had traversed less than half of their planned itinerary. Even though Châteauroux was a sizable town, every shutter was closed and the streets stood deserted. Anne would never admit it to the men, but she had been struggling to keep her eyes open ever since the trucks reached asphalt and left the muddy, mountainous roads behind.

A museum guard gestured for Anne to park in a large public square where the other guards had been organized to watch over the vehicles and their contents. Anne pushed her way across the square, searching for Monsieur Dupont. She found him directing a small group of guards to locate a military canteen nearby.

"Monsieur!" she cried. He turned to her, his mouth in a grim line. "I'm Anne, from the archives . . ."

"I know who you are." A sharp, gruff reply.

"Please. I'm looking for my brother, Marcel. Can you tell me where he is? I heard he was transferred."

For a long moment, he looked her up and down, squinting. "What did he tell you?"

"Nothing," she said. "You sent him somewhere?"

He nodded. "Along with others." A few other guards butted in, and he directed them to streets snaking away from the square. Anne's shoulders fell with relief to think that Marcel might just be somewhere else, somewhere safe.

"Please," she said again, stopping herself from grasping his hand. "Please tell me where I can find him."

"You can't," he said. Reading desperation on her face, he

continued. "I'm sorry. Look. I've been at this a long time. I recognized your brother's type. Careless. Maybe stupid. But I also saw potential. I was in the Great War with a few men like that. I recommended him for a position that required a bit of . . . fearlessness. I can't tell you any more. The information is confidential. It's for your own good—and his." He turned away toward a cluster of guards.

"Wait!" she called. "That means he's safe. Out of Paris. Right?"

Anne watched the ox of a man hesitate. He ran his broad hand over his mouth for a moment before responding. "He knows how to protect himself."

"Anne, come with us!" Lucie cried from across the square.

The drivers and museum staff had split into groups and left the square in search of food and accommodations. Reluctantly, Anne followed Lucie and Jacqueline, but they found every shop and restaurant battened down. They went from one block to the other until Anne felt so tired she thought her legs couldn't hold her up anymore; Jacqueline's face was solemn, and Lucie's red eyes spoke of lonely tears wept in the truck.

"It's no use," Lucie said when they reached the end of another street of closed shops and homes. "Let's go back. Maybe the others have found something."

In the square, they discovered that Christiane, armed with little more than her rusty Citroën and some diplomatic skill, had convinced a local bar owner to open his doors to the group. The two dozen men and women dragged themselves gratefully into the garishly lit establishment, happy for a stiff drink and some stale cashews the barman scrounged from the storeroom. The older staff sat at the wobbling tables, while the younger ones found spots on the sticky floor, silent, their backs to the walls. A few filed out onto the narrow strip of a sidewalk.

On the stoop of a battered-down tailor shop, Anne found Corrado, alone. She heaved herself down heavily beside him and then pressed her hand on his forearm. "See," she said, trying to cheer him. "Everything worked out all right."

Corrado slapped his hat on the sidewalk between his feet and ran his fingers through his hair. "We're only ninety kilometers from Chambord, Anne," he said. "And still more than three hundred to go before we get to Loc-Dieu. Three. Hundred . . ." An exasperated sigh. He met her gaze. "I'm an *idiota*. I can't believe I got us so lost."

Anne shrugged. "You didn't mean to. And look! If it weren't for you, we'd never have found this lovely establishment." She gestured to the dingy, striped awning of the luridly lit bar.

Corrado managed a thin smile. "At this point, I'm pretty sure my reputation is dirt. And all I want is a hot meal and bed."

At that moment, two of the guards appeared in the bar with rations they'd secured by knocking on the door of a nearby military canteen. When they entered the bar with their arms laden with food, however meager, a communal cheer went up. One of the men handed rations to Anne and Corrado. They opened their tins and ate together in silence.

AS THE RAGGED caravan moved south, Anne's sole focus was on keeping the ungainly truck centered in her lane. The roads became narrower and more twisted while the golden countryside slipped by slowly, kilometer after kilometer. As they moved through the single street snaking through a village, people leaned out their windows to watch the strange procession. A little boy whooped loudly, proclaiming the circus had come to town at last.

But there was no rejoicing on the staff's part. Anne and the guards in her truck had fallen silent, their hearts and minds back home. Before leaving the garish bar in Châteauroux, they'd gathered around the wireless, desperate for news. Waves of bombs had rained on Paris, the disembodied radio voice had said, but they had landed in the outskirts rather than the city center. Anne imagined Kiki safe in their little apartment and Marcel somewhere far from the dangers of the city. But she had no way of knowing.

On their way south, Lucie and her husband, André, had retrieved their daughter, Frédérique, from her grandmother's farm. More vehicles joined the ragged convoy as several other museum staff had begun to gather their families. Anne was left to despair over knowing nothing of her mother and Marcel.

Anne shifted stiffly in the driver's seat and watched the enormous, wrapped paintings in front of them teeter with the movement of the truck. Suddenly, she saw one of the tarp corners begin to billow and flap, and then they heard screeching truck brakes. Anne jolted the truck to an abrupt halt.

"*Merde!* What is it?" one of the guards from the back seat called.

"Look! One of the straps on those giant paintings has broken." She jerked the hand brake. "We need to help."

The convoy shuddered to a halt. Anne's stomach lurched. A strap holding one of the massive canvases had snapped; the painting was now listing dangerously to one side. Corrado clambered onto the truck's bed; veins stood out on his bare forearms as he strove to push the heaving picture upright. André and several guards joined him. Anne scrambled out of the truck, the guards close behind her.

She could hardly bear to glance at the great painting. It all felt so unjust, so wrong. That beautiful work of art should be hanging safely on the wall of the Louvre, touched only by the adoring eyes of those who'd come from all over the world to see it. Instead, it had been bundled onto a flatbed like a piece of cheap furniture and here it was, about to topple into a muddy roadside ditch.

"Come on!" Lucie gasped. She hitched up her skirt and struggled onto the truck bed, smearing her clothes with dust. Leaning down, she gave Anne a hand up, and they both braced their shoulders against the armature and pushed to straighten it.

"How did it break?" Lucie asked, after the painting was finally judged stable.

"Look." Corrado pointed to the remaining straps; their edges were frayed, fibers sticking out in all directions. His expression was grim.

"It's all the bumping around from yesterday. The friction must have worn the straps thin," André said. There was nothing accusing in André's tone, but Corrado's eyes darkened, his lips pressed into a thin line of disappointment. "We need to stop the whole convoy and check all the others," he said. "We can't afford a casualty."

It took hours to secure the frayed straps. Anne wished they could open the *Mona Lisa*'s truck and check on the painting, but nobody wanted to take the risk.

"The sooner we get these to Loc-Dieu, the better," Anne said quietly to Lucie.

"Yes. Too bad the trucks have to turn around and return to Chambord right away."

Anne felt her jaw fall. "What?"

"Not you and me," Lucie said, squeezing Anne's forearm. "We'll have our work cut out for us with inventorying everything that comes in—again. But the trucks will need to go right back to Chambord."

"But Pierre says Chambord will be the Germans' next target. I don't think it's worth the risk driving back there."

"We can only hope we'll have an armistice with the Germans by then. Pétain wants a cease-fire. But either way, there are artworks at Chambord that could never be replaced," Lucie said, "not to mention the rest of the archives and inventories still there."

For a moment, Anne's eyes flitted to where Corrado was tightening down a strap to the truck bed.

"Don't worry," Lucie said, as if she'd read Anne's mind. "They'll only be gone as long as it takes to pick up the next load."

"Of course," Anne said, her heart like a lead weight.

She leaned against the truck door and watched Monsieur Dupont approach Corrado's silhouette in the dim light.

"You're the one who sent us down this path in the first place," he barked at Corrado. "And now we're in this mess."

LEONARDO

Florence, Italy
1502

On the doors of our cathedral's ancient baptistery is an image of a man ready to slay his own son. I press my face closer to contemplate the forms of Abraham and Isaac in the cold morning air. I have only myself to blame; I sent myself on this path in the first place, and now I'm in this mess.

I should have known things with Cesare Borgia wouldn't last. Perhaps Salaì was right; working with Borgia was like stepping directly into the lair of a beast. Now, gazing up at the bright winter sky above the baptistery's peaked roof, I admit I feel relieved to have escaped Borgia's side with my body and mind intact.

Florentine citizens bring their infants to this ancient place to be born anew with holy water and the mark of a priest's thumb on their foreheads. As much as I hate to admit it, there is something comforting about returning to these old, familiar places. After months away from Florence, somehow it feels like home. Perhaps it's when we might lose it all that we finally gain an appreciation for things we once took for granted.

Yes, I know. Salaì has every right to stay angry with me forever. He might have moved on to another master. And yet when

I arrived in my abandoned rooms at the monastery of Santissima Annunziata, he returned to my side. Loyal boy.

The monks, too, seem resigned to forgive me for running off after a known tyrant, absent for months without so much as a word. The prior even launched a celebratory dinner in the refectory of Santissima Annunziata upon my return from the clutches of Cesare Borgia. He then announced, to my surprise, that the monks would open their chambers to allow the public in to see my preparatory cartoon for the central panel of their altarpiece.

Perhaps it is only a ploy to force me to finish the commission. At last, one final chance before the monks give the commission back to Filippino Lippi, as they had originally intended. Behind the façade of the jolly, simple monk, that old prior is as cunning as a fox. He knows we artists live and breathe public acclaim. And perhaps he is right; the pressure of a public display might be the only way I'll make good on my contract.

Looking again at the baptistery's magnificent bronze doors, I can only admit that we Florentines love a good public competition. For nearly a hundred years, such contests resulted in each of the three sets of doors on the baptistery. The most incredible of these, in my view, is the set of bronze doors that faces the cathedral, those crafted by the goldsmith and sculptor Lorenzo Ghiberti all those generations ago. They say it took Master Ghiberti more than twenty-five years to cast these Old Testament scenes. There is even a self-portrait of the old man, poking his gilded head from one of the roundels. I lean in close to the face of the balding man with a smug smile.

When Old Man Ghiberti won this commission all those years ago, the doors were just the latest artistic competition to grip Florence by the neck. I stand back with the realization that all these public contests are at the same time political, idealistic, contentious, biased, and unfair. Florentines revel in the controversy surrounding these displays of artistic prowess, and the impressive results that add layers to the city's ornate decoration.

Even the cathedral and its hulking tile dome appear as much a monument to incompletion as a testament to Florentine ambition. During my entire life, the Duomo has formed an active construction site, busy with the chaotic comings and goings of stonecutters, brick makers, ironsmiths, and other craftsmen working from dawn to dusk.

Ah, yes. To work . . .

It is time I return to the monastery, where the monks have asked me to pin up my drawing for all to see. No doubt Salaì is already directing assistants to mix the glue and tacks to attach it to the wall. The prior has even brought in a carpenter to erect a wooden barrier so people won't get close enough to touch the parchment. They're expecting a crowd, the novice called Stefano has told me. The young man with the startling amber-colored eyes has been assigned to make sure I have everything I need. It seems strange to think I might have made a name for myself in Florence, even as I have done my best to gain employment far from here.

I make my way past a cluster of aromatic leather workshops, turn into the square near Santissima Annunziata, and stop dead in my tracks. The prior was right. There is already a crowd waiting outside the monastery walls. Are people really lining up to see my meager drawing? It is little more than a picture of the Mother of Christ filled with gladness at seeing the beauty of her Son, whom she holds tenderly in her lap. I have added John the Baptist as a little boy playing with a lamb. That's all. This line of people extending around the corner has come to see my unfinished idea for an altarpiece? It is nearly unfathomable.

And yet . . . Outside the monastery door, the city's most elegantly dressed people have assembled. There are women with ponderous silk skirts and men with velvet hats. Then a gaggle of a family together with their servants and small children. They've brought the entire family out to see the spectacle of my meager drawing tacked to the wall.

As I step closer, I see a servant woman holding a small girl on her hip; the little girl looks at me with large, brown eyes, fingers in her mouth. There is a sad-looking woman in a fine silk dress of black and a little boy. Then a broad-shouldered man turns, and I recognize the face of that silk broker my father has been trying to introduce me to ever since I left Milan years ago. I struggle to recall his name.

Ah, yes. Now I remember. Francesco del Giocondo.

Florence, Italy
1502

Bellina followed Francesco del Giocondo's broad back into the cold shadows of the alley outside their house. She balanced Camilla on her hip. At three years old, the little girl showed no signs of relinquishing the habit of sucking on her fingers; she laid her head heavily on Bellina's shoulder as they made their way into the crowd waiting to see Leonardo da Vinci's drawing of the Madonna and Child. In the cold air, Bellina was grateful for the girl's wriggly, warm body.

Lisa had never asked Bellina to accompany her on such an outing. They were to dress in their finest clothing, Lisa had said, and walk together to the monastery of Santissima Annunziata, where Master Leonardo da Vinci's preparatory cartoon for an altarpiece was being put on public display. Bellina couldn't remember a time when the whole family went somewhere as a group. Still, she could hardly think of anything duller than going to look at a drawing.

All the same, she was grateful for the chance to get out of the house. A pall had been cast over the household. Feeling helplessly unable to rouse Lisa from her endless hours of staring out the window, her lying in bed until the midday meal, Bellina had redoubled her service. It was the least she could do, she thought, to dress the children in fresh clothing, to change Lisa's bedding, to put a wildflower in Camilla's hand and ask her to present it to her mother. With this family outing, Francesco also seemed to want to cheer his wife after the long months of sadness. Bellina had done her best to duck out of the room when Francesco discussed politics; she could not afford to get involved. In fact, she could feel nothing but gratitude toward the man who wanted only to pull his wife out of the darkness. He had corralled the entire household, including Madre and all the servants and children.

Bellina followed behind Madre as they made their way a few short blocks until the elegant arcades of the Servites' mother church came into view. Bartolomeo, now eight years old and the spit of his father, held Francesco's hand as the two of them led the family across the sunlit square. Lisa had said Bartolomeo was being tutored in French so he could take over the international trade of the branch of Francesco's company with his brothers in Lyon. Lisa carried little Marietta in her arms. Bellina could see the baby's bright eyes over Lisa's shoulder. Marietta was just learning to walk, but she insisted her mother carry her every moment. Bringing up the rear, Bellina carried squirming Camilla. Bellina attempted to hang on to little Piero's hand, but the boy pulled away, darting to the edges of the street, picking up rocks and sticks, and soiling his leather shoes in the puddles in spite of Bellina's scolding.

Bellina couldn't imagine why anyone would bring a gaggle of unruly children to see a drawing, but as they approached a side door in the alley alongside the monastery, they found dozens of people waiting. Men and women nodded their heads in respect to Francesco as he passed, and two men stepped back to allow the family to squeeze into the queue. At last, they entered the doorway and followed a potato-shaped monk down a long corridor. This part of the monastery was a semipublic space carefully concealed from the quiet, private living and sacred spaces of the monks. At this back service door, farmers delivered cabbages and herbs fresh from the countryside, and the monks took delivery of altar cloths from Francesco del Giocondo's workshops.

Was Stefano there, Bellina wondered, just the other side of this wall? She couldn't help it; the old mixture of attraction and repulsion welled up in the center of her gut. What did he think now, she wondered, that his austere monastery housed an esteemed artist? That the monks made a public display of a drawing that, just a few short years ago, Stefano himself might have thrown onto Savonarola's great blaze in the Piazza della Signoria?

After a long time, they finally made their way through another door into the dim interior. Bellina grasped Piero's hand tightly as the family jostled their way to a wooden barrier that had been put in place to keep people from getting too close to Master Leonardo's cartoon. Before them, several pieces of parchment had been glued together to make a large drawing surface. It was an idea, Bellina had been told, a preparatory sketch that Master Leonardo would soon turn into the monks' altarpiece.

Bellina set Camilla down on the tiles so she could squeeze herself between two tall men to get a better look at the drawing. In the filtered light, she could make out three figures. In the background, there was a large, seated Saint Anne with heavy folds of drapery. Another adult woman—the Madonna, Bellina realized—perched on Saint Anne's lap. The baby Christ, perhaps the same age as little Marietta on Lisa's shoulder, had just escaped from his mother's arms. The Christ child reached out to a small lamb as if trying to squeeze it tightly. The Madonna seemed to try

---

to stop her child from squeezing the lamb. In turn, Saint Anne was rising from her seat as if trying to stop her daughter from separating the baby Christ from the animal.

The drawing, Bellina realized, was little more than a series of lines drawn with charcoal or perhaps some type of pen. And yet, Bellina had to admit she had never seen anything so beautiful. She knew it was wrong to worship an image; Brother Savonarola's admonitions swam up from the dark recesses of her mind. But Bellina pushed them away. It was impossible to deny the beauty and power of this simple picture. If the surrounding crowds were any indication, she wasn't the only one held in rapture.

She turned to Lisa, who was staring at the drawing as if she were far away from Florence. "What do you think, *polpetta*?"

"It's a miracle," Lisa said. It was the first time in months that Bellina had seen light in her mistress's eyes.

Francesco stepped forward. He reached his arm around Lisa's shoulders and pulled her tightly to his side. "Yes," he said in a low voice. "Impressive. And I have begun talking with Ser Piero about engaging Master Leonardo to make a portrait."

ANNE

Loc-Dieu, France
1940

Francesco del Giocondo. He was the man who commissioned Lisa's portrait, according to the scholarly tomes in the Louvre archives that Anne had read. A self-made silk merchant in fifteenth-century Florence, Francesco probably had common business interests with Leonardo da Vinci's father at the monastery of Santissima Annunziata. Little more was known about the circumstances of the commission, and Anne was left to wonder what Lisa might have thought about having Master Leonardo paint her.

"Twenty-three. Twenty-four," Lucie said, bending over a crate stored in the shadows. "Is that right?"

Anne grimaced. "The first time, we counted twenty-one," she said, tapping her pen on a stack of pages worn and tattered from handling.

"Ugh." Lucie sat down on a crate, pushing her hair out of her eyes. "We'll have to count again. Our notes got so scrambled in our rush to get here."

"Just figuring out how many crates we have here is hard enough," Anne agreed. "When we start making an inventory of what exactly is in each crate . . ."

The two women surveyed the mass of wooden containers

around them, stacked and arranged in messy rows with ragged paths to walk between them. From the inventories, Anne knew they must have more than three thousand works of art in their possession now. Many boxes filled the austere, vaulted nave of the giant medieval abbey church of Loc-Dieu, stretching back into the dark side chapels as far as the eye could see. The church resembled a warehouse more than a house of worship. The great vaulted space was garishly lit with makeshift electric bulbs that made the jumble of crates cast looming shadows into the dark crevices.

Lucie had explained that out of an abundance of caution, the curators would need to open each crate and unwrap the pieces one by one to inspect their condition, and also send confirmation of their inventories to Paris. Large paintings that had been rolled would need to be laid flat so the pigments wouldn't be damaged. Lucie and Anne would need to be present to cross-check the inventories so nothing went missing. One crate might house multiple works of art, each separately wrapped in packing paper and fiber plugs to prevent excess movement. How long would it take to document everything in their care? Anne wondered.

"It could take months to unwrap everything," Lucie said, seeming to read her mind. "And we'll have to repack it quickly in case we need to leave again."

Anne shuddered. "Is there a chance we'd have to do that?"

"I hope not, but at this point, I can't predict what will happen."

Anne couldn't imagine what they had heard about German Panzers already crunching across the gravel paths of Chambord. The fairy-tale château had been a refuge—at least Anne had thought it was. Now, Nazi troops were using the typists' former dormitory for barracks, taking meals in its elegant halls, marching with their dirty boots up and down Leonardo da Vinci's double-helix staircase. If the Germans could take over a fortified castle so quickly, Anne wondered, then how long would it take them to find them here, inside this vast medieval church stacked with thousands of priceless works of art?

It had taken four more days of driving and three more days to unload the nine trucks that had finally traversed the distance. It had been tempting to race the darkness, to spirit all the crates inside the safety of the cavernous abbey church as quickly as possible, but as always, the work was slow and painstaking. Great sculptures had to be wheeled gently down ramps; paintings had to be carried carefully, always two or more men to transport even a small crate. Anne and Lucie busied themselves with ordering the inventories and doing their best to keep the ever-shifting puzzle of records straight. Anne couldn't imagine loading everything up and moving it all again.

Besides, here at Loc-Dieu, Anne had begun to feel something like peace for the first time since their traumatic departure from Paris. As soon as she had stepped into the austere, empty, fortresslike medieval church, she felt it wrap her in its serenity. She imagined the white-robed monks once bustling silently about their business here, all those centuries ago. The Germans wouldn't be interested in this, not the way they were in Chambord, she thought. She hoped. The curators told stories about how a branch of austere Cistercian monks had built the abbey in the twelfth century. The English had burned it down during the Hundred Years' War, and later it was sold as national property during the French Revolution. After that, a family bought it; their descendants had moved out to make room for the Louvre staff.

Their first few days in Loc-Dieu were so peaceful that there were times Anne could almost forget about the looming threat of German soldiers. There were no large towns nearby, only a few villages where some of the guards and other families had gone to find accommodations. She spent hours walking the serene grounds that surrounded the abbey, Corrado often by her side, listening to the babble of the stream and watching swallows loop and dive above the chestnut trees. She told him about her brother's mysterious transfer by Monsieur Dupont, who had now moved on to another depot. They also spoke of small things that didn't matter and shared their very different childhoods in Florence and Paris. As much as she loved Paris, the utter peace at Loc-Dieu soothed her soul.

Within the first few days at Loc-Dieu, more people came. Soon, there were dozens of families—Louvre staff, their spouses, children, and extended families, living together in the abbey's outbuildings. Lucie's daughter, Frédérique, and the other children played for hours without a care for what went on beyond the abbey gates. Many of the staff had lured family members away from Paris and other cities. The abbey's grounds now resembled a family reunion rather than an evacuation. Anne continued to write letters to Kiki that went unanswered.

Small though Loc-Dieu was compared to Chambord, it was better set up for large groups. Each family had a bedroom in the abbey cloister with a trunk for their clothes. Anne, along with a small group of single women, occupied the former monks' dormitory, each with a narrow bed spread with fresh, clean linens. At night, grateful to her core, Anne crawled into bed, buried her face in the pillow, and slept.

In the evenings, the staff and their families gathered around the tables in the monks' refectory while Pierre fiddled with the wireless until crackling voices brought grimmer news each day. As idyllic as the medieval abbey seemed, Anne couldn't ignore the tinny voice coming from the squat machine in the corner.

"Paris is no longer safe for its government," the reporter was saying. "Officials have left the city, and the government will move to Tours for safety as the Germans continue to advance. We urge Parisians to evacuate the city as soon as possible as the prisoner-of-war count continues to rise. There are now more than one and a half million French POWs imprisoned by the Germans." *One and a half million*. Anne could hardly comprehend that number, and she feared Marcel was among them. She wondered if Kiki would leave Paris now that even the government had abandoned its capital. If Kiki was still alive. Fear tore at her with black claws.

The Louvre staff also fretted over their Jewish colleagues still in Paris. Curators and other staff from Paris needed to leave but had nowhere to go.

"Can't they come here to Loc-Dieu with the rest of us?" Anne asked.

"One of our best paintings curators is Jewish," Lucie said, shaking her head. "Charles Sterling. He needs to get as far away as he can. Monsieur Jaujard is trying to help arrange passage for his family to another museum in New York. There are also Jewish curators at the Musée Guimet and other museums across the city. They have to leave. The sooner the better. Still, this was a mistake," Lucie said, shaking her head.

"What was a mistake?" Anne sat on a crate and kept her pencil point on the page to keep her place in the great stack of inventory pages on her lap.

Lucie sighed and placed her hands on her hips. "This whole thing. We were in such a hurry to get the *Mona Lisa* here safely, but we should have never left the archives at Chambord. I don't know what I was thinking."

"It's all right," Anne said. "We have a good record here." She flipped through the dozens of handwritten pages she had compiled in recent days, complicated, cross-referenced systems to track the ever-shifting, ever-moving works of art. "I think."

"But we have more than three thousand paintings alone here now," Lucie said, "not counting the many other works we've taken from the Louvre. And there will be more coming."

"I'm just glad we're finally settled in one place," Anne said.

But Lucie only shook her head. "I don't like it. We should be safe from the Germans, at least for a while, but it's too damp in here. I'm worried for the paintings but more than that," she said, looking into the blackness of the vaults, "I'm afraid we're all going to get the Black Death." She pressed her hand into the small of her back. "I think we both need a break."

Anne stood and stretched, then walked through the main portal of the church to a heavy, overcast sky bearing down on a flat, grassy plain that stretched to the forest line. In the distance, Lucie's daughter, Frédérique, was playing on the lawn outside with two other girls; she couldn't hear their laughter, but their faces were beaming.

Then Corrado suddenly appeared, running ahead of Frédérique and two other girls who had traveled here to safety with the Louvre staff. They were playing some kind of game of tag, and

Anne could see that Corrado was letting the girls win. She smiled. The girls ran to him, grabbing his hands and towing him across the lawn.

"I told you I'd bring him back." Lucie came to stand next to Anne. They gazed out at Corrado and the children.

Anne felt heat rise to her cheeks. Was it so obvious that she was taken with this charming Italian driver? Emile's betrayal had seeped into every crevice of her heart like spilled ink, but now, with a little time, she thought, she might begin to trust again.

"There you are!" From a shadowy corner of the church, Lucie's husband, André, strode toward them. "I'm afraid it's bad news."

Anne's stomach clenched. Was it more bad news from Paris?

"What is it?" Lucie said as André joined them in the shade of the church portal. He lit a cigarette at the end of a long, ebony holder.

"Mussolini has declared war on us. That's trouble not just for us but for everything in our care, too," he said, gesturing to the crates behind them.

"What?" Lucie's mouth hung open.

"If they march north, they'll want their pictures back." He swallowed hard. "We'd lose some of the most important works the Louvre has ever had."

"*La Joconde.*" Lucie's voice was barely a whisper.

Anne knew she should be worried about the five-hundred-year-old portrait sitting in its airtight box in the church, safe for the moment yet suddenly in peril thanks to this news. Instead, she was staring across the flat plain again. Corrado was sitting on the lawn, his hands gesticulating wildly, forming the shapes of the story he was telling to the enraptured children around him.

André followed Anne's gaze to the distant figure of Corrado, flapping his wings like a ridiculous, man-sized goose while the children nearly fell over with laughter.

"Poor sap," André said. "He's just become our enemy."

ANNE'S GIGGLES FLOATED around her like bubbles. "Wait for me, Marcel!" she cried.

He was too quick. Flaxen hair swirling around his face, Marcel glanced over his shoulder as he sprinted down the sidewalk, sending startled pedestrians scrambling out of his way. "Last one to the corner smells of pâté!" he chanted over and over.

Anne laughed breathlessly, redoubling her pace as she followed her brother's weaving form on the sidewalk. Suddenly the coins clutched in her hand, a reminder of the errand they had to run for Kiki, were forgotten. Marcel had made it fun. He made everything fun.

"You smell! You smell!" Marcel taunted, pausing on a street corner. He didn't see the truck coming. He put his foot out over the curb. Anne felt her heart fall through her shoes.

"Marcel, stop!" she cried. "I've got you!" Anne lunged forward, one arm outstretched to grab him.

But when her fingers met his coat, they fell through him like smoke. She stumbled to a halt, staring at him, but Marcel was fading in front of her eyes, his form dissolving as she watched. "Marcel!" Anne screamed, but he had disappeared, and she was standing alone on the sidewalk. Something boomed above her head, and she whipped around as a plane swept by in a thunderous shudder.

Gasping, Anne sat bolt upright. Her sheets were tangled around her legs. Outside the open window, the aftereffects of thunder rumbled, and she heard the rush of a sudden summer rain that chilled her sweaty skin. She pushed her hair from her sticky brow, trying to slow her gasping breaths. The dream had felt so real. She lay back down, pulling the covers over her arms, and took a few deep breaths. There were no bombers. She was safe in the cavernous dormitory at Loc-Dieu.

Suddenly, a loud creak of the floorboards. Anne stared wide-eyed at the ceiling, listening. Had that been her imagination? Or had she just heard footsteps? Her heart hammered in her ears, and she sat up, regretting the fact that they'd left the windows open for fresh air. She swung her legs over the edge of the bed and reached for her flashlight. She tiptoed from the bed.

As soon as she stepped into the corridor, she felt the back of her neck prickle. Someone was there. Her fingers tightened around her flashlight, and its beam searched wildly in the darkness. Suddenly, a hand clamped over her mouth, stifling the scream that ripped through her lungs. She struck out, dropping the flashlight with a clatter, her hand slapping into a strong arm as the fingers tightened over her mouth. She was being suffocated; she was going to be killed.

"Shhh," a voice whispered in her ear, warm and familiar. "Hush, Anne, it's all right. Don't scream. You'll wake the others. It's me."

Corrado. Relief flooded through her. Anne stilled, and he removed his hand from her mouth. The faint glow of moonlight illuminated his face. His usual smile was gone, and the light cast deep shadows around his eyes. His usually pleasant face looked gaunt and pale.

"What is it?" Anne hissed, frightened.

"I heard Monsieur Schommer and the other men talking. The

museum is getting rid of all its Italian employees. We are no longer welcome here," he said.

"What?" She barely comprehended what he was saying.

"I'm not waiting for them to tell me what to do. You've already heard about the POWs. I'm taking my delivery truck and I'm leaving right now. While I still can."

Anne gripped his arm. "Surely they won't hurt you?" she whispered. "You're part . . . you're one of us." But she wasn't so sure.

Suddenly, he reached up, his warm palms on either side of Anne's cheeks. His big, dark eyes captured everything about her—her attention, her eyes, her heartbeat, even her breath was lost in the depth of his gaze. In an instant, she grasped his face, too. Their lips found each other. For a moment, time stood still as she lost herself in his taste and the gentle yet earnest grasp of his hands. A kiss worthy of a thousand masterpieces.

When he pulled away, Anne gasped for air. Then, as swiftly and stealthily as he had entered the room, Corrado vanished into the shadows.

BELLINA

Florence, Italy
1502

Bellina watched Dolce cross the square with a basket of laundry propped against her hip. At the washing well, several other servant women bent over their wooden bats and scrubbed their masters' careless stains of oils and wine until their fingers cracked and bled.

"You're hiding something," Bellina said. "I can tell."

"I don't know why you would say that." Dolce set down her basket and tossed her long, dark curls that had turned white at the roots.

Bellina wagged a finger. "Ha! I know you better than that. You *are* the neighborhood earful."

Immediately, Bellina regretted provoking her old friend. Did she really want to know whatever Dolce was hiding? Bellina was utterly resolved to focus on her role as Lisa's servant and confidante. The birth of a healthy baby boy had brought an outpouring of thanksgiving. Andrea, a fat little boy, was the third son for Francesco, who placed a beautiful green gem into Lisa's inlaid jewelry box.

"Perhaps I just have exceptional hearing." Dolce smiled and plunked a tired-looking linen shift into the shallow basin with a splash. "You'd know everything, too, if you would only rejoin us at our meeting place."

"Shh!" Bellina lowered her voice. "I have tried to avoid it, you know that . . . I just . . . My place is in Lisa's house. I promised her father."

"I know," Dolce said. "You may choose to avoid them, but you can't stop them from talking about you. You and your mistress. They're paying attention."

Bellina squeezed the water out of one of Lisa's underlayers and narrowed her eyes. "What's that supposed to mean?"

Dolce considered Bellina carefully. "They're saying Master Leonardo is going to paint your Lisa," Dolce said. "That Francesco del Giocondo has promised a handsome sum to lure him away from his frescoes for the monks. Is that true?"

Had Dolce's brother told her that? Bellina knew Bardo was employed in one of Master Francesco's silk workshops, but Bellina was surprised that sort of news had reached beyond Lisa's house. At Lisa's dressing table, she had noticed a collection of small glass and ceramic vials with cork stoppers, procured from the apothecary at Santa Maria Novella. Bellina had spent the morning plucking the remaining eyelashes and stray hairs of Lisa's brow with a pair of silver tweezers. She had plucked more hairs, one by one, from her hairline until Lisa protested from the pain and they resorted to a new concoction, recommended by the apothecary himself. This one, he had said, contained a mixture of vinegar, quicklime, and cat dung, and was good for removing hair from stubborn areas like the hairline and the underarm.

"Well," Bellina said slowly. "My master and his mother want this portrait done, it is true." At the mention of Francesco's mother, Bellina felt heat rise to her face. "But Lisa? She is . . . melancholy. I believe she has no interest in a portrait," Bellina said. "But what of it? I haven't shared this information with anyone. I suppose I don't intend to. Not anymore."

Dolce looked around to make sure no one was listening and then lowered her voice even more. "Bellina," she began, "what are your intentions, then?"

It was a fair question, Bellina thought. Sometimes at night, as she lay on her narrow cot in the quiet, she dared to ask herself what she wanted, and the answers came. To bring her mistress out of the darkness. To see Lisa's children safely into adulthood. To keep Gherardo out of trouble until he was old enough to have some sense. Ultimately, to find a purpose bigger than Lisa and her family, bigger than herself. And, perhaps one day, to find love? That one seemed a far-flung fantasy.

"You haven't changed your mind about becoming an . . . informant?" Dolce pressed.

"I . . ." Bellina paused. She knew that the *frateschi* had planted people in many households, and she would not be the first or the last to share news from inside. But now she knew her involvement with the *frateschi* had been mostly about seeking Stefano's approval, and that was in the past. She shook her head. "No. Anyway, I thought now that Piero Soderini has been elected for life, there's no risk the Med . . . that *they* will come back to Florence."

"How would you know?" Dolce said. "You no longer know what's happening since you haven't joined us in a while. Plus, the important information may not be far away with the Medici in Rome. It might be right in front of you."

Bellina examined a persistent stain on one of Bartolomeo's gowns; she pressed it down into the soapy basin again. For a few long minutes, the two women worked together in silence. "And you?" Bellina asked. "You're still going to the riverbank every week?"

Dolce's face glowed suddenly, and her mouth spread into a wide grin. "Yes, but not because I care so much for the cause anymore. I go for what comes afterward. You remember that wool comber's oldest son. Vanni."

Bellina slapped Dolce's shoulder with the back of her parched hand. "Stop! You're in love!"

Dolce nodded. "And he's promised we'll be married as soon as he can arrange the papers with his father and the notary. It can't come quickly enough. I'm done with the Old Man."

"What?" Bellina's mouth fell open. "I knew you were hiding something! You're leaving your master's house? How? Your family's been serving the Salvini for generations! Your own mother promised you to them."

Dolce shrugged. "Shh! I haven't told anyone. But look: My mother's dead. I don't belong to the Old Man, and he can't make me stay in his service. If I want to be married, he can't stop me. I can make my own choices. I'm not a slave, Bellina. Neither are you."

Bellina's mouth was still hanging open as she watched Dolce pick up her basket and walk across the square. At the edges of the rooftops, the late-afternoon light turned the color of gilded silk, and suddenly, everything was illuminated.

THE GOLDEN AURA still colored the air when Bellina emerged from Lisa's house an hour later. She wended her way toward the riverbank without thinking how to get there. Her footsteps knew the way, tracing a well-worn track down the center of the alleys.

In the inner pocket of her linen shift, she felt the charred bones of Girolamo Savonarola bump against her thigh, bones as brittle and hollow as a baby bird's.

Once, a few years ago, they had seemed like relics that might hold some power of their own. Now, Bellina thought they seemed only the product of a dim-witted decision.

She left the shadows of the alleys and turned onto the quay-side bordering the Arno. The air was crisp, biting. She inhaled its scent, a mixture of fresh fields beyond Florence, the muddy edges of the river, and the stench of the cloth and leather trades. Along an embankment, she stopped and looked out at the sparkling expanse of the river and the cobbled-together colors of the Ponte Vecchio, as patched and mismatched as an old, mended blanket.

She thought of Dolce then, and the promise of a new life outside her master's house. A man she loved, a house of her own, a different future than the one either of them had imagined at the washing well. Dolce had hinted that Bellina might make a choice like that, too, but she could hardly imagine it.

Bellina didn't know what awaited her ahead. But she could at least put the past behind her.

She reached into the pocket of her gown and removed the bones, which now seemed so fragile, nearly weightless, as she rubbed them together between her fingers. Then, with a rush, she flung them into the air. For a moment, they twirled in the cold, suspended there, then Bellina lost sight of them as they fell toward the water and disappeared in the spangles.

LEONARDO

Pisa, Italy
1502

A portrait of a lady. Somehow, I've said yes.

Was it a moment of weakness that caused me to agree to my father's request to paint a portrait of Francesco del Giocondo's wife? Or perhaps the vision of Francesco del Giocondo himself, having dressed in the fur-lined cape of the Twelve and led his bustling family to view my cartoon at Santissima Annunziata? He may wear the crimson and ermine of the Dodici Buonomini, but anyone with eyes knows better than to think he is an adherent of Soderini's new republic. No. Look inside the outer wrapping, and anyone could see that Francesco del Giocondo is the very picture of a Medici supporter.

But I cannot afford to ally myself to any one faction. That will not serve me well. I follow the power, and power might shift at any moment.

I make a few hatch marks on the hairline of a woman in my sketchbook while I sit in the shade of a long arcade, shielding myself from the blazing sun. Beyond, the Camposanto of Pisa stretches out, green and lush, a carpet of green leading the eye to that strange, tilting tower. I admire the sweeping green expanse and the strangely skewed tower of white marble against a blue sky.

I suppose that some three hundred years ago, the engineers might not have known that the damp ground would cause the campanile to settle and begin to pitch. But there it is. A strange, leaning tower that has somehow made itself a monument to fallibility as much as a thing of beauty.

It has been many years since I've set foot in Pisa. For most of my life, it's been enemy territory. If we had come only months ago, the Pisans would have slaughtered us without a thought. But now, thanks to our superior military cunning, Florentine forces have taken the city at last. As powerful as our republic may be, Florence is landlocked. We can only extend our influence if we control a seaport. When the *gonfaloniere* asked for my help to engineer a new seafaring base for our Florentine forces, how could I refuse? Niccolò Machiavelli, my old friend now thankfully returned to Florence, has secured the commission for me.

While I wait for Salaì to bring me something cool to drink, I lay out my drawings on the table. First things first. I flip through the pages of my sketchbook, past the experimental designs for a new type of silk loom that might produce the *braccia* of fabric more efficiently. Past the many renderings of ladies' faces, hands. Of embroidered sleeves. Of small dogs and ermines in their laps. Enough. Instead, I turn to the proper task at hand.

In the distance, down the seemingly endless corridor of white marble arches, I recognize Salaì's silhouette. That boy, the joy and curse of my life. He has returned to me. Wherever he has been carousing across Florence during my absence, he has returned to the comfort of my employ. Whatever our disagreement before my departure to work for Cesare Borgia in the Romagna, it is now forgotten, forgiven with a simple nod. We have been together long enough that no words need be spoken.

As he approaches, I see he carries a large ceramic pitcher. Perfect; watery beer to slake our parched tongues. My mouth waters. His fine curls move in the breeze, his lanky frame silhouetted by the streaks of light and white marble.

"I found a few bits of ice left in the coldhouse," Salaì says, setting the pitcher down on the table next to my drawings, careful not to let the beads of condensation wet my papers.

I smile. "Thank you, my lovely."

He looks at my open sketchbook and frowns. "You've turned back to the riverworks?"

His endless questions, his endless questioning. He is like my sickness and its cure in the same dose. Life might be less complicated if I had never pulled him from the streets of Milan.

"Yes," I say, trying not to sound exasperated. "Now that we can safely set foot in Pisa again without getting our throats slit, the Signoria has accepted my proposal to divert the Arno."

"The Pisans won't have any water left?"

"Not only that! It will give Florence a seaport for the first time in history. It will of course require the moving of vast amounts of earth, but I have created the construction plans for that as well."

I turn my page around so that Salaì can peruse my sketch of the Arno. This river, my old friend. The waters of this same river— waters that are the first to enter and the last to leave Florence— also feed life to Pisa's port. The flow of water through the land is like the flow of blood through a body. The smaller tributaries feed the larger ones in ever-growing perfection.

But Salaì does not see these things. He only continues to frown. I try again. "Machiavelli is coming to see my drawings. He's the sole reason we have support for this project in the Signoria. The future of Florence hangs on what we do here." I hear myself pleading like a child, and I cringe.

Salaì pulls at a corner of one of the drawings, and it emerges: a fast sketch of a lady's serene face. Salaì looks at the drawing for a few moments, and then puts his eyes on me.

"Master, what of the lady?" Salaì asks, thumping his finger against the quick rendering of what might be a Madonna or a real woman; I'm not sure yet. "Francesco del Giocondo's wife?"

The boy asks important questions so innocently. I sigh. What shall I say? The truth is that I have laid aside the portrait of Lisa and the other small projects I was working on to create a series of technical drawings for the Signoria. These plans are suitable to guide the construction of the levees, canals, and gates for diverting the Arno and the creation of the water system we need.

"Were you in my shoes, my friend, would you deny Soderini for a mere portrait of a silk trader's wife?"

Salaì sits across the table from me and breaks open a pomegranate. I detest the fruit; it stains my fingers and clothing, not to mention my drawings. He thinks for a moment before speaking. "It's just that . . . Working with men like these never ends well for us. They will turn on you as fast as a snake if it suits them. Yet you keep returning, seeking favor, like a climbing vine that cannot stand on its own, scaling a giant tree. You *can* stand on your own, you know, Master. You will stand throughout history long after these men are forgotten." He is beautiful when his passions flare.

In the distance, a cluster of men cross the piazza and seek the shade of the arcade where the afternoon heat reaches us. I recognize Niccolò Machiavelli and a few other men. They will be with us before too long.

"I'm sorry, Master," Salaì persists. "It's just that . . . there are men like . . . like Michelangelo Buonarroti . . ."

Suddenly, the angle of the sun shifts, and I feel a searing beam on the back of my neck. "What of him?"

"They say he has managed to make something of that old marble block in the cathedral workyard after all."

Michelangelo Buonarroti. A *teppista,* a common troublemaker of the streets.

Salaì continues. "They say it will be a colossus, a wonder never seen in Florence."

"He is little more than a glorified stonecutter," I snap.

"But, Master . . ." He struggles. "It's not the fact that it's a sculpture. I can only think that glory like that should have been yours—if you had only stayed in Florence. If you had only . . . *painted* something."

The group of men approach my table, and I stand. Before I wave my hand to dismiss this pest, I whisper, "Salaì, let others carve images. My creations will give Florence a seaport, wealth, power, influence . . ."

Salaì just shakes his head at me and walks away from the table, taking the rind of the bitter fruit with him. Perhaps he is right.

"Leonardo." Niccolò Machiavelli's face lights up with a bright grin as he approaches the table.

"My old friend."

Machiavelli sets his dark, intelligent eyes on me, then he grasps my shoulders and I feel his clean-shaven jaw against my beard.

"I HEARD YOU were back in town."

The apothecary squints at me as I leave the white light of the street behind and step into the shadows of his workshop. The interior seems a place of magic, stuffed to the brim with containers filled with concoctions of medicinal plants and powders in every color God has made.

"Seems you're an old man now."

"Greetings to you, too, Master Sanguini," I say, smiling.

He scoffs, his grumpy exterior a thin veil over what I know to be one of the warmest hearts in Florence.

"I suppose my father has been spreading misinformation about me while I've been away."

"Your father?" the old apothecary says, raising his eyebrows and pressing his palms on the worn wooden countertop. "No. I saw your name re-inscribed in the account books of the Confraternity of Saint Luke. That's how I knew you'd come back to grace us with your presence again," he says, scanning me, taking in my rose-colored cape, my floppy hat, my newly shined buckles purchased from Ludovico Sforza's best metalsmith back in Milan. Of course. It is only natural for old Sanguini to keep track of all the painters in town. Their livelihood is also his. "What can I do for you today, Master Leonardo?"

"A new panel for a portrait of a lady," I say. I hesitate. In Milan, I've become accustomed to painting on fine specimens of walnut. I consider requesting a fine piece of walnut for this portrait, too. But surely it would not be of the type available in Milan.

Signor Sanguini nods and disappears into the darkness of the back room, where I hear him rifling through panels stored vertically in wooden racks along the wall. He already knows the type of piece I prefer.

"Make sure it's well seasoned," I call to him anyway.

"You already know it is," he calls back.

"Yes. That's why I come."

"And your usual gesso?" he asks, returning with a fine rectangle of poplar and placing it across the countertop. I run my hand across its light yellowish surface streaked with gray. It will do for a portrait of a lady. Salaì was right, after all. I should start the portrait and soon be done with it.

"No. I think I'll use lead white for this one."

Signor Sanguini nods smugly, as if I've guessed the right answer to a trick question. I don't need it, but I appreciate his recognition of my choice for this dense, thick base layer. If I stay away from the walnut, I'll need the base to compensate. I'll paint on the outer face to prevent warping. Later, I'll be back for cinnabar as red as dragon's blood, blue ultramarine from the exceedingly rare and costly lapis lazuli stone. I'll mix the rich colors with oil, slower to dry than the smelly eggs I once used in Verrocchio's studio. But first, the drawings. I buy a stack of parchment from the apothecary.

I've relented. I've accepted the commission for a portrait of Francesco del Giocondo's wife. My father has all but carried me to the man's house on his shoulders.

Soon enough, I'll gather my sketchbooks and walk to his well-appointed house on the via della Stufa to discuss the painting, meet the woman, and set the fee. Francesco del Giocondo is no fool. By hiring me to paint his lady, he will flatter himself with his patronage. He will tell his friends. And he will honor and please his wife at the same time. The more I think about the commission, I think I might ask for a higher fee than I've ever asked before. He will surely guarantee a hefty deposit; such a fee is nothing to him. He might even offer to accommodate me in his house. Then surely I will be free of those pesky monks at last.

I see the scene clearly in my mind. Even if he does not offer me a room under his roof, Francesco del Giocondo will be a gracious host. He will offer me food and drink, which I will politely accept. We will walk in the shade of his home's inner *cortile,* admiring the first blooms of spring. After some idle conversation, the lady will appear. She will blush and avert her eyes; she is not used to having a man who is not her husband stare so intently at her. After an appropriate interval, her husband will send her away, and we will seal our working agreement with a toast of our glasses.

"You staying for a while this time?" The apothecary squints at me again.

"I'm considering it," I say noncommitally.

He nods. "Our city seems a stable place at last, now that Soderini has been elected for life. If you play your hand right, the Signoria might give you a commission."

I don't tell him I have written to the duke of Ferrara with a newly proposed design for fortifications. I've drafted a missive to the sultan Balazeth, promising a bridge on the Bosporus. And meanwhile, there is a letter from Milan demanding my return to take on an old altarpiece, promised but never delivered.

"Where else would I want to be but Florence?" I smile.

"Good," he says. "We need you."

"*Buon lavoro,*" I say, forcing myself to smile. Panel under my arm, I make my way back out into the searing light of the street.

Wending my way around the apse of Santa Maria del Fiore, I glance up to admire the slabs of pink and green marble. At the gates of the cathedral workyard, a small crowd has gathered. Several women pause to press their faces through the bars of the wrought-iron gate. They speak in excited whispers and giggles. I hesitate.

Deep within the shadows of the workyard, among stacks of raw lumber, dusty marble slabs, and the loud rustling of pigeon feathers, young Michelangelo Buonarroti has built a wooden hut. I bristle. Of course he doesn't want anyone to see what he's doing. How would such an unruly youngster be so self-assured? I am confident enough to show an unfinished drawing while he labors in private and has even constructed tall, wooden walls to keep out curious onlookers.

And yet . . . In keeping them out, he has piqued their curiosity instead. Hiding it makes people want to see it even more. A brilliant idea; I don't know why I haven't thought of it. Perhaps I have been too eager, too quick to share my work.

A few more people stop their errands to press their faces through the openings of the wrought-iron gate. A giant, someone says. *Un gigante.* He's sculpting a colossus like the world has never seen behind that wooden enclosure, they whisper. Michelangelo is using an entire block of Carrara marble for the figure.

I cannot help it. I stop. I linger. For a few long moments, there is only the distant ringing of a chisel on the marble.

Suddenly, I see that no matter how hard I try to stay, the streets of Florence remain my personal Hell. I cannot escape this city of broad piazzas and narrow minds. Florentines have no vision beyond their trappings of status, their marble giants, their portraits of ladies.

"WHAT DO YOU MEAN, he's not paying?" I ask.

My father pinches his lips together and crosses his arms. He paces slowly across my monastery cell bedchamber, gliding his hand over a set of bone-handled silverpoint pens procured in Milan and now neatly arranged on my worktable. My father says he will accompany me to Francesco del Giocondo's house, where his wife, Lisa, is waiting. But the news isn't what I expected. "He doesn't trust that you will finish the portrait unless he withholds payment until the end," he says.

It is early. The sounds of roosters, the clop of hooves, the creak of wagon wheels, and the calls of water vendors fill the street outside my window. In the church, the monks have finished singing Prime and are preparing to break their fast in the refectory, where a cook clangs a metal ladle against a pot of steaming porridge.

I awoke in the dark to wash and groom my body with water, scented soaps, and powders. I dried myself with the linens, looped each curl carefully around my finger until each one reformed, and combed my beard. I dressed myself in colorful silks and satins to the point that I might resemble a silk trader myself. It is what such patrons expect.

But instead, my father informs me that Francesco del Giocondo expects the worst of me, not the best. He drums his fingers across the worn planks of my worktable. "I'm afraid your reputation precedes you," he says, glancing toward the door to the monastery cloister. I know the monks are unhappy with me for leaving behind nothing more than a sketch for the altarpiece project while I went to Pisa with Machiavelli. But what has that to do with a portrait of a silk trader's wife?

"But . . . that's ridiculous!" I say. "I've completed plenty of things for the duke of Milan. That reputation should count for something." I don't tell him about the letter sitting next to my father's drumming fingers, the one from Giovan Antonio de Predis demanding my return to Milan, without delay, to deliver the terms of my contract with him for an altarpiece at the Confraternity of the Immaculate Conception. "Plus, Francesco del Giocondo and his entire household have already seen my drawing for the altarpiece. They know my skill."

My father nods. "Yes. And I've already patched things up with the monks," he says, following my gaze to the door.

My saving grace is that the prior of Santissima Annunziata, for all of his public renunciation of worldly goods, likes to have me in his presence. I've come to learn that I'm something of a marker of status for the prior and for his entire monastery. My good humor, conversation, and appearance of luxury in this drab, dreary place keep me in the prior's good graces.

My father frowns. "You're lucky you have me to intercede on your behalf to save this commission, Leo. Otherwise you might be out on your ass. The least you can do is carry through with the portrait of the lady, deposit or no deposit."

Only yesterday, I had thought I might convince Francesco del Giocondo to pay his wife the highest compliment by having a portrait by my hand. And that he might pay me the highest price . . . But I was wrong.

I am wrong about so many things.

BELLINA

Florence, Italy
1503

From the cabinet in Lisa and Francesco's bedchamber, Bellina carefully removed a series of ceramic vessels and inlaid wooden boxes to be displayed around the house for the benefit of the prestigious artist soon to make a visit. On the bed, Bellina laid out three brightly colored gowns so Lisa could choose which one to wear when she sat before Leonardo da Vinci.

"Bellina, can I ask you something?"

"Anything, *polpetta*." Bellina removed a finely wrought brass candlestick and placed it on the table near the window.

"Do you think that . . . that God is punishing us somehow?"

Bellina hesitated. "What do you mean?"

"I just keep thinking." Lisa sat heavily on the edge of the bed and fingered a beaded cuff on a shimmering sleeve of silk the color of copper. "All these luxuries. They lead to greed. Envy. Perhaps they lead to . . . terrible consequences. I can't help but wonder," she said, "if we're being held accountable."

Bellina came to sit beside Lisa and took her hand. For a few moments, the two women sat in silence. Bellina surveyed the luxurious objects that had come into the house ever since she had followed Lisa's elaborate marriage procession across the river to Francesco's house some eight years earlier.

"I used to think the same," Bellina said.

Lisa turned, her eyes wide and brimming with doubt. "You did?"

Bellina nodded. "I thought maybe material objects—if we coveted them—might be the very thing to drag us down to Hell." Bellina hesitated again. Lisa had known nothing of her involvement with the *frateschi,* all those evenings at the riverbank, the ragged scars on her back. For a moment, she considered telling her everything, but she hardly knew where to begin.

"Perhaps the work of Master Leonardo is different," Bellina said. "When I saw that drawing, that Madonna he was preparing for the monks, for a minute I thought such a thing might not lead to sin. Instead, I thought it might lead us to the divine."

Lisa stared at her lap. "I don't know."

"Well, what does Francesco say?"

Lisa clucked loudly and wrinkled her brow. "He says it's silly of me to think that God has taken our child because we own ceramic plates."

Bellina put her arm around Lisa's thin shoulders and for a moment, she quietly soaked in these terrible, lonely ruminations of a grief-stricken mother.

"Where are the things they made for us in Montelupo?!" Madre's voice echoed up the stairwell, a spine-tingling screech.

"You'd better go down," Lisa said.

Bellina nodded and squeezed her mistress's hand. Then she carefully picked up a ceramic ewer and headed for the stairwell. At the bottom of the stairs, she froze.

"Francesco! You must see reason before that artist arrives in our house." Madre flapped like a buzzard over a carcass.

Throughout the house, the servants took cover. In the kitchen, Alessandro stopped his evisceration of a melon and ducked out to the herb garden. The new wet nurse bundled Lisa's new baby boy and hurried out into the alley, bouncing little Andrea on her shoulder.

But Bellina could not leave. As quietly as possible, Bellina entered the room and set down the ewer on the marble tabletop. She ran a clean rag over its smooth surface.

"The least you could do is offer Master Leonardo a room in your house," the old crone continued, squawking in her son's wake.

"He is living just fine with the monks from what I've heard," Francesco answered his mother as he headed across the room toward the stairwell. He looked like he was trying to duck into his office as quickly as possible, but Madre stopped him.

"Leonardo da Vinci is doing you a great favor in accepting your commission," she persisted. "He has many offers, and perhaps some of them are higher than ours. If he chooses to paint your wife, you should honor him by—"

"I *am* honoring him." Francesco stopped and spun toward his mother, interrupting. "I am honoring him with the opportunity to paint my most virtuous and upstanding wife. Besides, we are putting on a show for him already." Francesco waved his hand toward the beautiful things Bellina had pulled out of the cabinet.

The old shrew's eyes narrowed. "Your friends have done much more than that, *figlio*. They pay their artists large deposits in advance. Their servants prepare bedchambers to accommodate them in their homes. They serve them meals and offer them spare rooms so they might paint under their own roofs."

"Mother, you fail to see that I am being smart in this deal," Francesco said, and for a moment, Bellina caught a fleeting image of a whining little boy in the body of a man.

Madre only scoffed. "How are you being intelligent? You will bring dishonor to us. Our friends will not see the logic in failing to pay even a small deposit up front for your wife's likeness. He is the most sought-after painter in Florence."

"I wasn't going to pay a deposit at all, but now I've agreed with his father to pay a nominal one in good faith." Francesco shrugged and paced. "I am simply making sure Master Leonardo upholds his end of the bargain. The monks say they have been waiting three years for him to finish their altarpiece. That drawing we saw at Santissima Annunziata? It's all he has produced so far."

Francesco walked over to the table where Bellina had just laid out the ceramic ewer from Montelupo. Bellina retreated, running her rag over the dusty windowsill. Francesco paused, caressing the reflective curve of the vessel. "When the portrait is complete," he said, "then I will pay him a fee commensurate with the result. And anyway, Master Leonardo's father assures me he will agree to my terms."

"And where will he be staying while he does you the honor of painting your wife?" Madre looked down her nose.

Francesco only shrugged. "I suppose that is his own affair."

Suddenly, there was a ruckus in the stairwell. Four-year-old Camilla ran into the room, chasing the cat. Bellina heard the children's high-pitched voices, and she turned to see Lisa with baby Andrea in her arms and little Marietta hanging onto the skirts of the black mourning dress Lisa had worn nearly every day for the past three years.

For a moment, there was an awkward silence.

Bellina looked at Francesco, dressed in the signature blue silk of his workshop, and his mother, draped in a silk shawl that shimmered when the sunlight caught the pink warp and orange weft. To Bellina, they looked like the horses bedecked with the arms of the silk guild on the feast of Saint John the Baptist, but she would never say such a thing aloud.

"Lisa!" Madre said in shock. "Such a drab color? Have you forgotten that Master Leonardo is on his way to paint your portrait?"

"Of course I haven't forgotten," Lisa said, her head held high. "I wanted to wear this," she said.

Camilla scampered through Madre's billowing skirts as the cat leapt just out of reach. Madre scoffed loudly, and then turned to Bellina. "Is this your doing?"

Bellina felt her blood boil, but she said nothing. Instead, she took a step back and kept her head down. She was just as surprised as Madre to see Lisa still in the severe black dress, but she kept her mouth closed.

Lisa met her mother-in-law's gaze. "Bellina has nothing to do with this. I can choose my own gowns."

Francesco stepped between his wife and his mother. "*Tesoro*," he began gently. "Of course you can choose your own gowns, but . . ." His voice trailed off. *Why did you wear this one?* Bellina knew he wanted to ask. Instead, he said, "You have been wearing this same dress for . . . many days. And besides, I have had new colorful gowns made for you with silk from Flanders. It's the latest fashion. Would none of them do for a portrait?"

"Your husband has given you new gems with the birth of each child," Madre insisted. "You haven't worn any of them."

Lisa let her gaze fall to the zigzag patterns on the tile floor. "We are in mourning," she said.

Another long silence.

"Lisa," Francesco said finally, reaching for his wife's hand. "It has been more than three years."

"Yes." Lisa pulled her hand away and kept looking at the tiles. "This is what I want to wear."

Madre sat heavily into a velvet-upholstered chair as if defeated. "A mourning dress . . . for a portrait," she mumbled to herself, and Bellina imagined Madre must already be thinking what their neighbors might say.

"But we are no longer in mourning!" Francesco boomed. Bellina supposed it wasn't the first time he had made this argument in front of his wife. "Lisa. God would not be so cruel as to take a child before her time simply to punish her parents. Women and children die when there is new life. Everyone knows that," and Bellina saw a shadow pass over his face, perhaps a thought of Bartolomeo's mother. "We have healthy children," he said, gesturing to little Marietta, who sucked her fingers and pressed her face into her mother's black skirt as if it were a baby's blanket. "Does that not show that God has rewarded us instead?"

In Lisa's arms, Andrea began to fuss and gnaw his fists. Simultaneously, Marietta began to sob, and Camilla cried, "You said we could get a *biscotto, mamma!*"

"Come, *tesoro,*" Lisa said calmly, heading for the staircase and the kitchens below. Francesco followed his wife and children out of the room. Bellina wished she could find a reason to follow them instead of being left behind, alone, with the old crone.

She began carefully dusting the lip of a bronze dish, hoping that Madre would find something else more pressing.

"What are you doing?" Suddenly, the old woman was standing at her back.

"I'm . . . dusting," Bellina said.

"You're needed in the kitchen," she said. Bellina knew Madre didn't trust her to be alone in this room with all the luxuries. She felt examined, as if she were little more than one of the ghastly insects Bartolomeo inspected under his spectacle glass.

"Of course, *signora,*" Bellina said. She moved from the old woman's oppressive gaze, pressed a feather duster into her apron, and made for the stairwell. She followed the sounds of the children, looking for Lisa. Bellina had to make sure her mistress could compose herself before she sat for a painting that might capture her image forever. She worried Lisa might be remembered by future generations for her mourning gown and her sorrowful gaze.

As she passed the entry hall, suddenly the bronze bell at the door rang its familiar, high-pitched jingle. Perhaps it was that painter who had caused such strife in the house before he even arrived, Bellina thought. She crossed the room and opened the door.

Part 5
UNSTITCHED

ANNE

Loc-Dieu, France
1940

Anne awoke the next morning hoping she had dreamt it all, even the kiss. But arriving at the breakfast table only confirmed her fear; Corrado's place beside hers stood empty. It stayed empty for the next three days, and no one said anything, but Lucie addressed Anne with soft eyes and a gentle tone. Sometimes the guards grumbled something derogatory about the Italians, but when Anne was near, they fell silent.

Outside, birdsong filled the abbey's midsummer gardens, and the hedgerows bloomed with color, but Anne no longer noticed. Instead, she sat at her rickety table among the crates, under the looming vaults of Loc-Dieu's austere church. Only days ago, the abbey had seemed filled with light and laughter; now, there were only shadows.

In the cool air, she cranked the roller of her field typewriter and did her best to focus on the inventories. After a few seconds, the typed rows of text blurred before her eyes, unreadable. She blinked and stared into the seemingly endless rows of wooden crates, stacked and ordered until they disappeared into an abyss of darkness. In the dank silence, Anne surveyed her tattered pages again. Would her silly typed list really stop the Germans from

coming in and taking everything? Now she felt stupid for thinking it would. What was the point? Anne thought. Would her efforts matter in the end? And with whom would she share their
triumphs?

All that mattered, Anne thought, was that no one had tried to
protect Corrado from being a target. He was only doing the same
as everyone else. They were all doing their parts, working together
for the common goal of protecting the treasures in their care. He
was a good man, working in good faith. Couldn't they have given
him another option besides fleeing in the middle of the night? She
had already lost contact with Marcel and her mother. Now, Anne
feared that Corrado, too, had vanished. Did she have control of
anything at all?

On the evening of the third day, Anne picked over a plate of
reheated cassoulet prepared by women lured from a local village
to work in the abbey kitchens. The only sound in the old monks'
refectory was the clink of cutlery; even Frédérique, normally so
energetic and full of questions, sat quietly as the aroma of meat
and onions left stewing for hours filled the air. Then the door
creaked, and Lucie's husband, André, entered the refectory. He
pulled out the empty chair next to Lucie and sat down.

"Good news," he announced. Everyone looked up. "The last of
the convoys has left Chambord, and just in time. The Germans
are following close behind. I just got word that our troops have
blown the bridges of the Loire to slow them down. With any luck,
the last trucks should reach us tonight."

Lucie sat back in her chair and let out a sigh. "Jacques has been
a hero," she said, speaking of the Louvre's director. "It'll be a relief
to have him with us."

But André only shook his head. "Monsieur Jaujard isn't coming. He stayed behind at Chambord."

Lucie sat bolt upright, and the other curators began murmuring. "What do you mean, he's stayed behind?"

"But that's . . . madness!" one of the curators cried.

André continued. "The Germans . . . They want to take everything—especially *La Joconde*. Monsieur Jaujard plans to face them—and stall them as much as he can."

Anne imagined the Louvre's director sitting alone in that vast and empty château, waiting for the Germans as they drew ever nearer. They wouldn't find the *Mona Lisa,* of course. But what was to stop them from shooting the Louvre director right where he sat waiting for them?

"Jacques," Lucie whispered, covering her face. "Brave fool."

At that moment, something inside Anne snapped. Why did this war have to take so much from her—from everyone? First Marcel and Kiki. Then Corrado. And now, the art they'd been working so hard to save? She scraped back her chair and stood.

"We have to *do* something." Silence fell in the dining hall. "We have to stop this . . . this thing," Anne said. "They're taking everything from us. Our friends and families, our city, now works of art that do not belong to them! We can't let this happen. We have to fight them somehow."

"Anne," Lucie said, touching her hand.

"Let her finish," Pierre the guard said, nodding.

"There has to be something we can do," Anne continued. "We can't just keep . . . *hiding.*"

"I feel the same," Antoinette said, her voice heavy. "I want to spit in their eyes and see them driven from France as much as you do, *chérie*. But right now, the best we can do is protect the objects in our care."

"Antoinette's right," André said. "We have to stay focused on keeping this work hidden deep within the Free Zone. France may negotiate for an armistice, but we still have Great Britain as an ally. We can only hope that they may overwhelm the Germans before they get this far south."

Anne was about to give herself over to despair when Pierre pushed himself up from the table and drew an ancient timepiece on a chain from his pocket. "Time for the evening broadcast," he said. He ambled over to the wireless and turned it on, static filling the air.

The crackling voice across the airwaves did little to lift Anne's spirits. German troops had occupied the whole of Paris, the announcer said. Anne imagined Kiki performing one of her sad routines for a gaggle of men in German uniforms in the dance hall. She'd said that they were good clients, Anne remembered. If Kiki was still alive, did she think so now? Anne sank back in her seat and lowered her head onto her arms.

"Shh!" one of the guards said. "Listen!"

The broadcast ended, and a new, fresh voice came onto the radio, one that rang with authority. Anne looked up. General de Gaulle. For a few minutes, the room fell silent as the general spoke stirringly about how the war wasn't over, how the French couldn't surrender even though Anne feared that was exactly what the government planned on doing. "Each small act—by each individual—can be an act of resistance," the voice proclaimed across the airwaves.

"Easy for him to say, from his little hideout in London," Pierre grumbled, and a few of the old guards nodded their agreement.

"Whatever happens," de Gaulle finished, his voice rising over the static, "the flame of French resistance must not and shall not die."

Anne raised her head from the cradle of her arms. "That's what I'm saying!"

LUCIE AND ANDRÉ strode across the vast nave of the abbey church. "There's a wire from Paris," André said, waving a slip of white paper in his hand.

Anne stopped typing. The rattle of her machine fell silent. She felt her heart seize. "What is it?" Her mind immediately raced to Kiki. Marcel. Corrado. Had someone found them?

"It's about the Italians," he said, stepping over a crate where one of the curators was overseeing the unwrapping of a picture to check its condition.

"The Italians!" Anne began.

"Not *your* Italian," Lucie said.

Anne closed her eyes, wishing she could go back just a few days, to the last time she and Corrado had sat here talking. She no longer remembered what they had talked about; it didn't matter. Her mind grasped for the memory of his hands on her cheeks, pulling her to him.

"No. The Italian government," André continued. "Ever since they signed the armistice, Monsieur Jaujard warned us this might happen. They want their pictures back."

"What?!" Anne cried. "They want to take paintings?"

André nodded. "Everything of Italian origin."

"That's . . . impossible! They can't be serious." Anne gasped as the enormity of it sank in. She knew many Italian paintings came into the Louvre's collection after they were seized during the Napoleonic wars, including Paolo Veronese's gigantic *Feast at the Wedding in Cana*. Anne supposed she could see why the Italians might try to get them back. But then the realization hit. "The *Mona Lisa*." It came out as a whisper. She thought of the crate with the three red dots, tucked away in André and Lucie's bedroom.

"Yes," André said. "Especially *La Joconde*."

Anne felt something rise within her, something hot and roaring. "No." Anne stood up, crossing her arms. "We can't just hand it over—to the Italians no less than the Germans. Not after everything we've been through. The *Mona Lisa* . . . Leonardo da Vinci . . . He brought that portrait to France himself nearly five hundred years ago! It belongs to us."

"I know," André said. "And we're not going to hand it over. We have a plan."

Lucie wove her way through the crates, lowering her voice as she approached Anne. "Another wire also came, a secret one meant only for us. We have new orders from Monsieur Jaujard." Anne thought she saw Lucie's hand tremble as she unfolded the thin slip of paper. "He wants me to go back to Chambord and get the original provenance documents for the *Mona Lisa* and the other Italian paintings. If the Germans destroy those documents, there's no proof the *Mona Lisa* rightfully belongs to the Louvre. We need to put our hands on those records before they do."

"You're bringing all the archives back here to Loc-Dieu." Anne thought of the rooms and rooms of files they had moved. It had meant days of work and organization. It would be a massive effort to bring everything out of the old château, much more than one person could do.

"It's too late for that," Lucie said. "We should have brought them with us from Chambord to begin with. It was stupid of us to leave them there."

André nodded. "Now, those archives have to be kept just as safe as the *Mona Lisa* itself. Monsieur Jaujard won't leave Chambord. He needs someone to come and fetch the critical documents, someone who would seem nonthreatening to the Germans crawling all over the place now. Someone like a female archivist."

Anne felt her throat tighten. "She's going?"

"There's no one else who can do it," André said.

Lucie nodded. "I'm going. But, Anne . . . I need you to come with me."

Anne blinked.

"You know as much about the archives as I do," Lucie continued. "You've worked with the inventories as much as I have. If something were to happen to me . . ." She swallowed.

Anne's eyes widened. "You want me to come with you to Chambord. With the Germans there."

Lucie only nodded.

"To the Germans, you're just a typist," André said. "No one will expect you to know everything."

For a moment, Anne's mind flickered with the thought of the shells exploding in the sky above Paris just a month ago; of the arduous journeys to Chambord, Louvigny, and Loc-Dieu; of sleeping on the floor and eating out of tins; of the brave curators driving back and forth through German checkpoints. If she and Lucie returned to Chambord to retrieve the provenance documents, would it save the *Mona Lisa*? If so, she was going to do as de Gaulle had said, Anne thought. She was going to do whatever she had to do to make sure the Germans didn't get to their collection.

"Yes," she said, taking a deep breath full of new resolve. "We've come this far. Of course I'll go with you."

"THERE ARE TANKS lined up and down the rue de Rivoli. You wouldn't recognize it." From the passenger seat of André's car, the Louvre's Egyptologist, Christiane Desroches-Noblecourt, tilted her head out of the open window and into the heat of the day. The buzz of cicadas and the sewing-machine sound of the old Peugeot's engine vibrated in their ears. Anne gripped the steering wheel and stole a glance at Christiane, eyes closed behind oval glasses, her blond hair whipping toward the window. She'd heard that Christiane was an acclaimed archaeologist who had undertaken many excavations in Egypt. With the car chattering along peacefully through sun-drenched country roads, Anne struggled to imagine Christiane in an Egyptian tomb just as she struggled to envision German tanks guarding many castles of the Loire Valley up ahead, and farther north, Paris itself.

"Montmartre," Anne said. "Has it been hit?"

"I don't think so." Christiane shook her head. "The bombs fell mostly around the outskirts. More of a threat, I think. The Germans want to keep the city center intact so they can enjoy it themselves. Nazi officers are hosting lavish parties in the finest homes of the city as we speak."

Anne allowed herself a tiny breath of relief at the same time that the thought of German officers clinking glasses in requisitioned city mansions made her feel sick. If Kiki had stayed in the apartment or at the dance hall, then she was probably still alive. If she hadn't provoked a German soldier, that is.

Anne shifted in the hard, creaky seat. Compared with the ungainly pack animal of a truck she had maneuvered across southern France, André's old Peugeot felt like a racehorse. She navigated out of the flat marshlands of the Marais Poitevin and the first rolling hills of the Loire Valley came into view. The car purred along the empty roads, easily taking the turns in its stride as it swooped from one bend to the next. How long would it be before they encountered a German checkpoint? A line of Panzers?

"But it's no longer the city of light," Christiane continued. "In the middle of the night, you hear the thunder of engines. There are warplanes flying over the Louvre—and even swastikas hanging on the façades."

Anne didn't want to imagine such a sight, but she couldn't help conjuring up the image: the stately pillars of the Louvre, the symbol of French culture, the world's stronghold of beauty and creativity, the place she loved more than anywhere else, with the ugly Nazi flags fluttering across its windows.

"*Les allemands* have parked their tanks in the middle of the Cour Napoléon. It made my stomach turn to see it," Christiane said.

"I can't imagine it," Lucie said, leaning forward from the back seat. "Their dirty boots stomping through the galleries."

"Yes," Christiane said, "but remember, there's almost nothing left. You should have seen their faces when Monsieur Jaujard and I showed them from one empty gallery to the next."

For the last weeks, Christiane had gone back and forth, armed with her old car and a pile of stamped papers that allowed her to travel from one side of the Occupied Zone to the next as an esteemed Louvre curator. And now, Lucie and Anne carried similar piles of hastily stamped papers, expedited from Paris, ready to present in case of an inspection.

Anne couldn't resist a smile of satisfaction. "They must have expected to find a treasure trove!"

"*Oui*," Christiane said. "Clearly. Instead, they found a very beautiful, mostly empty building."

"Are the sculptures all right?" Lucie asked. Anne thought of the *Venus de Milo*, Michelangelo's sandbagged *Slaves*, and the other works that had been too risky to move from Paris.

"For now," Christiane said. "They just look lonely in those empty galleries. The Germans were furious, of course. They demanded to know where everything else was."

Anne gasped. "But it belongs to us!" she insisted.

Christiane only shrugged. "Not really, my dear. Do the Elgin marbles or the Rosetta stone 'belong' to Britain? These treasures have come to us at the Louvre through various circumstances; they have passed through many places and hands. They are not ours. We are only custodians. Our job is to protect and save them from damage and destruction. But they belong to all of us, all of civilization. They belong to the future."

The women rode in silence for a while, and Anne wrestled with the idea that she was only a temporary set of hands, only one generation of protection for the masterpieces in their care. Masterpieces that would endure long after she was gone, if she had anything to do with it. Only the perspective of an Egyptologist, she thought, could have helped her see beyond the bounds of this current conflict.

Lucie leaned forward. "Do you think they know where the depots are?"

Christiane nodded. "We told them nothing, but it didn't take them long to focus their attention on Chambord. And I think they know where some of the other depots are. But they don't seem to know about Loc-Dieu, at least not yet."

"What do you think they will do," Anne asked, "if they get into one of the depots?"

Christiane brushed a lock of blowing hair from her face. "They demanded right there that we bring everything back to Paris," she said. "They want to reopen it and show everyone that cultural life will return to normal under German occupation."

Lucie snorted from the back seat. "What a lie."

"Of course it's a lie," Christiane said. "I saw some of the higher-ranking officers picking out treasures for their own homes. Leonardo da Vinci's *Lady with the Ermine* has already been taken from a private collection in Poland and put into the hands of a high-ranking officer. The Nazis have vowed to steal every work of art by Leonardo."

Anne conjured up an image of the *Mona Lisa* hanging on the wall of Hitler's office. She might not be able to control her mother's or brother's choices, but surely there was something they could do to protect the precious objects in their care? "We have to stop them."

"Well, considering the Louvre doesn't have a standing army at its disposal, we're doing everything we can," Christiane said. "And we're trying to find a way to get some information to the Allies so our collection isn't bombed by mistake; a dangerous proposition, needless to say. Right now, the riskiest place is Chambord. There are still some valuable artworks there—not to mention the archives, inventories, and even the provenance documents that you and Lucie have to retrieve."

"But haven't they already taken control of Chambord?" Anne

asked. "What's stopping them from moving everything back to Paris right away? Why are they letting us in?"

"Monsieur Jaujard . . . ," she said. "I can only say that he's a hero. He's using diplomatic channels. He's trying to stall them. He's been tireless, pretending to be collaborating with the Germans to catalog everything, but actually stalling as much as he can. He's put his life on the line."

"As are we," Lucie said.

Anne steered the car into a long bend through silent wheat fields. She recognized the rolling hills from moving from Chambord to Loc-Dieu. Anne asked nervously, "Are there many soldiers at Chambord?"

"Yes." Christiane nodded. "But not as many as in Paris." She wrapped her arms around herself as if suddenly cold. For a while, the three women rode in silence.

"I can't believe how quickly we're moving compared to that trip to Loc-Dieu," Lucie said at last.

"That's because Anne is a skilled driver," Christiane said.

"For a girl, you mean," Anne laughed.

"For anyone," Christiane said.

At the first inkling of twilight, Anne recognized the familiar, rolling landscape of the Loire Valley, with its manicured trees planted symmetrically along the roadsides for as far as the eye could see. The fields that had always looked so open and glorious when Anne had first come to the Loire Valley were shrouded in purple dusk.

At last, she saw the lonely country road that led to the castle. The narrow tires of the dust-covered Peugeot rattled onto the now-familiar gravel drive. Chambord lay in wait before them, black shadows etched sharply into all its nooks. Anne slowed the

Peugeot, and for a few long, silent moments, the three women stared up at the looming château. Nazi flags stood rippling quietly from its wedding-cake towers.

If Anne had any illusion that Chambord was the haven they had left behind only a few months before, it vanished in the evening shadows. Chambord was enemy territory now.

LEONARDO

Florence, Italy
1503

The servant woman who answers the door is suspicious of me. Over my years of working within the walls of the ducal palace of Milan and the militia camps of Cesare Borgia, I know how to read distrust, even when masked beneath a veneer of courtly manners. For a servant who's never learned such things, there's no hiding it. Her dark eyes rake over me from my tight-fitting emerald-colored cap to matching hose tucked into laced shoes. I introduce myself. She nods and steps aside to let me pass.

The house, two steps away from the San Lorenzo church, is as I expected for a man such as Francesco del Giocondo. Through the warm, stuccoed entry hall, I see cats lounging in a lush inner *cortile* planted with herbs, oranges, lemons, and olives. To my left, there is a richly decorated room with a desk piled with ledgers and a large abacus. I smell onions and tomatoes stewing from kitchens I cannot see. The servant woman leads me up a broad staircase past richly carved wall panels and beneath lofty, painted ceilings to the *piano nobile*.

There, I find Signora Lisa with her hand on the sill of a parapet, overlooking the light-filled courtyard. We exchange pleasantries.

"My husband sends his regrets," she tells me. "He is occupied with his trade."

Ah. So there shall be no discussion of paltry deposits and payment arrangements today. No libations poured. No compulsory walk around the courtyard to examine his lily blooms and orange trees. No discussion of politics, the design of treadle looms, or the price of a *braccio* of Lyonnaise silk.

Bene. Instead, I shall focus on sketching.

Lady Lisa seats herself in a large *poltrana,* an elaborately carved chair that looks like it has passed through several generations of her husband's family. "Where is the panel? And your pigments?" she asks.

"For the first few sittings of a portrait, *signora,* I begin with drawings," I tell her, turning a page of my sketchbook and pulling a new silverpoint pen from my worn leather case. "It allows me to see the core of my subject. To capture the essence of your virtue, your honor, your . . . beauty."

But I flatter her. For as attractive as she is, something is not right about Lisa Gherardini del Giocondo. For one, she wears a black silk gown, the type a woman might wear during a period of mourning, and certainly not to sit for a portrait. It is faded and frayed as if she has worn it for weeks. Her eyes, though carefully plucked of lashes and brows, are swollen and lined. Her hair is uncovered, disarrayed, without ornament. She wears no jewelry. Have the ladies of the house not advised her on how to prepare to sit for a portrait? Even the servant attending her might have put in a word.

But it's more than that. I see instantly that Lisa is troubled. Melancholy even.

The servant woman who answered the door seems oblivious

to Lisa's overall shabby state. Instead, the woman, who must be some fifteen years older than her mistress, seats herself in the light by the sill of the parapet, drawing her embroidery needle through a swath of linen. She is remarkably skilled with her needle; I can see this even from a distance, her neat rows of colored threads. She pretends to ignore us. If she is any good as a servant, I'm certain that instead she's paying close attention. How many secrets has she overheard in this house? I wonder. How many details of Francesco del Giocondo's trading schemes against his rivals in the cloth guilds, his exchanges with other supporters of the Medici? She is trained to feign ignorance. But I know better.

I begin with a few brief drags of red chalk across the parchment. I trace a hint of a jawline, the shape of the brow.

"Bellina," the lady says, as if she senses I am paying attention to the servant, "please bring Master Leonardo something to drink. This heat is infernal."

"Yes, *polpet*—my lady." The servant woman sets down her embroidery ring on the chair and walks toward the stair landing.

"And have Alessandro give you a block of that new cheese from our estate in Chianti. Perhaps Master Leonardo would like to bring some home with him."

"Thank you, my lady." I open the latch of my old leather case and draw out several sheets of parchment. "I imagine your husband might be occupied right now, *signora*," I say, "between managing his silk workshops and his country estates. And I understand they have reelected him to the council of the Dodici Buonomini."

From my peripheral vision, I see the servant woman—Bellina—pause at the threshold of the door. Yes, just as I thought. She is paying attention. As am I.

ANNE

Chambord, France
1940

As the Peugeot's bare tires crunched slowly along the sweeping gravel drive of Chambord castle, Anne took in the metallic gleam of armored vehicles shining dully in the evening's last light. Surely the Germans could have blown up the château with those big guns long ago, Anne thought. And then, all their efforts—the long months of planning, the trucks' slow crawl across western France—might have been for naught. Anne glanced briefly at Lucie, who sat still and white-faced in the back seat.

"Monsieur Jaujard will have told them to expect us," Christiane said. At that moment, two German soldiers emerged on the short bridge over the castle moat.

"Act like . . . like you have every right to be here," Lucie whispered, as if trying to convince herself. But we have every right to be here, Anne thought. The works of art, the archives, this castle—they are our responsibility to save. She brought the car to a creaking halt.

In the dusk, one of the soldiers strode up to them, the sound of the gravel crunching under his boots. Anne took in the gleam of his polished buttons, the helmet the shape of a turtle shell. The soldier leaned over and peered into the open window. His jaw was juglike, his eyes a piercing shade of pale green. High cheekbones gave him an imperial look as he glared down at them. Anne felt like a bug being scrutinized under the magnifying glass of some cruel little boy, the type of boy who pulls wings off flies just for the fun of it, she thought.

From the passenger seat, Christiane unfolded their paperwork and handed it to the soldier. While he examined it, two more soldiers approached, vigilant, their weapons cradled in their arms. For a breathless few moments, the men said nothing. Anne monitored one of the newly arrived soldiers, who stared at her with eyes as flat and black as a shark's. Then the first soldier barked something in German, returning the papers to Christiane. They rustled as she took them in trembling hands. The men stepped aside. Anne steered the car a little farther over the gravel and came to a stop.

The risk of air raids behind them, Chambord was now lit up in all its glory, yet it seemed to Anne to be darker than ever. Surrounding the palace, Anne took in the formal gardens and lawns where she and Corrado had enjoyed picnics and light conversation—just a few months and a lifetime ago. Now, German soldiers were pacing among the geometrically trimmed hedgerows. The men stared at the women as they stepped out of the car. Under watchful eyes, they moved inside the château.

Just months ago, the Louvre staff had worked as a team to move precious works of art up and down Leonardo da Vinci's double-helix staircase. Now, a pair of Nazi guards stood in the stairwell instead, still as tin soldiers. The men led the women into the dining hall with its familiar table. Portable German typewriters and stacks of paper were spread all over it. Lucie shuddered at the sight. The tin soldier guards halted, and then took their places alongside the door.

From behind the piles of paper on the table, a man in a rumpled suit rose from his chair. If he had been clean-shaven, and if he had looked less like he hadn't slept for a week, Anne thought he would have been handsome. He had been, in fact, the last time she saw him back at the Louvre. Jacques Jaujard, the Louvre's director, stepped forward.

"You made it," he greeted the women.

"You look terrible," Anne heard Lucie whisper to him as they exchanged loud kisses on each cheek.

Monsieur Jaujard stepped back with a tight grin. "Nice to see you," he said. Anne realized they wouldn't be able to exchange anything important with Monsieur Jaujard now. They couldn't risk saying anything that might be overheard by the soldiers and later used against them.

Loud footsteps sounded in the hallway, and a new set of German soldiers marched into the room. The one at the front of the group seemed more distinguished than the others; when he raked Anne with a glance, his eyes were commanding. "Monsieur," he barked, his French sounding harsh and accented. "You may have your people begin work now."

"*Oui*," Monsieur Jaujard said. "We will begin at once to get everything in order." He led Anne and Lucie back to the table and indicated the inventories. Anne recognized some of the ones she'd typed months ago during frantic hours spent in the Louvre archives.

"Our trucks will depart for Germany as soon as everything is in order," the soldier was saying.

A swift inhale. Germany. Were they taking what was left?

The arrogant German seemed to sense her fear. He glared at her. "Who is this?"

"You know Madame Desroches-Noblecourt. Madame Mazauric is our head archivist. And this is one of our typists," Jaujard said, shooting Anne a quick glance.

"Good." The German nodded. "Make it quick. We will return to Germany at the first opportunity." He sighed, turning to Monsieur Jaujard. "I still think all of this is unnecessary."

"Monsieur, as I have explained, the archives were badly scrambled on the trip from Paris," Monsieur Jaujard said calmly. "It will waste a lot of time if the paperwork isn't in order, and that could mean more damage to the paintings and other artworks. It'll be best and quickest to have Lucie and Anne here review all the inventories to make sure there are no further delays. They know the records better than anyone."

Anne met Monsieur Jaujard's eyes as he spoke. They were as serious as ever, and she knew he couldn't care less about inconvenience to the Germans.

"Very well," the officer said through the row of straight lower teeth. "You French dogs are as disorganized as ever. The women may continue."

The door had scarcely closed behind the men before Anne sank down into a chair. "Now they want to take everything to Germany? After everything we've done?" she whispered.

Lucie laid her hands on Anne's shoulders. "No!" she whispered loudly. "Don't you see? Monsieur Jaujard isn't having us do this to speed things up for the Germans. He's stalling them."

Anne looked up. "I can't bear to lift a finger for them."

"We're not working for them," Lucie whispered. "We're working for the Resistance. For the art. For our own future." She squeezed Anne's arms. "We're not going to help the Germans; we're going to help Monsieur Jaujard stall them. We just need to figure out how."

Anne nodded, and the two women waited in heavy silence. Lucie walked over to a large window and stared at the formal gardens outside, her mind calculating.

"I have an idea," Anne said finally. She came to stand next to Lucie. "You and I are the only ones who know how the paperwork is organized. That means we can scramble the inventories just as easily as we can keep them straight. We make ourselves look busy, typing away and making copies—we'll mix them up inside these boxes and boxes of documents." She leaned closer, terrified of being overheard. "And while we're at it, we'll retrieve those provenance documents for the *Mona Lisa*."

"Anne," Lucie whispered, turning to her, "you're a genius," and Anne saw Lucie's eyes glitter with resolve.

AFTER THREE SEEMINGLY endless days, Anne and Lucie departed Chambord. Frazzled and sleep-deprived, Anne was sure the only thing keeping her awake at the wheel was the white-hot fear that the Germans who had been watching their every move in the castle might now follow them. Through the hours, she gripped the steering wheel and studied her side mirrors for the smallest movements on the road behind them. Under Lucie's seat lay the provenance documents for the *Mona Lisa* and other important Italian paintings.

Hours later, when the crumbling medieval abbey of Loc-Dieu came into view at last through the dusty windshield of André's

Peugeot, Anne couldn't help it; she wept. There were no Germans here; there was only a beautiful, green, wet summer valley, the rolling hills all around that knew nothing of bombs or occupations. The abbey still lay tucked in its bed of flat fields. Anne pressed back in the driver's seat, letting the car putter toward the sturdy abbey church.

Lucie gave her a haggard smile. The three sleepless days they had spent at Chambord felt like months with German guards looking over their shoulders.

André was the first out of the abbey's gates to greet them. He spread his arms wide as he watched his wife step out of the car. Lucie said nothing. She just walked into his arms and let him hold her for a long time. "*Maman!*" cried Frédérique, rushing out of the gates and grasping her mother's skirt.

Anne gazed at the abbey's looming façade. She stayed in the driver's seat, brushing hot tears from her cheeks.

No one was waiting for her.

OVER THEIR NOW-EMPTY plates of the midday meal, the curators lit cigarettes and sat back in their seats, listening to Anne and Lucie's account of how they had scrambled the inventories at Chambord under the watchful eyes of Nazi soldiers.

Most of the staff, and especially Pierre, were delighted to hear of their small act of defiance, but now, Anne saw that André's face remained shadowed.

Finally, André said, "Monsieur Schommer wants us to have everything ready to go in case the Germans come here next."

"But they're still a long way from Loc-Dieu," Jacqueline Bouchot-Saupique, the drawings curator, said. Around the refec-

tory tables, there were new aunts, uncles, cousins, and siblings.
More refugee family members had arrived from towns across
northern France, along with a new crop of guards from museums
around the country whose contents had been evacuated to the depots. The men's uniforms were shabby, and their tired eyes spoke
of injustices far beyond the walls of the Louvre.

Anne didn't want to think about what might happen if the German soldiers rolled their Panzer tanks into the peaceful grounds
of Loc-Dieu, especially not before she had a hot bath and a full
night's sleep in her narrow bed.

"Whether or not the Germans come, we have other problems,"
André said. "I told them this place was too damp, but they continued on anyway."

"What do you mean?" Jacqueline asked.

"Come see," he said, pushing back from the table. "It's the
Mona Lisa."

Anne followed André and the small group of curators to the
abbey church, whose hulking space was filled to the brim with
wooden crates. She looked on as two curators carefully eased the
Renaissance masterpiece out of its box. They had been so careful;
Anne had seen it herself. It was wrapped in waterproof paper,
cushioned by velvet, and carefully supported by a series of foam
wedges. Anne's heart thudded as she wondered what might be
revealed when that wrapping was opened.

"It's the moisture," André was saying. "It was so hot and dry
when we arrived, we didn't know how much of a problem it would
become. But we've had so much rain this month, and the chapel
is getting damper with every shower."

"Look!" cried Anne. "What are *those*?"

The curators drew back in alarm. There was something on the

velvet. Anne's skin crawled. Lucie backed away, and Jacqueline cautiously lifted out a cushion. "Mites," she said. "They've started to eat the velvet."

André stood speechless. The curators lifted out the *Mona Lisa* and slowly unwrapped the waterproof paper. Anne hadn't seen the painting outside its crate since they'd left the Louvre. She held her breath as the paper fell away, and there she was, the lady with the enigmatic eyes, smiling her secret smile, as perfect and beautiful and expressive as if she were sitting right in front of them in flesh and blood just as she'd sat before Leonardo da Vinci to be painted hundreds of years ago.

That smile. It was the thing everyone talked about. What was Lisa smiling at? Anne had read many theories. The Renaissance art historian Giorgio Vasari speculated that Leonardo da Vinci had hired jesters and musicians to entertain Lisa while she sat for him. Later historians came up with more outlandish ideas—that she had rotten teeth or some disease; that she might be hiding a pregnancy or another secret; that Leonardo might have captured a memory of his own mother smiling at him.

But for all her reading about the reasons for Lisa's mysterious smile, Anne had always found something sad in the lady's expression.

Looking at the portrait now, Anne laid a hand on her chest as if to still the thunder of her heart. Lucie let out a long breath.

"She looks all right for now," said the paintings curator, leaning closer. "But we opened her up just in time. Those pests could have destroyed her."

"What can we do about them?" Anne asked.

"The mites aren't so hard to deal with. We can brush them out of the velvet and air out the crate," said one of the curators. "Then we'll put on new packing material and seal it to keep them out. We had feared those wedges might warp the painting, but even those can be removed and replaced with other cushioning." He turned to André, his expression worried. "The bigger problem is the damp."

André took a quick, audible drag on his cigarette and crossed his arms, glancing at Lucie. "That's what we've been saying."

"Can't we just store the painting in another room?" Anne asked.

"She's already in our bedroom," André said. "At least it's on a high floor with some sunlight to keep things dry. But Loc-Dieu is damp all over. There is no crawl space; they built it right on the swamp, directly on the ground. Last week, one of the government architects came to see what could be done, but he says that the moisture is coming from too many sources. We measured ninety-five percent humidity here just a few days ago while you two were still at Chambord." He shook his head. "Look at the number of paintings here. This damage to *La Joconde* might be the tip of the iceberg."

"We have two options left," the paintings curator said. "We've been in contact with Monsieur Jaujard via telegram. We could either install enough heating to dry out the air in the abbey—which won't be easy since they designed the building long before heating existed."

"Or we have to move everything," André said quietly.

Anne sat down hard on a nearby crate. She hated the thought of leaving peaceful Loc-Dieu behind. It had become a haven in a terrifying world. And she couldn't imagine repacking, re-inventorying, and re-transporting the thousands of objects under their care. "Surely the heating would be better," she said.

"I wish that were the case," André said. "But the cost would be astronomical, and most of the heating firms big enough to tackle this project are in the Occupied Zone. There are too many obstacles."

"And the Germans will still come, sooner or later." Lucie's voice was resigned. "There's no other way. We have to get *La Joconde*—and the other things—out of here."

BELLINA

Florence, Italy
1503

So far, the drawing consisted of only a few lines, but Bellina could already see why Leonardo da Vinci was considered a master. With just a few strokes, he had suggested the flesh and nails of Lisa's hands. At the window, Bellina pulled a fuchsia thread through a swath of linen with her embroidery needle and watched his hand drag the silverpoint pen across the page. Careful, yet somehow effortless.

"Perhaps you have heard the news, *signora*?" he said. His eyes didn't stray from the page. "Piero de Medici has been killed."

"Madonna!" Lisa exclaimed, a sharp intake of breath. She kept her pose.

Master Leonardo's hand halted. "Drowned in the Garigliano River along with his artillery train," he said. "I hear they were fleeing the Spanish."

Bellina worked to capture Master Leonardo's words at the same time that she pretended not to listen.

"And his wife and children?" Lisa asked.

Master Leonardo nodded. "Safe, as far as I've heard. I'm told they had already fled Rome, in the care of their mother."

Bellina watched the artist carefully run his silverpoint pen over the piece of parchment again. Leonardo da Vinci had made several visits to Lisa and Francesco's house with a stack of pages and a case full of pens and charcoal. And yet, after several months, there was still no painting.

Watching Lisa from across the room, Bellina had to admit that Master Leonardo had begun to pull her mistress out of the gloom. Neither Bellina nor Francesco, and certainly not Madre, had convinced her to change out of her black mourning gown or don one of the many gems stored in her wooden boxes. But as Master Leonardo pulled Lisa into conversation while he drew, Bellina saw color in her mistress's cheeks for the first time in months. He seemed to know how to put his subjects at ease with only a few gentle words and a smile, even as he discussed a difficult subject.

"Piero de Medici's wife is a Roman, and his children are very young," Master Leonardo continued. "Hardly old enough to launch a coup here in Florence."

"I see," Lisa said. "And Piero's brothers have never lifted a finger against Soderini."

"No," Leonardo said. "It seems unlikely the Medici will launch a campaign to return right now. Perhaps impossible. Is that good or bad? I suppose that depends on your position."

There was a long pause. As she pulled her needle through the linen again, Bellina observed the artist's face. Was he trying to fish for information about where Lisa and Francesco's loyalties lay?

But Lisa said nothing. Bellina's mind began to spin. If there was no chance of a Medici return to power, were Lisa and her family safe? Would the efforts to persecute the nobility be finished? What did it matter if they aligned themselves with the Medici if there were no Medici left?

But after a period of heavy silence, Lisa changed the subject.

"Master Leonardo, have you heard about the statue to be un-veiled?" Lisa asked. "The *David* that Michelangelo Buonarroti is sculpting in the cathedral workyard?"

From the corner of her eye, Bellina saw Leonardo da Vinci bristle. For a few moments, his hand wavered over the page. "I have heard . . . some things." He cleared his throat.

"They say it is to be a colossus," Lisa pressed. "I heard they are taking down one side of the wooden enclosure at Carnival so everyone can have a peek."

Bellina watched Master Leonardo force a smile that looked more like a grimace, but he didn't reply immediately.

"You're not curious to see it, Master Leonardo?" Bellina couldn't help it. She butted into the conversation and for a moment, she was afraid she had overstepped her bounds. But Lisa sat unruffled, and Master Leonardo only turned to her.

"I have already had a preview of the block of marble in the workyard," he said. "Just another David versus Goliath. I can tell you that the clamor over it is little more than . . . titillation."

Lisa continued. "Maddalena Strozzi says her husband saw a sculpture made by Master Buonarroti in Rome. Our Lady, he said, with the adult Christ on her lap. A marvel."

"Who can account for what happens in Rome, my lady?" he said, shrugging. "All I can tell you is that here in Florence, few have heard of the young man. And anyway, this . . . colossus . . ." For a moment, the artist seemed to be rendered speechless.

"If it is to be a *gigante*," Lisa said, "then it may be like nothing ever made."

Bellina watched the artist set down his pen. He sighed. "I can tell you already that the body is too massive," he said, "and too muscled. The proportions are all wrong. If he had been humble

enough to let someone see it in advance or to accept help, some-
one might have advised him. But he insists on working alone.
Stupid pride, nothing more." He picked up his pen again, but
Bellina thought he looked agitated.

Lisa's face turned dark again. Bellina struggled for a way to
continue the conversation. "Mistress, we could make another outing," she said, "just as we did when Master Leonardo's beautiful
cartoon was exhibited at the monastery. When the door to the
sculpture's wooden box is taken down at Carnival, perhaps we
could go have a glimpse."

For a moment, Lisa's face brightened. "Yes. Bellina has a good
idea. Master Leonardo, would you come with us?"

Bellina saw Master Leonardo seem to hesitate, calculating, but
then he nodded. "I suppose I would come with you to the cathedral workyard, if your husband accompanies us."

"I shall inform him," Lisa said. "Surely he will agree."

Bellina wasn't sure of how Francesco would feel, but she hoped
he would at least recognize the excitement in Lisa's voice. It was
many months since Bellina had seen her mistress take an interest
in something, and more than anything else, she hoped to see her
smile.

ANNE

Montauban, France
1940

Anne peered into the awkwardly mounted side-view mirror of the truck to take in the strange sight of Lucie astride a motorbike. Her scarf whipped in the wind as they bellowed along another curve in the mountain pass. It took all of her attention to control the heavy truck as it swayed and struggled around the mountainous curves. Ahead, Frédérique sat in the passenger seat of a large truck with her father, teetering canvases lashed down and covered in tarps in the back.

They couldn't be far from Montauban now. Even though the distance from Loc-Dieu was only a little over sixty kilometers, it had taken them hours to struggle their way toward their new destination with the scores of paintings, sculptures, artifacts, and antiquities tucked into their crates and loaded onto the trucks once more. Another trial of loading the fragile works. Another excruciatingly slow journey to endure. As she watched the trucks sway and teeter before her, Anne hoped it would be their last.

As the convoy made its slow progress through the countryside, Anne's only solace was that this time, their destination was not some dank medieval church or a castle that was an easy target. Instead, they were going to a real art museum. At the Musée

Ingres in Montauban, she had heard, the Louvre director's office had secured a safe space for them—and the artworks. Still, it had made Anne's heart sad to leave the peaceful grounds of Loc-Dieu.

But when they rounded the next turn and Anne saw the town of Montauban spread out in the valley before them, she began to hope this wouldn't be so bad after all. The town lay deep inside the Free Zone, and from this distance, Montauban looked untouched by the conflicts that had flushed people from their homes with their belongings strapped to their backs. The lazy loops of the Tarn wound through the town, languid as a resting python, fat with rain. There were no bombs or German uniforms or swastikas here.

Anne was starting to relax when there was an appalling squeal from the truck in front of her. Then a cloud of smoke burst from its axles. Cursing, Anne stamped hard on the brake. The rattle of crates in the back of her truck made her cringe. But André's truck didn't slow down despite the approaching bend. From her motorbike, Lucie was waving an arm frantically; the truck hurtled toward the bend, swaying, and Anne could only watch helplessly as it headed for its doom. At the last moment, the truck swerved hard. It teetered, the bed tipping horribly, but the bend had slowed it somehow, and the truck rolled gradually to a halt along the precipice.

Anne stopped her own truck behind it and jumped out. Lucie was pulling off her helmet and disembarking from her motorbike, her face ashen. "André!" she cried.

As the women approached, they saw André press his forehead to the steering wheel. He was sweating, and his hands shook where he clenched the wheel. "The brakes!" he cried. "I pressed on the pedal with my foot but nothing happened."

"Fredi, are you all right?" Lucie called to the little girl in the passenger seat. The girl nodded, wide-eyed.

"She can ride with me," Anne said. Frédérique jumped down from the passenger seat.

Two other men ran up to the truck. "The painting is too heavy," André said. Everyone looked at the bed of the truck, where Veronese's giant *Wedding at Cana*, taller than the height of three men, was strapped into the back.

"More than this truck can take," André said, stepping down from the truck cab and shaking his head.

"What are we going to do?" Anne asked.

"We can't unload it here in the road," Lucie said.

"We're nearly there." André glanced down at the city where it lay below. Just moments ago, it had seemed so close, but suddenly Anne thought the river winding through Montauban looked a very long way away. "If I nurse the truck and we go very slowly, we'll be all right."

The convoy crept down the rest of the pass. Anne's heart beat wildly as she watched André's truck take each downward turn. At last, they crossed the great bridge over the Tarn as the afternoon sank into evening. Anne didn't have time to enjoy the glimmering river or the bridge with its arched supports, or even the majesty of the museum where its towers reached into the sky ahead of them. She just wanted to get inside and get the *Wedding at Cana* out of that truck.

The line of trucks finally came to a halt in the museum court-yard. They disembarked as an elegant man with a receding hairline and narrow mustache—Anne recognized him as René Huyghe, the director of the Louvre's department of paintings—strode out of the doors to greet them.

"Refugees from Loc-Dieu," he cried, opening his arms. "*Bien-venus!*"

Lucie removed her helmet and the staff lined up, greeting one another with relief.

"My mother has come down from Arras," Monsieur Huyghe said, leading them into the museum entrance. "She has insisted on making dinner for everyone. I would advise you that refusing her offer is a very bad idea."

THE MUSÉE INGRES occupied a seventeenth-century building that once served as a palatial residence for the bishops of Montauban. Anne considered it might take days for her to understand the building's complicated layout, with endless galleries and vaulted, underground rooms that looked like they might serve as torture chambers rather than paintings' storage. On the top floor, Anne found her sparse room in a narrow warren of servants' quarters.

After dinner, Monsieur Huyghe led Anne, André, and Lucie to his makeshift office while the rest of the staff began the laborious process of unloading the trucks. André and Anne carried the *Mona Lisa*'s crate between them, setting it carefully on the floor by the director's desk.

René ran his fingertips over the crate. "*La Joconde!* She has already been through so much. I'm glad to have her here—and forgive me for being overprotective, but I think she should stay in my office during the day, and my bedroom at night."

Lucie nodded. "Yes. We kept it in our bedroom at Loc-Dieu, too. And it slept with Monsieur Schommer at Chambord."

"I'm just glad she's back inside a proper museum again, with the right conditions," André said.

"Let's have a look," René said. "We don't have to worry about humidity here, thank goodness."

Anne and Lucie busied themselves with prying the crate open. André turned to René. "What is the news from Paris?"

René's face turned grim. "Not good, I'm afraid. Our Jewish colleagues are in grave danger. They are no longer considered French citizens."

"What?" Lucie cried. "How can that be?"

"All their visas have been revoked. No one will accept them in another country," said René, "and I'm afraid they'll be arrested for staying in France without the right paperwork."

"Carl Dreyfus . . . ," André said. "They put him in charge of the depot at the Château de Valençay. Thank goodness he's far from the city."

"I'm afraid not. Carl slipped out of the depot to stay at a hotel for a while, and then he just . . . disappeared," René said.

Lucie stuttered. "But . . . The *Winged Victory of Samothrace*! The other works at Valençay . . . They were all under his care."

"They're still safe," said René. "We just don't know what happened to Carl. We think he may have gone into hiding in the countryside. You know there are deep woods in this part of the country. He had some help to escape, we think, perhaps from one of the resistance cells. At least I hope."

For a while, everyone worked in silence, trying to take in the news that their Jewish colleagues were disappearing into the vapor. But Anne's head spun at the mention of resistance cells in the woods.

René continued. "And in Paris . . ." He shook his head and snorted. "The Germans reopened the Louvre to the public. Well, as much as they could open an empty museum," he said. "The only works left to see are the ones we had to leave behind because they were too fragile to transport. One of their officers, a Monsieur Wolff-Metternich, gave a speech about protecting what's there, which I suppose is a relief; even though he's a Nazi, he's an art expert. Jacques told me in confidence that he's been trying to help keep the paintings out of German clutches where he can, so that's a relief. The staff who were left wore black in solidarity to show they're mourning the Louvre falling into German hands."

"I can't imagine there was anyone left to attend the reopening," Lucie said.

"Parisians? No. But Germans did," René said. "Plenty of them, especially the high-ranking Nazis. They were looking for paintings to earmark for their personal collections. They must have been shocked to see that all the paintings were gone."

The crate was open now, and the face of the *Mona Lisa* stared out at them with her secret smile. Anne stared down at it, relieved to see it was as pristine as ever. Lucie reached out as if to touch the painting, and then drew her hand back.

"Leonardo da Vinci never delivered this portrait to Francesco del Giocondo and his wife, Lisa. Did you know that?" Lucie said. "She's been in France ever since Leonardo brought her here himself."

René nodded. "We won't let them take her."

"No. She belongs to us," André said. "Still, it is a mystery to me why Leonardo never delivered this picture to its patron. Wouldn't you love to know what happened inside Francesco del Giocondo's household?"

BELLINA

Florence, Italy
1503

In the raucous blur of Carnival, Dolce left her life of service and married a man she loved.

Bellina watched Vanni the wool comber's son lift her old friend in his arms like a calf. He twirled Dolce around, her hair flowing free, as if he had opened her eyes to the wonders of the tight, crowded piazza where the revelers had gathered. Horns blared and tambourines chimed. Garbage fluttered and collected in the doorways and dark corners of the square. Fireworks cracked in the sky, and the thick smell of smoke filled the air. The edges of the marriage celebration blended and spilled into the wider chaos of the Carnival festivities in the streets beyond. Young men clutched one another's necks and sang, their laughing, drunken clusters swaying down the alleys snaking away from the square.

"Come, Bellina! Dance with us." A pull on her sleeve. She waved it away and moved toward a group of rickety chairs that had been dragged into the square so the old aunts and uncles could sit at the edge of the marriage celebration.

Bellina tucked herself against the wooden battens of a wheelwright's shop and watched the ruckus. She recognized many faces from the dyers' warehouses. Just a few years ago, they would have felt nothing but revulsion to witness such debauchery. How quickly things had changed. Where once there was only a choice between sin and righteousness, now Bellina felt the communal urge for joy in its place—for a city full of people who might be free to choose their own destiny. How easy it seemed now for those who had once sat at Brother Savonarola's feet to let down their braids, to loosen their stays and dance through the night.

Bellina observed Dolce's glowing face and felt satisfaction for her old friend. Bellina then thought of Stefano, missing from his sister's celebration, locked behind the monastery walls. She watched Bardo, in the middle of the square, pull his own wife into a tight embrace and sway with the crowd. A petite, pretty woman, she tucked herself under his broad shoulder and smiled up at him.

But the longer Bellina stood at the wall and watched the swirling, pulsing crowd, the more separate from it she began to feel, as if a bird seeing it from the air. When the feeling of separateness loomed so large she could no longer bear to stay, she pushed away from the wall, slipped into a narrow alley, and headed in the direction of Lisa's house.

DAYS LATER, the Carnival celebrations continued, but there was a new attraction. In the cathedral workyard, laborers dismantled one side of the wooden box surrounding Michelangelo Buonarroti's new *David*. The workyard itself was little more than a dusty construction site, the place where stonemasons, carpenters, metalsmiths, and other artisans toiled on the details of the great, never-finished cathedral. Now, the gates of the old workyard had drawn an unprecedented crowd.

Bellina had pressed Lisa to ask Francesco to come along to see the new giant. He'd agreed, and Bellina hoped that an outing might cheer her mistress.

Now, at the cathedral workyard gates, Bellina held baby Andrea on her hip and pressed herself behind Francesco del Giocondo. Lisa looped her hand through her husband's arm. Master Leonardo stood alongside them, engaging Francesco and Lisa in a conversation just beyond Bellina's earshot, jostling among those who pushed their way toward the gates. Only Madre had stayed behind at home, refusing to take part in the ungodliness of Carnival season. Bellina's eyes scanned the group, keeping the children together. Around the red-tiled dome of Santa Maria del Fiore, the streets swelled with people.

Suddenly, Bellina felt a sharp pinch on her backside.

"Aya!" she yelped, instinctively swatting away a hand.

"*Ciao, bella,*" a male voice said. She turned to see Gherardo just as he reached an arm around Bellina's waist and kissed her cheek.

Bellina flushed and swatted him. "*Birichino!*" she cried, and in her arms, little Andrea giggled. Gherardo made a silly face and squeezed the boy's foot.

"You have seen the *David, signorina*?" Gherardo asked.

"Not yet. I do not understand the mad rush to see this thing," Bellina said.

He shrugged. "Maybe it's about more than the statue."

Suddenly, the crowd pushed against the wrought iron until it forced those in the front to press their faces into the spaces between the metal. Behind, there were whistles and calls echoing through the street. Bellina felt herself transported, as if borne aloft by the wave of the sea; their little knot of a family stood before the gates. Now, she heard Leonardo and Francesco's conversation.

"You're not a supporter of Buonarroti's work?" Francesco was asking Master Leonardo.

"Buonarroti and I work in different disciplines. Painting is the nobler art, while sculpture is little more than manual labor."

Francesco moved to the side and Bellina stepped forward, where she grasped the wrought iron and pressed her face through the bars. In the shadowy recesses of the workyard, she could see the large wooden enclosure Master Leonardo and Lisa had discussed. On one side, the wall had been dismantled to reveal a sculpture inside, as if unveiling a surprise inside a giant gift box.

Bellina had seen plenty of statues before, of course. The city was full of them. But now, before her eyes, was something she had never seen before. It was a nude young man holding a sling over his shoulder. Nothing more. And yet . . . It was a colossus, a shining, white marble hero taller than three men standing on one another's shoulders. A wonder.

Bellina turned her head toward Lisa and Francesco, to see if they saw what she saw. But then she heard Gherardo whisper in her master's and mistress's ears. "That statue will be destroyed before it ever makes it to its resting place," he said. "Mark my words."

The statue . . . Destroyed? Had Bellina heard that right?

"Don't be ridiculous," Francesco said. "The statue will have eyes on it day and night."

"You should not talk of such things here," Lisa whispered back to Gherardo. "Besides, if anything happens to you while you are under our roof, your mother will never forgive me."

Lisa turned to Bellina. "You were right," her mistress said. "It was good to get out of the house. And I'm glad I saw that sculpture everyone has been talking about."

Bellina cast her gaze to Master Leonardo. The artist stood with his arms crossed, but he couldn't seem to take his eyes off the *David*. Bellina thought he seemed mesmerized by the marble colossus, especially for a man who claimed from the start the statue had no merit.

FOR MONTHS, Bellina had watched Leonardo da Vinci do little more than make small sketches of Lisa's hands, eyes, and mouth. He had filled both blank and reused sketchbook pages with a nub of charcoal or a silverpoint pen. Then, weeks went by before the artist might appear in Francesco del Giocondo's house again. Bellina wondered where he was, what he was doing out there in the city.

But then, in the days following the Carnival preview of Michelangelo Buonarroti's marble colossus, suddenly, there was a painting.

In the *salotto* of Lisa's house, the artist had set up a collapsible easel and propped up a wooden panel covered in a white substance the artist had explained would allow the pigments to bind. Then, in a flurry of activity, the painting came together faster than Bellina would ever have imagined.

Bellina was glad to see Master Leonardo again because she wanted to ask more questions about Michelangelo's new marble sculpture. On the streets, people were saying the newly revealed *David* would stand as a symbol of Soderini's new republic. They claimed it was the very image of Florentines, fierce underdogs who, just like David against Goliath, might stand up to enemies larger and more powerful. The Pisans. The French. Maybe even the Medici. A man in God's image, at the same time it seemed a god in the figure of a man. Not too long ago, Bellina might have considered the image sinful. And yet now she could see its beauty—maybe even its ability to stand for something bigger than just a sculpture, just a man, just an ideal.

And was there really a plot to destroy such a beautiful human creation, something that might last for generations? That was a question for Lisa's cousin Gherardo, but he, too, had disappeared.

Now that Master Leonardo was back in the house, Bellina had moved her chair and embroidery ring to a spot in the room where she could better watch him paint Lisa. He was painting her from the waist up, posed as if she had turned to speak to someone who had just arrived. Her figure seemed to emerge as if from a smoky haze, with soft outlines and the careful painting of loose, frizzled tendrils of her hair. Then, Bellina had watched in horrified amusement as the painter put down his brushes and began to smooth the oils with the tips of his fingers. In the afternoon, he left the house with his fingers stained and the panel still slick with oils.

Bellina stood before the picture in the silence and stared at her mistress's face. It was Lisa. But it was more than Lisa. It was a woman of beauty, worthy of respect, worthy of happiness.

And there was something about her expression. There was a smile, yes. But somehow, Master Leonardo had captured the ambiguity of her mistress's emotions. In the face, Bellina saw the anticipation in leaving her father's house to follow Francesco del Giocondo to a new life across the river. She saw the joy in the birth of her children, and then the utter devastation of losing a child. She saw the acknowledgment of expectation of her role as

Francesco's wife. She saw joy, pain, disappointment, wonder, the striving to make her way in this difficult city.

For a long time, Bellina stood in the waning evening light and wondered if Lisa might also see her true self reflected there.

Bellina resolved that she would ask Master Leonardo about the smile, too. But then, days went by and the artist vanished.

ANNE

Montauban, France
1941

André was hiding something.

Anne watched Lucie's broad-shouldered husband from a high window of the Musée Ingres. He looked both ways to see if anyone was watching. Then he hurried across the museum lawn toward the tree line. The attic-level room where Anne slept was as small as a closet but its window projected from one of the museum's square towers, affording an unencumbered vista across the museum's lawn and gravel pathways to the sinews of the Tarn and a wooded expanse beyond. Anne pressed her palms to the windowsill and craned her neck. She watched André approach a gnarled old tree. The tree was partially hollow, with a large, protruding round knot like a swollen knuckle.

André glanced around furtively. Then he reached into the front of his coat and pulled something out. With quick, jerky movements, he pushed it down into the hollow trunk and stepped away. A nasty suspicion rose in Anne's gut. She grabbed a sweater and hurried out of the room. She made her way down a series of marble staircases to one of the grand galleries overlooking the grounds.

In the largest gallery, Anne found Lucie with a small cluster of museum staff. The curators had unfurled the giant *Wedding at Cana* on the floor. Veronese's colors came to life in the winter light. Filtered light from the great windows illuminated the beauty of the Venetian painting, nearly four hundred years old, in stunning detail.

"Monsieur Huyghe says that Maréchal Pétain is going to pay us a visit," one of the curators was saying as Anne drew nearer. Across the room, there was a communal gasp. Anne froze. The head of the Vichy government? Here? "A publicity opportunity, no doubt. We've been asked to open some of the crates and show him the paintings. He wants to see the *Mona Lisa*."

For months, the "Louvre refugees" had slipped into a kind of peaceful existence at Montauban. Monsieur Huyghe and the curators received visitors—journalists, publishers, artists, and other art experts—as if it were just another day at the office. The troubles of their colleagues still in Paris felt distant. In a large, well-lit gallery, the archives were taking order; the boxes and files now neatly organized. For the first time since they'd left Paris, Anne felt she could put her finger on anything they asked her to locate. Those staff who had brought their families along to Montauban also seemed to settle into a regular routine. Many had fanned out across town, finding small apartments, homes, and rooms to rent. Lucie and André had enrolled Frédérique in the local school, where she had begun to settle into a routine and make friends.

At that moment, André appeared at the door from the lawn. He rattled the door handle and let himself inside. He was heading toward the small gallery he had commandeered for a study when Anne caught up with him.

"André," Anne whispered more sharply than she'd meant. He stopped. "What were you doing just now?"

"What?"

"I saw you hiding something in the tree."

André's eyebrows flew up, and his eyes flitted to the window as if trying to work out how Anne had seen him. "Ah! It's a . . . diary."

"A diary?"

He shrugged. "I've been keeping a daily journal of our experiences. I think it's important that people should know what happened to the paintings of the Louvre. Maybe someday there will be a free France again, and people will want to remember that there were a few brave people, like you and my wife, who risked their lives to save these works."

"Why are you hiding it?"

André scratched his balding head. "Simple. I don't want it to be confiscated when the Germans come. If they put their hands on it, then they would know where everything else is located. It would be easy for them to take whatever they want."

Anne swallowed hard. Suddenly the wintry day no longer seemed so still and peaceful. "You still think they're coming here—after everything we've done?"

André nodded solemnly, and then walked over to the frosty window and looked out on the lawn. "That's why René insists that we have the government's authorization and the right paperwork in hand. Hopefully, that will make it possible for us to leave town if we need to, even with the Huns here. Maréchal Pétain and the others may make a show of things seeming normal here. But make no doubt about it. They are coming."

Anne felt desperation rise in her throat. "Isn't there something we can do? René said there were . . . resistance cells . . . somewhere."

André's eyes were hooded, and he remained silent for a few moments, perhaps gauging whether he could trust her with the information. Anne saw his tone was careful. "In the countryside, there are people who believe that we can still stand up to Germany. And there are resistance cells forming all over the Free Zone," he said. "Groups of men and women hiding in the woods, meeting in homes to organize weapons. Reconnaissance. Perhaps even here in Montauban."

That night, Anne tossed fitfully on her bed. When she finally slept, her dreams were filled with images of men and women hiding in the woods.

LEONARDO

The rain begins long before my mule reaches Pisa, and by the time I arrive at the canal works, it's too late to save it.

The wind whips the wiry hairs of my beard across my chest as I stand on a makeshift wooden platform and look at the disaster below me. Surely it is a bad dream, but no; I am awake. My ideas, my infallible designs. All of it destroyed.

For months, Machiavelli and I collaborated on the perfect plan. To divert the Arno would mean tunneling under a mountain and the labor of thousands of men. But if all had gone as planned, soon enough, the Pisans' crops would wither. They would have no way to bathe or drink. And the water would divert to Florence. At last, we would have a passage to the sea.

But now, the Arno spreads into wide plains. The earthenwork channels I designed have washed away, the retaining walls destroyed. The river has overrun everything and formed into pools that have bred mosquitoes and brought malaria. Machiavelli tells me that scores have died of the cursed disease. Machiavelli tried to break the news gently, but there is no way to soften the blow of lives lost.

The Signoria hired an engineer to divert the river according to my designs, but the imbecile did not follow my instructions. The builders dug the channels too shallow, leaving the reservoir above the level of the riverbed. When they released the water, it rampaged and destroyed the earthenworks because the water was not properly conducted to flow downstream. A force of Pisan soldiers left the safety of their city and attacked the project under cover of night, and finished the job the incompetent builders started by destroying the whole undertaking.

My name will suffer disgrace. They will hold me responsible.

All I want is to leave this place, but Florence will provide no shelter. There, my commissions—my altarpieces, my fresco for the Signoria, my portrait of the wool trader's wife—all of them remain untouched. And in the intervening months, all anyone can speak of is Michelangelo Buonarroti's lumbering giant. The cathedral committee has granted him what he wants; they will place the colossus in the Piazza della Signoria. A symbol of the Florentine republic.

And now this. This disaster will finish me forever. They will plow me under the dirt beneath the feet of younger men . . .

"Master Leo."

No sooner have I thought of Salaì than he appears at my side. The boy's face is white, his lip trembling.

"What's the matter? Are you ill?"

He shakes his head. "No, sir, not me." He looks nervously over his shoulder. "The messenger has just brought word from Florence. We need to go home. They said it would be better if I told you myself."

"Tell me what? What's happened?"

He touches my sleeve.

"Master," he says softly. "It's your father. They say he's passed to the Hereafter."

MY FATHER LEAVES behind a dozen legitimate children and one bastard: me.

As the oldest, I might be the leader. But as we gather around my father's old table to hear the reading of his last testament, these much younger half-siblings, chattering among themselves, feel like strangers. The teary woman who attended my father during his life brings trays of meats and cheeses. No one addresses me beyond the mandatory pleasantries.

My father's house is much as I saw it last: pretentious in some ways, scrappy in others. Just like him. There are fine boxes of intarsia along with his moth-eaten undergarments in the wardrobe. In the bottom of the cabinets, there are sprouted potatoes along with fine maiolica plates from Montelupo's best artisans.

As I look at the faces around the table, I see my father's imprint. These children of Ser Piero da Vinci have all modeled their lives on his. Some are notaries, others are accountants for wealthy clients; the women have all married well. All walk in the higher social circles of Florence. Only I, it seems, beg and scrape to make my living.

For a moment, I feel as if a weight—no, more of a ceiling—has been removed from my life. I feel like I can stand straighter now, taller, and I can see more clearly. Salaì was right. This man colored everything in my world, whether or not I chose to admit it. I have spent my energy trying to win his approval, and I did not see that it was an approval that could not be won.

Being a notary, naturally my father's testament is in order. The reading of the will begins and I listen as each child's name is called.

Part 6

RULES OF ENGAGEMENT

ANNE

Montauban, France
1942

The Germans were coming. Anne just couldn't see them yet.

From an upper-story balcony of the Musée Ingres, Anne gripped the wrought-iron railing and gazed out across the river Tarn, the icy air turning her nose and fingers numb. As far as she could see, bare branches glittered with a cover of frost. Her heart felt like the fields: robbed, empty, frozen.

The news had come to them the way it always did: Pierre, sharing information from the wireless. This time he was pale with shock, his usual smile beneath a scowl now wiped away. The Germans had invaded the Free Zone at last. After the Allies landed in North Africa and started pushing back Italian forces, the Free French—courageous citizens who refused to bow either to Nazi Germany or to Vichy France—had scuttled the French navy. Then German forces had simply strolled into France and taken what they believed was theirs.

For now, the town and the surrounding landscape stood eerily still. Nothing moved in the fields beyond Montauban; one lonely Citroën puttered unhurriedly along a winding road in the distance. Even the Tarn's current had turned sluggish in the cold. For a moment, Anne's mind filled with the explosions above Paris, the

blind panic of pigeon flocks wheeling above Notre-Dame's vener-
ated towers, the plane engines in the clouds between Chambord
and Louvigny. She shuddered. How long would it take before the
quiet turned to chaos? The conflicts had seemed so far away ever
since they'd left Chambord this time last year, but it seemed that
no matter where they ran, chaos would always, always catch up.

Anne heard the echoing tread of footsteps across the vast,
empty gallery behind her. Christiane stepped out on the balcony and leaned her elbows on the railing beside Anne. She said
nothing, only lit a cigarette and blew a stream of smoke into the
frosty air.

"We have to leave," Anne said dully.

Christiane nodded and then turned her back to the railing,
looking at her. Christiane wasn't yet thirty years old, but Anne
thought she had aged ten years in a month. Small crinkles had appeared in the corners of her eyes, and there were stress lines across
her brow. "There's no other choice. They will take everything
we've worked so hard to protect. Montauban lies along several
major roadways. We're a prime target from the air." She aimed her
skinny cigarette toward the still, winter sky.

Anne didn't want to envision the Musée Ingres blown to pieces,
but she could hardly imagine packing up the *Mona Lisa* and everything else again.

Christiane seemed to read her mind. "We've done too much to
give up now," she said.

Anne swallowed hard and nodded. "Where are Lucie and André?"

"Lucie hasn't said anything to Frédérique yet. She took her to
school."

School. They had done so much to help Frédérique live a

normal life here in Montauban. Anne wondered at how foolish they'd all been to believe they could ever find safety. "Where will we go this time?"

"They tell me Monsieur Jaujard is still trying to work it out," Christiane said, turning to gaze out at the countryside.

Anne only shook her head.

Christiane shrugged. "He's doing his best," she said heavily. "If the French government could just tell the British and Americans where we've hidden everything, they'd avoid bombing us if they could. I don't think they want these pictures destroyed any more than we do. But Vichy didn't seem to care, no matter how high Jaujard pushed it up the chain of command."

"Nobody cares," Anne murmured.

Christiane laid a hand on her shoulder, squeezing it. "We do," she said, "and all the people who will come to the Louvre in the generations after us to see the pictures we saved. Imagine our grandchildren. They deserve to look at the *Mona Lisa,* too."

Anne huffed in disbelief. "You really think the Germans might lose?"

"Their position is not what it was this time last year," she said. "The Allies are closing in from North Africa now, so the Germans are losing ground. And now that the Japanese have blown up Pearl Harbor, the Americans are finally ready to get involved. They're powerful."

"And they're on our side?"

"Nothing is certain," she said. "It will be a long time before this is finished, I tell you. But things are beginning to shift. The Germans can smell it. They are going to want to grab as much as they can before it's over. If you could have seen the officers prowling through the empty galleries of the Louvre . . ." She shook her head. "It was as if they were in a shop instead of a museum." Anne couldn't bear to think of the Louvre's paintings hanging in the homes of such monsters.

Anne knew René was still working on a plan to get them—and the artworks—out of the Musée Ingres. They had spirited away thirty more crates during three midnight runs between Montauban and the château of Loubejac.

"Isn't it risky for copies of the depot inventories to be in Paris?" Anne asked. "You said it yourself. The Louvre is now crawling with Germans—more so than here in the country."

She shrugged. "Someone has to deliver them to Monsieur Jaujard, and I'm the only one with the clearance to do it." Christiane seemed to hesitate for a moment, then she said, "Plus . . . we have to get the inventories to Paris because there we have . . . people . . . who can turn them over to the Allies for us."

Anne gasped. "I knew it! Resisters . . . They can help us!"

Christiane sucked again on her cigarette. "It's not clear yet how they might help us, but that's what we hope. We may run out of our own men to help us before long."

"What do you mean?" Anne asked.

"You have heard of the Service du Travail Obligatoire?"

Anne swallowed. "It doesn't sound good."

"It isn't!" Christiane shook her head. "The Germans have poured everything into this war, but mostly their men. They now have a shortage of workers back in Germany. The Vichy leaders are deporting French men in their twenties to Germany to replace the soldiers in the factories and businesses."

Nausea rose in Anne's throat. She backed away, unable to meet Christiane's eyes. Marcel was twenty-three.

"And you can imagine how they will be treated there," Christiane said. "To them," she said, nodding toward the landscape as if it were already filled with Nazi soldiers, "we are barely human."

Anne closed her eyes, but she couldn't keep the images out of her mind: Marcel, arrested, dragged from the only country he knew, shipped off with hundreds of other young men to labor away in some grim factory far from home. She couldn't imagine it. Anne shook her head sharply. She couldn't afford to give up now. "I think I should go and help pack up the inventories downstairs."

"You go ahead," Christiane said. "I'm going to check on the paintings in the main gallery—André should be done with them by now. And René is preparing *La Joconde* for immediate transport."

Anne hurried downstairs. The staff were moving around, rolling up paintings, wrapping what they could, padding them in their crates. There was a strange atmosphere of fear and silent resolve. Lucie flitted from crate to crate, a ledger in her hands, to ensure all the crate numbers and contents matched her records.

"Anne!" Lucie called when she reached the bottom of the stairs. "Would you let René know we're almost ready?"

Anne passed two of the younger guards, who were busy struggling to heft one of those giant Napoleonic paintings. Pierre was standing at the door, his arms folded, his squinting eyes never leaving them.

At the door to René's office, the wooden crate with the three red dots sat waiting. Anne imagined the painting sealed inside in the dark. The *Mona Lisa*. She was so real and yet so far beyond real. It seemed as if, should she touch the painting, she would be able to feel the warm and vibrant life of the dark-haired lady pulsing through the paint. The stillness of her—the serenity, the secret smile—none of it fit. Not in this frantic rush to once again pack up all the artworks of the Louvre and take them away to a new, ever more secret location.

Anne knocked gently on René's door. "Monsieur?" she called. "The Chamsons wanted me to let you know they're ready."

There was a grunt of effort from the other side of the door. Anne stepped inside René's office. She found him bent over a crate, the upper half of his body invisible inside it. He hadn't heard her enter the room. He was struggling with something inside the box.

"Can I help?" she asked, reaching the edge of the box.

René started and stood up quickly. He whirled around, stepping in front of the crate. "Don't . . ." He held up his hand.

But it was too late. Anne had already seen what was inside the box. A gasp tore loose from her throat, and then her hands flew to her mouth. Anne stared wide-eyed down into the wooden crate. Her heart thumped against her ribs unpleasantly, as if she'd just uncovered a nest of vipers. The crate was filled with weapons. A pile of rifles and machine guns shone dully in the pale light.

Anne recoiled. "René!" she cried. "What—"

René put a finger to his lips. "Shhh!" Fear shone in his eyes. "Please."

It stilled her. She swallowed hard. "What are you doing?" she whispered.

He grabbed a lid for the crate and put it on shakily, glancing over his shoulder. "We must protect ourselves and everything in our care," he said. "Surely you understand."

Anne gestured to the door. "But we have guards," she said.

René's eyebrows rose. "Pierre?"

As soon as he said his name, Anne realized how ridiculous it was to have the illusion that the hobbling old man—or *any* of the sagging, uniformed, unarmed men in the museum—might protect them from a regiment of Germans: young, strong men with a thirst for blood. Wearing felted caps instead of helmets, armed with rings of skeleton keys rather than machine guns, those old Louvre guards would never be a match for Nazi soldiers.

For a moment, Anne felt she needed to sit. Instead, she clung to the lid of the crate with the deadly weapons hidden inside.

"Ultimately, the Vichy government pays our guards," René continued. "What good will they do us? And . . . we must consider that they could put us in harm's way instead."

"You think our guards would betray us?" It had never occurred to Anne to see Pierre or any of the other guards as anything but allies.

René glanced at the door again. "I think we have to be ready to take matters into our own hands, *mademoiselle*."

Anne nodded, understanding. She looked into René's eyes. Tired. Resolute. "You think the Germans will come," she said.

A tight nod. "I know they will. Jaujard and the others in Paris are trying to arrange paperwork that will allow us to move to a new location. But it's too slow. By the time they get it done, the Nazis could try to requisition this museum for themselves." A shadow passed over René's face. "We have to stop them from taking what is rightfully ours—what rightly belongs to the cultural patrimony of all humanity." His voice wavered. For a moment, Anne watched the rims of René's eyes turn red, but he cleared his throat and gathered himself.

Anne reached for René's forearm and gave it a squeeze. "Then you can count on me to help you," she said, gazing down into the contents of the crate. "Whatever it takes."

IN THE CORNER of a dark museum storage room, Anne tossed and turned on a narrow sofa. There was no going to bed. She lay on the thin cushion, fully clothed. During the sleepless hours, her mind always returned to Corrado. She thought of the long afternoons they had spent walking across the lawns of Loc-Dieu, their hearts full of hope even under the threat that the Germans might find them. Mostly, though, she allowed herself to relive their kiss. The passion. The urgency in his touch. She closed her eyes but sleep would not come.

As weak dawn light finally appeared in the window glass, Anne rose, returned to the cold balcony, and looked out over the Tarn.

This time, she saw German trucks.

As the light began to turn orange, dark green trucks and camouflage-painted tanks approached with shocking speed along the sweeping roads bordering the river.

Within minutes, around the museum, men were piling out of the vehicles. They walked in groups down the middle of the streets, machine guns slung around their bodies. They cupped their hands and peered inside any shop window that wasn't battened shut. Anne watched a soldier relieve himself over a railing into the river.

As the sky turned light, a group of soldiers collected near the entrance gate of the museum. Their harsh voices and laughter reached up to the windows. Anne noticed that several of the men had giant cameras hanging from their necks, some more impressive looking than their weapons. They didn't seem ready for a battle. A few of the men were already snapping pictures of the town, a strange and unlikely bunch of soldier-tourists. One soldier raised his camera and raked it up the façade of the museum. He seemed to point his apparatus directly at Anne. She recoiled and slunk from the window.

For weeks, the staff had played an excruciating waiting game. Each day, they longed for the phone to ring, for a telegram to arrive from Paris or Vichy, giving them the clearance to load the trucks and leave Montauban for another safe location.

Now, it was too late.

What would happen if the Germans took over the depot, or worse, discovered they were hiding stashes of weapons and ammunition in some of the crates?

Anne heard a gasp behind her. She spun around. Lucie stood by the window, both her hands plastered over her mouth. Then she lowered her hands slowly, and her words had a forced calm, as if she'd beaten them into submission.

"We have to go," she said.

In the end, there had been no time for the Louvre staff to do anything other than what they were already doing: frantically packing the objects and keeping the inventories straight. But now it was too late. Anne turned around. The gallery behind them suddenly filled with frantic staff pulled from their beds. They scurried like mice in a trap, tucking ledger books into padded boxes, nailing the crates shut. Each smack of the hammer reverberated through Anne's bones like a gunshot. She swallowed hard and tried to keep her voice from shaking. "Do we still need the inventories at this point? Shouldn't we just . . . run?"

"We'll need them when we get to . . . wherever we're going," Lucie said. "Anyway, it's too late to run; we're out of time. There are too many Germans in the streets. And we don't have another plan."

"Where on earth are we going to find another safe place for all this—for all of us?" Anne said. Dismay bubbled in her like a tar pit.

"René and André are doing their best," Lucie said. Anne knew the men had spent weeks scouring the countryside, knocking on the doors of large, private country estates, using whatever contacts they had to secure a place large and safe enough. "They've found a few potential solutions," Lucie said, but her voice was flat, void of hope. "Nothing ideal."

Suddenly, André burst into the storage room. He strode across the room toward Anne and Lucie. Beads of sweat had formed on his forehead and thinly veiled panic registered behind his eyes. "Quick!" he said, his voice whispering and frantic. "We need one copy of the depot inventories. René has a plan."

Anne squared her shoulders. "What can we do?" Lucie rushed to one of the file boxes where they had stashed some carbon copies of the inventories Anne had typed.

André continued. "René is sending Christiane back to Paris. She's the only one with enough stamps on her papers to get through the checkpoints. We're going to try to get the lists into the hands of the British and Americans."

Anne gasped. Was there really a way to reach the Allied forces?

André seemed to read her mind. "René has some—channels—to the Allied forces. If they know what's here, they might prevent our works of art from being destroyed or stolen."

Anne tried not to look out the window, but it was impossible not to hear the tread of German feet outside. Could René hold the Germans off any longer? She thought of the *Mona Lisa* resting in Lucie's bedroom.

"Oh!" Lucie gasped from the window. "They're—I think they're coming inside!"

Anne hurried to the window. They gazed down into the street below. Two German officers, their chests glittering with medals, strode confidently to the front doors of the museum. Lucie leaned into André as if it were the only way she could remain standing. Anne slipped away. She tiptoed down the stairs leading to the museum entrance hall.

Just then, there were several loud bangs on the door. The sound made Anne jump; she had to bite her tongue to keep herself from letting out a shriek. She paused on the stairs, just out of view of the guards and staff collecting nervously in the entrance hall.

Anne watched René run his hands over his slicked hair. He was dressed in his finest suit, his tie neatly knotted. He looked as much a museum director as if he were calmly overseeing things in any Paris museum in peacetime. He knew this was coming, Anne thought. He was ready. She watched René pause to collect himself, and then open the door.

A shaft of daylight streaked across the threshold, and René stepped back.

"You are Monsieur le Directeur?" Anne heard one of the German officers say.

"*Oui,*" René answered, his head held high. "René Huyghe."

The German officer nodded and the two uniformed men stepped inside. For a few moments, there was nothing but dead silence. The Germans looked around, surveying the marble floors, the frozen staff standing around, the crates neatly staged for a getaway.

Anne swallowed hard, knowing some of those crates were stockpiled not with paintings but with weapons. She saw René follow the Germans' gaze and step in front of it, his grin suddenly broadening as a bead of sweat trickled down behind his ear.

One of the Germans met his gaze and Anne heard his harsh version of French echo through the gallery. "*Nous sommes ici pour voir les peintures*. We are here to see the paintings."

AT A BACK ENTRANCE to the museum, Anne helped two curators slide a crate quietly into the bed of a small truck parked in the alleyway. A sliver of moonlight provided the only illumination. Anne squinted into the blackness. Eight crates were now secured with ties on the truck bed.

For weeks, the Louvre staff and the German soldiers had done little more than surveil one another through the museum's great panes of glass. Anne could hardly believe how René continued to stall them. Each time an officer banged on the museum door, there was a stilted, hyper-polite exchange of "*Monsieurs*" and "*mercis*" and an exchange of paperwork. But in the end, the Germans only milled around the entrance hall while the Louvre staff continued their frantic packing in the upper galleries.

This particular regiment did not have the proper authorization from their superiors to enter the museum and confiscate the art, René told them. By German standards, the lack of paperwork was enough to keep them at bay. For how long? It was anyone's guess. Things could change at any moment, he said. What would happen when they tired of waiting for permission?

Meanwhile, René told them, neither could the museum staff afford to wait any longer for direction from Paris. The depot workers at Montauban had to take matters into their own hands now. They would do their best, René said, to spirit away as many works of art as possible, even at the risk of doing so under the Germans' watchful gaze. André and René had located a small, privately owned château at Loubejac, some ninety kilometers to the north. Some of the smaller, most important works would be transferred there immediately.

Anne watched the clouds skirt over the crescent moon as they waited for the final crate to emerge from the museum.

Finally, André, Lucie, and Frédérique appeared at the back door, their eyes heavy with exhaustion. Then a few, final, small crates. Without a word, André and Lucie slid the crates into the dark truck bed. Lucie gave Anne a quick peck on each cheek. "I'm leaving the archives in good hands," she whispered. "Thank you."

Anne nodded. "Godspeed," she whispered back.

Anne watched the Chamsons climb quietly into the truck. From behind, René, Anne, and the small cluster of curators and guards pushed the truck down the alley. Silently, it rolled out toward the main street, André leaning forward over the steering wheel with full focus. When they reached the main street along the Tarn, André kept the headlights off, but the engine roared to life. Anne watched the truck pick up speed and then disappear into the blackness.

After a minute, the town of Montauban returned to its slumbering state. Anne lingered on the museum grounds, taking in the gentle breeze, the rush of the river, the chirping and peeping of the night creatures. At the edge of the lawn stood the old hollow tree where Anne had seen André hide his diary. Anne approached the tree's silhouette, fuzzy and hulking in the darkness. She stood on tiptoe and slid her fingers into the hollow cavity. There. A flutter. She felt a piece of paper and pulled it out of the hole.

She moved to the back door of the museum, where there was

a small light by the entrance. She unfolded the page and imme-diately saw a hastily scrawled list of the new depots: Loubejac, Bétaille, Vayrac, Lanzac, others.

Anne stood in wonder. André had not only been keeping a di-ary. He had left behind a message—for someone. Did the Louvre staff have contacts outside the museum? Anne felt the back of her neck prickle. Dry leaves rustled in the branches above. She tucked the paper back into the hollow tree and hurried inside.

AS A GROUP of newly requisitioned, gazogene-powered trucks rumbled through the woods, Anne leaned forward over the steer-ing wheel and did her best to stay alert. It had been a long drive from Montauban after an exhausting day of double-checking their records. Even though the distance was little more than one hundred fifty kilometers, the trucks rumbled along at a snail's pace. To Anne, it felt like days.

Ahead, Anne kept her eyes on the small truck carrying the *Mona Lisa*. Once again, a truck had been hand-selected to carry the priceless masterpiece, and they had almost reached their des-tination at Montal. Perhaps they were going to make it safely there after all.

The past three months had drained nearly all Anne's resolve. It was tiring even to think about it: the endless struggle to keep inventories straight as works of art shifted; Monsieur Jaujard and the Chamsons scouring the surrounding countryside for new ha-vens; the struggle for paperwork and resources once they'd settled on moving the art to Montal.

In the meantime, Anne had continued to wrestle with the in-ventories as German soldiers marched through Montauban. It seemed only a matter of time before they claimed some priceless artwork for the wall of a German officer's bedroom. Eight hundred pounds of packing material had arrived just a couple of days ago at the Musée Ingres, and the massive task of resecuring all the art had gone on well into the darkness each night. Somehow, Monsieur Jaujard had scraped together permission from Germany and from the Vichy government to allow trucks to line up in front of the museum. Their movements would no longer be a secret. Everyone—especially the German soldiers posted outside the museum—would be watching.

But Anne didn't want to ruminate about that now. She just wanted to rest, and as the truck rattled and bumped through the rocky, hilly woods, she could almost dream herself back to three years ago on the road to Chambord for the very first time. Corrado's gentle voice, always tugging her out of her worried thoughts, keeping her from slipping too deeply into fear and despair. If he were here now, focusing on the bumpy road as he guided the truck toward safety, he would be telling her jokes. But Corrado wasn't there, and Anne had to accept that he might never be again. Italy and France were enemies now, and it didn't matter how he and Anne felt about each other. Instead, it was René in her passenger seat, and he had hardly breathed a word since they'd left Montauban and headed northeast for the next château.

A bump startled her out of her daze. René sat up, and she flashed him an apologetic smile, keeping a tight grip on the steering wheel. "Rocks are everywhere—I'm doing my best to miss them. I just hope the *Mona Lisa* is all right." They watched as the truck in front of them swayed over the uneven terrain.

"She's seen worse than this. Have you already forgotten her passage to Loc-Dieu?"

Anne's eyes scanned the woods along the roadside as the trucks slowed to a crawl. The first blush of spring had colored them; she could see an occasional blossom unfurling, a green shoot trying to nose its way through the thick, wet ground.

For a fleeting second, the undergrowth seemed to rustle, and something flashed from a bush to behind a tree. Too big to be a bird, Anne thought. A deer or fox? Anne leaned closer to the window, frowning as she tried to make out the figure. She stared deeply into the shadows of a thicket, and suddenly the form of a man took shape.

Anne recoiled. "René!" she gasped. "There's someone in the woods. Look!"

Another flashing movement caught her eye. There was more than one person moving in the heavy underbrush just beyond view. Anne's stomach burned with fear. This didn't look like one of the German or Vichy government checkpoints they'd stopped at repeatedly on their journey so far, and those had been stressful enough.

The trucks in front of them creaked to a halt. Anne felt her vehicle sway with the weight of the precious art it carried. She clutched at the door handle of the truck, her heart hammering. "What's happening?"

A figure stepped out from among the trees. It was a tall, sturdy young man wearing a tattered jacket and trousers buttoned just below the knee. At his hip, a large revolver gleamed in the dim light.

"René!" she gasped.

"Stay here," he ordered, opening the door.

"Wait!" Anne began, but he had already slammed the door behind him.

Anne gripped the steering wheel and watched. Blood rushed in her ears as René strode toward the young man. Some of the other drivers had also climbed out of their trucks. René and the young man spoke, and the latter gestured to the drivers. Moving briskly, they jumped up onto the nearest truck and began loosening the straps around one of the crates. Faster than Anne thought possible, they'd untied a crate. More people appeared out of the woods and rushed past the young man, seizing the crate as Pierre and the others handed it down.

"No!" Anne choked out. She couldn't stand by and watch them steal their art. She leapt out of the truck and ran toward them. "Stop! Leave that alone!"

"Anne." René whirled around, holding out both hands to her. "Stop."

"Don't let them take it!" Anne cried. The men were staring at her; she saw one of them reach for his gun.

René grasped her wrist. "Anne, stop," he hissed.

"But they're taking the art!"

"They're not taking the art," René said.

At that moment, the truth dawned on her. Anne recognized the crate full of weapons she had seen in René's office. The men were not taking art; they were taking weapons.

Anne blinked. She stared at the men, who were scuttling back into the woods already, the crate jostling and bouncing between them. She looked back toward René where he stood at the passenger door. In his eyes, there was concern but also a sparkle of spirit.

"*On y va*," he said.

Behind them, Anne watched as three more crates were unloaded and spirited off into the woods. Anne and René got back into the truck. The convoy rumbled off again. Anne stared into the woods, but she couldn't see the men anymore.

The adrenaline seeped out of Anne's veins after watching the resistance fighters sprint away with the smuggled weapons. Immediately, the trucks trundled onward through the woods, Anne's mind spinning with questions for René.

"You could have told me about the crates," she said.

He regarded her carefully. "I wasn't sure how serious you were when you told me you wanted to help us, *mademoiselle*. Your efforts in preserving and cataloging paintings have been exemplary, but there's a difference between smuggling paintings and smuggling guns."

Anne nodded. "But we're rid of the weapons now, aren't we?"

"Not yet," he said carefully. "There are more resistance cells in the woods near Montal that need supplies, too. We have a few crates left for them."

For a few moments, it filled Anne with wonder that the convoy held not only crates full of the best of human artistic achievement but also others filled with weapons and ammunition.

"Aren't we putting the paintings at risk?" she asked.

But there was no time for an answer. The convoy descended a hill and slowed at the sight of another roadblock.

This time, there were Germans.

A PAIR OF DUSTY German trucks stood diagonally, blocking the road. A cluster of soldiers stood by the roadside, and as the convoy came nearer, one of them stepped out. He was armed with weapons and ammunition strapped across his midsection. He held out one hand to stop them.

The trucks groaned once more to a halt. René glanced at her. "This time, you really have to stay in the truck, Anne," he said.

She nodded mutely as René got out of the truck. Anne rolled down her window as the German soldier approached. René was smiling submissively, his shoulders hunched as he pulled out a file full of paperwork.

"*Bonjour, bonjour, Monsieur,*" she heard him say, but she strained to hear the rest. "*Musées Nationaux . . . Paris . . . oeuvres d'art, peintures . . .*"

The German soldiers gazed suspiciously at the trucks.

"If you look at my papers, Monsieur . . ." Anne saw that René was trying hard to maintain the soldier's attention on the papers in his hand, but to her horror, the man gestured with the end of his rifle for the other men to fan out among the trucks. Anne watched her knuckles turn white as she gripped the steering wheel. A soldier's head appeared at her window for a few long seconds. Then she heard the back doors of her truck open.

She cowered, sinking into her seat as the soldier marched up to the truck bed and struck one of the crates with the butt of his rifle. There were words exchanged in German, then she heard René's voice again.

"They contain artworks, Monsieur. We have our paperwork," he insisted again. "We are on official government business." But she heard rustling in the truck bed and German voices just behind her head.

Anne's heart felt like it was beating in all the wrong places—her hands and feet and face. If they opened the wrong crate, they'd kill René. What would they do to her? To the others?

A new soldier with a row of stripes on his shoulders suddenly appeared. He quietly took the papers, skimmed through them, and then looked at the crates. He nodded at the first soldier, who only sneered and thrust René's papers back at him.

Anne watched the soldiers retreat to the roadsides, and one of the German trucks rolled out of the way to let them pass. Anne heard her own sigh of relief.

"*Merci, merci, merci,*" René simpered, backing away.

Anne only breathed again when René was back in the passenger's seat and the trucks were moving once more. For a while, they rode in silence.

"Those people in the woods . . . ," she said after a while.

René said nothing, only ran his hand over his stubbled jaw.

Anne pressed. "Tell me who they are."

LEONARDO

Florence, Italy
1504

An oxcart shuttles slowly into the piazza, piled high with wooden crates and trunks. Inside each wooden crate, there are paintings. Drawings. Small models and contraptions of wood and gesso. Brushes, pigments, and panels. We have packed them carefully in paper and wool plugs to minimize movement and damage in transit over the rough cobblestones between Santissima Annunziata and the great church of Santa Maria Novella.

There, Salaì and a half-dozen new pupils are waiting before the great façade decorated with colorful, geometric marble patterns. I watch the oxcart driver stop before a service door that leads to the rooms off the monks' cloister. The cart comes to a halt, and the young men spring to action.

"*Attento!*" Salaì calls to one of the new, young apprentices balancing the wooden crate over the crown of his head. They have much to learn, but I cannot be impatient with them. I am filled with optimism.

A new beginning. A new commission. A new place to lay my head. And a new chance to make my mark.

"I can hardly imagine it, Master," Salaì says, dusting off his palms and wiping his brow. "It seems you have rid yourself of the Servites of Santissima Annunziata at last."

"Actually, they have rid themselves of me. It's all a matter of perspective, my lovely." I touch his chin and he smiles. We follow the young men into the cool shadows of the great cloister. Behind us, the oxcart driver whistles and snaps his reins. The emptied oxcart rattles away across the cobbles.

In a suite of rooms adjacent to the great cloister, the youngsters are unpacking my crates. They are storing my silk gowns and hose in the cabinets, and carefully uncrating my stacks of parchments, my glass pots of ground pigments, my leather cases filled with brushes of fox hair and ermine. There is a panel with an image of Christ as Savior of the World that I began in Milan and have not yet finished. There is a *Leda and the Swan* that has occupied many hours, and other works in progress.

But none of that is why I'm here. Instead, the *gonfaloniere* of the republic, Piero Soderini, has arranged for my transfer from one monastery to another. As I have always said, it doesn't pay to pick sides in politics. Even Michelangelo Buonarroti has skillfully sidestepped that mistake by not answering people's questions about the meaning of his sculpture. Now, Soderini has instructed the prior of Santa Maria Novella to hand me the keys to the room the monks call the Sala del Papa. There, in an old, disused storeroom once used for the pope's holy entrance into the city, I'll have space to work on my cartoons for a new project: a great battle scene on a bare wall of the Palazzo Vecchio where the men of the Dodici Buonomini meet.

Salaì and I wander through the vast, silent space of Santa Maria Novella. At last, we come to stand before the family tomb of the Giocondo. There, the slabs of several generations mark family members in eternal rest. The newest, clean marble slab is small enough for a child.

Piera, it reads. A single word for a mere slip of a girl.

Salaì follows my gaze to the small tombstone engraved with the name of a little girl. "Master, what of the portrait of the del Giocondo lady? Is it finished?"

"Lisa? Nearly done. But it can wait. There are more pressing issues."

BELLINA

Florence, Italy
1504

Bellina found Lisa's cousin Gherardo in the kitchen, laying a slice of cured ham between two slices of bread, and then stuffing it in a small sack for his day at Francesco's silk workshop.

"There you are," she said. "I wanted to ask you something."

"Anything, my lovely Bellina," he said, tying a knot in the sack.

"The other night, at the cathedral workyard . . ." She hesitated, hardly knowing how to put it into words. She paced in front of the gaping, black hole of the brick oven. "You said something about that sculpture—*Il Gigante*—being in danger of destruction."

Gherardo flashed his usual charming smile, but Bellina thought she saw him hesitate for a moment. He reached into the fruit bowl. "Apple?"

"*No, grazie.*" She waved the apple away. "Gherardo . . . What did that mean?"

"Well," he said. "It's going to take a while for that colossus to make its way from the cathedral to the Piazza della Signoria," he said finally. He shrugged. "Anything could happen between here and there. That's all."

She narrowed her eyes. "And you know something about it."

He shrugged again. "Maybe."

"Gherardo. The last thing we need is to bring attention to this house," Bellina said. "I've heard . . . things. That . . . certain groups . . . are watching Francesco and Lisa. We would never want to put them in danger." For a moment, Bellina's mind flew to Master Leonardo's portrait. Was it in danger, too?

BELLINA JANGLED the small brass bell at the door to Bardo's family silk tailor shop and waited, watching her breath vaporize in the cold air. Stefano had said that, after he retreated into the monastery, Bellina could share any information with his older brother. But would Bardo even remember who she was, after all this time? And would he be able to do something with the information that burned inside her chest?

"My mother is not here," a dark-eyed little boy said, peeking through the opening at the door.

"I'm here to see Bar . . . your father," Bellina said.

She found Bardo seated at his tailor's workbench, running a long, wine-colored thread through a small wooden contraption used for heavy silk upholstery brocades. The studio was warm, comfortable, and inviting—part workshop, part living quarters. Bardo's wife ran the business, took in embroidering on the side, and raised their three small children while Bardo went out to work in Francesco's silk workshops. The brown-eyed little boy, around seven years old, sat alongside his father at the bench. Behind them, from floor to ceiling, shelves held silks of black, violet, crimson, azure, and green.

"Bellina Sardi! Haven't seen you since my sister's marriage celebrations. What can I do for you?"

She blushed to think he called her name so quickly.

"Yes," she said. "It's . . . your brother. Before he took his vows, he told me that any kind of information . . . I might share with you," she said. "That you might know what to do with it."

Immediately, Bardo bustled from behind the workbench and grasped her elbow with a firm grip. "Come," he said in a low voice. "We may speak upstairs."

They left the young boy threading a needle, and Bellina followed Bardo into a narrow, steep, and twisted stairwell. "My wife is at the market, and my cousins are out on business matters," he said as the worn stair treads groaned under Bellina's feet.

When they emerged at the landing, Bellina took in the details of an artisan's house: the hearth filled with the soot of thousands of meals, the children's woolen capes on their hooks, the basket of a daughter's embroidery, half-done. There were no gilded boxes, no hand-painted ewers, no portraits. No servants and their intrigues, no cooks with their unreasonable demands. Only a little family knit together by blood, love, and dedication. The details disintegrated into the whole, and Bellina felt a wave of comfort and satisfaction wash over her as if she had just arrived in a room that had been waiting her whole life. It felt good. It felt like family. It felt like home.

How her life might have been different if she had ever thought that marriage to a neighbor's son might have been a possibility for her. If only, like Dolce, she had envisioned a future for herself outside the boundaries of servitude. Now, she envied her friend.

With a pang, she thought of Stefano, surely now an austere figure in his Servite robes, his hair shaved into a tonsured fringe—and she berated her own stupidity. How naïve she had been, how completely under his spell. Bellina remembered how she had gazed at him and ingested his impassioned rallying cries. How she had believed they could change the world. How inspiring it had been to listen to someone who held the power of their conviction, and what a fool's dream it seemed to think he would have made her part of it.

Now, Bellina realized how easily she might have been satisfied instead by the smallest of family comforts. By the simple things that most people took for granted—a copper pot for the family meal, mending a child's woolens by the fire, a son to learn a father's trade, a daughter who might trade stories and help with sweeping and making beds.

Bardo pulled out a chair for Bellina near the window. "Tell me," he said.

Bellina hesitated. She picked idly at a loose thread on a piece of half-finished embroidery in the basket by her chair. For a moment, the two of them regarded each other carefully. Bellina could see little of Stefano in Bardo; Bardo was solid and broad-shouldered where his brother was lean and angular. Bardo was olive-skinned with kind, dark eyes like Dolce's, in contrast to the fire behind his brother's glare, so intense it seemed to burn. Could she trust him?

Bellina never thought she would get involved with the *frateschi* again. But then, she never thought she would consider betraying her mistress either. It wasn't Lisa she wanted to betray, of course, but there was no way she could separate betraying her mistress from spying on the household. She could only hope that if Lisa's husband came under suspicion, she could keep Lisa safe.

"I followed my mistress from the Gherardini house after she married Francesco del Giocondo," she said. "I've been there ever since."

"I know," he said.

"Ah," she said. Dolce had been right. They were still paying attention.

"I, too, am employed by Francesco del Giocondo, you remember." He smiled. "In the silk workshop at Por Santa Maria."

"And your upholstery shop?"

"My wife and sons keep it running while I spend my working hours at del Giocondo's. I've been there two years. He has made me a foreman."

Bellina couldn't help it. Her jaw dropped. "You're spying!" A loud whisper.

A wide, cat grin. He wagged a finger at her. "I am doing the same as you, *cara*. Only paying close attention."

Bellina huffed in disbelief.

"But there is something you wanted to tell me," he said. "Perhaps something you've learned in the house?"

"No, it's not that," Bellina said, feeling the heat rise to her cheeks. "My first duty is to Lisa, just as I promised her father. Plus, she needs me. No, it's something her cousin told me."

"Young Gherardo? I remember him."

"Yes. I . . ." She paused. "You have seen Michelangelo Buonarroti's new sculpture?"

"The *David*. No." He shook his head. "Not with my own eyes. Seems that it has caused a reaction, though. Some among our group are saying it's more than a statue. They're saying it's a mark of the future . . . a symbol of the new city. A symbol of those of us who oppose the return of the Medici."

Bellina paused. She hadn't thought of it like that. She had not realized that a sculpture or a painting could represent something for people to hang on to, something to make them band together, something to give them hope.

Bardo continued. "Some are saying it's a colossal man made in God's image. And others are saying it's a naked pagan god made into a biblical hero. That it's blasphemous in the end. And what did you make of it, *cara*?"

Bellina paused, searching for words to describe the marble colossus in the cathedral workyard, but she failed. Instead, she took a deep breath. "It was . . . astonishing."

Bardo smiled. "And you came here to tell me about a sculpture of a nude man?"

She blushed. Was he teasing her? "It's more than that," Bellina said, rubbing her sweating palms on her apron. "I have some information about it that might be useful. I don't know."

He cocked an eyebrow. His face was earnest, honest-looking, Bellina thought. "And you trust me with it?"

"I don't know who else to tell," she said. "You're the only one I know who might get the information into the right hands. I'm not as connected as I once was. I've been staying close to home. I . . . Lisa . . . She is suffering."

For a few moments, there was only the sound of wagon wheels in the street.

"I will keep any information you give me secret until you feel comfortable with me . . . using it . . . ," he said. He settled back and waited for her to speak.

"There is a plot to destroy the sculpture," she began. "It's strange. I suppose I shouldn't care, but since it came from Lisa's cousin, it felt close to home. I'm worried that Lisa's family is a target since they have profited from the Medici rule. And as much as I am against a Medici return—you know that—all the same, I would hate for anything to happen to Lisa or the children."

For a moment, Bardo rested his chin on his fist and considered

her carefully before he spoke. "Well. Since you have shared a secret with me, then I shall share one with you," he said, leaning
forward in his chair and putting his brown eyes on her. "I can
confirm that the *palleschi* are still fighting to bring the Medici back.
You know already that most of the Medici supporters in the city
have enough resources to do whatever they want. And there are
some . . . individuals . . . speaking of taking away what they have."

"Like what?"

"Like taking property. Perhaps burning. There have already
been fires set at several *palazzi*. You have heard? No." Bardo continued. "I tell you more as a warning, out of concern for your
own safety than anything else. Francesco del Giocondo is highly
visible in this city. You probably know that he has served on the
city's highest councils. And I've also heard that Master Leonardo
is painting a portrait. You have every reason to be fearful for your
Lisa."

It was more than Bellina could take in, more than she wanted
to know. She wished she could walk out the door and forget everything Bardo had shared. And yet, she had to know. If Lisa and
her family were in danger, she had to protect them.

LEONARDO

Florence, Italy
1504

Tell him I'm not here."

I press my back against the hard, cool planks of the wooden door.

The moment I heard the long, echoing clang of the great brass door knockers ringing through the monastery, then the scurrying footsteps of the novice at the door, I knew in my heart it was Francesco del Giocondo. He's coming to pester me about that portrait again. Doesn't he have bigger things to worry about? The anti-Medici factions are gathering like the swirling winds of the Adriatic Sea.

"Master!" A few more flat-handed slaps and then Salaì's rasping whisper. "Where should I tell him you are?"

"You'll think of something."

I hear Salaì's exasperated cluck, and then his receding footsteps.

The man is expecting the piece he commissioned. I know how long it's been. I glimpse the portrait in progress, the man's wife seated against a dark background, yet to be discovered. It's far from finished. The more I look at it, the more I see what needs to be explored. Her cheeks, the tone of the flesh, it must be as if she were sitting right before the viewer. She must seem to live and breathe as if she could come to life from the panel. But she hasn't come to life yet. The layers must be added gradually, lightly. It can't be rushed.

His voice now. I hear the proud, confident voice of Francesco del Giocondo in the hallway, speaking to the monks. The voice of a man at the top of the hierarchy.

"Where is the lout hiding?" Francesco del Giocondo's voice.

"He isn't here, *signor,* I swear it, upon my mother's eyes! He's gone to . . . to a meeting about . . . the Pisan levees."

A huff of disgust. "A squandering of the Signoria's precious resources. He wastes all of our time."

"Would you like a glass of cool beer, *signor*? It is hot out there."

I raise my eyebrows. Salaì is doing a good job.

But del Giocondo ignores the boy's pleasantries. "Where is the likeness of my wife?" I imagine his eyes scanning my stacks of drawings, my paint-stained pots of brushes, the panels stacked against the wall. "I will take it with me now."

"It's not here, *signor.*"

"Where is he keeping it?" A rush of impatience. I run my hands through my hair and take a deep breath, holding back my ire.

"I . . . I'm not . . ."

But Francesco del Giocondo doesn't let Salaì finish.

"I paid a significant deposit for that picture—against my better judgment. It is never a good idea to listen to your mother on matters of financial importance."

"I understand, sir . . ." Salaì's voice is crestfallen.

"And I have nothing, *nothing,* to show for it."

Ah . . . This picture amounts to little more than a business deal, the same as any of his suppliers. Francesco del Giocondo is a wealthy merchant with friends in high places. I can hardly afford to disappoint my patrons, but I know it's too late to reverse that sad course when one pounds on the door.

Another hard rap makes the wood rattle against my back. "Leonardo di Ser Piero da Vinci! If you're hiding in there, hear me! I'll ruin you! You'll be the laughingstock of all Florence, of all Tuscany! Your family name will be laid to waste, you . . . you lazy lout." The last part comes out deflated.

Every fiber of my being wants to open the door and shout down that brute. But of course, I say nothing. I only stand as if frozen on the other side of the door.

"He'll turn over that portrait," he says to Salaì, "or I'll have my deposit back in full."

Money, I can't help but think, *the stink of a rotting fish once tasty and fruitful. It ruins everything.*

"I'll give you one week to deliver it to my house!" Giocondo yells through the door. "After that, I'm throwing your contract on the fire."

His footsteps recede at last. I hear Salaì's muttered words of supplication as he escorts Francesco del Giocondo out of the monastery visitor's corridor.

I know what comes next. A long series of negotiations. My new portrait is going to be wrenched from me if I'm not careful. But it can't be rushed, and I won't allow that. My reputation, my life, is at stake at just the crucial moment.

What Francesco del Giocondo doesn't understand is that a simple portrait of a woman will never make my name.

ANNE

Montal, France
1943

The medieval towers of Montal castle rose from the forest in a shroud of fog. The convoy descended the narrow, mountainous paths toward the old château. Anne felt her shoulders fall with relief. This castle was isolated, a rising giant in a peaceful sea of green forests. There was something rugged and assuring about the outlines of its fortified walls and narrow towers. If Chambord was a magnificent palace, Montal was a fortress. Small windows punctuated the sturdy brick walls; its towers cast looming shadows over the landscape. Even though she knew the convoy could be stopped or attacked at any moment, each time the Louvre staff arrived at one of these depots—whether Chambord, Loc-Dieu, or even Montauban—Anne felt as though she had escaped into a fairy tale where nothing bad could happen.

But not this time. Montal, this looming fortress that Monsieur Jaujard had worked so hard to secure for them, was already crawling with Nazi soldiers. Anne spied the now-familiar helmets as soon as they turned off the main road and approached the imposing walls of the castle compound. As they moved forward cautiously, they saw soldiers at the gates, German vehicles bristling with weapons standing among the manicured hedges. Anne gripped the steering wheel and exchanged a wordless glance with René. She guided the truck to a halt in the gravel courtyard.

"Stay calm," he murmured as they stopped in front of the castle. "Just act confident. Our paperwork is in order."

Our paperwork isn't quite honest, Anne thought, but her voice had left her. She didn't know how many crates in the back of their truck still held guns instead of works of art. And now that René had confided that he had been supplying resistance cells in the countryside with weapons and supplies, Anne felt every pore on the back of her neck prickle as she watched René walk toward the front door where a tall German soldier stood waiting. As Anne emerged from the driver's seat, she saw René hand over his stack of papers.

The castle was smaller than the other depots, she could see now, but André and Lucie had told her it was still big enough. Four of its huge vaulted rooms on the ground floor would be enough space to fit the sixty-five truckloads that were coming here from castles and museums around France. There was little risk of fire in this impressive structure, and there was plenty of lodging for the staff in the nearby village. The castle's owners had lent the entire château to the Musées Nationaux. It was perfect, Lucie had said. Now the sharp eyes of the German inspector standing at the door made it seem anything but perfect.

The German swept his eyes briefly over the papers. He said nothing but returned them to René and gave him a curt nod. The curator turned around, relieved, and started calling to the drivers and guards to help offload the crates. Anne hurried to help. She grabbed a large file box full of inventories from one of the trucks and followed the guards inside as they started carrying the crates into the enormous entrance hall. Her feet echoed, and the weight of the inventories in her arms made her wonder how many of them had made it safely to Paris with Christiane.

There were more German soldiers inside, watching every move Anne and the other staff made. Anne tried not to stare, but she could feel their eyes penetrating her skin like bullets as crates were unloaded from the trucks. She knew that René and the other staff were anxious to open the *Mona Lisa,* but they would open nothing in front of the soldiers. Anne's heart sank as she realized that the German authorities probably already knew about their efforts to hide the Louvre's collection. All this time they'd been trying to keep the paintings safe from these Germans. Now, with them all over the château, it felt as though they'd already failed.

Only nightfall brought relief. As the forest of Montal became a silhouette against the setting sun, a pair of German soldiers remained stationed at the castle's fortified gate. Anne watched the men lounging inside their truck, smoking cigarettes, their legs hanging out of the trucks and their guns sprawled across their laps. The rest of the German trucks rumbled off to what Anne assumed were lodgings secured in the nearby village.

At last, Anne and the others allowed themselves to slump around the enormous table in the castle's dining hall. One of the curators tended the great hearth. Soon, a crackling fire cast looming shadows in the great dining room. Anne watched Pierre, still dressed in his now-shabby Louvre guard uniform, tinker with the knobs of the wireless they had brought with them from Montauban. The sound went scratchy and screechy until the familiar French voices of the news announcers emerged from the static.

In the vast rooms throughout the castle, the crates stood in disarray, waiting for the long days ahead of reorganizing and re-cataloguing everything. Anne knew that many days of tedious work stretched ahead, as the archives staff would begin the painstaking task of piecing together the giant puzzle of where everything was located. Aside from the paintings they'd moved from Montauban, there were now dozens of crates newly arrived from other depots in the countryside. Anne was sure that Jaujard had considered Montal safe. Who could have foreseen that the Germans would arrive even before the Louvre staff?

In the dark attic, the crates holding the weapons stood quietly in the shadows. René had overseen the operation of moving these crates up the winding staircases personally. Hopefully no one would think to look there for paintings, or at least, for what the Germans thought were paintings.

Now, everyone gathered, quiet and exhausted, around the dining table. Tireless, René's mother brought some life back into the group with her cooking. It was a watery but welcome stew cobbled together from leftovers packed in the trucks, and Anne could almost feel it fortifying her as each savory mouthful slid down her throat.

Suddenly, a British voice crackled through the speakers of the wireless. Anne's English was fair, but she felt too tired to follow the BBC broadcast closely. She scraped around listlessly in her bowl, scooping up a last mouthful of the fragrant stew.

Suddenly, beside her, one of the curatorial assistants squealed. Anne jerked upright. "What—" she began.

"Did you hear that?" She grabbed Anne's arm and looked around the table. "Did you all hear that?!" she repeated.

"I can hardly believe it," René breathed.

"What?" Anne said. "What is it?"

For a wild moment, she hoped that someone was going to say that Italy and France were no longer at war, or that the deportation of French men to work in Germany had stopped. Instead, when the girl turned to Anne, her words made no sense. "Van Dyck thanks Fragonard," she said.

Anne stared at her.

"It's what we've been waiting for," René announced, his eyes sparkling. "A secret message from the British via the BBC . . . They're letting us know they've received our inventories."

The young assistant grasped Anne's hands. "It worked!" she cried. "Your inventories worked! Christiane . . . She did it! She got them to Paris, and then they made their way into the Allies' hands. They know where these paintings are now. Thank God! Just in time."

A rush of joy flooded Anne's heart, and she wrapped her in a hug. "We did it! We did it!"

"The government wouldn't help us, but we helped ourselves," René said, nodding.

Anne grinned, feeling something like fanfare in her heart. It was a little triumph, as if a small victory had been won.

ANNE WAS HEADING to bed when René stopped her in the darkened corridor.

"Anne." René glanced around nervously. For a moment, he said nothing, only studied her. "I wondered if you were still serious about wanting to help with our efforts to . . ." His eyes flitted toward the window at the end of the hallway. Below, German trucks lined up in the courtyard and soldiers milled around aimlessly. Anne thought the hours must tick by at a snail's pace; the men did little more than stroll back and forth in the courtyard.

"Yes!" she interrupted in a loud whisper.

René's mouth spread into a tight grin. "*Très bien*. I had a feeling you would say that." René began to pace. "I have a message that needs to be delivered to . . . our friends. They're in the woods nearby," he said, gesturing toward the window.

"They're here?" Anne asked, her mouth agape. "Your . . . friends?"

He nodded. "And you would be the perfect person to deliver the message: a young lady taking an afternoon walk along a wooded path after a long day's work . . ."

Anne faltered. "You want me to walk past the Germans and go into the woods. Alone."

René nodded. "They would suspect me in an instant, but I don't think they will bother you. The message will be encoded on a scrap of paper. You can simply put it in your pocket and . . . go for a stroll." He gestured toward the window again.

"What's the message?"

"Ah!" said René. "Only the thing you know best. Where these priceless works of art are located. If our people in Paris can't keep us safe from the Germans," he said, gesturing toward the guards at the entrance of the château, "then we must protect these works—and our own lives."

Anne stared at him, nervousness churning in her gut. "I'll do it."

"Perfect!" he said. "I don't mean to give you the idea that this little errand is without risk."

"I know," Anne said, gesturing to the crates. "None of this has been without risk, not since leaving Paris. Please—just tell me what to do."

LEONARDO

Florence, Italy
1504

A portrait of a lady. No chance it will make me famous.

The lady. I've pushed her off again for as long as I can. Instead, I pin my hopes on the fresco for Gonfaloniere Soderini and his Signoria. Surely, I have a better chance at leaving a legacy with such a prominent commission in the halls of Florentine government. And besides, the citizens of Florence already want to see it. On the pavement outside Santa Maria Novella, a crowd has gathered. Beyond the monastery walls, I hear their voices, their laughter and calls to one another. How often I have been guilty of the sin of pride, yet it seems the only path to the next commission.

The Sala del Papa has become our workshop and our staging area. One side of the room is filled with our stacks of paper requisitioned by the Signoria, our pencils and pens, our supplies for making rabbit-skin glue. Several of the boys are still high on the scaffold, attaching the pages of the cartoon together to create a surface as large as the wall. It's fragile, but it won't have to last long. They have made good use of the unique scaffold I've designed, made to collapse and rise like the bellows of an accordion.

When we finally move to the Palazzo Vecchio, this complicated drawing will serve as a kind of map fixed to one wall as a reference. They will easily transport the scaffolding across town. Once we set up in the Palazzo Vecchio, my apprentices will be ready to prepare the wall for fresco. I'm eager to experiment with an old technique that modern artists seem to have forgotten, mixing pigment and wax. Encaustic paint uses beeswax as a binder, a technique originated by the ancient Greeks.

Our Signoria has asked for a scene from the battle of Anghiari on one wall of the Palazzo Vecchio in the Sala del Gran Consiglio. It's to feature a tumble of men and horses locked together in a fierce battle, a tangle of forces of energy pushing against one another in a sheer demonstration of might and will. For me, it represents so much about what's going on in the world around me. Empires clash, man and beast collide.

Outside the door, I hear the rising voices of the crowd, like a tide that threatens to turn over and spill into the room.

"I don't know how much longer we can keep them waiting, Master," Il Fanfoia calls.

I climb down from the scaffold and dust the chalk from my hands. I take my favorite lilac-colored silk cape from a nearby table and sweep it around my shoulders.

"Then let them in."

"I SUPPOSE BY NOW you have heard about the other wall."

Niccolò Machiavelli raises his eyebrows to assess my reaction, then turns again to look closely at my cartoon. Hands laced behind his back, he leans forward to examine a small detail of a warrior's helmet, the swish of a warhorse's tail. I watch Machiavelli's lean silhouette as he paces back and forth. He is skilled at this . . . this asking of important questions and then waiting in silence.

"What other wall?"

"Hmm." He presses his lips together in concern. "So they haven't told you. I was afraid of that."

Behind me, Salaì oversees the laborious process of mixing the rabbit-skin glue and adhering the individual papers together. Slowly, the design for Soderini's fresco in the Palazzo Vecchio is taking shape as a series of pages as tall and as wide as the wall.

"Tell me what?"

Machiavelli turns to face me now. "Soderini has engaged Michelangelo Buonarroti to . . . to make a fresco on the wall facing yours in the great hall of the Palazzo Vecchio."

For a moment, it feels as though my very heartbeat stops. "I . . . Buonarroti? But he is a sculptor, not a . . ."

Machiavelli shrugs. "You have seen the colossus in progress. Apparently, Buonarroti can do anything he wants."

I swat the air with my hand. "I don't care. Let him come."

Machiavelli nods, judging my reaction again; he is good at this. "The Signoria has given him a suite of rooms across the river at Sant'Onofrio. Not exactly on the order of your accommodations here," he says, waving a hand at the large room and my dozen laboring pupils. "The difference is that Buonarroti has locked himself away. He will hardly allow even his assistants in to see what's behind the doors."

I have no choice. Soderini did not consult me before he made his decision. I cannot cancel my commission. I would if I could. Instead, I will create a wall to surpass my *Last Supper* of Milan. I will stake my future on painting.

It is all I can do.

It was decided the moment I learned I was the only child to whom my father left nothing. Nothing. The moment my half-siblings left me sitting alone at my father's table, left with my own thoughts and his servant woman silently tidying the crumbs and peels. His disapproval complete.

A portrait won't get me there.

No, a big, public commission. A painting worthy of our time, of our city. Of myself. A painting to end all ages.

My father was wrong about me. Soderini was wrong, too. They all are.

My destiny lies beyond painted ladies, beyond the walls of the Signoria, and beyond the noose of this city.

Now is my chance.

They will see.

To Master Leonardo da Vinci at Santa Maria Novella in Florence

Whereas a deposit has been made by Francesco del Giocondo of the Arte della Seta to Leonardo da Vinci in exchange for a painted portrait of his wife Lisa;

And whereas no portrait has yet been delivered;

Now, wherefore, Master Leonardo is demanded to return to the portrait within the next thirty days; otherwise, the deposit must be returned.

Witnessed on this day by Gaetano Soldini
Notary on behalf of Francesco del Giocondo

BELLINA

Florence, Italy
1504

Bellina watched Master Leonardo lick his thumb.

It was not what she expected, this thumb-licking. In fact, everything Master Leonardo did surprised her. Bellina had never given much thought to what went into painting someone's likeness. Now, she realized, the seemingly dull act of putting paint on a wooden panel was the most fascinating thing in the world.

While Lisa stared out the window and turned flushed in the suffocating heat, Bellina was only entranced with the image of Lisa. The image seemed to imitate Lisa as she was in life, a woman of true flesh and blood. Bellina could almost believe the woman in the picture might breathe or speak.

Although she had not felt inspired to sit for Master Leonardo, Lisa was growing more comfortable being immortalized in paint. Perhaps it was simply the fact that she seemed to enjoy her conversations with the painter. As she watched the painting take shape, Bellina saw exactly why Leonardo was regarded so highly. His images moved her soul in the same way as the statue of the *David*. How could something so beautiful be sinful? And how could anyone want to destroy it?

She had heard nothing from Bardo or Dolce since she had

shared her secret about the *David*. Had she done the right thing, sharing what she had heard of the plot to destroy the sculpture, a plot that perhaps was connected to a larger series of events to usher the Medici back into Florence? Only time would tell.

Bellina was so lost in this swirl of complicated thoughts that when Lisa spoke, it took her a moment to register it.

"Do you think today will be our last time together?" she asked, as she sat on the armchair that had become her regular perch.

"For a while," Leonardo replied, as he settled down and dipped his paintbrushes in the jar of water that had been provided. "At least until this layer of paint dries. Besides, I have my work for the Signoria. When I return, the picture will be ready for the next step."

Bellina stepped closer to Master Leonardo's back to look at the portrait. "He has done you justice, *polpetta*."

"Thank you," Lisa said, standing. "Please excuse me, Master Leonardo. Bellina will show you out."

For a few silent moments, Bellina watched Leonardo da Vinci pack up his brushes into a wooden case.

"Master," she began, but she struggled to find the words.

"What is it?" he said.

"Surely you won't leave the painting here?"

He looked at her. "And why not? I'm sure the lady's husband will like to see it. He must see that I have made good progress according to our . . . agreement."

Bellina reached for a response. She did not want any harm to come to Lisa or Lisa's image. "But . . . you're just leaving it here. Out in the open?"

"It must sit out for a while," he said. "The oil pigments take some time to dry. Anyway, I imagine a man like Francesco del

Giocondo might like to see it, and to show it to his friends. They usually do."

"But . . . ," she tried again. "What if something happens to it?"

"What could happen to it, Bellina? You are not threatening to do anything to my lovely picture, are you?" he teased.

"Of course not," she said. "I just . . . wanted to make sure it was safe."

"Well, perhaps you can make it your concern to keep the children and the cats away from it while it dries."

She felt like she had no other choice but to nod and avert her eyes.

"I will show myself out. Thank you." He left Bellina alone with the painting.

The room fell silent. Bellina stepped forward and looked at the portrait in progress. With a few strokes of a brush and a wet thumb, Master da Vinci seemed to have breathed life into Lisa's face. It was so beautiful. And more than that. The portrait was a symbol of their wealth, of the family's status. And now, she had gone to Bardo. With whom would he share her secrets? Bellina now regretted that she'd drawn attention to the household. Perhaps she had even put the picture in danger.

Bellina jogged down the stairwell and pushed open the door. Master Leonardo was strolling down the center of the street, swinging his wooden box, a splash of color in the dingy street. She caught the artist's billowing silk sleeve. He stepped back in surprise.

"Please, Master Leonardo," she whispered. "Please take the picture with you. It is so beautiful. I don't want anything bad to happen to it."

"Is there something I should know?" The painter stopped and scrutinized Bellina's face.

"Nothing," she said, trying not to sound desperate. "Won't you take it back to your workshop?"

Bellina thought she saw Master Leonardo hesitate. "If you want to know the truth, I am waiting for the balance of Signor Francesco's contract, which has not been paid. I expect that a nearly finished portrait of his wife might inspire him to pay it."

"Oh," said Bellina. She had not considered the financial side of this commission. She took a step back.

He continued. "I appreciate your concern. However, I am certain that in such a grand household, there are many more valuable things between those walls. My half-finished portrait should be the least of your worries, I assure you. Now, I bid you a good day, my dear." With that, he turned and walked away.

Bellina felt her breath catch in her throat as he walked away. She could not help but feel as if she had lost an opportunity she would never get back. She plodded back to the door of the house. She would have to do her best to keep the portrait out of sight; she only wanted to protect her mistress's family. Bellina climbed the stairs back into the *salone*. She stood before the portrait again, taking one last look at Lisa's rare smile, which the painter had captured so perfectly.

Bellina could never forgive herself if something bad happened to the picture. Careful not to touch the wet paint, Bellina lifted the panel from the easel. Step by step, she climbed the back staircase toward the servants' quarters. What possible excuse could she use if someone caught her tiptoeing up the stairs with Master Leonardo's portrait? Her heart pounded in her chest with each step up the wooden treads.

In her tiny bedchamber, Bellina slid the panel under her bed, careful not to let anything touch the wet surface.

When she returned to the room where Master Leonardo had been painting, she found Lisa standing before the empty easel.

"Where is the portrait?" She turned to Bellina.

Bellina clasped her hands behind her back. "Master Leonardo took it with him."

BELLINA TOUCHED the surface of Lisa's portrait carefully with the tip of her smallest finger to make sure it was dry.

Then she covered the picture in a faded, green velvet cape, once the proud possession of one of Francesco's ancestors, now discarded on a hook in the servants' hallway. She slid the velvet-covered portrait into the far reaches of the worn cabinet in her bedchamber. Then she hurried out to join Lisa and her family.

In the street, Lisa and Francesco, their children, and the other servants had gathered to walk together to see Michelangelo Buonarroti's colossus move from the cathedral workyard to the Palazzo Vecchio. The moon hung low in the sky, a great, white ball that bathed the nearby church of San Lorenzo and its chapel housing the Medici tombs in silvery light.

"Where is Gherardo?" Bellina tucked herself in beside Lisa.

She shrugged. "Who could keep track of that boy?"

The family pushed its way into the boisterous crowd snaking toward the cathedral of Santa Maria del Fiore. Bellina and Lisa skirted the edges of the street, making their way around the clusters of merchants, guildsmen, women and children, shopkeepers. Francesco walked ahead of them, his mother's hand in the crook of his arm. They turned a corner and the tiled dome came into view. The chants and shouts grew louder. Everyone in Florence, it seemed, had gathered to witness the latest public spectacle: the emergence of a marble giant into their streets.

"I heard the cathedral committee decided to open the doors of the workyard in the middle of the night to avoid a riot," Lisa said.

"It seems they have failed," Bellina said.

"You're right." Lisa nodded. Instead, the midnight spectacle had drawn a frenzied mob. Bellina felt a chill run down her spine. The last time she witnessed such a feverish crowd was when, only a few short years and a lifetime ago, she had watched Girolamo Savonarola hang and burn in the Piazza della Signoria. The image was forever seared into Bellina's mind.

And now, Michelangelo Buonarroti's new colossus might stand in the same spot. Would it be a symbol of the new Florence, like Bardo had said, a marker of all the madness put behind them? Would a block of marble have the power to shift the Florentines' minds again, to take them from an old order into the new? Would it also be the same place where the sculpture would crumble before the crowds, ushering the Medici back to power? What had Bardo done with the information Bellina had shared? Bellina's eyes scanned the streets for Gherardo.

Bellina and Lisa moved with the swirl of the crowd toward the back of the cathedral, where the church's workyard lay in the shadows. While the chapels and apse of Santa Maria del Fiore were inlaid with marble slabs in pink and green pastel shades, the façade remained little more than an ugly wall of dingy stone. Bellina wondered if she would live long enough to see the façade finished. Perhaps one day, it would be beautiful to behold.

Suddenly, Bellina felt the energy of the surging crowd around them. She scanned the faces around her. Was it as Bardo had said, that right now, there were Medici partisans and their Roman supporters waiting just beyond the city gates to usher in a new era of their reign, one the Medici family saw as their birthright?

Bellina heard the rattle of iron gates, and the chants and cheers of the crowd grew louder. She and Lisa locked arms as they inched their way alongside one of the hulking stonemasons guarding the iron doors. Through the bars, Bellina spied the large wooden enclosure that Michelangelo Buonarroti had constructed around the block of marble. It was a strange sight, this rough-hewn wooden box with a levered roof open to allow light from above, constructed to ward off curious onlookers. It seemed strange that the sculptor might try to keep people out, Bellina thought, when Master Leonardo let throngs of people freely see even a sketch.

Suddenly, a group of workmen appeared alongside the wooden box. The street clamor settled. Then, from the shadows, the artist himself appeared. Even in the darkness, Bellina recognized a man who could only be Michelangelo Buonarroti, the man known for his dingy gown coated in marble dust, his greasy hair, and his stature, small and stooped, yet disarmingly intimidating for a man who had not yet reached his thirtieth birthday.

Bellina watched the sculptor draw a skeleton key from the pouch of his gown and unlock the iron padlock that secured the door of the wooden enclosure. The stonemasons gathered with their sledgehammers. It only took a few moments. The wooden barriers of the box fell to the ground. In the moonlight, clouds of dust and marble rose into the air. Bellina heard the gasps of the people at the workyard gates, but she could see nothing but dust and shadows.

Lisa lost her grip on Bellina's sleeve then, and Bellina found herself caught up in the vortex of the pushing, swirling, surging crowd.

INTO THE NIGHT, workers inched the sculpture forward from the cathedral workyard. Amidst the chaos, stonemasons broke down a lintel and part of a wall to let the sculpture pass. Bellina had given up trying to rejoin Lisa or Francesco now. She positioned herself in the deep doorway of a linen vendor and watched a group of laborers slathering grease on some two dozen smoothly hewn logs, which rolled slowly together as the Signoria's guards pushed back the crowds. The sculpture was suspended inside an elaborate wooden contraption that looked as if it had leapt from the pages of the sketchbooks Master Leonardo had brought with him to Lisa's house. Inside the rough timbers, the colossus was suspended by pulleys and ropes that creaked and grated as they stretched under the heft of the marble. The moving of this marble colossus would progress slowly down the street of the shoemakers, Bellina realized. Perhaps it would even be days before it arrived in the Piazza della Signoria. Vendors hungry to take advantage of the pressing crowds never before seen on this street opened their shuttered doors and streetside counters in the predawn hours. One smart craftsman created tiny slings for children to pick up rocks and try their own hand at slaying a giant.

As dawn broke, sunbeams suddenly streaked over the tile roofs and the crowd parted. Divine light illuminated the white marble sculpture and for a moment, the chaos seemed to fall away. Now, in the dawn light, Bellina caught sight of Michelangelo Buonarroti walking alongside the wooden contraption. The sculptor's dark eyes darted through the crowd. With every tiny forward movement of the colossus, Michelangelo took a step toward the pushing crowds, toward the cheering, toward mayhem. His piercing gaze scanned the high windows of the buildings bordering the square.

Suddenly, Bellina felt a rain of dirt and dust across the back of her neck. She heard several small stones pelt the dust, scattering dirt and pebbles in the street like spilled grain. The crowd surged sideways, nearly knocking her to the ground. A woman beside her let out a bloodcurdling scream and a sizable rock hit the dirt. Bellina turned around just in time to see a cluster of youths slinking along the wall of a building bordering the square. One youth was clapping dust from his hands. Another young man was reaching down into the cracks of the cobbles, dislodging a decent-size stone.

Bellina's breath caught in her throat. Gherardo.

Part 7

A CONVOY

ANNE

Montal, France
1943

The job was simple enough. Walk into the woods, hand off the note according to René's instructions, and then return to the castle.

Anne patted her skirt pocket to make sure the slip of paper was still there. She pushed back a swath of lace curtain to watch the German guards pacing idly in the castle courtyard, staring at their boots as they kicked up gravel dust. Then she went down the staircase and set off through a crumbling, centuries-old servants' entrance to the castle kitchens. The morning frost had given way to a calm, peaceful afternoon without the slightest rustle of the bare branches. Trying her best to appear inconspicuous, she imagined that taking a walk through the splendid Dordogne countryside seemed like the most natural thing to do. She glanced back at the guards in the castle courtyard, and then walked more quickly toward the tree line.

She felt the first blush of spring sunshine as she strolled along the gravel footpath. Entering a narrow lane, Anne pushed aside the stretching boughs with their faint buds of green poking their shy heads through the rough bark. Just as she began to entertain the illusion that this part of the countryside might be untouched by war, she heard the familiar rumble of a gazogene engine. She froze as a German truck appeared around a curve in the road, loaded with hunkered-down soldiers. For a moment, she stared at them, caught in fear. But she had to act as though she had nothing to fear, and besides, they didn't turn their heads. She walked on, the piece of paper weighing in her pocket, heavy as a bomb.

At a gnarled old oak tree along a bend that René had described to her, Anne turned off the lane. The leaf litter crunched under Anne's feet as she made her way along a winding path among the trees. She ducked through a thicket, and suddenly the barrel of a rifle was pointing at her face and a sharp, French voice called out: "Stop! I'll shoot!"

Anne froze, her heart pounding. She held up her hands and had to try twice to get the words out of her dry mouth, her scattered brain struggling to remember what René had said. "The *Victory of Samothrace* is taking a stroll," she said, her voice shaking.

The barrel lowered, and a young woman stepped forward. A mass of unkempt wavy hair appeared from beneath her felted beret and her face was smudged, but her eyes were cast-iron.

Anne's voice wavered. "René Huyghe said you would be expecting me."

"Shhh! Don't say his name." She grasped Anne's arm with a small, firm hand. "Come with me." The young woman pulled Anne through the thicket, moving quickly and stealthily over roots and rocks. Anne stumbled along behind her.

All at once, the woman pushed back a branch and they emerged into a small campsite. The ashes of small fires smoldered among a circle of ragged tents. Men and women watched warily as Anne and the young woman appeared from the brush. Some were lying in their tents or hanging laundry on a line, while others were talking together in low voices as they cleaned rifles, played cards, or sipped from tin mugs. Among the soft scents of the forest, it was a surprise to smell tobacco, the campfire, and gun oil.

Anne's mind raced. "What is this place?" she whispered.

The woman ignored her. "She's here!"

Anne watched a tent flap open, and a slender, bearded young man appeared. He was as haggard as the rest, his knee-length woolen pants stiff with dirt, his hair long and greasy beneath his black beret. The girl who had pointed the gun at Anne's head heaved herself onto a stump by a circle of ashes.

"You have a message for us," the young man said.

"I . . . ," Anne said. "I work as an archivist's assistant at the Louvre; we've been carting around paintings for months now. We've been on the move since the Germans came . . ."

"I know," he said, brushing a lock of hair from his face.

"You do?" She felt her hand brush the folded letter in her skirt pocket.

He nodded. "Your boss has been getting messages to the *maquis* for months."

Anne was stunned. René had been involved with resistance cells—for months? "What's a *maquis*?"

He grinned, an expression that made dimples appear in his cheeks, in contrast to his intimidating demeanor. "You really are fresh, aren't you?" He swept his arm to take in the campsite. "The *maquis* is us. Well, you could say we are *maquisards*."

"Scrub brush . . . people?" Anne said slowly.

He nodded and gestured to the others lounging around the campsite. "As you can see." Anne noticed now that, whether women or men, these so-called *maquisards* were wearing a uniform of sorts, trousers buttoned below the knee, long socks, a woolen field jacket, and a beret.

"You're all here to . . . fight?"

"We are all here for different reasons," he said. "Most of us men are here to avoid the obligatory German service, but there are women, too. There are also some Jews among us, just trying to survive until we can defeat the Krauts. There are *maquis* cells all across southern France . . ." He stopped, as if worried he had shared too much already. "I'll take that note from you now. I'll make sure it gets into the right hands. You'd better get back before anyone gets suspicious."

Anne reached into her pocket and handed over René's folded piece of paper, with its encoded message, and then he led her back to the path leading toward the castle.

"See you next time, *mademoiselle*?" he said, his strange, amber-colored eyes surveying her carefully.

Anne pushed back a branch and began to walk away, but she turned around. "Wait! I don't even know your . . . name."

But the trees had already swallowed him, and Anne was left standing alone on the footpath.

THE TASK WAS FAMILIAR, but this time, it felt sinister. Anne leaned over a crate like she'd done a thousand times over the past three years, propping her ledger open on the edge of the wood as she counted, then wrote the names of weapons she was just beginning to learn.

For weeks now, René had entrusted Anne with documenting the arrival of weapons from his sources—still unknown. With

René's apparent connections to the Resistance, at some point Anne expected the weapons would also leave the castle, perhaps going to *maquis* groups in the woods like the one she'd encountered.

Instead, crates piled up in the château's attic. Little by little, Anne had come to learn the strange names of the weapons. Just as the vocabulary of art history had once seemed like learning a foreign language, Anne was beginning to recognize the familiar forms of rifles, handguns, grenades, and ammunition.

Still, Anne felt relieved to be doing something, *anything,* to resist the Germans, but there was a brutal juxtaposition between cataloging artworks and taking inventories of weapons. The art felt important, precious. The weapons were cold, savage, and Anne hated them, but she knew they were necessary. They would have to be used if they were to stand a chance against the Germans. Over time, more contraband filled the crates—armbands stuffed with French francs rolled into tiny packets, leaflets describing the locations of bridges, roads, and German checkpoints.

"Anne!" Lucie's insistent whisper came from the stairwell. Lucie and her family had joined them at Montal, and after some consternation, Lucie had reluctantly agreed to René's request to let Anne slip away from her work on the Louvre inventories in order to help prepare and track the crates tagged for resistance cells. Anne walked to the narrow attic doorway and looked down the steep stairwell to see Lucie peering up at her.

"They're reopening the crate with the *Mona Lisa* to check for parasites," she said. "I thought you might want to come have a look?"

It was a relief to leave the stuffy attic, down a winding staircase and through a network of narrow hallways, and finally into the bedroom where the *Mona Lisa* was being kept, safely tucked away among Lucie's things. René, André, and several curators and guards gathered around the now-familiar crate sitting on the bed.

The *Mona Lisa*'s crate was easily opened; here in the dry conditions of Montal, she was safe. Anne watched Lucie gently lift the velvet wrapping away from it, revealing the timeless, ambiguous smile.

"The other works we opened at the Musée Ingres were incredible, but there's still nothing that can match the *Mona Lisa* for me," René said. "Hard to believe how many times she's been in harm's way."

"WHERE'S YOUR FAMILY?"

The young man—Ravel was what they called him in the camp, Anne learned—stretched back in a makeshift hammock strung between two trees, one hand behind his head. With the other, he held the stub of a cigarette and watched Anne with those arresting eyes that seemed to burn with an internal fire. Another message delivered, Anne had lingered in the campsite. She was fascinated by these scrappy *maquisards* living in the woods. The first time she'd encountered them, she had been so rattled that it was only later that she thought of a thousand things she wanted to ask them. She heaved herself down on a large rock and stared at the embers of a smoldering fire inside a ring of stones that the *maquisards* had cobbled together to cook their camp meals.

She shrugged. "It's just my mother and my younger brother, Marcel. I haven't had any word from them since I left Paris. Nearly four years ago now."

"That's awful," he said. "So, you came here as an intelligence specialist?"

"Who, me? No," Anne laughed. Why had she come here? It was a fair question. She inhaled the damp, earthy smell of the campsite and folded a blade of grass between her fingers. In her mind, she made a list of all the reasons she had said yes to Lucie's request to travel with the Louvre's collection: to escape the pain of losing Emile, to leave the city behind for the first time in her life, to embark on an adventure. To turn her back on the resentment she felt for bearing the burdens of her family. To save the works of art she had come to treasure. To find a purpose bigger than herself.

"I'm just a typist," she said. "But . . . I wanted to help René as soon as I found out about this," Anne said, waving her hand toward the tents. "I wanted to make a difference somehow . . . to find a way to set us all free."

Ravel nodded and took another puff of his cigarette. For a few long moments, they sat in silence, only with the rustling of the dry leaves above. Then he leaned forward and set his fiery gaze on her. He lowered his voice. "They talk about you in the campsite, you know," he said, a foxlike, dimpled grin appearing on his face as he gestured toward the circle of tents. "A lady driving priceless works of art from the Louvre—in a truck—all over France."

Anne felt heat rise to her cheeks. "I'm not the only one."

"Is it true you helped to transport the *Mona Lisa*?" he asked. "That it's here at Montal?"

Anne struggled to push down the strange mixture of attraction and unease under his intense gaze. "Now why would I tell *you*?" She smiled.

"Fair enough." He tapped a new cigarette on the heel of his hand and lit it with a match.

"I can tell you it's been a long, hard road from Paris with our hoard," she said. "But compiling inventories seems pretty boring compared to the wild and adventurous life of the *maquisards*. How did you get involved with . . . with this?"

The young man spat out a laugh and surveyed the ragged group of resistance fighters now lounging in their tents. Anne glanced around at the people she had begun to recognize. Guy-with-Gap-in-Teeth. Pale-Girl. Gray-Haired-Smoking-Man. Boy-Trying-to-Look-Like-a-Man. "We all have our reasons for living in the woods, I guess. It's not as romantic as it seems. The last thing I wanted to do was board a train to work in some godforsaken German factory. So I left Amiens. Just walked out of town without saying goodbye to anyone. The next day, the Germans came."

Anne shuddered to think of it. "You're the leader of this group?"

"Yes." Then he laughed and shook his head. "I'm joking. Actually, we're pretty disorganized, but around here, several cells have been gathered under one leader. Each camp has a commander, and then there's the commander of our whole area—a *commandant*. Code name *Chopin*. We've never seen him."

Anne looked at him sideways. "And I suppose *Ravel* isn't your real name either, is it? You don't strike me as a nineteenth-century composer."

It was his turn to blush. He paused, pushing his flaxen hair from his face. Then he met Anne's gaze. "Étienne. That's my real name."

"So, Étienne . . . What do you do, apart from taking delivery of weapons from innocent-looking museum officials?" Anne asked.

He regarded her carefully for a few moments over the wisps of curling smoke. Anne noticed his fingernails were dirty, his brow lined. Although he looked as if he hadn't bathed in months, there was something magnetic about him, Anne thought.

"Mainly we've tried to develop our networks with the other groups," he said. "We share weapons and explosives, yes. But also food, money, leaflets of information so we can recruit others to our cause. Some other groups are doing bigger things, like exploding bridges and roads so the German trucks can't pass. And we've worked to get information to the Allies—like what you're doing."

"You think it's working?" she asked.

He shrugged. "Some days it seems like an impossible task. But you tell me . . . You're working for something bigger, too. And if you save one life—or even one work of art—from destruction, then would it have been worth it, in the end?"

IT WAS ALREADY DARK when Anne ducked behind a hedgerow, beyond view of the German soldiers in the courtyard. She crept into the castle's back kitchen door.

Anne pushed open the door to the makeshift dining hall to find the Louvre staff huddled around the wireless. English voices crackled across the airwaves and this time, she strained to understand: a British announcer's voice; something about Hitler visiting Mussolini. With a pang, Anne wondered where Corrado was now.

Lucie looked up, relief filling her features. "Oh! There you are," she whispered. "You disappeared."

"Sorry I'm late." Anne slid into her usual spot alongside Frédérique.

"You had a pleasant walk?" René studied her carefully.

"Perfect," she replied, meeting his eyes long enough for him to understand. Then she dug into the simple, hearty potato soup, warm and fragrant, that René's mother set before her. It was savory and satisfying in a way that Kiki's cooking never had been. She felt a pang of longing as she thought of Kiki. Her mother had never really cooked for her and Marcel; they'd lived on bread and jam most of the time until Anne had started to teach herself how to make meals. René's mother's cooking made her nostalgic not for what she'd once had but for what she'd always lacked. Still, she missed her mother and wondered what had become of her.

As the radio voices continued, Anne listened more closely. It had become a habit for them all to listen to the entire BBC broadcast, whether or not any of them could understand English; they were all desperate to hear code words to indicate that the Allies had received their inventories.

She struggled to focus on the English voices. "Bolivia has declared war on Germany, Japan, and Italy," the broadcaster read. "The Allies hope that this will improve access to Bolivian tin mines for supplies." He read the weather, and Anne listened, silence falling over the table. Finally, the sentence they'd all been waiting for came through the tinny wireless.

"*Mona Lisa* is smiling," the voice said.

At once, there was a roar around the table. "Thank God!" someone exclaimed.

"It's working!" Lucie said, grasping Anne's hands. She grinned. "I can't believe it's working. The English and Americans are getting our messages!"

"Mark my words," René said, standing suddenly, his eyes now shining with pride. "You mark my words—this is only the beginning."

LEONARDO

Florence, Italy
1504

This is only the beginning. That's what Salai said, and I fear
he must be right.

In the Piazza della Signoria, the air is stifling. I feel a drip of
sweat trickle to the small of my back as I tuck myself into the
doorway of a fruit seller. A deafening, rhythmic drumbeat accompanies the cheers and chants of the crowd.

It has taken four days since leaving the cathedral workyard for
that blasted colossus to arrive in the square. Around the clock,
some three dozen vigorous men worked in rotation, rolling the
logs joined beneath the wooden contraption, reapplying grease,
and then transferring them as the sculpture makes its way toward
the piazza. Around the base of the contraption, Soderini's militiamen pressed people back from the rolling logs to make room for
the *David* to inch forward.

There is more litter in the streets than I have ever seen. Above
our heads, men, women, and children lean over their windowsills
to watch the colossus make its slow progress toward the Piazza
della Signoria. They cheer, clap, and whistle wildly as the statue
creeps slowly past. Some residents collect coins in exchange for
the chance to climb the stairs into the upper floors and rooftops

of their homes for a better view. A tavern owner lures passersby with quail roasting on an outdoor spit. Nervous whispers ripple through the crowd as the bound colossus teeters, causing the wood and ropes to squeak and stretch. The crowd is so thick that I barely see the sculpture at all, can only hear the strange, creaking wooden crane that delivers it to the square at last.

Now, I see Soderini has assembled scores of his new militiamen under dozens of tottering flagpoles. The men are finely dressed in their bright uniforms, in a dramatic public display of military strength and public pride.

As the days have passed, I have found myself wracked with uncertainty as I watch the crowds rally around this sculpture, at all hours of daylight and darkness, chanting and singing. As it's made its slow progress toward its new pedestal before the city hall, it's become clear that the people see the sculpture as a kind of new hero. Some say that Michelangelo has outdone even God in creating a perfect man. Rubbish.

Still, for the last four days, I have eaten little and have found it nearly impossible to sleep. Beyond my cloistered suite of rooms at Santa Maria Novella, I hear nothing but the cheers, the rallying cries, the impromptu explosions of homemade fireworks that light up the night sky. Even the monks' cloister at Santa Maria Novella cannot shut out the sounds. I am compelled by a force beyond myself, as if lured by the statue itself with its constant squeaking and twisting of the ropes, strained by the heft of the marble.

Suddenly, the drumbeats stop. The noon bell. The clanging metal reverberates through the still air.

I see that laborers have already dismantled the bronze statue of Judith beheading Holofernes, which has stood at the entrance to the Palazzo Vecchio for as long as I can remember. They have constructed a new pedestal for the colossus. As the complicated wooden contraption lifts the great *David* to its ultimate place on the pedestal, the midday sun warms the square and illuminates the white marble against the rough stones of the old palace with its tall, narrow watchtower.

The *David* stands still but is not at rest. The young boy-king is nude in all his glory; I am left stunned. It's the first time I have ever seen a sculpture like this: a larger-than-life nude. The boy's weight is shifted to his right leg in a relaxed stance, yet this idealized youth seems to boil beneath the skin. His muscles flex. In the dawn glow, the sculpture seems alive, with blood rushing through his sculpted veins, which crackle the surface of his transparent skin. I stand in the middle of the street, frozen.

I don't want to admit it, but . . . I note the moment that Michelangelo has chosen, just before the Old Testament's unlikely hero prepares to strike the fatal blow to the giant by launching a stone from his slingshot. David cradles the stone in his right hand. With his left, he grasps the strap of the sling, which trails over his shoulder and down his muscled back. It is the tensest moment of the battle, just before the boy loads his rock into the sling. Goliath is physically absent from the scene yet powerfully present at the same time. Michelangelo has captured this formidable opponent only through the hero's fiery gaze and furrowed brow. He's captured the intensity of the boy's struggle to corral his strength in the face of a fearsome enemy. He has somehow reconciled the contradictory idea of "human" and "divine" in a single figure.

Of course. Anyone might grasp that, for Florence, the sculpture is a symbol of an underdog confronting stronger opponents—

Siena, Milan, Rome, France. It sums up all the courage and as-
piration of our people. By changing locations from a cathedral
buttress to a civic square, the *David* has turned from a religious
allegory into a political and patriotic statement for defiant, independent citizens in a struggle for their own sovereignty.

The biblical boy-hero sets his intense gaze beyond Florence,
toward her rivals, Pisa and Rome. He is the great underdog of
the Bible, a scrappy youth audacious enough to face a formidable
enemy. A boy brave enough to face a giant, to pick up a rock, set
it in its sling, and let it go. A symbol of the new Florence.

I cannot say anything good about it. And yet . . . Michelangelo
Buonarroti has created both an Adam and a Hercules, a man
made in God's image, God made flesh. The giant sculpture is an
achievement of never-before-seen proportions, and already, I can
see that this sculpture is indeed a new hero for the city.

It is his city. And I am just an old man. Past my prime. In the
pit of my bowels, I know it is time to move on. No painting in a
building, and no portrait of a lady could ever rival it.

ANNE

Montal, France
1943

One night on the wireless, Anne heard the BBC announcer.

"The *Victory of Samothrace* is riding a bicycle," the voice said.

"I have to go," Anne said. In the back kitchen hallway, she picked up a dark rucksack and headed out the door into the twilight.

For weeks, Anne had studied the comings and goings of the German soldiers outside the castle. It had become like a job to know their routine; she watched how they changed guards as the sun rose, the men extending their arms in salute as the night guard prepared to leave and a new one took his place at the door. She had found a rusty bicycle discarded in a toolshed, and she located a path out of the castle grounds with high grass that helped shield her from the guards' view.

Anne pedaled harder as her worn bicycle tires shuddered into the muddy ruts of the wooded path. This time, aside from her satchel filled with armbands and leaflets, the bicycle's worn leather saddlebags were filled with ammunition. The old bicycle creaked and heaved under the weight as she made for the tree line. The sooner she disappeared into the woods, the better.

Anne had grown to look forward to her clandestine trips into the woods, into the circle of tents. Their number had grown considerably since her first visit there in the summer, and she could see the signs of greater organization among the *maquisards*. Each time Anne emptied the contents of her rucksack, more of them came over to talk with her as they unloaded cash armbands, boxes of ammunition, leaflets calling for a united French Resistance to throw off German shackles, padded boxes of deadly grenades. For a moment, Anne wondered at how things had turned out. Just a few years ago, she had spent her days as a lonely typist in the Louvre archives, and her afternoons strolling its vast galleries. Now, all those masterpieces were hidden away, and here she was, pedaling a rickety bicycle into the woods to save them. She was part of something bigger than herself, something important, a great network of people who, like her, believed that art mattered. And they depended on her. She had become the *Victory of Samothrace* riding a bicycle. She smiled.

The sun spilled through a filter of gilded leaves: bright gold, deep bronze, blazing red. Anne listened to them crunching under the wheels of her bicycle as she steered it along the lane, bouncing through holes filled with the first rain of the coming winter. She had to resist the temptation to close her eyes. Instead, she sat back on the saddle, letting the breeze of her movement comb through her hair, and took a deep breath of the sweet forest air. It felt good to get out of the château—and out from under the watch of the soldiers who loitered around the front entrance. Now she was cycling quietly through the woods, the weight of her rucksack hanging on her shoulders. Before long, the silhouette of the familiar gnarled old oak was before her, and she turned the bicycle onto the footpath. She followed its twists and turns to the *maquis* camp.

These days, pointed guns no longer greeted her. Instead, the grubby resistance fighters gathered anxiously around her as she reached the outskirts of the camp. She found Étienne sitting on a low stool behind a tent flap, a circle of others around him. When he saw Anne lean the bicycle against a tree, he stood and came to greet her.

"We heard the Germans searched the château," he said. "Are you okay?" He ran his hand down her arm, and Anne felt a tingle down her spine at his touch. His piercing eyes were full of concern.

She nodded. "They didn't find anything. We stayed up all night getting everything in order. Thankfully, Monsieur Jaujard has been working with the Kunstschutz in Paris to keep them from taking over the depots. He's made phone calls, written official memos. We're lucky it was only one inspection. Next time, it might be more. That's why René was insistent that we get this stuff out of there."

"Your Monsieur Huyghe has been a godsend for us," Étienne said. Over the weeks, René had instructed Anne and the other staff to pull the leaflets, armbands, weapons, and inventories out of the various crates of art. All of it went into the woods, piece by piece. Anne had made countless trips to the *maquis* camp.

"And Monsieur Jaujard has been ours," she said. "He's got us extra vehicles, gas, phones, and water pumps in case there is fire. Jaujard is coming to inspect the château tomorrow."

"I'm sure he'll be happy to see you," said the young woman who had first pulled Anne into the camp. Now, she knew her name was Amélie.

"Me?" Anne said. "No, he probably doesn't even remember who I am. I'm no one."

"How could he not?" Étienne said, looking at her so intently that she stared at the toes of her worn leather shoes. "Out here," he said, "you're famous."

MONSIEUR JAUJARD'S DARK EYES brimmed with concerned anticipation as René opened the lid of the crate that had been stashed safely behind a hinged panel in his bedroom wall. They widened when the painting was loosened from its velvet and the *Mona Lisa* smiled up at him. The director took a step forward, reaching out as if to touch the painting. Thinking better of it, he allowed his hand to fall to his side.

"The portrait that made Leonardo da Vinci's name live for eternity . . . *Bonjour, Madame,*" he whispered to the painting.

Monsieur Jaujard straightened. His face had grown pinched and gaunt since Anne had last seen him; there were lines on his cheek that hadn't been there when she went to fetch the provenance documents from Chambord with Lucie.

The director continued to look into Lisa's face and Anne thought it striking that the Florentine lady seemed to smile up at him. "It's good to see you after all this time," Monsieur Jaujard said to the picture. "I'm relieved to see you haven't fallen into the wrong hands."

BELLINA

Florence, Italy
1504

Until things change, none of us should attend public events."
Madre cooled herself at the dinner table with a brightly
painted silk fan. "The last thing we need is to bring more attention to this family."

Even though weeks had passed since the attack on the statue, it
seemed to be the only topic in Florence. No one could believe that
someone would try to destroy such a work, let alone a member of
one of the city's important families. And as much as the sculpture
had awed her, Bellina would be happy if she never had to think
about it again. Madre, however, seemed to allow it to occupy her
every waking moment.

"Mother, you cannot make such sweeping statements," Francesco said. "It had nothing to do with me or you personally. And
it could have been worse for Gherardo and his friends. He is fortunate that he only spent a week in the Stinche prison."

"A disgrace to all of us," Madre spit, as if she had just sucked
on an orange pith. She pushed her plate away.

Lisa sat hunched between her husband and her mother-in-law.
Bellina's mistress had spent more and more days in her bedchamber, and no longer wanted to leave the house.

Meanwhile, four young men had been prosecuted for throwing stones at the sculpture, their names called from the steps of the Signoria: Martelli. Spini. Panciatichi. And Gherardini. All four boys from families of Medici partisans. Only Agostino Panciatichi had avoided prison time by fleeing the city; the other boys were caught and sentenced to short stays behind bars.

"It has brought dishonor upon your wife's name," Madre persisted, as if Lisa were not present at the table and Gherardo's own seat at the table were not conspicuously empty. "And by extension, upon all of us."

Bellina froze. Had she drawn attention by sharing the news with Bardo? Had she inadvertently made the family a target of the anti-Medici factions?

THAT EVENING, Bellina gripped the stair railing, feeling exhaustion down to her bones from the day's chores and the weight of the anxiety in the house. She could hardly wait to put the day behind her, to pull the woolen blanket up to her neck, and surrender to sleep.

But as she neared her bedchamber door, she froze. Rustling. Movement. Someone was there. Cautiously, Bellina stepped forward and peered through the door.

Madre.

For a few suspended moments, her mind struggled to process the image of Francesco's mother poking around through her things. In all the years she'd spent in the house, Bellina had never seen Madre on the upper floor at all.

The old woman stood before the cabinet, her fingers on the latch. Bellina's heart suddenly leapt. Lisa's portrait. No possible story could explain why it was here, inside Bellina's cabinet, inside her own bedchamber. She would be out on the streets with nothing and no one to help her.

"Sig . . . Signora . . . ," Bellina stuttered.

Madre turned slowly, frowning. For years, Madre had suspected Bellina of stealing. She would be only too self-satisfied to find she'd been right all along.

"What . . . Can I help you find something?" Bellina asked.

"I'm inspecting all the rooms in the house," she said. "My son doesn't believe me, but I have good information that there are fires being started in certain homes. We need to make sure ours is not one of them."

"Surely there's no danger of fire here, Madre," Bellina said, holding the old woman's gaze. "Who would do such a thing to us?" For a long few moments, Madre scanned the bare floor, the thin blanket tucked neatly into the corners of the narrow bed, the table with its comb and mirror, the empty chamber pot.

"Hmm," she said finally, and brushed past Bellina into the dark corridor.

"WORD HAS SPREAD that Master Leonardo is painting the likeness of our Lisa," Francesco said. "People want to see it."

Another Sunday meal with Francesco's brothers and their wives. Bellina pressed herself against the wall. Had she heard that correctly? They wanted to see the portrait? She thought of the velvet-wrapped panel hidden in her bedchamber cabinet, and felt her heart drop to her scuffed leather clogs.

"A public showing of the portrait?" Francesco's sister-in-law raised her sparse eyebrows.

"No, not a ridiculous spectacle like the one for that Buonarroti thing," Francesco said. "Rather, a private viewing. For a few friends, for anyone who matters."

Bellina could no longer hold her tongue. "But it's not finished!" she exclaimed. Immediately, she regretted her outburst. Now, she was no longer one of many invisible servants waiting in the shadows. Everyone's eyes were on her.

Her mistress rescued her. "Bellina is right," Lisa said. "Master Leonardo told us the layers of paint must dry before he comes back again to work on it. And he hasn't finished yet." She picked at her food. Lisa looked haggard and skinny in her worn black dress.

"What?" Madre asked. "Why would we want to show an incomplete portrait?"

"Exactly," Francesco said, licking oil from his fingers. "He needs a little prompting to get it finished."

Madre looked skeptical. "Well, you have not paid Master da Vinci more than a paltry deposit for that picture, much less fed him a meal or accommodated him in your home, so it's no wonder he hasn't come back to finish it. Besides, I don't know why we would want to bring more attention to our family right now."

"I'll pay him when he's done," Francesco said matter-of-factly. "The man is skillful and silver-tongued, but he's not known for finishing projects. But I'm on to him. When the portrait is done, he'll get paid. It's that simple. Perhaps an imminent showing will prompt him to complete it before he leaves Florence again."

Bellina gasped, but she held her tongue this time. Master Leonardo was leaving Florence? She felt panic well in her chest. Master Leonardo believed his portrait still stood on its easel in the house, where Francesco might be calculating how much this treasure was worth to him. In the meantime, everyone in the house believed the artist had returned to his studio with the picture. In reality, the beautiful portrait still languished in its velvet wrapping, in Bellina's own servant's bedchamber. She had to get it out of there as soon as possible. But where could she take it? And if Master Leonardo left town for some unknown period, then what? Eventually it would be discovered and they would brand her a thief. Plenty of house servants snitched small baubles, but . . . a painting? What would happen to her? Surely she would be out on the street, if not in jail herself.

"He's leaving Florence?" Iacopa asked.

"Heading back to Milan, from what I've heard," Francesco said. "He's been granted another commission."

"He cannot do that to us!" Madre said.

"It appears he can," Francesco said. "You see, Mother? I told you he cannot be relied upon, no matter his skill." He gestured with his hands. "He . . . flits around like a colorful butterfly, chasing one bright flower, then another. The prior of Santissima Annunziata warned me of that even before Master Leonardo came into this house."

Bellina was worried another fight was about to ensue between them, and she took another step back. She didn't know what had possessed Francesco to allow his mother to live with them when they fought so bitterly.

"May I speak?" Lisa said suddenly. Everyone turned to her. Her tone held no anger, and her eyes were soft. "If my opinion matters . . . I do not care if this portrait is finished or not."

For a moment, everyone stared silently at Lisa, who sat hunched and morose over her plate.

"But Lisa . . ." Francesco said softly. "You said you loved it."

"Please don't misunderstand, Francesco," she said, touching his hand. "I know you commissioned Master Leonardo to paint my likeness as an honor to me, and I am grateful. But it's a luxury, a painting that stands for pride and envy of the rich classes . . ."

"Don't be ridiculous!" Madre fired from across the table.

Francesco chuckled. "You *are* of the rich class, *carissima,* whether or not you like it. You speak as if you've gone mad. What's the—?"

"But just look at . . . all these vanities," she interrupted, scanning her eyes over the inlaid wooden panels, the painted walls, the deeply coffered ceiling, the wrought-silver candleholders on the table. "You don't think we won't be punished somehow for our greed?"

Bellina pressed her back against the wall and felt the old, familiar dread overtake her. Her mind searched desperately for what to do with the portrait. But . . . Was her mistress right? Would they be punished? And if she was the one responsible for putting Lisa and her children at risk, she would never forgive herself.

LEONARDO

Florence, Italy
1505

An inspection. The thought of it sends a shudder through my body.

The last thing I need is to hear the opinions of these supposed authorities on my unfinished fresco in the great hall of the Signoria. As if these wool brokers would know what it takes to prepare a plaster for pigment, to render the anatomy of a horse in battle. They draw my attention away from what counts above all else: the careful application of the color before it dries and is too late to change. By the window, I watch for the arrival of the men in the long, scarlet robes. Instead, there is only an ominous, black cloud descending from the sky, pressing down on us with its weight.

"The azure is dripping, Master!" The new assistant, the one I call Il Fanfoia, calls to me from his place on the accordion scaffold. "We can't seem to stop it."

"Add more binder!" I call, but the men in uniform distract my attention.

They are good, these young assistants. Better than they give themselves credit for. They don't need me coddling them, watching their every paint stroke over their shoulders. Over days, the fresco has slowly taken shape. Our novel mixture of pigment and wax, though an experiment, has seemed stable so far. Those vital, rich colors have thrilled me in a way I haven't felt in a long time. The Roman historian Pliny wrote a description of a process by which paints could be fixed to a surface using heat. I have brought flame pots to fix the work already done before I move on to the next section.

The image, when it is complete, will measure as wide and as high as the entire wall of the council hall. I have designed it to be three separate but yet continuous scenes from the famous battle. I have created massive images of horses and men in desperate collision in an intense, personal, life-and-death struggle projected on a scale of immense proportion. The picture shows four riders and their war-hardened steeds caught in a moment of time, battling for control of the standard at the Battle of Anghiari. The central figure, the Florentine commander, is about to wrench the standard away from the Milanese leader. All portray a sense of power and emotion along with the exploding fury and violence of war.

Suddenly, outside the open windows, there is a crack of thunder; a shock of lightning brightens the sky like a firework. The men in uniform scatter in the courtyard below, taking cover in the arcades or running inside the building, slamming the doors behind them. A trickle of rain suddenly becomes a downpour.

"Master Leo, come! Look at this." Il Fanfoia gestures from where he stands on the scaffolding. I grasp the wooden rails lashed to the supports and climb up.

I'm barely over the edge of the scaffold when I see it. The paint has started to bleed and blend on the wall, in spite of our best efforts with the wax binding. I'd thought it might bring greater permanence, but the skies were mocking me, the elements demonstrating their terrible dominance. The young men collect around me; we stand still as the paint melts before our very eyes. Outside, another crack of thunder. The rain suddenly comes down in sheets outside, roaring like a wave on the sand.

There's nothing I can do. There's no sketch or invention or notion or dream that can conquer this mistake. Il Fanfoia rushes up to me, looking from the parchment to the fresco, to me and then at the others with a frantic urgency. "Master," he asks in a hushed tone already filled with defeat. "What do we do now?"

But there is no good answer. I can only survey the damage.

"Master."

I have to search for words, head shaking as the rain comes down even harder, making certain what had almost been within hope's reach. There's little more to say than, "There's nothing more to do, Il Fanfoia. What's done . . . is done."

I can only step back and accept that the fresco is forestalled, that the weeks of work are for naught. Now it has to be replicated, reborn. The wall has to be scrubbed and relined and work started again.

The painting is ruined. Surely, I am ruined, too.

Suddenly, the men in uniform are at the door. I turn to face them.

ANNE

Montal, France
1943

Y ou already know how to load those paintings quickly on the trucks." Étienne pointed to the map spread between himself and Anne. "Once the crates have been secured, we'll head for the woods in the Massif Central."

Anne and Étienne clustered among a group of *maquisards* inside the stained flaps of his dank tent. Inside, there were a few oil lanterns, a pack of leaflets, and a low table. Against one side of the tent was a bedroll of woolen military blankets, just wide enough for two people. Étienne and Amélie . . . were they lovers?

"We'll cover you while the museum staff helps us unload everything into our hiding places—bunkers, old stone barns, people's homes." When Anne looked at him skeptically, he said, "We may not look like much, but our network is wide. There are places to hide paintings here, here, and here." He tapped his finger on the map where a series of red Xs had been marked. "If the Krauts retreat, the rest of us will regroup here to avoid leading them to where we've hidden everything."

Anne nodded, rubbing her temples. "Okay. But let's assume the Germans *don't* find the art up there on the plateaus," she said.

"I'm still worried that some of the art wouldn't survive being stored in those conditions."

Étienne put his amber eyes on her. "This is the best plan we've got. You want to go over it again?"

"No. I think I know it well enough to propose it to René," Anne said, standing. "I hate to think about having to recapture all those works of art after they've been stolen. But I know we need to consider the possibility." She rubbed her palms together to thaw her frozen fingers. "I should get back to the château before dark."

Étienne said, "You could stay here and eat something with us . . ." His gaze was intense and searing. She turned her face toward the campsite.

Beyond the tattered tent flaps, clouds of steam emanated from a giant metal cauldron where it seemed there was an endless supply of watery gruel with the occasional addition of stale bread, a piece of cheese, or a hard sausage pulled from the garland hanging under the rafters of an old farm building. They had set long wooden planks with meager rations. In some ways, Anne longed to join in the babble of conversation, the camaraderie of the ragged little group. Inside the castle, the constant presence of German inspectors had created an atmosphere of tension and silence, dampening everyone's spirits. Here in the campsite, the cold lay thick and her breath steamed in the air, but there was solidarity and a shared purpose, Anne thought as she looked around at the crowd of men and women around them. The Nazis had tried so hard to separate all kinds of people from one another, but here in this ramshackle campsite of *maquisards,* their actions had had the opposite effect.

Suddenly, running feet crashing into the camp sent Anne,

Étienne, and Amélie lurching upright. But the man rushing into the camp was one of the *maquis* scouts, a mousy man with a bushy mustache and a giant smile. "Come, come!" he said, laughing. "Christmas has come early!"

Amélie grabbed Anne's hand. "Come with us," she said.

Étienne, Amélie, Anne, and others followed the little man almost dancing with excitement ahead of them into the woods, their feet crunching on the dead leaves. Étienne stepped down a bank and onto a strip of ice that had formed across a stream. He held out a hand and Anne gripped it gratefully, letting him help her over the icy water and up the next bank. Then he did the same for Amélie. She grasped his hand and when he pulled her up, she pressed her body against him and kissed his cheek. Anne looked away. They scrambled out of the frozen stream's bed and found themselves in a thicket of stately trees. Among the trunks, something huge and metal shimmered. Anne followed them to the big metal container enmeshed in a tangle of parachute fabric and strings.

"The Brits dropped this in for us," he whispered. Simultaneously, everyone fell silent and looked up into the air to see if they could see one of the great planes that had dropped this treasure.

"Whoo!" the scout cried. "We're going to fight for ourselves at last!"

Could a parachuted crate filled with rifles, hand grenades, and long belts of bullets lead them back home? Anne closed her eyes and allowed herself to dream all the way back to Paris, to her city bustling with life, to its church spires and towers, to the magnificence of the Louvre. She dreamt herself back to walking on the sidewalk with her brother, listening to his laughter as the traffic flowed around them. She dreamt herself back to a small Parisian sewing machine repair shop where a funny Italian with strong arms and a warm smile might be waiting.

But the arm that slipped around her waist now was not Corrado's, but Étienne's. In one hand, he held a shiny revolver pulled from the stash of British weapons parachuted into the forest. Standing behind Anne, he encircled her, lifting the weapon and lining up their view in its sights.

"I heard you drive like a madwoman, *mademoiselle,*" he breathed into her ear. "Do you know how to shoot, too?" He smelled of the campfire, cigarettes, and stale coffee.

"Not at all," Anne said, laughing nervously as her neck tingled under Étienne's hot breath.

"Then let me show you."

"I HAD A FEELING it was bad news."

In the light-filled gallery, René held a small, nearly weightless telegram from Jacques Jaujard.

"What does it say?" Lucie said, sidling up to René and looking over his shoulder.

"*Tieschowitz from the German art protection unit came to see me,*" René read, his face drawn and pale. "*Local German military authorities now have the right to search any depot and open any crate in order to look for materials like leaflets—anything that might be used in resistance efforts. Remove all such materials from the depots at once.*"

"*Mon Dieu!*" Lucie's hands flew to her mouth.

"We have to follow his instructions. We don't have a choice," René said. "It's one thing for the Germans to uncover the *Mona Lisa,* but if they find the other crates instead . . ."

"But there's so much of it here," Anne said, thinking of their stash in the attic. At least, she thought, she knew exactly what was in each crate. By now, she had the inventories nearly memorized.

"I know," René said. "It seemed such a good idea to hide them in the art crates, but now they're not safe there anymore. Not even in our own quarters. We'll have to move them right away. And I'll have to let my . . . supplier . . . know not to send any more until further notice."

"René," she said, "where do these things come from?" Perhaps he wouldn't tell her, she thought.

He hesitated, but then said, "I have a contact inside the Louvre. Someone involved with museum security."

Anne gasped. "Monsieur Dupont!" she cried.

René's eyebrows flew up. "You're acquainted."

Anne grasped his sleeve. "Can you contact him? I need to know where my brother is, if only he will tell me."

René nodded grimly. "I can send him a message. But for the moment, we have to find a new hiding place for the most valuable paintings—especially *La Joconde*."

Anne glanced out the window at the sunlight sparkling on the frost of the castle lawn.

"Looks like a nice day for a bicycle ride."

ANNE WEAVED BRISKLY down the footpath on her bicycle, sweating in spite of the crisp air. She needed to make at least three trips today if she was going to move the materials quickly enough. Her head swam with the news that Monsieur Dupont was linked with this mysterious network of resistance fighters.

"Bad news," Anne said as she saw Étienne cross the campfire

circle. He took her rucksack and they headed toward the ramshackle wooden hut the men had built from skinny trees. Anne
pushed her bicycle and propped it against the structure. "We just
got word from Paris. The Germans are allowed to search the depots. Even open our crates."

Étienne sucked in a breath. "The paintings . . ."

"Yes, but if they find the other materials, that's even worse. We
need to move everything we can into the woods."

As the smell of campfires reached them, Anne expected to find
the regular circle of *maquisards,* but instead, the camp circle was
empty. "What's going on?"

"Seems you're not our first surprise visitor today," Étienne said.
"Come see."

Anne followed Étienne's lean silhouette through a narrow trail
that opened to another clearing. Friendly greetings surrounded
her as Étienne pulled her to the center of the circle, and two fresh
faces stared up at her from their spot at one of the long tables
where they sat with bowls of watery coffee.

"Meet John and Patrick," said Amélie. "They just dropped in
this morning." A roar of laughter rose from the table. "With the
help of parachutes."

The men wore dusty uniforms with leaf camouflage on their
helmets.

"*Bonjour* . . . ," Anne said. "Hello!"

"This is Anne, the one we were telling you about," Amélie said.

"The famous lady on the bicycle," the man called John said.
"The Victory of Samothrace . . . Am I right?"

Anne hesitated.

"We heard about you," he continued, his eyes wide. "About how
you brought the *Mona Lisa* from Paris the day the city was bombed,

and how you scrambled the inventories at Chambord, and now you're looking after those things around here somewhere . . ."

Anne felt her cheeks heat. "You make it sound more glamorous than it was."

"Don't be modest," one man at the table said and grinned. "The other *maquisards* have been bragging about you; even Chopin knows about you now."

Étienne caught Anne's eye as he cupped his hands and lit the butt of a cigarette. From across the crowd, he gave her a warm, intimate grin.

Anne took a deep breath and turned back to the Englishmen. "You brought supplies with you?"

"Yes, ma'am," the younger Englishman said. "Our mission is to strengthen the Resistance across this region of France, however we can."

"Good," Anne said. "We need you."

ANNE STRUGGLED to steady her hands as a German soldier peered over her shoulder at her diligently recorded inventory pages. He stood so close that Anne could smell the dankness of his unwashed field jacket and the musk of his hair. His eyes, black and cold as a snake's, raked over her neatly compiled ledger pages of artists' names, painting titles, dimensions, and accession numbers. The boy hardly looked older than seventeen.

They were obsessed with paperwork, these Germans, Anne thought. It seemed the only thing standing between conducting a tense meeting and blowing their brains out was a metal seal dabbed in ink and stamped with the swastika on an official document, the hastily scrawled signature of a senior officer, or an endless list of artworks on an official museum inventory.

The boy's commanding officer said something to him in German and he moved to the crates Anne and Lucie had lined up for their inspection.

Anne hoped the steel-eyed boy couldn't see her hands trembling as she leafed through the ledger pages. But no. Instead, everyone's eyes were on Pierre the guard, struggling to open one of the wooden crates with a small crowbar. René looked on nervously while Pierre wedged it into the lid of the crate. Behind him, a line of curators watched in silence. Two dozen more German soldiers stood watching behind them. Despite the number of people in the castle great room, there was a tense near-silence, save for the loud tick of an ancient clock in the hallway.

Anne marveled once again at Monsieur Jaujard's diplomatic skill. Somehow, from Paris—which now seemed very far away—their museum director had stolen back a tiny bit of ground from the Germans. They had had to give notice before they were allowed to search the châteaux, and French staff had to be present to help them handle delicate objects. For now, the Germans seemed to respect the rules. All the same, they were becoming impatient.

As their commanding officer followed Pierre and René from crate to crate, he slung his automatic rifle to his back and began leaning into the wooden boxes. He hardly glanced at the priceless paintings that René, Pierre, and the others lifted out of the boxes, digging instead through the packing material, searching for weapons. His annoyance seemed to rise every time he found the crates empty except for paintings, sculptures, and artifacts.

Anne read out the contents of each crate from the pages in her hands. One by one, each box's contents matched her inventories exactly. With the opening of each crate, the Germans got more and more impatient. It became clear to Anne that this officer didn't care about the works of art. He was looking for something else.

Finally, the commanding officer's patience broke. "Upstairs," he barked.

Anne met René's eyes, and for a fleeting moment, she saw naked fear. René gathered himself. "This way," he said, his voice sounding bone dry. He cleared his throat and began mounting the great staircase. The legion of soldiers and curators followed.

The black-eyed German boy stepped away from Anne and followed the others up the stairs. Anne felt the heat of the men's eyes on her back as she climbed the stairs. She walked slowly, dragging out the seconds, dreading what might happen if they found their hiding place for *La Joconde* just behind a piece of false wall paneling. The officer pushed roughly past her when they reached her bedroom door at the landing.

A loud bark in German made Anne flinch.

The black-eyed young man sprang to action. He kicked the door open and immediately commenced to tear her room apart. Anne sucked in her breath. There was a landscape she'd painted hanging on the wall; they ripped it down, cast the painting aside, opened the back of the frame. Other guards pulled off her bedclothes, throwing them carelessly on the ground. They opened her drawers, threw her dresses on the floor, pulled down her curtains. Anne tried to hold back hot tears.

Another series of barks. Anne understood nothing, but the

meaning was clear. Immediately, the men fanned out, moving on to ransack all the bedrooms on the top floor.

"Where are your quarters?" the head German asked René in French. Anne watched his mouth twitch, then he led them to his bedroom door and opened the latch.

"I have nothing to hide, sir," René said stiffly.

A giant lie. Anne's heart thumped in the back of her throat.

As the soldiers entered René's bedroom, Anne's heart thundered against her ribs. She did her best to look unfazed as the guards pulled out his drawers and threw them on the floor.

The two men seized the bed, and Anne's heart froze, keeping perfectly still. She couldn't move or breathe, frozen as entirely as the true *Victory of Samothrace,* as they slid the bed away from the wall. One of them pulled off the bedclothes; the other stomped on the wooden floor, seeking a loose floorboard. René was holding his breath. Anne felt as if she had no breath left. The *Mona Lisa* was hidden behind paneling at the soldier's side.

The men seemed to lose steam in their search when suddenly, one man began to run his fingers over the wall.

Anne felt darkness buzzing around the corners of her vision. He was so close. She didn't want to take a breath now, even if she could have; surely she would make some strangled sound and give it all away. The officer walked back and forth in front of the wall, his eyes scrutinizing every panel, then turned away. His eyes blazed with fury.

A few more snapped words in German, then the soldiers filed back down the stairway.

As soon as their footsteps receded down the stairs and out of the château, Anne's legs buckled. She crumpled to the floor, and buried her face in her hands. René staggered over to the wall, gripped the loose panel, and stood there quietly, his chest heaving. Safe and sound in the dark nook beyond, the crate with three red dots rested, out of reach of the Germans for now.

THE CRACK OF the gunshot rippled through the air, the rifle kicking into Anne's shoulder. Muzzle smoke wafted into the cold winter day. The target painted on a tree trunk remained unmarked, but Anne felt a little better. It felt as though each bullet that left the rifle took some of her tension with it.

From behind, she felt Étienne's firm hands on her shoulders. He shifted her position. "Aim a little more to the right."

Anne cocked the British rifle again and leaned her chin against it, sighting down the long, shining barrel. Placing the sights slightly to the right of the target, she closed her eyes for a moment and drew in a deep breath. When her lungs were full, she opened her eyes. Her trigger finger closed and the rifle cracked again, jabbing her shoulder. This time, there was a crack of wood, and the bullet punched through the center of the target.

Anne lowered the rifle to see a wide, boyish grin across Étienne's face and his dimples in their glory. "No one's going to want to cross you now, *chérie*." She felt a tingle down her spine as Étienne cupped his hand around a match and cigarette, then smiled at her again.

Anne shook her head. "I was picturing the face of that German who tore my room apart," she said. "It sounds so silly to be upset by that, considering everything else they've done. But it was so personal, so . . ."

"No need to explain," Étienne said, taking the rifle from her hands and opening the barrel. "Those Krauts took everything from me, too. Anyway, that's why we're starting with the plan next week."

"Do you think it will work?"

"Chopin has assured us," he said, closing one eye and looking into the open barrel. "Taking out the bridges is an important part of weakening their forces as they try to move through this area."

Anne sighed. "I hope Chopin knows what he's doing. Do you think John and Patrick are right? That the Allies are coming to help us?"

Étienne sat the weapon down on a nearby stump, then returned to place both hands on her shoulders. "I'll tell you a secret," he whispered, looking into her eyes. He leaned in so close to her that for a moment, Anne thought he would kiss her. She felt a strange mixture of warmth and unease well up inside her as her senses suddenly filled with his scent of tobacco, coffee, and the smoldering ashes of the campfire.

But instead, he brushed a lock of hair away from her face and studied her eyes. "Everyone is counting on the Brits and the Americans to come help us, but I can't say for sure. All I know is that we must take care of ourselves. And if the Nazis come here, then we have to do whatever is in our power to take them down."

Étienne's presence—his smell, his intense gaze—all were suddenly overpowering. Anne stepped back. She picked up the rifle from the stump. She set her jaw and reloaded, then set her sights again at the target on the tree.

"Then I need to get better at this."

BELLINA

Florence, Italy
1506

I need to get better at this. I may be a servant but I am a grown woman and I ought to speak my mind, Bellina thought as she opened the door and walked out into the white daylight.

Bellina wished that there was something she could say to convince Lisa that the beautiful portrait was not about greed. Even Bellina herself had begun to see that. But she was afraid that too many people in Florence still saw things that way, and the last thing she wanted to do was put her own future at risk by hiding the portrait in the house. Winding past the rough brown stones of the chapels where the Medici family tombs lay, she headed down a narrow street toward the monastery of Santa Maria Novella.

There was only one thing to do at this point: convince Master Leonardo to take back the painting. To do that, she had to catch Master Leonardo before he left town.

"Make yourself comfortable." The young, curly-haired assistant gestured as he escorted Bellina through a back entrance to the monastery that saw the arrival of family members, of servants and vendors delivering bread, wine, cloth, and other supplies. "Master Leonardo will be with you shortly." The young man led

Bellina into an antechamber and then he disappeared behind a heavy wooden door.

Bellina sat awkwardly on a stone bench near the doorway and looked around the chamber, a small sliver of the monastic complex open to the outside world. Around the room, several easels had been set up with drawings glued to wooden panels. It seemed the monastery celebrated the fact that a well-regarded painter lived in their midst. Bellina smiled to think of the silk-enveloped Master Leonardo among these austere men in their sackcloth, crude sandals, and knotted belts.

Bellina waited patiently, trying to keep her gaze at the stone floor, but she could not help but look at the drawings surrounding her. It seemed that each one was more beautiful than the last. Master Leonardo did not just make religious pictures or portraits. As he had told Lisa, he found inspiration in many things. There were sketches of Madonnas, yes, but also strange contraptions, vehicles with rolling treads, odd spears, trebuchets and crossbows that looked ominous.

"You see something you like?" Master Leonardo said, appearing suddenly. She jumped.

"I'm sorry!" she cried, averting her eyes. "I was just looking. I thought . . ."

Master Leonardo smiled. "No need to apologize. Pictures are made to be admired."

"Yes," Bellina said. "Which is why I have come to see you."

"Oh?" he asked. "Perhaps your master sends word of a progress payment for the portrait of his wife?"

"That . . . ," Bellina said. "No. I'm afraid that is none of my business, sir. But I have come to ask you to take back the portrait. We've heard you are leaving Florence."

"Yes," he said. "My assistants and I are preparing to leave for Milan. But unless your master changes his mind about the payment terms, I'm afraid the portrait is as finished as it will ever be. Best to leave the portrait in Master Francesco's house for safekeeping . . . and as a reminder of his debt."

Bellina did not know that Francesco had not paid, but if she was honest, it did not surprise her. Francesco del Giocondo was shrewd. What Master Leo didn't know was that no one in the house had laid eyes on the portrait.

"My master said he will pay . . . when the portrait is finished," Bellina said, but stopped herself. She quickly added, "But Master Francesco didn't send me here, Master Leonardo. I came of my own volition."

"I see," the artist said, looking at her skeptically. "Well, it seems your master and I are at an impasse."

"But . . ." Bellina rushed forward to grasp his billowing silk sleeve, the color of lavender. "You cannot just . . . leave the portrait in the house! Please, sir! Take it with you to Milan!" she blurted out.

He looked her in the eye and a long period of silence fell on the room. "Why?"

"The last thing we need right now is to bring more attention to Lisa's family." Bellina surprised herself by repeating Madre's words.

"What unnecessary attention to the household?" he asked, but she only shook her head. "My dear," he continued. "Do you understand that painting is how I make my living?"

"Yes."

"And do you understand that the more attention comes to my work, the more patrons I attract? But . . . I cannot make my living if someone does not pay me?"

"Of course." Now Bellina felt stupid for not realizing this simple concept.

"Then understand that if I take the painting back, and your master does not see it every day, it will easily slip his mind and he won't pay at all," Master Leonardo said.

"But . . ." Bellina sucked in a breath. "You don't understand. Please. I want it finished so my mistress . . . She is in despair."

"What has happened?"

"It is not what has happened . . . ," Bellina replied. "It is what could happen."

Master Leonardo said nothing to this. Instead, he turned to look out the window at the light. "She does not like the portrait?"

"No, it's not that!" Bellina said. "She has . . . expressed some concern about what the painting stands for . . . but that is not what the problem is . . . Please . . . just believe me."

The door opened and Master Leonardo's curly-haired assistant appeared again. "Master," he said. "They are waiting."

Leonardo da Vinci stood. "I'm sorry. There is much to do to prepare to leave town, and we have no more room for another painting. Unless Master Francesco is prepared to make another payment, the portrait will need to wait until I return."

THAT EVENING, Gherardo made his way up the stairs to the servants' hallway. He leaned against the doorjamb of Bellina's bedchamber, watching her rinse her hands in a bowl of water on the table. She tried not to let her eyes wander to the cabinet where Lisa's portrait remained hidden.

"Say, Bellina," Gherardo said, "they've been talking about you in Master Francesco's silk workshops." He grinned.

"Me?" she huffed. "I doubt that."

"It's true," Gherardo said. "Seems word has spread about your stitching skills. I heard Bardo mention it."

"Bardo . . ."

He nodded. "Says he's suggested to Francesco to let you out of this prison of a house and come work at the loom instead."

Bellina froze. Bardo wanted her to work in Francesco's workshop? Was that true?

"What?" He smiled, reading her expression. "You think you can't do something outside of here? There's more to life than what goes on inside these walls. Open your eyes, Bellina. *Buona notte,*" he said, disappearing into the shadows.

If Gherardo had been trying to draw Bellina's attention away from the troubles of the household, he had succeeded. Her mind swirled. On one hand, Bellina could hardly imagine a life outside Lisa's house. On the other, she had been thinking about it more and more.

ANNE

Montal, France
1944

Viens, chérie. Come." Étienne squatted at the top of the ditch and extended his hand.

His hand was rough, stout, and strong. His fingers were ice cold where they gripped hers. He lifted Anne from the deep ditch and into the undergrowth along the side of a country road. The movement made the straps over her shoulders bite into her flesh with the weight of her rucksack. This time, they did not fill her bag with leaflets or cash armbands. It was heavy with the weight of explosives. Anne had traded her tidy Louvre skirt for canvas trousers loaned to her from the girls in the woods.

"It's too early in the morning to be blowing things up," Amélie grumbled as she scrambled up the ditch beside them. "Chopin couldn't have chosen a more civilized hour?"

"That's the point," Étienne said. "This way, we won't have any civilian casualties. See?" He parted the scrub. "There's no one on the bridge or anywhere near it."

Étienne was right. In the distance, the old bridge was empty, its imposing stretch lonely and deserted against the canvas of the winter sky. Anne could hardly believe the explosives in her rucksack might be enough to bring such a hulking structure down.

Her eyes picked out the weak spots in the supports, just as Étienne had explained to her.

"Ready?" Étienne whispered. Anne took a deep breath and nodded. She would never admit that she was scared to death.

"Remember the signal," Étienne said. "I'll whistle like a bird three times if Germans come or if anyone walks out onto the bridge."

Anne and Amélie scrambled off through the brush, moving as quietly as they could. Every snapping twig sounded as loud as a gunshot, and Anne strained her ears for Étienne's signal, but behind them, there was only silence.

At the bank of the river, Anne paused and glanced back. She made out the faint gleam of the sunlight on the lenses of Étienne's binoculars as he scanned the bridge for movement. Amélie's face was pale. Anne reached back and touched her hand. "Come on," she whispered.

They stepped out onto the riverbank, their feet crunching on the pebbles, and hurried along to the nearest support of the bridge. Anne's hands were shaking with cold and fear as she wedged the explosives into a crook in the stones, as high up as she could climb.

"Hurry!" Amélie hissed from below. "It's nearly ten past seven. The others should be done laying the charges on the other side."

Anne attached the last wire to the improvised bomb and slipped back down to the ground, reaching it with a grunt. Amélie helped her roll out the wires along the riverbank. They reached the brush at last and scrambled through it to where Étienne was hiding with the detonator.

"Well done, *mesdemoiselles*," he whispered.

The wiring was fiddly work, difficult with shaking hands. She struggled to wire up the detonator to the explosives as they had shown her, and at last, it was done. Anne looked up one last time at the bridge. "Ready," she said, her hand on the switch.

"Wait," Étienne said, holding out his hand. "We need to go at the same time as the others. Thirty more seconds now." He stared at his watch.

A few lonely chirps soon crescendoed into a cacophony of birdsong in the surrounding countryside, drowning out the quiet lullaby of the river on the rocks. She could almost imagine that there was no war here by this calm riverbank. She could almost feel as oblivious as the birds swooping over the water, as the fish that flashed beneath the clear surface.

"Ten seconds," Étienne said, examining his watch.

Anne stopped her ears, following Amélie's example.

"Five. Four. Three. Two. Now!"

Anne flicked the switch. It was a tiny movement, almost effortless. Suddenly, a fireball bloomed around the bridge's supports. The roar filled her ears, a burst of unstoppable sound that swept through her entire being like a tidal wave. Smoke poured from the bridge, and there was a long moan as metal snapped and twisted. As they watched, the great bridge teetered. Voices started yelling from the nearby village, but the bridge was already toppling. It struck the water with a burst of noise and disappeared in a cloud of smoke, dust, and spray.

"Run!" Étienne grabbed Anne's hand.

They fled as quickly and quietly as they could. Behind them, trucks and tank engines roared to life. Sirens began to wail as the dawn light emerged. She almost believed she could feel German eyes on her back, and she ran with all her strength, Amélie and Étienne on either side of her. Anne's lungs burned, muscles aflame as they approached the ditch. Étienne took a flying leap, landing on the opposite bank, his hands digging into the mud. The thunder of the falling bridge was still in their ears. Anne scrambled down, slipped, fell on her hands and knees in the mud. Amélie grabbed her arm. "Come on! Run!" she gasped.

Dragged back to her feet, Anne followed Amélie up the other side of the ditch and, in a flash, they dove into the tree line. Anne's legs were growing numb, and her heart felt like it had swollen up to fill her entire chest, crushing her lungs. "Keep going!" Étienne gasped, turning to watch the women catch up. "We're not in the clear yet!"

Ahead, a diesel engine rumbled. Without hesitation, the three of them threw themselves into the undergrowth. Anne's cheek pressed against the sharp edges of a branch. She hoped wildly that the sound was just a farmer driving past, but when the voices floated toward them on the cool breeze, they were German.

Anne held her breath, not daring to stir even an eyelash. She could hear Amélie panting beside her. After a long minute, the truck rumbled on, finally disappearing down the crest of the road. Anne cautiously raised her head.

The brief rest seemed to have given Étienne and Amélie a second wind, but Anne was not used to the physical demands of the *maquisards,* and she struggled to keep pace as they sprinted deeper into the woods. At last, they saw the familiar wisps of smoke coming from the *maquis* camp, and they came crashing into the clearing. Anne collapsed on one of the makeshift wooden benches, her heart raging in her ears. She had never run so hard in her life.

"We did it!" Amélie cheered, leaning with her hands on her

knees. She let out a small whoop. "We blew up the bridge!" The few remaining *maquisards* clapped Étienne and Amélie on the back.

"It was Anne who flipped the switch," Étienne said. She sat up on the bench and wiped the sweat from her brow.

"Excellent," one man said, smiling at Anne over folded arms. "Chopin would like to meet you. Come."

For all its wild thumping, the words made Anne's heart go still. The man pointed, and they all turned to a tent on the other side of the camp. The front flap rustled aside, and a boot appeared. Anne's heart was moving again, and it was hammering in all the wrong places, stealing her breath.

Then Chopin stepped out into the sunlight. Anne saw a tall, slim frame, and then luscious blond hair and wide blue eyes gazing at them with a mixture of gentleness and ferocity.

"*Bonjour à tous*," she said. "Is this the famous *Victory* you've been telling me about?"

ANNE WAS DEEP ASLEEP inside her ransacked castle bedroom, her mind shifting with images of Chopin as glamorous as a film star, when the sound of gunfire made her eyes snap open.

Rat-tat-tat-tat-tat-tat-tat!

For a long moment, she lay frozen on her cot. Had she dreamt it?

It came again, a harsh, distant popping, a sound that had become familiar to her from her time spent on the *maquis'* makeshift shooting range. She pushed back her blankets and stared out the third-floor window onto the grounds of the château.

Rat-tat-tat-tat-tat-tat-tat!

Machine guns.

Groping for the doorknob, she rushed out of her room and almost ran into René in the hallway.

"Wake everyone!" he said, his brow covered in beads of sweat. "We have to secure the château."

Still disoriented, Anne groped along the dark hallway, banging on each door as she went. "Wake up!" she cried. "We need help!"

She heard doors opening and footsteps in the château's hallways.

She ran down the stairs and passed the door to René's bedroom. He was struggling to move the crate with the three red dots. It made Anne's heart thump somewhere in the back of her throat.

"*La Joconde,*" she whispered.

"We have no choice now, not with the fighting so close," René said. "We have to move her. Give me a hand. We'll take her to the basement, damp and all." Anne followed René into his bedroom.

There was another burst of gunfire from somewhere outside while René was dragging the crate from its hiding spot in the wall. "It still sounds far," she said, trying to remain hopeful.

Another round of gunfire answered the first; the sounds meshed into one continuous drone of noise, and Anne thought she heard a scream. She looked up at René, her heart hammering. Then, Anne ran ahead of him, pushing doors open so that he could move down the stairs to the basement. They had used pallets to build makeshift pedestals so that the paintings wouldn't rest on the floor. They had stacked crate upon crate in the musty interior. There were large canvases in great rolls, the looming shapes of wooden crates. Anne helped René to put the *Mona Lisa* down safely on one of the pallets that had been laid on the dirt floor.

There was another yelp, and Anne recognized the voice of Madame Huyghe, René's mother.

"*Maman!*" gasped René. Anne followed him as he ran up the stairs to the kitchen.

Madame Huyghe spun around as they rushed into the kitchen. She said nothing, but pointed with a trembling finger to the small window over the kitchen sink. Beyond, the hedgerows stood as looming silhouettes in first morning light.

"*Merde,*" René whispered.

A large band of *masquisards*—dozens of them, Anne saw—were hunched over, scrambling through the hedgerows of the château, guns in their hands, black berets cocked on their heads, their eyes darting across the brightening landscape.

René pushed open the window.

"René!" Madame Huyghe hissed. "Stop it! What are you doing? You will only incite them!"

He ignored her. "*Hé! Messieurs!*" he shouted. "Get away from here! You're putting everything at risk!"

The distant thunder of the guns continued as a few of the *maquisards* stopped and stared at him. After a moment, they disappeared into the hedges, and René turned to Anne, his face pale.

"They've gotten too close," he said. "They'll draw the Germans to us. Come away from the window, *maman*. We have to cover the glass."

René corralled the Louvre staff to pull all the mattresses from their beds and cover the windows. The mattress operation proceeded quickly, and soon enough, the interior of the château had returned to darkness as if it were night.

"Do you think they will try to attack the château?" Anne asked, gesturing to the front door.

At a large window, Pierre pressed the soft bulk of a mattress to the side and peeked out a front window toward the gravel drive.

He shook his head. "I don't think so," he said. "The Huns are leaving." Anne spied a cloud of dust through the sliver of light. Then the thunder of engines grew distant.

"Surely no one would attack us?" Lucie asked. "Everyone knows the art is being safeguarded here—the Germans, the *maquis,* even the Allies. Those youngsters that came past just now were careless. I don't think they were trying to endanger the château on purpose."

"But we might get caught in the crosshairs if things turn violent," Pierre said.

Suddenly, there was a deafening crack of gunfire, and this time it was closer. Much closer. It reverberated through the room, the unanimous thunder of numerous guns being fired at the same moment. Anne couldn't help jumping. René blanched, and Pierre's face darkened. They stayed very quiet for a few moments, but there was no more shooting. Long silence stretched out among them. No one moved a muscle.

"What's just happened?" Anne whispered.

"Three shots like that, all at once . . . Then silence." René shook his head. "An execution."

The words stirred something inside Anne, something hard and fierce, something that burned and consumed and spat and struggled. Something that roared up in her chest and blazed through her veins, tearing at every cell in her, driving it to action.

"We have to fight!" She made for the kitchen door.

"No!" René shouted, but it was too late. Anne was running up the stairs toward the attic where some of the last remaining weapons were kept. She could hear voices shouting to her, but she ignored them. Opening a crate, she reached for the long, smooth, heavy shape of a bolt-action rifle. She grasped the weapon and ran down the steps, feeling the weight of it, strange and somehow galvanizing, in her hands.

"Anne!" René sounded horrified when she appeared at the bottom of the grand staircase, looking as if she might blow everything up in a heartbeat. "Come back here!"

Pierre was at the door. He stepped into her path, holding out a hand. "*Mademoiselle,* wait . . ." Pierre met her eyes. "What are you doing?"

Anne met Pierre's gaze. "Fighting for all of us."

"Stop her!" someone yelled behind her.

Pierre nodded once. Then he stepped out of her way.

Anne opened the front door and ran out into the searing daylight.

LEONARDO

Florence, Italy
1506

There is something exciting about loading pictures on a mule train. The promise of an adventure. A new passage.

Outside Santa Maria Novella, the mules stand ready. The one at the front drops her head and flicks her ears, sending a pair of flies buzzing. Poor beast; she knows what's coming. She's already resigned herself to a long journey ahead.

The sun is no more than a glowing band on the horizon, but already, beads of sweat collect in the hollow of my back. Better to strike out early and cover as much of the road northward as we can before the midday heat forces us to seek shade—and before my assistants realize I've departed the city.

"Master!" Ah. Too late. A voice from the cloister echoes in the street. They have spied me. "You're leaving us?" The young man rushes into the alley, shrugging his pudgy shoulders and looking at me with pitiful eyes, like a faithful dog watching its master walk out the door, imagining that he may never return.

I look over the mules with their leather satchels, the wagon with my trunks of clothing and supplies. Salaì and Il Fanfoia have already loosed the reins from the great iron rings on the walls. My loyal, capable boys. They help me believe I'll do well enough in Milan if we manage to get there unscathed.

"Not to worry, my friend," I say, trying to placate the assistant with his pitiful-dog eyes. "We'll be back before you know we are gone."

I don't begin to tell him the rest, that leaving Florence behind will be a welcome respite, even if I am forced to return to an old Milanese contract and to a city that no longer resembles the place where Ludovico Sforza once reigned before the French soldiers led him away in shackles. That I've perhaps taken a step longer than my leg. Pride is a mortal sin, of course, but I could hardly wipe the smirk from my face when I got word that Charles II of Amboise, the French king's new governor in Milan, had called for my services.

I may be the butt of people's jokes in Florence, but at least in Milan, I still have something of a reputation. They need not know that I'm only being called back to finish the Virgin of the Rocks altarpiece for the Confraternity of the Immaculate Conception before some other hungry young whelp comes to scoop it up. Never mind the details of the long, legal wrangle, the letters back and forth on the post-horses between Florence and Milan. At last, Giovan Ambrogio de Predis has agreed to withhold further prosecution against me if I finish the piece within two years. No one in Florence need know the details. They only need to know that I am in demand elsewhere. I must keep them wanting me.

And anyway, suddenly, I'm inspired.

"But . . . the fresco . . . ," the young man persists. "You're leaving it unfinished?"

"For now."

"But, Master, what are we to do with an unfinished fresco?"

His poor, drooping face. I can only smile. "What do you do

with a daughter not yet ready to be married? Keep her covered, of course." A flutter of laughter echoes in the alley. "Three months," I say, patting his shoulder. "That's as long as the Signoria will let me be away from the city."

"Three months? You can't be serious! It's like . . . like leaving an open wound for an entire season!"

I try to keep a light tone. "The work will stand for ages, my friend! What difference does half a year make in that scope?"

"You see? Now it's gone from three months to six. There will be icicles on the face of the Duomo when we see you again."

"Months, my friend, not years, not decades . . . not centuries." He seems to wrestle with the notion. "Patience. We will return from Milan. I promise you, nothing in this city will take precedence over the completion of our project. Agreed?" He looks around, seeming to know he has no choice. We kiss both cheeks and at last, the poor boy lets me go.

I nod at the two men I've hired to protect my mule team, tough men with quivers and bows and big knives strapped to their legs. The roads beyond Florence are plagued with criminality. I supervise the last motions of packing and preparing the mule train before climbing aboard my own miserable mount.

Milan is the lifeblood of commerce, so my reputation there is paramount. I must finish the Virgin of the Rocks, and then design a new villa for Charles d'Amboise, who will host my little group—my loyal Salaì and Il Fanfoia. It's all about appearances, in the end.

The sun's rays have already burned the fog from the streets when the wagon wheels creak into the ruts in the cobbles. We head toward the northern city gates, leaving the still forlorn-looking assistant behind in the alley.

BELLINA

Florence, Italy
1507

B ellina had not expected God to answer every prayer, but she
hoped he might answer the most important ones.

One night, after hours of thrashing, clenching and unclench-
ing, the spikes and ebbs of labor, a beautiful baby boy came into
the world. Bellina had never been afraid for Lisa's life the way she
was that night, whispering in her ear between the great wanes
and flows, the piercing clamps, and the final release of a wailing,
slippery newborn.

For seven days, Francesco del Giocondo's household lit up with
joy at the birth of another son—and his mother's survival of the
ordeal. But then, the little one turned sickly and by the twenti-
eth day after the birth, the family was dressed in black again,
bundling the little body into the family tombs in the shadows
of Santa Maria Novella. At home, curtains in the finest black
silk from Francesco's workshops were hung from the windows,
and Bellina watched the gloom return to Lisa's face. Her mistress
simply stared off into the distance, and when Bellina spoke to her,
she only waved her away.

Bellina busied herself with boiling water to wash rags, with
changing bedding, dusting dirt from the corners, removing

cobwebs from the coffers. She did her best to stay unobserved; she did not want to bring attention to herself or the contents of her bedchamber, where Master Leonardo's old portrait of her mistress still lay hidden.

So when Francesco called for her, Bellina couldn't imagine what to expect. All the same, her heart flip-flopped.

She knocked tentatively on the half-opened door to Francesco's ground-floor chamber. "You wanted to see me, *signore?*"

"Bellina," he called. "Come."

She stepped inside. No one was allowed inside Francesco's home studio and for a moment, Bellina was overcome by the stacks of dog-eared account books, with lines describing complicated international orders of sheepskins from Provence and bales of wool from Lyon. There were samples of sugar from Madeira; of leather and hides from Ireland; and folded, tattered maps marked up with sea and land routes.

"I'll get to the point," he said. "We all thought you would be occupied with a new baby right now. I'm sure you did, too?"

"Yes, I expected so, sir," she said. For a moment, panic seized her heart. Was Francesco dismissing her from the household? Had she proven herself dispensable now that she was older and there was no longer a baby to care for? Was she no longer needed? Or wanted?

"You see," Francesco said, "my textile workshops in Por Santa Maria have expanded their production. We have new orders from Flanders and Portugal. It seems the new circumstances are favorable to my family's enterprises."

Bellina nodded. She still didn't know what this had to do with her.

"Now that things have turned out differently than we had

hoped, I thought I might utilize your skills in my largest work-shop. We have enough staff to care for the household for now. And you are skilled with the embroidery needle, as everyone can plainly see."

It took Bellina a few moments to process what Francesco was saying. "You want *my* help in your workshops?"

"Yes," he said. "My foreman, Bardo, mentioned your name, and that you knew one another already."

Bellina felt her face warm. "We . . . I knew his family when I was young," she said.

Francesco nodded. "Very good. I only bring in those who are skilled—and trustworthy. Anyway, perhaps you would enjoy a change of scene away from . . . the troubles of the household."

Bellina didn't know whether Francesco was talking about his despairing wife or his domineering mother, but her head spun with the information. She had barely allowed herself to imagine working anywhere but by Lisa's side, but for a moment, she felt lighter, as if she had just set down a basket of wet laundry.

Bellina hardly knew what to say. "You think you could teach an old dog like me new tricks?"

Francesco spat out a laugh. "I'm sure you will be current in no time. You could begin right away. Bardo will show you what to do."

She swallowed hard and nodded. "If you think it's best."

"You do not think it's best?" he asked.

"I . . . I do not wish to cause any trouble," she said.

"But you do not agree." He came closer and looked in Bellina's eyes. She took a step back.

"I only wonder who will look after Lisa," she said. "She is dev-astated. And she's been my charge for so many years now. She doesn't want anyone else."

For a long moment, Francesco tapped on the desk, seeming to consider Bellina's assessment. "That may be true," he said, "but in time, she will see that the world still turns. And if no one is there to dote on her, then eventually, she will have to come out of her room."

LEONARDO

Milan, Italy
1507

Three months in Milan have stretched to a year. I've had the joy of seeing another harvest in my vineyard outside of Santa Maria delle Grazie. I've felt the strange mixture of pride and wretchedness as the Dominicans slap my shoulders in appreciation for their *Last Supper* in their refectory, at the same time that it pains me to look at it now, so many years later, when there are a hundred things I wish I could change.

But as I stroll along the canalside at the Naviglio Grande, I see that not everyone is happy to be back in Milan. Il Fanfoia, for one, wants to return home to Florence; there's no hiding it. He's grown weary of the long winter, the thick fog that descends over the city as if it might suffocate us. As we walk past the used housewares sellers' barges on the canal, Il Fanfoia is remote, responding with little more than hunched shoulders and mumbled responses.

"Do you see, Master? The pontoons were developed especially to transport lumber along the canals." The new boy. He, on the other hand, is filled with excitement. And he is brilliant beyond his years.

And now, as we walk together, I see the true source of Il Fanfoia's unhappiness: there is someone else. Someone new. Someone filled with the youthful aspirations of art and invention. Francesco Melzi. They are used to new assistants; a fresh gaggle of young men seem to latch on to me wherever we go. But now, Il Fanfoia and even Salaì, who might have been happier to return to Milan, look as if they might just as well throw themselves into the murky canal waters instead.

"You see, my friends," I say, gesturing to Salaì and Il Fanfoia, who trail behind Melzi and me. I try my best to pull them back into my circle. "If it were not for engineering projects such as the canal locks, Milan would still be a swampy backwater. The locking system allows for boats to transport salt, wheat, and ash north to lakes. In return, the barges bring wood, marble, granite for the great cathedral workyard—right into the heart of the city."

Melzi smiles at me, filled with emotion. It was something of an accident that Francesco Melzi came into our lives. I might have encountered him at Ludovico's court had things worked out differently and the duke had not been taken prisoner. Melzi's own father, a nobleman, worked in Ludovico's service after my last departure from the city. But a new era has dawned in Milan. The French governor, Charles d'Amboise, has me working for King Louis XII. Things seem to develop well enough. I've even managed to straighten things out with de Predis on that blasted altarpiece at last.

I feel happy to stay here among these impressive canal works, among the rag dealers, the used-goods sellers with their fascinating storefronts of tin wares and chipped crockery, among the old women washing their linens in the dark canal waters. We skirt around a mule cart laden with cattle skins headed to the tanneries. The Naviglio Grande is a tranquil respite from the flurry of activity in Milan, carts and horses and mules and people all scurrying in every direction.

As I pull my woolen cloak tighter around my neck to ward off the chill, I think the role of the artist is to rise above petty squabbling. These young assistants should feel only gratitude for the things I have afforded: fine accommodations in San Babila, the hospitality of Charles d'Amboise, tables laden with roast pheasant caked with rosemary, thick gravy, wines of every flavor and hue.

"You do not have such river mechanisms in Florence?" Melzi asks.

I hesitate, my heart squeezing with the painful memory of my disastrous Arno project, which now seems a lifetime ago. "No," I say. "We have only the workshops of the cloth trade on the Arno."

"I should like to see such a thing, Master," Melzi says innocently. "Along with your other achievements there. I have heard of your cathedral in Florence. They say it is a marvel."

Florence.

I must admit that my home city has pulled at my heart again. For days, I've hidden a letter in the pocket of my cloak. I haven't told the boys yet.

My uncle has died. They are calling me to come home again.

I cannot say I feel much. We were not close, and the man lived a long life. What's remarkable is that he found it within himself to leave his entire estate to me. I can hardly fathom it. There lies my uncle's entire fortune, waiting for me in the bank. Perhaps he felt a certain pity that his brother ignored his oldest son. They say I must come home and sign for the inheritance. I will sit before one of my father's colleagues and sign the papers. I would be stupid to leave such a sum in the hands of notaries.

"Perhaps we will make a trip to Florence sooner rather than later," I say, raising my eyebrows and pausing a moment to gauge their reactions. As I predicted, Salaì is the first to question my motives.

"Master!" he says, already pulling at the embroidered trim of my cloak. "You can't be serious. It's not safe to travel right now. Surely we are better off here in Milan." I don't have to say it. They know I hate the thought of leaving Melzi behind.

Il Fanfoia jumps in. "Salaì is right, Master. There's talk of a new attack on Venice to drive King Louis out. We might find ourselves in the middle of it if we're on the road."

For a moment, I hesitate, thinking of the monks of Santissima Annunziata, the Signoria, and Francesco del Giocondo still expecting me to finish my projects. And I want nothing more than to fulfill my obligations. Forces are still closing in on me from all sides, no matter which way I turn.

"Perhaps young Melzi will consider coming with us," I say.

Melzi's eyes grow wide and he stumbles over his words. "Florence! Are you serious, Master Leonardo? You would bring me with you—all the way to Florence?"

Another Milanese boy; I'm little more than a guaranteed passage to Florence. I can only smile to think it was the same when I made the same offer to Salaì years ago. That's it, then. We're going home. I can no longer avoid it.

"Indeed," I say. "It is as simple as arranging a mule train."

BELLINA

Florence, Italy
1508

Bellina had been born in Antonmaria Gherardini's house.
Lisa's father set her on a lifelong mission to be his daughter's
servant and protector, even while she herself was still a girl. As a
servant, her life flowed with the consistent rhythm of daily tasks,
each one performed thousands of times over, with little thought.
What else was there?

But as Bellina pulled a gilded thread through a fresh swath
of linen by the light of the window in Francesco del Giocondo's
textile workshop, she felt a rush of excitement course through her
veins. Who could have imagined that the simplest act of pulling
a silk thread through a plain piece of linen might have the power
to change her outlook? To change her life?

"You make beautiful stitches," one woman sitting beside her
said. Bellina hadn't learned all their names yet. The women doing
handwork sat close together in neat rows. Behind them, the relentless slap and clack of the old looms filled the great workspace
with noise.

Bellina felt she had just been pulled into a large, happy family
she never knew existed. As they worked, the women chattered,
sharing stories and gossiping, smiling, and helping one another

with their work. Bellina realized it was the one thing she missed most in her life. It was true that from time to time, she had laughed with Dolce at the washing well, but it was always tied to a larger agenda. And Lisa hardly wanted to laugh or share stories at all anymore.

Now, as Bellina made stitch after stitch, she imagined herself as a single bee within a hive. She had feared she would be overwhelmed and under-skilled, but she had no trouble keeping up with the others.

"Thank you," Bellina said. "I never imagined I would be suited for this type of work."

"I'm called Innocenza," the woman said. Bellina detected a strong accent. "You come from Florence?"

"Yes. I live in Master Francesco's house," Bellina said.

Innocenza raised her eyebrows. "You work in the grand house *and* here? Why?"

Bellina wondered how much she should reveal. She decided that it wouldn't be wrong to tell the other woman how she had come to work in the factory, so she told the story of her dedication to Lisa and her mistress's despair. It made her feel better, Bellina realized, to unload the sadness from her own shoulders.

"And you?" Bellina asked. "You are not a Florentine . . ."

"I was born in a small village south of Rome," Innocenza said. "My entire family's still there."

"Why did you journey so far?"

"I needed work," she said. "I didn't want to follow my mother's life as a servant. My aunt told me about this position working in one of the silk factories in Florence. This one is famous, you know."

But Bellina didn't know. She had never thought about it like that. She, like Lisa, thought that luxury goods could be the root of evil. However, hearing things from Innocenza's perspective made her realize that they also kept the city running and provided sustenance to those who might otherwise be out on the streets.

"Well. I am glad to hear that my master puts food on your table," Bellina said.

When Bardo emerged from the foreman's office, the women in the stitching circle fell silent and worked diligently at the pieces in their laps. Hands clasped behind his back, Bardo made his way slowly around the circle, carefully observing each woman's work. When he got to Bellina's place, he stopped and nodded. She couldn't help it; she smiled and somehow, her heart lifted.

"You ladies might learn a thing or two from Bellina," he announced. "And to think it's only her first day among us."

Once he was gone, Innocenza turned to Bellina. "That is surprising," she said. "Bardo is a kind man but his standards are high and such compliments are rare. You have impressed him."

Bellina flushed and she couldn't help a smile from coming over her face. She didn't want to admit that she knew Bardo already.

"Hurry, ladies," one of the older women said. "The sooner we are finished with the pile in front of us, the sooner we can all go home." Already, the sky had turned orange, and Bellina imagined that the sun had already sunk below the cathedral dome. Bellina worked quickly through the pile of embroidery in front of her. She picked up the basket of the day's work to take to Bardo. When she placed it on his worktable, he looked up with a surprised expression. She worried he would examine every stitch and small error. Instead, he pushed back in his chair and regarded her carefully. "I'm impressed."

"If that's all for today, then I am eager to return to my mistress," she said.

Bardo nodded, and then said, "Wait." He reached into his desk drawer. "Such hard work deserves a reward." He pulled out a small tassel ornamented with gilded threads and silver beads, and handed it to her. It was small, and Bellina's previous self must have thought it was extravagant—even sinful. But now, turning over the small luxury in her palm—as silky as the tip of a cat's tail—she only smiled. Then she felt her cheeks flush.

"Simply being told the job is well done is gift enough," she said, but she tucked the tassel into a pocket hidden in her skirts.

Along the riverside, she passed the old dyers' warehouses, now so cleaned up she hardly recognized the place where the *frateschi* had held their secret meetings, all those years ago. She watched the sun sink behind the Ponte Vecchio, making every façade appear as if God had gilded it with a paintbrush. As she walked, she flexed her aching hands open and closed a few times. She was getting old—nearly forty-five years now, she thought to herself, looking down at her lined hands.

She put her hand in the pocket of her skirts and fingered the tassel of silken threads that Bardo had given her. A small treasure. This time, she hadn't stolen it. She hadn't longed for something that seemed out of reach and found herself undeserving. Instead, someone had given her something as a token of appreciation for a job well done. For the first time, she felt rewarded. Worthy.

When she reached the great wooden door of Francesco del Giocondo's home, she took the stairs two at a time to find Lisa. She hoped that her absence had not caused any problem. She put her hand in her pocket on the tassel, and hoped it might bring a small smile to her mistress's face.

Bellina knocked gently on Lisa's bedchamber door. When no

one answered, she peeked inside. Lisa was lying on the bed, her eyes closed. Whether Lisa was lost to sleep or the dark oblivion of her own mind, Bellina did not know. She turned the latch quietly and stood for a long few moments with her palm on the door.

Then she went up the narrow staircase to her small room, intending to make sure nothing had happened to Master Leonardo's portrait while she was gone.

BELLINA WALKED HOME from Francesco del Giocondo's workshop at Por Santa Maria in high spirits. That morning, she had convinced Lisa to don a new yellow dress instead of the old black one. A small triumph. Bellina had not shown her the tassel yet, but she had plans to show her as soon as she got back from her work in the embroidery circle.

The last thing she expected to see was black smoke issuing from an upper window.

For a moment, Bellina froze. She couldn't believe the scene before her eyes: black clouds billowing from a window—from the servants' quarters—and flames licking the edges of the roof. It was the room where she slept, where she kept her meager belongings. It was the room where she had hidden Master Leonardo's painting before he left for Milan nearly two years before.

Inside, the household was in chaos. The servants were running up and down the stairs, tossing heaps of silk clothing and linens out into the walled garden. Bellina had a brief thought of how ridiculous it was to save the valuable objects, when there were people inside.

In the street, voices rose up between the buildings. The neighbors were already rallying to put out the fire.

"The mistress—the children!" She grabbed Alessandro's arm. "Where are they?"

"I don't know." Alessandro broke her grip and ran up the stairs toward the growing fire. Bellina turned her head and she saw Lisa coming down the stairs with the children grasping her skirts.

"There you are!" Lisa said, when they reached each other. "Thank God. I was so worried. I did not know where you were and—"

"Get the children outside!" Bellina pleaded, as she pulled her mistress through the growing smoke. She was terrified that they would not make it out before the smoke took over the house.

"Lisa!" Francesco came from the other side of the house, with Madre on his arm, pressing a cloth to her face. Bellina took a swift look at the older woman, and realized it was the first time she had ever seen Madre look anything but angry or disappointed. Now she looked terrified. "Quick! Go out into the street."

The family moved swiftly down the staircase toward the front door.

"Bellina!" Lisa cried. "What are you doing? Come outside at once."

On the landing, Bellina hesitated. Then she thought of Master Leonardo's portrait hidden away in her cabinet, and she ran up the stairs instead.

Part 8
A SINGLE THREAD

LEONARDO

Florence, Italy
1508

At my uncle's doorstep, Francesco del Giocondo's servant woman stands there, carrying a panel in her hands. She's done her best to cover it with a worn, emerald-colored velvet garment, but of course I would recognize such a flat rectangle anywhere.

"Master Leonardo." She hesitates. "I'm relieved to see you. We heard of your return." She looks nervously down the street. "May I come in?"

I step back to let her into the shadows. Behind us, the smell of roasting meat fills the house that belonged to my uncle, the house that's now my own. In far-flung rooms, Salaì, Il Fanfoia, and Francesco Melzi make themselves comfortable among the spacious bedchambers, the collection of books, the broad hearths, and the well-stocked scullery.

Francesco del Giocondo's servant woman sets down the panel on the stone floor, and I carefully remove the velvet covering. The lady. Lisa Gherardini del Giocondo. The woman with the mourning dress, the plucked brows, and the quiet questions. The melancholy woman who, for a moment, smiled.

The servant woman suddenly grasps my hands. I feel her cool, hard and calloused palms on my wrist. "Please, *signore*. I beg you. Take the picture back. It was nearly destroyed by fire."

ANNE

Montal, France
1944

Anne ducked behind the château's formal hedgerows and hurried toward the road. Once perfectly clipped in geometric patterns, the shrubs were now ragged and overgrown, the perfect place to hide a young woman with a heavy British bolt-action rifle slung over her chest.

Distant machine-gun fire burst somewhere ahead of the château, but it seemed to come closer. The dawn had broken into a golden summer morning, with only a quiet breath of wind and white clouds scudding peacefully over a perfectly blue sky. Occasional clouds cast shade across the verdant landscape.

She had nearly reached the road when there was a rustle in the hedge in front of her. She raised her gun in that direction before she could think; she tried to steady her wobbling hands.

"Anne! Don't shoot!" The hiss of a familiar voice.

"Étienne." She lowered the rifle. Now Anne saw the smudged faces and black berets of other *maquisards* hiding behind the thickly entwined branches.

"Chopin sent us to cover the château," Étienne said. The shadows under the hedge cut deep lines in his brow. "Are you all right?"

"I'm fine, but you managed to scare everyone half to death.

René says you need to get away from the castle. You're bringing the conflict too close to us. We can't afford to have you put the art in danger!"

"Too late," he said. "Come!" He grasped her wrist and pulled her into the hedge and down a steep bank. Nearby, an ancient stone bridge crossed a narrow creek. Anne slung her gun onto her back again and crawled down under the hedge. Sticks and leaves poked her face and hair, and the ground was wet and cool, but she was glad to be under the shelter of the hedge. "We have a little cover here. If the Germans come down the road, we can fire on them before they realize we're here."

"How far away are they?" she asked.

"Well, if you're talking about the ones who are fleeing northward, they're still some ways away." Amélie came to squat down close to Anne. "About three kilometers, we think. But a group of them have gathered in the village."

"The Germans guarding Montal left the château in a cloud of dust," Anne said. "Maybe they will leave us alone at last. I hope to God."

"Shhh!" one of the men said, listening closely to a radio.

Anne heard a man's voice through the static. "German guards captured three *maquisards* in Saint-Céré. There was a . . . public execution in the town square."

There was an exhale of communal grief as the reality spread through the group. One of the men stood and marched away from the group, his face in his hands.

"They are trying to make an example for us," one of the men said.

But the reeling from grief didn't last long as there was the sudden crunch of tank treads on the gravel.

"Krauts," hissed Étienne, pulling Anne down by the arm.

Anne's eyes snapped wide open. She hunkered down, her eyes searching the tar road that lay gleaming in the late sun like a dropped ribbon across the landscape before them. The rumble of an engine was coming closer.

A lone German truck came over the rise, soldiers sitting in the back, guns gleaming in their hands. Anne hesitated, and for a horrifying moment, she saw their features in the sun, their faces and eyes, their hands and lips.

Suddenly, one of the *maquisards* fired.

There was a burst of blood and a brief scream, and then gunfire exploded all around them.

It was somehow quieter than it had been on the *maquis'* secret shooting range; a series of *pop-pops* as the world slowed around her and she was firing half-blindly into the crowd of Germans. There were muzzle flashes and growing clouds of smoke. Someone was yelling profanities beside her, his shotgun spitting into their ranks. One jumped down from the truck among the hail of bullets, took aim into the hedge, and fired. The *maquisard* with the radio did not make a sound. He simply rolled over beside Anne, blinked at her once, and then was completely still.

Above her head on the roadbed, there was confused shouting in German. Then the gunshots slowed and the trucks swung around. Some soldiers were still shooting from the backs of the trucks. Anne lowered her gun as the headlights of the German truck swept across the landscape, staring eagerly in order to see who it was that had come to their assistance.

It was Chopin. When the headlights struck her, they lit up her blond hair like a halo, and she stood with a gun in her hands, chin raised in triumph. For a splendid moment, she herself looked like the *Victory of Samothrace*: a ragged, filthy version, but the same expression of victory glowed in every line of her body.

That was when Anne saw him. Standing beside her. Bearded, so she couldn't be sure, but the face. There was no mistaking it.

"Marcel!" she shouted.

But the headlights just flashed over for an instant before the darkness swallowed him. Anne started forward. Étienne grabbed her hand. "Anne, get down!" he hissed. "They're still shooting!"

She collapsed to the hedge, feeling as though her world had been yanked out from under her, utterly disoriented. Étienne was shaking her. "Anne? Anne! Are you hurt?"

"No!" Anne managed. She realized the gunshots had stopped; she sat in stunned silence. "I'm all right. I just thought . . ." She shook her head.

"You did well, *mademoiselle*," Étienne said, lighting a cigarette. "But this is no place for you. You'd better get back to the château."

"No!" she said. "I'm not going back. I think I just saw my brother."

ANNE RAN BEHIND a small cluster of *maquisards* through the wet grass. Her eyes followed the dark track of Amélie's footsteps in the tall, wet, rustling grass. The dusk had lasted only moments, it seemed, and now, the rising moon was bright enough to make Anne feel exposed, her gun in her hands.

Muzzle flashes burst from the hedge ahead. Anne flung herself on her belly and crawled, the wet grass soaking into her jacket, until she found herself sliding into the hole beside Étienne under the hedge.

He was grappling with his gun. Bullets sprayed above their

heads, close enough that dirt splattered in Anne's face. At least she hoped it was dirt.

"*Merde!* They're back." Étienne wrenched a magazine into place and met Anne's eyes briefly. "Stay down." Étienne's gun was already rattling beside her.

Gun first, Anne slithered to the top of the ditch and took aim. The moonlight etched out the shape of a German truck on the road; it bristled with gun barrels as soldiers used it for cover. Anne took a deep breath, laying the sights of her gun on something that gleamed like a helmet. She squeezed the trigger and it spat fire into the night. Bullet holes peppered across the door of the truck. Screams and shots echoed through the darkness for a few moments before the truck picked up speed and disappeared over the rise. A jubilant voice rose above them.

"They're running!" Amélie cried. "They're retreating north."

"Wait!" Anne pulled Amélie down again, then scrambled to the top of the ditch, her heart hammering.

"Get down, Anne!" Étienne barked, grabbing her ankle. "They're still out there."

Anne slipped down. She reloaded her weapon with a sturdy, metallic sound. "I think they're heading for the woods."

Amélie's eyes widened. "They're moving toward the camp!" she gasped. "We have to warn the others."

"We have to *stop* them," said Anne.

Then they were running, their worn shoes slapping on the road, Anne clutching her gun close as she ran into the fields. The long grass snagged at her; she heard Amélie yelping in panic behind her, but she didn't have time to turn back and help because the first German had appeared ahead of her. He was limping, laboring, his helmet flashing in the moonlight.

"Stop!" Amélie was yelling, her gun raised. "Put down your weapon!"

The German spun, raising his weapon. Amélie's gun banged, and he fell without a sound. Anne vaulted over the fallen man's body, seeing another far up ahead at the fringe of the woods. Anne didn't want to run across that silver field alone, but she had to.

"Stop!" she shouted at the soldier, pushing her burning lungs to croak the sound. "Drop your weapon!" She tried to take aim, but it was impossible while running; the sights swung crazily across the landscape. The German stopped at the edge of the woods and spun. For a moment, he hesitated, and Anne thought he'd surrender. Then he raised his weapon. Anne fired, the gun spitting bullets madly, her aim useless; she saw splinters fly from the trees above the German's head. His shotgun rattled, flashing in the night. She dodged. It was almost too late. A pain struck through her left calf, but she could still run, so she did, firing madly, and the German turned and disappeared into the woods.

Anne's heart was beating all over her chest now. The *maquisards* were well-hidden, but if the German kept running blindly in this direction, he would appear right through the middle of the unsuspecting camp. She prayed Étienne would make it in time. What if the Germans saw him? Up ahead, she glimpsed a shadowy figure dodging from one tree to another.

The time for yelling was over. It was time to shoot now. She fired off another string of rounds, prompting the shadowy figure to stop and turn back, raising his shotgun. The nearest tree exploded beside her, spitting wood shavings into her face. She let out a wordless yell—she wasn't sure if it was fear or fury—and kept firing. The man turned and disappeared into the trees.

She ran after him, but her legs were tiring, and there were no trails. Staggering to a halt among the stately trees, Anne put her back up against a sturdy elm nearby and leaned against it, scanning what little she could see of the woods. The moonlight hardly penetrated through the thick canopy here; it painted small dapples on the forest floor and cast deep shadows under every bough. Each one of those shadows looked like the German. Anne kept her gun up, searching for him, sweeping it back and forth, but all she could see were shadows and all she could hear was her own harsh breathing.

Then, a soft thump, and the tinkle of something rolling. Anne looked down, and the moonlight gleamed on the shape of the grenade that was gently tumbling over the leaf litter toward her.

She didn't think. She spun and ran, tossing down her gun, knowing it would be useless if she couldn't get away, branches snagging her, holes tripping her, running. Light filled the night, hot and red, and the boom burst through her mind and grabbed her by the torso and threw her into the air. She was flailing, flying, bits of branches stabbing through the air alongside her, and the ground rushed up and she struck it and then darkness.

BELLINA

Florence, Italy
1508

"We have an enemy under this very roof." Bellina turned to see Madre's eyes well up with the familiar look of accusation.

Bellina ducked her head and gathered fine, white ash into a dustpan. She tied an old kerchief behind her neck and adjusted it to cover her nose and mouth while she swept the corners of the *salone*. She thought it a miracle the fire had been extinguished before any family members—or the portrait—were harmed. Now, the servants spent their days wiping down furniture with wet rags and sweeping fine dust that seemed to rise into the air and resettle on all the surfaces.

"Why do you jump to that conclusion, Madre?" Lisa asked. "Perhaps a candle was knocked over by accident."

"We'll discover the truth," Francesco placated his mother. "Mark my words."

She persisted. "But of course I'm worried! What's to stop someone from 'knocking over a candle' while we are asleep—or slitting our throats in our beds? Especially after they've already shown themselves willing to burn us all down to ashes?"

"Mother. Calm down. No one did this to us on purpose,"

Francesco assured her, but Bellina thought his voice sounded less than certain. "And if they did, they will never do it again. I will make sure of that. Alessandro is questioning everyone—the kitchen help, the gardener, even the messengers."

Bellina tried to make herself invisible, but the talk of servants suddenly put attention on her. Bellina thought she could see Madre's lips beginning to move, as if she were formulating another one of her unfounded accusations.

Lisa stepped in before Madre could say anything. "Bellina," Lisa said, "come help me in the bedchamber."

"Yes, *polpetta*," she said. The two of them made their way down the sun-filled corridor to Lisa and Francesco's room. Lisa sat on the edge of the draped bed.

"Thank goodness the damage didn't reach this far," Bellina said as they entered the room. She moved to the windows and adjusted the wooden shutters against the sun's heat.

Lisa sighed. "I hate to admit it, but I think Madre is on to something. Someone is targeting us."

"You think someone set the fire on purpose?" Bellina said. She came to sit beside Lisa on the bed.

Lisa nodded and lowered her voice. "There have been fires set in other *palazzi*," she said. "Anyone who has shown loyalty to the old regime. Perhaps someone is watching us."

Bellina whispered, "I have heard there is a plot to assassinate Gonfaloniere Soderini. But . . . people report nonsense at the washing well. Francesco—you think he is involved?" She saw Lisa's eyes well up with fear. "Well, is he?"

"You know he doesn't tell me anything," she whispered. "Have the servants said anything to you?"

"No," she said. "And anyway, I am sure it is not like that. Perhaps it was just a candle, as you said." But Bellina's heart was beating nearly out of her chest. Suddenly, Madre rushed into the room, her skirts rustling with her heft.

"There you are," she said, putting her eyes on Bellina.

"What is it, Madre?" Lisa asked.

"I told you . . . We can't trust anyone in this house."

Madre opened her hand. In her palm was the gold tassel with beads that Bardo had given her.

Bellina stuttered, "Where did you find that?"

"This," she said, wagging the tassel before Lisa's eyes, "fell from the pocket of your maid's skirts while she was sweeping."

"Don't be ridiculous," Lisa said. "Bellina cares for nothing of the material world."

"It's . . . It was a gift!" Bellina stood and attempted to take the tassel from Madre's hand, but the old woman crossed her arms, pressing the bauble against her body.

"What?" Madre snorted. "Who would give you such a thing?"

"Bardo . . . the foreman of Francesco's workshop. He said that I did well with my stitching," she said. "And so he wanted to reward me."

"I do not think that you are such a good stitcher that he would give you such a costly gift," the old woman said. "You have stolen from my son's workhouse."

"I did not take anything!" Bellina insisted, turning to Lisa.

"Madre," Lisa said. "If Bellina says it was a gift, then I believe her."

"You are a fool," Madre said, peering down her nose at Lisa. "Your maid is hiding things from you. You will regret taking her side. Mark my words." She pressed the tassel down on the bed next to Lisa. Lisa only stared at her mother-in-law's back as the old woman swished out of the room.

Bellina sat on the edge of the bed in shock, and she turned to Lisa. "Bardo really did give it to me as a gift," she said. "He said that I did better than the other women who had been sewing for years."

Lisa picked up the tassel and turned it over in her hands. "It's lovely," she said, and placed it back into Bellina's palm.

"I wanted to give it to you," Bellina said. "I have no use for such luxuries. Plus, I thought it might bring a smile to your face."

ON A WINTER'S DAY after the house fire, Bellina watched Lisa latch an old wooden trunk, then stand and pull her oldest daughter, Camilla, into a tight embrace. The girl was nearly as tall as her mother now, a skinny thing with her mother's dark hair woven into a braid. The nuns of San Domenico were waiting.

In the wardrobes, her gowns of green and pink silk were left behind in exchange for a plain woolen cloak. Her dozens of hand-made shoes were passed down to Marietta, just a year younger. Only the bare necessities made up her monastic dowry—a few headscarves and gloves, undergarments for warm and cool weather, a pair of practical leather shoes, slippers, and a special bronze spoon passed down from Francesco's mother.

She would leave behind even her own name in the big house on the via della Stufa. She would be called Suor Beatrice. And she would spend the rest of her days praying for her family's souls.

Within the hour, a carriage would carry her small trunk to the doorstep of the convent just a few blocks away. Francesco would kiss his daughter's head and hand her over to the nuns along with a sum equal to a bride price. Inside the convent walls, she would be safe. She would never know the carnal pleasures of a man, the suffering of childbirth, the heavy weight of a child in her arms. In exchange, she would be tucked away, sheltered from the temptations of the city—and from its dangers.

In some ways, Bellina felt she, too, had lived in a gilded cage, as much as Camilla would live inside the walls of the convent. But it was the temptations, the slippery, shifting machinations of the city, that still tormented her.

BELLINA WALKED AMONG the rows of looms and pretended she didn't notice Bardo watching her. *Ignore him.* At her waist, a large key ring jangled as she observed the clusters of women focused on their embroidery work. When he called out to the errand boy for orange thread, she looked away.

In Francesco's workshop, Bellina's reputation had grown. She learned that she had a talent not only for stitching but for teaching and supervising others. Bardo had quickly promoted Bellina from the stitching circle to supervise a group of women skilled in the working of gilded threads, pearls, and jewel-studded headpieces prepared for export far beyond Florence. Her keys opened the complicated metal locks that secured an array of gilded threads and sparkling beads used to decorate Francesco's famous silks. She would never have imagined herself satisfied surrounded by luxuries, but she had to acknowledge that working in Francesco's textile workshop gave her a sense of purpose and worth she had never before experienced.

She didn't want to admit it, but each day, she looked forward to seeing Bardo a little more. She caught shards of information, none of it verifiable. Bardo had a singer's voice. He raised doves. Doted on his children. Was a marvel with numbers. Had traveled to Lyon with a silk merchant. He was always the first to compliment her, the first to flash his kind smile when she arrived in the mornings.

"Bellina." She felt his hand at the small of her back. She sucked in her breath as he shuttled her into a small corridor between the silk looms and the rows of worktables.

"It's originating from inside Santissima Annunziata," he blurted out in a forced whisper.

"What?" she gasped. "They're starting fires from inside the monastery?"

"Shh! Not exactly. I have been to see my brother."

"Stefano!" For years, Bellina had pushed Stefano from her mind, but now, at the mention of his name, Bellina felt a flash of emotion—a strange blend of hurt and resolve. Was he throwing another lightning bolt at her from inside the walls of the monastery? Was he behind the fire that threatened to destroy Lisa's family and her home?

"It's not how it sounds," he said. "Stefano has become an important leader there; I'm sure you can imagine it. But there is also a group of monks with connections far beyond the walls of the cloister, beyond Stefano's influence. They are targeting Francesco. Stefano is trying to turn the focus away from your house, but I am telling you for the sake of your own safety. And I know you care about your mistress and the children. Be careful."

"Bardo!" one of the other foremen called from across the workshop. Bellina only stared at her shoes, reeling. At last, she gathered herself and turned away.

"What was that about?" Innocenza leaned her head and whispered when Bellina returned to the embroidery circle. Bellina knew that Innocenza would be watching. Innocenza reminded her of Dolce. She seemed to see and hear everything in the workshop.

"Nothing," Bellina said as she picked up one of the women's embroidery and untangled a thread. "One of the looms needs repair." She handed the piece back to the young woman in the circle.

"You lie," Innocenza said with a mischievous grin. "I have seen the way Bardo seeks you out."

"Now *you* lie," Bellina teased, and tried to look offended and unruffled at the same time. "You are not accusing me of doing anything indecent, are you? The man already has a wife. He is not free, and neither am I."

"You know to watch out for him, right?" she whispered. "I have heard he has connections with those who are keeping the Medici out of Florence."

"I don't know what you mean." Bellina picked up another woman's embroidery and picked diligently at a tangled thread.

LEONARDO

Vaprio d'Adda, Italy
1511

In the end, we return north. This time, I take the portrait of the lady with me.

The silk trader's wife, the melancholy Lisa. There is something about her. I never saw it before.

I set the half-finished painting on my easel and contemplate her expression. She has just begun to smile, that moment when delight reaches to the corners of the eyes. One might see a loving, maternal gaze. And yet, there is something flirtatious, perhaps teasing—the charge, the flash of a real person emerging out of the darkness.

We were set to return to Milan again, but with conflicts raging north, south, and east, Melzi pled with me to let him take us to his family's villa on the banks of the Adda River. We can wait there, he said, until things calm down and our patrons might once again turn their attentions away from war and toward art.

Melzi's family villa is our calm respite from the violence that seems to rage in the cities. The villa sits on a high bluff overlooking a curve of the Adda River, where willows drape over the riverbank and swans glide. Melzi's mother, a stout woman around my age, cooks and tends to us as if we were her own personal flock.

In the afternoons, I nap. In the evenings, I stand on the riverbank and listen to the babble of the water. I breathe.

The hours, days, weeks, months stretch out. I draw. I paint. I contemplate the portrait of the puzzling Lisa. I have turned my attention to the landscape in the background, practicing the layers of haze. I consider what to add next. For years, I thought little of this commission for Francesco del Giocondo. And yet, now, the picture resists my refusal. I can't seem to finish it. I can't seem to let her go.

At midday, Melzi's mother serves the others succulent cuts of lamb, making a separate plate for me and taking care to cater to my preference not to eat the flesh of an animal. Melzi relishes his mother's attention. Salaì has accepted that Melzi is here to stay. And Il Fanfoia decided to stay in Florence. Salaì and the young apprentice seemed to have struck up a genuine camaraderie. It is gratifying to have played some small role in creating a friendship. For now, we live on my uncle's inheritance and the hospitality of Francesco Melzi's family.

At every meal, there is talk of war and of machinations far beyond us. "There is to be a new canal built at San Cristoforo," Melzi tells me, "if Milan is ever returned to peace."

"It can't go on forever," I say. "The French are already celebrating their victories. I've been asked to ready a triumphal celebration for King Louis XII to commemorate his defeat of the Venetians. Milan may be next."

Melzi's mother lays a cake on the table. Already my mouth is watering in anticipation of the crumbling texture of almond flour, cornmeal, butter, and a dusting of sugar on my tongue.

"*Auguri,* Master Leonardo!" Melzi says. "How old are you?"

I take a moment to calculate.

"I believe I'm nearly sixty."

ANNE

Montal, France
1944

The sound in her ears was a thin, shrill whine, slicing through her splitting head. Anne coughed and opened her eyes. There was dirt in her mouth, smoke in her nose. Everything hurt. She slammed her hands down onto the dirt to push herself upright. Everything was ringing and spinning.

Grenade. It was a grenade. The German. There was a German here who'd come to kill her—

The world was tipping and bucking under her. Her eyes combed the dark branches, but there was only silence. After a long few seconds, Anne's head began to clear and she rose shakily to her feet. Had the German moved on after throwing the grenade? Had he left her for dead? She had no idea how long she'd lain there in the woods. Anne made her way through the tangled branches in near darkness. In her right arm, there was a fierce sting. Which way was the château? Or the *maquis* camp? She was no longer sure.

She stepped into a clearing, and suddenly, the silver slice of the moon appeared. She turned and caught sight of the road. There were figures. Immediately, her heart pounded until she recognized them. It was dark, but not so dark that she could not make out their shabby clothes. These were not neatly uniformed Germans. They were the dirt-caked, cobbled-together uniforms of resistance fighters who had lived in the woods for months on end.

"I'm here," Anne said before she fell to her knees and her friends came running.

WHEN THEY DRAGGED Anne into the camp, she collapsed.

"Clear a cot for her!" She recognized Étienne's voice and her chest heaved in relief.

"I'm okay," she said. "I just can't hear too well. And my arm hurts."

They laid her down and for a long, thankful moment, she closed her eyes. She was safe. She had killed a man. Maybe more than one. Had that really happened?

When she opened them, she saw Étienne's crooked grin and Chopin's concerned expression. There was another young man Anne recognized as a medic, even though he didn't look a day older than seventeen.

"You may still have a few tiny bits of shrapnel in there," the young medic said, watching Anne's face while he wrapped her throbbing upper arm. "But it should heal up just fine." She winced.

"Your target practice paid off, *chérie*," Étienne said. "They were trying to kill as many of us as possible on their way out. If you hadn't slowed down that Kraut with the grenade . . ."

Chopin smiled. "You would have earned a medal, if we had one to give you. Don't move. Our *commandant* wants to meet you."

"You're the big boss, I thought," Anne said, grimacing.

Chopin shook her head. "No. Someone bigger than I am." She turned her head as another face appeared beside the cot.

"Anne!" A familiar voice. "*Dieu!* It's really you!"

Suddenly, there was an unmistakable, lined face so familiar it was like slipping on a favorite pair of shoes.

Her brother.

But he had to be a hallucination. Anne stretched her numb fingers as she stared at him; his mouth was moving, but though the ringing had quieted a little, all she could hear was a vague warbling somewhere beyond it. He stepped toward her, still talking. Marcel? No. He had to be a dream. Ever since she had left Paris, she had been seeing him everywhere. Without hearing his voice, there was no way of knowing if it was really him.

He reached out and took her hands in his. Then his arms enfolded her, and he pulled her against his chest. He was warm, and solid, and when she flung her good arm around him she felt the thump of his heart on her cheek.

Marcel.

It wasn't her imagination. He was alive.

"YOU WON'T BELIEVE IT," Anne said as she led the way through the tangled forest toward the château of Montal. "The *Mona Lisa* is hiding in our depot director's bedroom."

"*La Joconde?*" Marcel's jaw dropped.

She smiled. "I'll show you."

Marcel pushed through the brush with the confidence of one who had lived in it for nearly five years. Anne watched him carefully as they picked their way to a narrow footpath. His once baby-faced cheeks were tan and weathered; where he'd grasped her hand, his skin was hard and calloused. He'd matured into a lean, strong man with broad shoulders and an angular face. He'd grown a full beard. A small pink scar traced its way from the corner of his left eye up across his temple and into the tumult of light hair. That once-unruly kid had matured into a man. Competent. Courageous. The head of a resistance network.

Before they departed the *maquis* camps, someone had pushed a newly loaded British rifle into Anne's hands. The ringing in her ears had almost gone now, and Anne was just happy to have her brother back, weapon or not.

"All this time you've been running with your girlfriend. Chopin. She's Jewish?"

He nodded. "I suppose Kiki told you about her. Guess I should have, but I thought you'd do something to keep me from her because you'd be worried for me." He gave her a sheepish look. "As soon as the trouble started, I knew I had to get her out of Paris right away. If you knew where we were, you might get yourself into trouble trying to follow us." He shook his head. "I didn't know you were capable of getting yourself into trouble all on your own."

"You've been living in the woods all this time?"

"We hid on her uncle's farm near Clermont-Ferrand for a while," he said. "Then Monsieur Dupont helped us get to his contacts in Lyon. After that, others began to join us and we started to organize. It grew so big . . ."

"All this time, you've been so close," Anne said, huffing in disbelief. "To think how hard I've been trying to reach you and Kiki!"

"I've been getting messages to her," he said. "Last I heard she was dancing on a table for a regiment of Germans."

Anne looked concerned for a moment, then burst out laughing. "Somehow I knew she'd find a way to survive!"

Even though Anne wanted nothing more than to talk with her brother, her questions died in her throat as soon as they reached the road at the edge of the forest. Anne felt a pang as she saw the broken window glass and bullet pockmarks across the stone façade of Montal's old castle. Silence settled on them, tight as violin strings. They hurried across the castle lawn as dusk fell.

ANNE FOUND her Louvre colleagues in good shape yet shaken from the days of gunfire. The German guards had disappeared in a cloud of dust, leaving behind little more than empty bullet casings and the imprints of truck treads in the mud.

Even better, they received the news that Allied forces had reached Paris at last. Though the Germans were doing their best to hold the city, Monsieur Jaujard had already ordered the French flag raised atop the Louvre once more. In the castle dining hall, there was a communal cry of joy. Anne closed her eyes, smiling, allowing herself to imagine it. Cleansing away her memory of the sandbagged Louvre, sponging gently the thought of a Louvre under a Nazi flag out of her mind, she thought of the Louvre as she knew and loved it when she was just a naïve art student. A proud, pillared building, towering above the streets, the pride of Paris, the flag of a free France flying over its roof. Marcel squeezed her hand.

René, Lucie, and the others welcomed Marcel into their fold, amazed to hear the story of how Anne had found her brother amidst the chaos of a gun battle in the woods.

"That young man is famous among the Resistance, you know,"

René told Anne, smiling over a cigarette and cup of coffee. "And to think he's your brother . . . Now I see that a certain recklessness runs in your family," he teased her.

A familiar smile broke across Marcel's face. "It's a family tradition."

BELLINA

Florence, Italy
1512

Mark my words. The pope's soldiers are coming," Bardo said, but Bellina couldn't see them yet.

From an upper-story window of Francesco's workshop, Bardo and Bellina stood side by side, gazing out across the Arno, the afternoon sun turning the stone sill hot enough to scorch their fingertips. As far as she could see, the trees lining the river were lush and heavy with fruit.

Bellina felt strangely secure, as if nothing bad could happen as long as Bardo's sturdy, solid presence was beside her. And yet, word had spread like a wildfire across the city: In the countryside, papal troops were assembling, organizing their march northward to Florence. Bellina had watched Bardo's tan face turn pale as he shared the news with the workers: Soderini, who had been expected to rule for life, had suddenly lost his French supporters. Now, Bardo had said, the *gonfaloniere* might have little choice but to flee the city.

"If Soderini leaves," Bardo said in a low voice, "it will be easy for them to stroll into Florence and take what they believe is their own." Were the Medici really going to return to Florence after all these years? Bellina could hardly believe it.

For now, the city and the rolling hills beyond it stood eerily still. Nothing moved in the distant landscape; a single, lonely ox-cart rattled unhurriedly along the cobblestones toward the Porta di San Brancazio. Even the Arno's current had turned slow and sparkling in the heat as the cicadas made a sound like upholstery shears sharpened on the grinding stone.

For a time, Bellina had harbored the false illusion that things would always be this way. She spent her days strolling through the rows of weavers and embroiderers, watching for imperfections, for lapses that might slow down production in Francesco's workshop. In the ground-floor trading offices, Francesco and Lisa's sons were being instructed in the ways of the family business. Andrea, a strapping ten-year-old, now followed his older brothers, Piero and Bartolomeo, to visit the shops of their best customers. Gherardo was now tasked with sitting at a large desk, tallying sums in a leather-bound ledger. Francesco was determined to make a responsible man out of him.

Bellina had already noted that Francesco was more absent from the workshop than ever, as he became more involved in the city councils where the silk guild continued to elect him. He had also turned his attentions to other painters, as a new haul of paintings from the studios of the city's most esteemed artists filled the corridors of the house. And it seemed that Master Leonardo's portrait of Lisa was now all but forgotten.

In the spring, Lisa and Francesco had led their youngest daughter to the Franciscan convent of Sant'Orsola. Marietta was bundled into a carriage along with her trunk of meager belongings. Soon enough, her hair was shorn, and Francesco made a donation to the sisters that might rival the most generous bride price in the city.

And as soon as she sent Marietta off to Sant'Orsola, Lisa followed. Now, Lisa spent many days in the convent's great weaving room, working alongside other noblewomen who were the invisible hands of the nuns' work. The women wove white cloth on ancient looms, embroidered sacred vestments, and wound long strands of gilded thread that would fill the convent's coffers and fund their charitable work. Day by day, Bellina watched Lisa pull herself out of the darkness by serving others.

Bellina wished she could say that her own work in the textile trade served a charitable purpose. But if she was honest with herself, her motives were mostly selfish. Her attraction to Bardo seemed to grow with each passing day. She continued to think of him on her walk home and at night as she turned down the silk coverlet on Lisa and Francesco's bed. She struggled to push away the thought of him.

"I'm going home to make sure my wife and children are accounted for," Bardo said, turning to set his large brown eyes on Bellina. "I think we should close up early and return to our homes. Don't forget to shutter your windows tonight."

Ignore him. Nod and look away.

Instead, she looked at him and squeezed his forearm, as solid as a tree trunk. "Stay safe."

Bellina took one last look toward the southern hills. Right now, were the pope's soldiers fastening their chain mail, watering their horses, and sharpening their swords? As Bellina looked out over the haze, she struggled to imagine it. Were the Medici coming back to Florence? This time, with Soderini ready to flee the city and a Medici pope on the throne of Saint Peter, it looked like they might succeed at last.

"SHE HAS DONE nothing but bring shame on this family!"

In the corridor outside the *salotto*, Bellina froze. Madre's voice made the hairs at the nape of Bellina's neck stand on end. Were they talking about her?

"Don't be ridiculous, Mother!" Francesco's voice. "Lisa has been a faithful and upstanding wife." Bellina winced. No. Word had spread that Lisa's younger sister had allowed male suitors into the convent of San Domenico. It seemed that the entire city was aflame with the news of the men's breach of the convent walls.

"And the same place where you have sent your own daughter!" Madre continued. "I shudder to think what the neighbors are saying."

Francesco only scoffed. "They have no place to say anything because Lisa spends many days there, giving her time. Plus, we have funded their coffers generously over the years. They won't do anything to put our funding at risk."

Bellina peered into the room. It was dark, the windows shuttered against the infernal heat and the threat of riots in the streets. For days, supporters of every political faction in Florence had come out of the woodwork, throwing garbage and lighting fires until smoke curled from every square in the city and Bellina's clothing, hair, and skin smelled of embers even though she had done her best to stay home. Even in the shadows, Bellina could see that Francesco's face looked haggard and drawn.

Madre went on relentlessly, wagging a finger at Lisa. "It is bad enough that your sister has brought shame upon the family, but your daughter is in the same convent and carries the Giocondo family name. We cannot afford to put it at risk."

Bellina thought Lisa was remaining remarkably calm under

Madre's relentless condescension. "I am as stunned as we all are," Lisa said, "but this is not my doing, Madre."

"Of course it's not," Francesco said. "It will blow over."

There was a knock at the open door and all of them looked up to see Alessandro standing in the doorway, his face pale and unreadable. Bellina could see at once that his hands were shaking. "Master," he said, "there are some men here for you . . ."

"What men?" Francesco asked and Alessandro lowered his voice.

"They . . . ," he began, but did not finish. At that moment, several guards of the Signoria, big men with swords, appeared at the door.

"Francesco del Giocondo. We arrest you in the name of the Signoria under charges of treason to the Republic of Florence."

Lisa gasped and clutched desperately at her husband's arm.

"Treason!" Madre exclaimed, and for a moment, Bellina thought the old woman might fall to her knees.

"There's been a mistake!" Lisa cried. "Who has accused him?"

But the strong men did not answer. They only grasped Francesco by either arm and led him to the stair landing. Francesco did not try to put up a fight. Instead, he turned to Lisa and said through gritted teeth, "They cannot keep me."

Madre seemed to regain her strength and she struck out at the men, beating futilely at their backs all the way to the stair landing.

Francesco called back to Lisa as the men bundled him down the stair treads. "Go see Fabiano the notary—the one who worked with Master Leonardo da Vinci's father. He will know what to do."

LEONARDO

Between Florence and Rome, Italy
1512

'm an old dog now, if you haven't taken note," I call to Salaì and
Melzi, who have reined in their mounts ahead of me. At the top
of a rise overlooking a vast panorama of green hills, Salaì watches
my horse hobble over the stones.

"Take your time, Master," Salaì calls back. "We don't want any
harm to come to those pictures."

The trunks behind us contain several panels I've worked on
over the course of years: the John the Baptist, which Salaì says he
wishes he still resembled; a Leda and the Swan I've continued to
tinker with; and the portrait of Francesco del Giocondo's Lisa.
These pictures have now traveled between Florence and Milan
multiple times. And now, to Rome. My little entourage heads
south once again.

Of all the powerful men I've written to over the years, I would
not have gambled that His Holiness would be the one to lure us
away from our comfortable retreat at Melzi's family villa along
the Adda in Lombardy. There is no refusing when the pope calls
you to Rome, I suppose, no matter which pope it is. Even the son
of a Medici, who has promised us our own suite of rooms adjacent
to the papal apartments.

One evening at nightfall, we ducked through the gates of Florence, Salaì and Melzi under strict instructions not to tell anyone. For a few glorious days, I retreated to the comfortable, quiet chambers of my uncle's house, venturing out only long enough to collect money from my accounts and to see if what they say is true: the Medici have returned not only to the papal throne but to the Signoria of Florence.

I am only gratified that we were not here to see the terror of fires in the squares, the throwing of vanities from the windows of fine homes, the wailing and shouting through the streets, the arrest of the city's most esteemed men. Even my old friend Machiavelli was charged with corruption and put on trial. And Francesco del Giocondo, who has always seemed invincible to me, was imprisoned for several days before he was released on bail. Soderini capitulated easily enough and fled the city with the clothes on his back, fearful that the troops would lay waste to Florence just as they did in Prato.

And now, a reversal. No sooner have the Medici returned than Francesco del Giocondo once again serves as prior of the Signoria. They say he has even pledged five hundred gold ducats from his own reserves in support of the new regime.

It is as if that ugly business with Savonarola never happened at all, as if no one remembers the upturned coffers and vanities burning on a great pyre. The wool and silk traders rake florins into their accounts. Their wives, buttressed by an entourage of servants, totter around the filthy streets in high-heeled clogs, in layers of silk and velvet. The notaries flitter around the city from guild hall to fine home, their gowns flapping. The old dyers' warehouses on the Arno have been renovated, and the workshops on the Por Santa Maria keep their looms operating until well past the evening bell. Just a few years ago, no one would have believed it.

At last, resupplied with a round of pecorino, a few loaves of bread, dried venison, and figs pickled in vinegar, we continue on to Rome. We pause periodically to see to the animals, to fill our flasks with water from a stream, to make camp in a grove of trees. With each trip, my mule train grows longer, and the slow progress takes its toll. My beard is white now, my bones brittle. Just a few more days to the gates of the holy city.

On the way to Rome, I've made careful observations in my notebooks about the light's effects over distances of terrains. I've awoken before dawn to watch the shadows and the dark, the infinite variation over the hillsides and valleys. I've watched the smoky horizon disappear at dusk. These beginnings and ends of shadows may be infinitely diminished and infinitely increased.

When we arrive in the papal apartments, I'll carefully unwrap my paint-stained easels and bundles of brushes. I'll open the small pots of pigments and smell them to make sure they've not turned rancid. I'll pull the pictures from their velvet and twists of cords. At last, I'll be able to experiment with these newfound observations. Lisa's likeness has become a field of games, a place to experiment with the lightness and dark. The background is now populated with craggy mountains pulled from my imagination of what might be, with a distant river running through a valley.

The letters of Francesco del Giocondo's notaries—demanding the return of the portrait—will now only stoke my hearth. No. No matter how powerful he is, he will not get his Lisa back. Not now.

BELLINA

Florence, Italy
1512

After only a few days in prison, Francesco returned home. And just as quickly, it seemed, the Medici returned to Florence. Bellina could hardly believe it.

With the Medici reinstalled in their offices near the Piazza della Signoria, Francesco's textile business suddenly ramped up production to a height Bellina had never seen before. Dozens of new workers were pulled from the city and countryside. The workbenches were rearranged, and among the old faces, there were many new ones. Bellina walked up and down the rows, correcting, organizing, coordinating. Because Francesco had proven himself a loyal supporter, the Medici and those close to them were ordering textiles from his workshop. Bellina could hardly count the number of busy hands in the workshop and the *braccia* of fabric piling up in the storehouses below them.

At her usual place at a south-facing window, Innocenza looked up and smiled at Bellina.

"You are keeping up?" Bellina asked.

Innocenza nodded. "Many in the guild are complaining about the extra work, but I am glad for a chance to get out from under my husband's eyes." She smiled. "And I hope Master Francesco is compensating you for the added responsibilities you have now, with all these extra people to watch."

"Oh, I do not ask for more." Bellina blushed, then wondered why it hadn't occurred to her to ask. Innocenza raised an eyebrow.

"Why not?" Innocenza asked. "You are being expected to work harder. And I hear that your master has money to give away."

"What do you mean?"

"It's no secret that he gave five hundred gold florins to the Medici cause," Innocenza said. "He must have plenty to spare."

Bellina froze. Five hundred gold florins . . . It was more than she could imagine earning in a lifetime of manual labor.

Bellina picked up a gilded trim a young girl sitting alongside Innocenza was stitching. With a small metal pick, she carefully picked out the seams. "Do this part again," she said to the girl. "Straighter this time."

"You are good at the gilded trims," Innocenza said. "I wish I could get them so straight."

"Practice," Bellina said. "That's it. I've been doing it since I was barely old enough to sit still."

"I am not sure," Innocenza replied. "I have tried the trims half a thousand times. Bardo used to take them away from me and give them to someone else."

Bellina gave her a pained smile, then glanced at the empty office at the end of the row as the two women fell silent and Bellina's mind drifted back to all the time she had spent in the workshop with Bardo.

"Where did he go?" Innocenza asked.

"Back to his family workshop," Bellina said. She didn't say that she suspected Bardo had felt so disillusioned by the Medici return that he had left Francesco's workshop and returned to his upholstery machines.

"Did you and Bardo . . ." Innocenza seemed unsure how to proceed. "Was there something between you?"

Bellina felt her face flush. She stared at the embroidery trim in her hands and picked harder at the seams. "Don't be ridiculous."

"You never . . . got together with a man?"

Bellina gave her a sad smile. "My life has been dedicated to caring for Lisa."

"You've never been in love?"

Bellina stopped pulling at the stitches and looked out the window toward the muddy banks of the Arno. "I thought I was once," she said. "But maybe I dreamt it."

Innocenza lowered her voice and looked ashamed for asking. "Oh. I'm sorry."

"It's okay," Bellina said. "There was a time I thought he was the one God had sent for me." She paused. "But it turned out He wanted him for the monastery instead."

"Then that means God has someone for you still," Innocenza said.

Bellina coughed out a laugh as she finished her square of fabric and picked up the next one. "I'm an old dog now, Innocenza, in case you haven't noticed. My chance to marry and have children has long passed."

"I don't believe that," Innocenza said. "Surely the love of your life is waiting out there." She gestured to the window.

Bellina shook her head. "Just consider how many husbands mistreat their wives. My mistress loves her husband and I am satisfied with that."

"Does she?" Innocenza asked, incredulously. "Then the *signora* is fortunate. Those types of marriages are rarely founded on love."

"Yes," Bellina said. "I guess Lisa is luckier than most."

"Does he shower her with gifts?" Innocenza said.

"I suppose," she said.

"And your master . . . I thought he commissioned a portrait by Master Leonardo da Vinci to paint your Lisa. I imagine it must be beautiful to behold."

Bellina paused, thinking of the portrait and wondering where it was, after all these years.

"Yes," Bellina said. "Yes it was."

LEONARDO

Florence
1515

I t's been many years since I last saw Lisa. In that time, I have come to regard her as something more than a real woman. In my mind, she is an idea. No. An ideal.

All that time, as I have washed thin layers of varnish over a smoky landscape or mixed colors with the edge of my smallest finger, Lisa has lived only in my imagination. She has become the sum total of everything I know and understand, and at the same time, everything I do not.

And yet she *is* real.

She stands before me for the first time in perhaps twelve years, a woman in the flesh. She is older, of course, her body softer, her cheeks more hollowed. All the same, there is something more alive in her appearance than all those years ago, when she sat before me, a forlorn woman in a mourning dress. Now, I see a vitality and vibrancy about her that was missing before. Is she flushed with new life, or is it simply that I have been staring at her face in two dimensions for so many months? For a moment, I struggle, thinking of a thousand things I want to change in her portrait.

Lisa's servant woman is back, too. For her part, she has turned more gray-haired and hunched like those who spend their days at the washing well or the loom. The two women hesitate in the doorway. For a few long moments, I forget my manners. I only stand, my mouth agape, and stare at the woman whose face has stood on my easel and been my project for all my months in Rome.

"Master Leonardo." Lisa speaks and the spell is broken. "We heard that you had returned home to Florence."

"Only for a short while, yes, before I return to His Holiness. But forgive me, my lady. How gratified I am to see you. Please. Come in."

The women follow me into my uncle's old *cortile,* where water babbles in a small fountain and a stray, striped yellow cat who has taken up with us trots across the stones to swirl around our ankles. The tinkling of cutlery, the singing of the cook, and the smell of roasting onions waft from the rear kitchens. We settle on a stone bench in the courtyard where Salaì and Melzi spend days filling their notebooks until their inkwells run dry.

"I trust that you have been thriving in Rome?" she asks, settling on a stone bench in the shadows of an arcade.

"Indeed. His Holiness has been lodging us in the papal palace and offered me several important commissions."

An exaggeration. Perhaps. But how do I begin to explain that even though Giovanni de Medici—now called Leo X—has provided my assistants and me a comfortable suite of rooms in the papal palace, he has mostly left us alone? Meanwhile, he's asked Michelangelo Buonarroti—I can't seem to rid myself of the annoying runt, even in Rome—to fresco the ceiling of the old chapel of Pope Sixtus. And even Raffaello Sanzio, another youngster with a better demeanor at least, has followed us to Rome and has managed to win other important commissions.

Meanwhile, as a seeming afterthought, His Holiness has asked me for little more than a plan to drain the marshes outside the city and to design an astronomical telescope. And I've been tasked with writing letters to a German mirror maker who's defaulted on his commission. As if I might know of such things.

"It's been a very . . . busy time," I manage to say.

Lisa nods. "I can imagine how occupied you must be. I won't take up too much of your time. I came to ask about the portrait you did of me, years ago now," she says. "You remember it?" She looks at me with her dark eyes, nearly black as coal. So innocent. So trusting. The servant woman next to her stares at her fingers, fidgeting with the edge of a silk cord of her dress.

The portrait. I feel a pang in my gut and it's all I can do not to turn my head in the direction of my bedchamber, where the very portrait she's asked about stands on an easel. That portrait. It has become my obsession.

How could I possibly begin to describe how her likeness has tormented me in Rome? How, in my idle hours in the Belvedere wing of the pope's palace, I have returned to it each day? How I've swept aside the clutter of my notebooks, scientific instruments, books, and clothing so I might reposition the portrait around my bedchamber in the changing Roman light, how I have tinkered with the hands, the hair, the smile? How I have experimented with various brushes and my own fingertips? That it is among the smallest number of things I brought with me to Florence?

"Of course I remember the portrait, *signora*."

She nods. "I would like to see it finished so I may give it to my husband as a gift. A surprise. You see," she continues, "after a period of . . . darkness . . . Francesco has taken on new responsibilities on the council of the Signoria. I might like to surprise him with my likeness."

Only natural, of course. The display of opulence is even greater than before the Medici fled the city decades ago. Even household servants like Lisa's look as if they might pass for merchants' wives.

"You must be very proud, *signora*. But the portrait . . ." I clear my throat and try not to stammer. "It was never really finished, you know."

"Yes," she says. "I thought we might make some time to finish it so I may give it to Francesco when he is inducted."

"Ah, a lovely idea." I drum my fingers on my knee. "Generous. Yes."

I do my best not to let my eyes wander to the door of the next room, where, if the ladies were to enter, they would find said portrait on the other side of the door. As soon as she leaves, I see that I will need to change at least a dozen things now that I have seen the lady again in the flesh.

"I'm sorry, my lady. I'm afraid your portrait is not here," I say, hoping she won't see the bold lie written all over my face. "You see, I've left it behind in my studio in Rome."

Part 9

NORTHWARD

ANNE

Montal, France
1944

Anne carefully pried away the velvet wrapping and turned the 450-year-old poplar panel toward the window of René's office. Marcel gasped and this time, Anne didn't look down at the lady with the secret smile. She looked instead at her brother, soaking up the surprise and wonder of his expression, followed by a deep and inexpressible awe. She had seen that look on the faces of so many people walking through the Louvre's galleries. This portrait had a powerful, inexplicable effect; it left every viewer a little different, a little changed by what they'd beheld.

"*Dieu*," breathed Marcel. "So this is what you've been carrying across the country since we left home."

Anne nodded. "Yes. Along with countless other treasures."

"You know, when our group first heard of moving these paintings away from Paris, well . . . Even though I worked inside the Louvre briefly, I always wondered why anyone would bother—you know, in a war with so much suffering and death. But now . . ."

"I know."

By the hearth, Pierre leaned over and stoked the fire while Anne and Marcel continued to stare into the face of the *Mona Lisa*. Outside, snow had begun to fall in a steady pattern of tumbling flakes. Alongside the hearth were stacks of old newspapers full of stories real and exaggerated. Anne hoped that the most recent papers were correct: that the Allies were pushing the Germans back to the north and east. That Paris was back in French hands, and France itself was all but liberated; that Luxembourg and Belgium were free, that the German city of Aachen had been captured by the Allies, and that there was a stalemate with Italy. Could they dare to believe that the war might come to an end? Anne watched Pierre lean over awkwardly, crumpling the yellowed newspapers and tossing them one by one into the fire.

For now, all that mattered was that Marcel was safe, that he was with her now.

"She's breathtaking," Marcel said. "But I think there is also something melancholy about her. No?"

"I have always thought so."

"How soon will you take her back to Paris?" he asked.

"René says we should be ready within a few days. We've gotten good at packing up and leaving," she said. "Hopefully this time we'll have enough room and enough trucks." She squeezed Marcel's hands. "Come with us," she said.

A hesitation. "I will go back to the woods first," he said.

"Of course. Silly of me," Anne said. "You will want to return with Chopin."

He nodded. "Sara."

"Sara." Anne nodded. "You love her."

Marcel grinned. "Now tell me. All this time we've been apart, what about you? You haven't found love amid this war? It seems as though you've wooed at least one *maquisard*." He grinned.

"Étienne." She felt heat rise to her cheeks, then she shrugged, feeling the now-familiar mixture of attraction and uncertainty.

"Well. There's Amélie, and anyway, I don't think I could ever steal someone away."

But then, Anne's heart took wing. It flew effortlessly, taking her all the way back to a night at Loc-Dieu, to the frantic hope in the dark eyes of an Italian tailor, to the pressure of his lips on her own. At that moment, she wanted nothing more than to return to Paris. "Was I in love? Maybe for a little while. At least I thought so. But perhaps I dreamt it."

"Then perhaps you will come with us instead?" he said. "God willing, we'll end up back in Paris soon, too."

Anne shook her head. "No. My first duty is to see these things returned safely to the Louvre."

LEONARDO

French Alps
1516

I gather my wool cloak around my neck as our mule train rattles over another mountain pass. The cold moonlight brightens the snow-covered forms as if it were day, drawing the world of night in scales of gray. All the beauty, solidity, and color of the Alpine landscape, transmuted to shadow play.

A cold rush of wind blows through me and my lungs take a deep, wheezing breath. Gone are the familiar smells of the city: rotting horse feces, rancid laundry water, the stinking battalion of dye vats on the riverbanks. I know the future of our kind lies in those busy streets, but how I've come to loathe them in my old age. They represent so much of what is base and poor in the human condition.

Here in this strange, windswept, shadowed world, all of that seems so far away, a place God surely intended to be His own masterpiece. The steep slopes, snow-caked crags, rugged angles and curves; it is the most magnificent sculpture that could ever exist. No rowdy upstart sculptor could ever attempt such a creation.

It is not my first trip over the Alps, but now, as my lower back aches with the rolling of the mule beneath me, the blood in my legs is halted and my feet become numb, I wonder if it is to be my last. My mind is still eager, but my body can no longer keep up. A month-long journey over this strange and wonderful landscape may kill me.

"You all right, Master?" Melzi reins in his mule and waits for me.

"Fine as ever," I say, but I wonder how long it will take the boys to figure out I am lying. I haven't told them that some mornings, I awake to find my right hand numb. For a man in my position, a painter and sketcher, it is a death sentence. My muscles and tendons are contracting beyond my ability to counter it. I am losing the deftness I've always had, and upon which I have so strongly relied. I haven't told the boys; they would only flit and fuss over me. Salaì now treats me as if he is my mother. But before long, I fear they will notice it.

I'm fortunate to be able to use my left hand, in the end. It seems cynical to me, the left hand being the sinister side, where the devil would sit to whisper in one's ear. I've never had much interest in or time for such nonsense, but with every step closer to the grave, it's hard not to give these matters at least a passing thought.

But what's on my mind most is my right hand. I've long been ambidextrous, and that gives me an edge over my encroaching decrepitude. But I can't outrun it much longer. My fingers curl, my muscles lock up. Even Salaì looks at my hand with a growing concern he cannot disguise. The unrelenting cold of the Alps, this treacherous wind, only makes things worse. I can only hope that by the time we stop for a spell in Lyon, it improves.

I'm not the only one. The ravages of aging have taken my friend and a valued patron, Giuliano de Medici. The brother of our pope and a man of great generosity, his passing has changed things for me.

But it's the promise of a new, powerful patron that propels me forward, along this strange and beautiful winter's journey. The king of France has offered to make me a royal painter, even to provide me with my own manor house in the valley of the Loire, where, I am told, there are many fine castles and estates. I look forward to returning to court life; I have missed it after so many years away from Ludovico's side in Milan.

They've promised I'll be treated the same as the royals who surround me, and I cannot lie; I'm looking forward to it. I've been up and down our peninsula constantly over the years, even as war has torn its own path across our beloved lands. I've survived this long, and I feel I've got a bit of travel left in these old bones.

The sharp wind cuts through me, the mules grumbling. They carry my panels and easels, others with stores of dried, smoked meat; pickled vegetables and small vats of wine. The beasts push on, their odor wiped away by these frigid winds. But they are tireless, and so must we all be. There *are* good times waiting in France, I believe that; it's no matter of bravado. But we must survive the journey first. The winds push us back, the Alps echo with their howling cries. But there's not much farther to go, and I am determined not to be found in the crags of the mountains, under a sheet of snow.

When we arrive, I will unpack my *Lisa* and decide what to do with her next. My Florentine lady. She has become my constant companion, my consort to the lonesome end of our shared journey. We've been through war and peace together. She will be finished in France, if it's the last thing I ever do.

ANNE

Paris, France
1945

Nearly six years had passed since Anne left Paris and she could hardly believe the city lay just around the bend. Her hands gripped the steering wheel as the truck bumped and rattled. The road was trampled with tank treads and she steered the truck's worn tires around gaping holes glittering with last night's rain. In the end, it had taken months to put everything back together for transport back to Paris. Now, fear crept into the shadows of her mind. She had a feeling that the Paris she returned to would not be the same as the city she had left.

Flexing her left arm, Anne felt the hitch in the movement that was left there by the grenade shrapnel that had ripped her flesh apart. There was still a piece wedged in the muscle, the *maquis* medic had said, but taking it out might be trouble. She would always carry a fragment of the war inside her.

So would Paris, she guessed. How many homes would she find destroyed or left vacant? How many people would be dressed in mourning in the city of light? But they told her that the Louvre was undamaged. The Louvre would be the same, and so would the many paintings that weighed down her truck as it groaned around the bend. She changed gears, steadied it, easing it around the turn. Not a single one of the Louvre's paintings had been permanently damaged. They would go back to their places untouched by evil. They would be a symbol of something lasting amid a world that had, in just six short years, seemed on the brink of succumbing to the darkness.

They rounded a turn and there it was. Paris. That unmistakable, pencil-like steel tower. La Tour Eiffel. Her city. Home. She felt tears prickling at the corners of her eyes.

Sitting beside her, Pierre pressed his palm to his lips and Anne saw that he, too, struggled to push back the tears.

"I can't wait to get home," she said, diffusing the emotion that had grown heavy in the silence between them.

"You'll be back in the archives soon enough, I suppose?" he asked, gathering his wits.

She took a deep breath, feeling something tremble deep in the pit of her heart. "As soon as possible. Yes. But there are a few things I have to do first."

BELLINA

Florence, Italy
1518

Bellina arrived home from the workshop to find black silk hanging from all the windows of Lisa and Francesco's house. Death.

It was the only thing it could mean. Bellina felt her heart fall to her worn shoes. She watched the black, shining fabric wave and flap from the open windows.

For months, a new wave of plague had blanketed the city. Market vendors were selling nosegays of mint, sorrel, and butterbur. In the churches, people covered their faces with wet cloth. And in Francesco's workshops, weavers had disappeared one by one as the looms stood still and forlorn in the shadows.

Each morning, Bellina had knelt on the floor, thanking God that she was strong and healthy, and so far, the plague had managed to stay away from those she loved. But now . . . Who had died during the hours when she was occupied with overseeing the remaining embroiders in the circle? She shuddered and asked God for courage. Then, she forced herself to open the back servants' entrance.

The kitchen stood silent and empty. Bellina moved up the stairs with trepidation. In the *salotto,* she found Francesco and his mother sitting together in a silent stupor. Madre rocked back and forth, running her arthritic fingers across the purple glass beads of a rosary. Bellina's eyes flew around the room.

"Master . . . ," she began. "Lisa?" She knew that she should not address them in such a manner, without an invitation or a greeting, but she could not wait a moment longer.

Francesco stood. "Lisa is upstairs. She's fine."

Bellina felt all the wind release from her lungs. "Who then? Who has died?"

Francesco said, looking up with red-tinged eyes, "It's Camilla."

Bellina stumbled against the wall in shock. "Camilla!" She would never have guessed the young woman, in the flush of youth. "What happened?"

"Pestilence has spread through the nuns' dormitories at San Domenico," Francesco said. "By the time they realized it, it was too late. It was swift for her. I suppose that is a mercy," he said, but then his voice cracked. He pressed his fist to his lips and sat back down.

"I . . ." Bellina could barely form words.

Francesco took a deep breath. "It's spread south as far as the Ponte Vecchio. It's touched many families around my workshops at Por Santa Maria. Even Bardo, my longtime foreman, has lost his father and his wife."

"Hopefully this plague is done with this family now," Madre said. Bellina felt guilty to wish that the dreaded disease had taken the old woman instead of a girl in the flush of life. Although Madre was older and frailer, Bellina had a feeling the old crone would live forever. And Bardo . . . a widower. Bellina struggled to process the information, which shifted like sand in her mind.

"I suppose I must shut down the workshop for a while," Francesco said. "It's the last thing I want but I must do the right thing by the workers."

Bellina nodded. "Lisa . . . ," she said, already feeling the loss of Lisa's daughter as if someone had stabbed her in the gut. "I will see to her." Bellina began to turn to the stairs.

"Don't bother," Madre said. Bellina hesitated.

Francesco said, "She has locked herself away in her room. Mother and I have tried all day but she won't see us." He hesitated. "But if anyone has the power to reach her, it's you, Bellina."

"Yes, sir," she whispered. Bellina turned toward the stairs and made her way slowly into the corridor. The black cloth on the windows had cast the entire house into shadows. Bellina grasped the stair rail and trudged upstairs, where her mistress awaited her in the darkness.

BELLINA DIDN'T THINK she would ever see Lisa smile again. But then, a grandchild changed everything.

Piero's new baby was a wiggling girl named for Camilla. And the little one, with her bright plum eyes and a coat of dark hair that made her resemble a duckling, was the one thing with the power to bring Lisa from the darkness and into the light.

The wave of pestilence subsided at last, and the city reawoke from its confinement as if it had pushed aside a heavy winter blanket. Bellina followed Francesco's broad back as the family made their way to the baptistery with the baby swaddled in the finest silks. From above, neighbors and friends opened their shutters and called their congratulations into the street. A flower seller emerged from his market stall and put a white blossom into Lisa's hands.

In a pocket of her linen *camicia,* Bellina carried the tiny coral amulet she had hidden in her cabinet ever since Antonmaria Gherardini had carried baby Lisa to the old baptistery nearly four decades ago. It was just a small thing, really, but it weighed heavily in her pocket. She hoped that, if she fastened the bauble around baby Camilla's neck, it might protect her from a lifetime of misfortune.

The family collected at the doorway to the great, octagonal building as more relatives emerged from the adjacent alleys to join them. The great white, pink, and green marble panels gleamed in the sudden rake of morning light. Lisa came to stand next to Bellina, looping her arm through the crook of her elbow. Andrea, now taller than his mother, pulled himself into their group and laid his cheek affectionately on top of his mother's head.

Bellina squeezed her mistress's hand. "Your father put you in my arms right here when you were just a few days old. He made me promise to protect you for always. I was scared to death."

"And look at me now, Bellina," Lisa said, her teasing smile returning. "I am an old grandma. I think you have done your job."

IN THE BEDCHAMBER, Bellina watched Lisa loop a long, heavy golden chain over Francesco's head. The chain glimmered across his crimson silk cloak, the uniform of the city's most upstanding citizens who were called to serve a two-month term on the Signoria.

There was excitement in the household again as Francesco

kissed the top of his wife's head and left the house to walk the few blocks to the Palazzo Vecchio. In the kitchen, Madre was wagging a finger at Alessandro, who was listening patiently as he chopped vegetables for the evening's celebratory meal. She should go upstairs and change into her best dress, Bellina thought, as she knew the family expected even the servants to look their best on this day.

"Bellina, wait," Lisa said. Bellina paused in the doorway. "I have something for you." Lisa unlocked the old cabinet with an iron key. She reached into it and removed a small wooden box inlaid with small strips of wood arranged in floral designs. She handed the small box to Bellina, but Bellina only stood frozen for a few moments.

"Open it."

Bellina set the box on the bed and raised the lid. She gasped. Inside was a collection of necklaces—soft, silk cords with colored gemstones.

"Lisa," she began. "I don't . . . Surely you're not giving these to me!"

Lisa nodded. "It's not much," she said. "They are hand-me-downs, of course. But I wanted you to have them. You have always been here for me. You are the most trustworthy of servants. Besides, I have more than I will ever need."

Bellina pulled out a large green gem on a silk cord. She ran her fingers over its hard, iridescent surface. Then she held it up to her neck.

"Look at that," Lisa said. "*Perfetto.*"

Then, Lisa smiled.

Bellina thought it was the most certain type of smile—and

the most beautiful. The kind that made the corners of your eyes crinkle, just this side of breaking into laughter. The most contagious of all. Bellina couldn't help it. She smiled, too.

THE STREET CORNER in the Por Santa Maria was the right one; Bellina had walked by it a thousand times. What was more, she could hear it: the sounds of silk looms chattering down the narrow street. Her eyes scanned the buildings. There.

Bellina spied a small building, tucked comfortably between the silk workshops, tailors, and merchants lining the cobbled street. The period of mourning now past, the black curtains had been taken down from the windows. Now, they shed a warm, yellow light from the oily wicks of the lamps inside. Soon enough, the merchants would be latching their wooden battens and returning to their tables for the evening meal.

On the corner, Bellina paused and gathered herself. Beyond the row of shops, the surface of the Arno glittered as the evening glow turned the riverside and its dyers' warehouses a brilliant shade of gold—nothing but a beautiful yet shifting, hazy illusion. Only darkness and a depthless struggle below its sparkling, irresistible surface. Suppose Bardo wasn't there—or didn't want to see her? She swallowed hard. So much time had passed since they worked side by side. Would he still be in the clutches of grief? Would he invite her to step across the threshold into the warmth—or turn her away?

As she walked toward the river, she reached her hand into the pocket of her dress. She fingered the small tassel ornamented with gilded threads and silver beads that Bardo had given her without the smallest hesitation. A gift. She kept it there always.

Each time she felt her fingers run over the threads, as soft as a puppy's ear, it was a quiet reminder to Bellina that she had dared to dream of something larger than herself. That she was valued for her skill and service, yes, but not only that. She was worthy of something not only earned but freely given. Something of beauty and value, of inherent worth without any expectation of sacrifice in exchange.

When at last she arrived at Bardo's door, she pulled her hand out of her pocket and took a deep breath. Summoning all the courage she had, she pushed the shop door open as a little brass bell chimed above it.

ANNE

Paris, France
1945

The street corner in the garment district was the right one; Anne had checked it a thousand times on the map. What was more, she could hear it: the sounds of sewing machines chattering down the narrow street. The garment factories of Paris were up and running again after being battened closed for so long. Her eyes scanned the address numbers, each number in a blue square along the doorways as she passed: 32, 34, 36. There.

Anne spied a small building, tucked comfortably between the squat shops lining the street. A small sign advertised upholstery and the repair of sewing machines. Anne recognized the same lettering from the side of the old delivery truck that had carried her all the way across France. Seeing the familiar lettering advertising Corrado's shop made her head swim. How many long hours had the two of them spent together in that squeaking truck? How many confidences exchanged, how many fears and hopes expressed, even those she had never shared with anyone else?

On the corner, Anne paused and gathered herself. She swallowed hard. Suppose he wasn't there anymore? Or was already taken? He'd known her for less than a year, and that had been almost half a decade ago. Plenty of time for him to take a wife and start a family. Anne raised her fingers to her lips as if she could still feel his kiss. Five years. She was a different person now; had he changed still more, transformed among the turmoil of the war?

Summoning all the courage she had, Anne walked toward the shop. But as she got closer, she saw the rusted, rolling metal shutters, the familiar, shabby façade of an abandoned shop with its metal *volets* to keep out mal-doers as well as every speck of daylight. The windows must have once glowed with welcoming, yellow light, but now, they were battened with an ugly, dusty barricade. It was like watching the life go out of someone's eyes. Before the door, a crumpled newspaper page fluttered and caught at her feet.

LE JOUR EST ARRIVÉ, the headline read. The day has arrived. PARIS BRISE SES CHAÎNES. Yes, Anne thought. The chains were broken.

For a moment, she stood silently, watching the crumpled newspaper spin in circles on the sidewalk. Then, the door of the shop next door opened, and a man in a white apron emerged with a broom.

"Monsieur," Anne said. "*Excusez-moi*. Do you know what happened to Corrado?" She gestured to the shabby, rusted metal shutters. "The man who used to work here?"

The shop owner stopped sweeping and leaned on his broom handle, looking her up and down.

"*L'Italien?*" He shrugged. "I heard he returned to Italy with his family. It's good to be back home at last, *n'est-ce pas, mademoiselle?*"

Anne turned back to the main street but she scarcely noticed the cafes and shops that had begun to reopen, the Parisians who had begun to open their shutters, put on their nicest clothes, and come out into the sun. Instead, as she walked, she imagined

Corrado in the fold of his Florentine family. She hoped that he had found satisfaction in returning to the trade of his forefathers, and that he felt himself belonging there.

Then, Anne turned northward toward her apartment, where Marcel and her mother were waiting. She had made them promise they'd all be together at the dinner table.

Yes, she thought. It was good to be home.

LEONARDO

Amboise, France
1519

I t's because my arm has gone limp that the boys want me to sign my final testament. I don't want to do it, of course. Who wants to sign away their final wishes—to concede their end?

Salaì watches as I select a new quill from the box and struggle to attach a new tip with my one good hand. He will benefit greatly in my estate; surely he knows it. But I know this is not at the forefront of his mind. They are only looking out for my interests. Salaì and Melzi have been nothing at all if not loyal.

This signature might as well be on my own death certificate. I feel as if I'm putting my name to my last panel, and with the numb hand having gotten even worse before arriving in Amboise, I can barely do that. I rely on my left hand and try to hide the twisted knot of bones and muscle that my right hand has become. But like so many endeavors in my life, I am failing; this time, the whole world seems to know it.

They go out of their way to tell me how much value I still have to them. It only drives the point home. They say, "*You can still impart that great wisdom to others, Leonardo,*" and, "*You've earned your easier years, Master.*" But I hear only, "*This way to the grave, Master.*"

Ah, well. There is also good. I live well in the ample brick home provided for me, only a short walk away from the king's side, down a long, secret underground corridor. The king dotes on me, enamored of my name and reputation. And I'm grateful for it. Every luxury is made available to me and I no longer wish for the great travels of my past. I want for nothing: delicate, flaky pastries and crusty bread; stews and soups to warm my bones; a fine wardrobe fit for a king along with a thousand other daily comforts; interesting and intelligent visitors from the ends of the earth. These visitors. They come to see my drawings, my paintings. They copy my work. They stand before my picture of the Florentine lady and stare into her eyes.

My *Lisa*. We cling to each other in our final years, like a doddering old couple, shuffling through the final years together, sharing a sweet and simple smile. Only death will separate us. I look at her, those eyes meeting mine. She is tranquil, hands folded over her lap, her brief smile captured in paint. Behind her, floodwaters rise, threatening the languid calmness of the world around her. Who can say what others may make of her little smile? In this way she is life itself, beautiful and blushing, carrying the burden of both vitality and mortality. She looks back at me just as I have looked upon her—as a lover, a wife, the second part of my soul. A quiet yet teasing helpmate.

Salaì seems to understand. I know the dear man is worried for me, and for himself, though he needn't be. This onetime street thief shall inherit my vineyards at San Babila and several paintings. His life will be one of leisure and reward, one he's well-earned. One day, he will return home to Milan.

And as for Melzi . . .

"Master," he says as he approaches, his voice most soft and reverent, "the portrait of the Florentine lady . . . Your *Lisa*."

"Yes . . . What of her?"

He seems to struggle for words, and pauses to scan the list compiled on my last testament. "Francesco del Giocondo, her husband . . . He will want her portrait at long last, will he not?"

"Perhaps," I say. "But not yet." Melzi nods and steps back. I press my hand on my last testament and turn to the poor boy, who is only looking out for me. "Hand me my pen."

THE KING OF FRANCE never bathes alone.

At the doorway to the royal bath, two men with colorful stripes and halberds stand guard. His Royal Highness has asked me to join him in the warm waters but I decline. Even if my mind hasn't failed me yet, my old body has. Sometimes I think these powerful men desire my friendship more than my art. The most important men in the world struggle to find a single friend.

In the end, Francesco del Giocondo will never lay eyes on the now-completed portrait of his Lisa. No. But it's not because I refuse to let her go. Rather, it's because the king has insisted on hanging the panel in his royal bath chamber. There, as he lounges in the warm waters, he watches her sly smile, as if she is chuckling at his stout, mole-covered pale body in the giant basin.

I sit on the edge of the tub, sweating in my lavender silks. We converse, he in rusty Italian, and I in my halting French. Droplets hang from his thick beard as the steam rises from the surface.

"What do you see when you look at the lady, Master Leonardo?" he asks.

For a moment, there is silence as the two of us old men look back at Lisa Gherardini del Giocondo. We consider her smile, a smile that just reaches the eyes. Teasing. Secretive.

"I suppose she reminds me of home," I say at last.

"And surely you know the truth about her," His Royal Highness says, pointing his finger higher in the air. "This Florentine lady."

"What is that, Your Royal Highness?"

"This smiling lady, this *Lisa*. She is the masterpiece of your life."

MELZI

Amboise, France
1520

To Signora Lisa Gherardini del Giocondo, in Florence

My most esteemed Lady,

Perhaps you have already received word that Master Leonardo da Ser da Vinci passed to the World to Come. My master was not well in his final months and lost the use of his right arm. As long as I have breath in my body I shall feel sadness. He was like the best of fathers to me.

The portrait that Master Leonardo began of you many years ago is now in the hands of His Majesty King of France. For the last few years, it has hung on the wall of the king's private bath chamber. I thought you might like to know of its whereabouts, and that it has brought joy to the king and his court as much as it has brought honor to you and your family.

I commend myself to you,
Francesco Melzi
In Amboise

BELLINA

Florence, Italy
1520

"Where do you think you're going?"

At his worktable, Bardo stopped sewing and peered over the top of his magnifying lens at his fourteen-year-old son. The boy shrugged his shoulders. It was impossible to see his face through the fringe of hair that hung from beneath his cap and over his large, brown eyes.

"To the river," the boy said. "Some of my friends are meeting down at the old dyers' warehouse."

"No good will come of it, son . . . ," Bellina began. But she stopped herself. I'm not the boy's real mother, she thought.

But Bardo came to her aid. "Bellina is right," he said. "Keep your head down and stay with your stitching. We have orders to complete by Saturday for Giocondo's factory at Por Santa Maria."

"But they are saying there's a plot . . . There are people gathering to talk about . . . ," the boy stuttered.

Bellina pressed her lips together to avoid commenting. But no comment was needed. One more intimidating stare over the concave glass from his father and the boy acquiesced. He set down his small rucksack and returned to his workbench. He picked up a swath of silk and ran a silk thread through pursed lips before threading the needle. Bellina and Bardo exchanged wordless glances.

"I'll go check on dinner," Bellina said, rising from her bench. She grasped the worn handrail and pulled herself up the dark, twisted stairwell to the second floor, where Bardo's two daughters chopped carrots pulled from the tiny garden behind the house. Bellina listened to their whispers, their giggles, their shared confidences.

"Almost done," the older daughter said and smiled at Bellina when she emerged from the stairwell. The girls were so responsible and self-sufficient that Bellina hardly had to lift a finger. She would never replace their mother, yet they pulled Bellina into their fold as easily as if she had always been there.

Bellina turned into the tight bedchamber she shared with Bardo. The bed was neatly made with a thick woolen cover and it smelled of the hearth. A leaded window looked out over the rooftops and beyond, to the Arno.

From under the bed, Bellina pulled out the beautifully inlaid box of gems that Lisa had given her. She had no need for such luxuries. Perhaps one day, when one of Bardo's daughters married or survived the ordeal of birth, she would pull one of the baubles out and offer it as a gift—a talisman, some protection. Until then, best to keep them safe.

Bellina opened the creaking door to the old wooden cabinet and pressed the box deep inside. Then she turned the iron key and locked them away.

ANNE

Paris, France
1945

Anne made a note in her ledger and walked to the nearest of the hulking windows, pushing it wide to lean out over a bright, midsummer morning. Her eye followed the lines of the building to a street utterly hidden under the swarm of people. Outside the museum entrances, hundreds, maybe thousands, had gathered. Anne saw young women fanning themselves as they chatted in little knots; young men pushing each other around in lumbering bravado; mothers trying to organize scattered clutches of overexcited children; fathers lifting little boys and girls on their shoulders.

"So many people," said a soft voice behind her; she felt a hand at the small of her back.

She turned to smile at her brother, who looked handsome in his Louvre guard uniform and cap. "Just visiting a museum . . . I suppose it's the best way for us to feel like we have our lives back," she said.

On the other side of the empty gallery, Pierre talked animatedly with Kiki about a painting of a nymph and a satyr. Anne smiled at the old guard—still in his shabby uniform jacket but leaning on a new walking cane. And her mother—gaunt, wrinkled, and bedecked in a dress of frayed fringe. Like Pierre, she had endured. Anne shook her head and smiled. They were quite a pair.

"Ready?"

Anne turned to see Lucie standing there. Lucie, André, Frédérique, and other family members of the Louvre staff had gotten a preview of the galleries before they opened to the public. In the Galerie Daru, a ground-floor space usually reserved for ancient sculpture, the curators had hung the *Mona Lisa* against dark red velour, and placed a metal barrier so the crowds couldn't get too close.

André appeared on her left, his cheeks glowing with pleasure. He peered at the crowd waiting outside the museum. "This place is the heartbeat of Paris; and Paris is the heart of France itself. They must have been lost without it."

"*I* felt lost without it," Anne admitted. For a few moments, she stood in awe that everything taken out of the Louvre all those years ago had made it back. It was incredible to think about the scale of their efforts to save even the smallest item, and that she had played a small role. "We had all the paintings with us the whole time, but in this place, they finally feel at home," she said.

Lucie turned to Anne. "When we left the Louvre, well, most of us were high-ranking staff who'd been dedicated to it for many years. You were barely out of school, and yet you let us drag you along." She squeezed Anne's hand. "Do you regret the fact that you agreed to come with us?"

Anne paused. She thought of the loneliness of Louvigny, mites in the velvet of the *Mona Lisa*. The cold eyes of German soldiers. The wrench of leaving Montauban. The crack of a grenade, and agony blossoming through her arm. Corrado's kiss, locked away forever inside her heart.

Looking across the room, she saw her entire world: Marcel, wiry, battle-hardened, all grown up. Chopin—beautiful Sara—no longer a hero of the Resistance but simply Marcel's better half, her hand clasped firmly in his. Kiki smiling merrily, fanning herself with a gloved hand. They stood together and gazed at the Florentine lady in the black dress.

"No," Anne said to Lucie. "Where else would I have gone?"

The doors at the far end of the gallery banged open. René strode into the room, his eyes glowing with excitement. There was color in his cheeks again, and he moved with a sweeping decorum befitting a hero. "Come!" he boomed. "It's time."

They gathered around the place where a small painting, a painting that looked at first utterly unremarkable beside the sweeping magnitude of *Wedding at Cana,* hung unassumingly on the red velvet. Yet when Anne looked at it, everything else in the world seemed to melt away except the dark eyes of the lady who smiled out at the world, her expression filled with mystery.

It was the secret that an artist conveys from his heart to the heart of the viewer, that thing beauty does to all those who behold it. A stirring, a personal and private flicker in the soul of those privileged enough to gaze upon something unique in the world. Anne had traveled the length and breadth of France to save it, and she would do it all again.

"That's my daughter!" Anne heard her mother say to one of the guards. "She was always so responsible, but then she did something so . . ."

But Anne couldn't hear the rest because all at once, the museum doors swung open and the people of Paris rushed into the Louvre. There was only the sound of a crowd barging in, thousands of footsteps in the galleries and past the stairs, past the impressive *Victory of Samothrace,* her winged arms opened to welcome them after six long years.

Anne headed over to where Kiki, Marcel, and Sara were standing, admiring the Florentine lady, who smiled at them as if she had known all along that everything would turn out all right. Anne pushed against her brother's warm bulk. "Are you ready?" she said. "All of Paris is coming through the doors of this place."

"Of course," he said. "They have come to see the lady."

Together, they listened to the crowd trundle toward them, a sound like the roar of the sea.

ACKNOWLEDGMENTS

Over the course of writing this book, I felt a special bond with Anne and her *Mona Lisa*. You see, I too found myself suddenly untethered from my normal life.

When the global pandemic hit the United States in March 2020, I was deep into writing this book and my family was in the midst of a cross-country move. In the mornings, I worked my way through the story of *The Stolen Lady*. In the afternoons, I packed the belongings of our family of six into a series of boxes and crates, then moved everything to storage for, well, who knew how long. Among the last things I packed in my study was a small oil painting on panel, Italian and very old, of a woman with a mysterious grin on her face. I don't know much about her, only that a painter long ago tried to emulate Leonardo da Vinci.

For months, our family waited out the situation at our vacation home, feeling gratitude for such a place to quarantine. We adjusted to the adventure of homeschooling and videoconferencing from various corners of the house. We worried about and missed our loved ones. We let go of planning for the future and lived in the moment. I rose early every day and revised my manuscript. When the kids returned to a hybrid schedule, we transitioned to a temporary apartment near school. Then we found a home, gutted it, and began renovating. As I went through the final round of copyedits on *The Stolen Lady* more than a year after packing up, our new house was mostly finished. The moving truck arrived, and we unloaded crates and boxes. When I pulled my mysterious smiling lady from her box at last, I felt our peripatetic year come to a close. It had been a long haul.

With each book I've written, my family has always been at the top of my list of people to thank. With this one, they went above and beyond. My husband understood when my alarm went off at 4:30 or 5:00 A.M., seven days a week. My children understood when I shut the door, went out to a lawn chair with my laptop, or fell asleep on the couch with the dog. They all understood when I booked myself into a nearby hotel and shut off my phone for forty-eight hours to work through a particularly tough stretch of revisions.

In a year when no one could leave home, traveling vicariously with Anne, Bellina, and Leonardo da Vinci truly kept me sane. In my imagination, I whisked myself away to Renaissance Florence, over the Alps to the Louvre, to the breathtaking châteaux of the Loire Valley, and to the hulking medieval abbeys of southern France. What an incredible imaginary journey during the strangest of times.

Books have the power to transport us, to allow us to escape to another time and place, just by reading some words on a page or screen. That's the closest thing to magic I know. If the pandemic has taught us anything, it's that art matters. In times of strife, we turn to stories—books, movies, dance, the visual arts. Stories and creativity help make meaning out of chaos and fear. They make us human.

Of course, nothing would have made me happier than sitting

amongst a pile of acid-free cartons, inhaling the wonderful scent of historical documents in the Florence state archives or the reading room of the Bibliothèque Nationale, just as in the old days. All the same, I am grateful to the staff at the Archives Nationales, the Bibliothèque Nationale, and the Louvre archives for patiently answering my questions, so poorly expressed in French via email. Many thanks to Éditions Plon for permission to translate and share a portion of Lucie Mazauric's fascinating memoir.

Special thanks go to Jessica Hatch, editor and early reader extraordinaire, for her unique brand of tough love and thoroughness. When I get an email from Jessica, I know it's time to brew some coffee, take a deep breath, and find my highlighter. Thanks to my agent, Jenny Bent, for her eagle-eyed insights, and to the team at the Bent Agency for helping me behind the scenes. Thanks to Madeline Grubb for creating the map showing the itinerary of the *Mona Lisa*. Thanks to the production team at William Morrow and especially to the book designers, who pour their creativity into each project. Last but certainly not least, thanks to my editor, Tessa Woodward. I am so happy for our continued partnership in putting beautiful books into the world. For me, it is truly a dream come true.

About the author

About the book

Insights,
Interviews
& More . . .

Meet Laura Morelli

Davide Mandolini

LAURA MORELLI is an art historian and *USA Today* bestselling historical novelist. She holds a Ph.D. in art history from Yale University and is the author of fiction and nonfiction inspired by the history of art. She has taught college students in the United States and Italy, and has developed lessons for TED-Ed. Her flagship shopping guidebook, *Made in Italy,* has led travelers off the beaten track for more than two decades. Her award-winning historical novels include *The Painter's Apprentice: A Novel of 16-Century Venice, The Gondola Maker, The Giant: A Novel of Michelangelo's David,* and *The Night Portrait: A Novel of World War II and Da Vinci's Italy.* Learn more at lauramorelli.com. ᴄᴪ

About *The Stolen Lady*

The Louvre is arguably the world's most famous museum, and the *Mona Lisa* is its most famous treasure. Much like Anne and millions of Louvre visitors, I stood before the *Mona Lisa* as a young person and felt the old Florentine lady change me. The mystery of her smile sparked a curiosity. It helped set me in a direction to study art history and everything it has to teach us about our own time. This wonderful image is in part responsible for the years I spent living and studying in Paris, the French countryside, and Italy.

The *Mona Lisa—Ma Donna Lisa, La Gioconda, La Joconde*—had already gained a certain level of notoriety after the French Revolution, when the painting moved from the French royal collection to the Louvre. But after an Italian worker stole the painting in 1911—and after it was returned to the Louvre two years later in a widely publicized event—the *Mona Lisa* was suddenly propelled to fame. In the intervening years, the *Mona Lisa* has become more than just a famous painting. She is an icon, a symbol, an image immediately recognizable to every person on the globe, regardless of their knowledge of the lady or her history.

In the years since that dramatic theft, credentialed scholars, art enthusiasts, and conspiracy theorists have developed hypotheses about this portrait. Most ▶

accept that Leonardo da Vinci is its maker, but theories about the lady and her mysterious smile range far and wide. The traditional interpretation is that Lisa represents the wife of Francesco del Giocondo, a Florentine textile trader. But it's been proposed that she's inspired by Salaì, that she's a latent portrait of Leonardo's mother, or that she's a self-portrait of Leonardo, among many other suggestions. (You can learn more about these and other compelling—often zany—theories about Lisa and her smile on my website at lauramorelli.com/lady.)

As a twelve-year-old visiting Paris, I wrote in my diary that even though I had seen the *Mona Lisa* smiling, something about her expression seemed sad to me. The idea of the melancholy Lisa stayed with me, and many years later, I still wondered about it. What was behind the enigmatic expression? Just why was Lisa smiling—or perhaps not? As I began to immerse myself in art history and learn more about the portrait's probable circumstances, I wondered why it was never delivered to its patron, Francesco del Giocondo, and why Leonardo kept it with him for the rest of his life. What was it about this picture that might have obsessed the artist so much that he worked on it until his death? Because I couldn't find any truly satisfactory answers amid the vast scholarship on the *Mona Lisa,* I began to think about these questions instead as a historical novelist.

To the best of my ability, Lisa, Francesco, their children, and their extended family are all based on the piecemeal evidence we have for these historical figures. We know, for example, that Lisa Gherardini del Giocondo gave birth to six living infants, but three, perhaps four, of the children predeceased her—a common enough occurrence at the time but one whose impact on women and families, I think, is underrated. (For many more biographical clues about Lisa herself, I recommend Dianne Hales's excellent book, *Mona Lisa: A Life Discovered*.) We know Francesco concentrated his textile operations in the Por Santa Maria section of Florence, and that his brothers opened branches of the family business in Lyon and Lisbon. In his will, Francesco referred to Lisa using the unusual term *mulier ingenua*, which translates to something like "noble wife." Francesco and his sons were buried in a family tomb at Santissima Annunziata, while Lisa was interred in the convent of Sant'Orsola, where she had donated much of her time toward the end of her life. As always in a historical novel, I have taken some license with these Renaissance characters. For example, Francesco's mother was probably deceased by the time this story unfolds. Francesco and Lisa's daughter, Camilla, entered the convent in 1511, not in 1508.

Gherardo Gherardini, Lisa's cousin, is documented along with three other youths who were arrested for hurling ▶

rocks at Michelangelo's *David* as it made
its slow, four-day procession from the
cathedral workyard to the Piazza della
Signoria in 1504. All four boys were
raised in families with pro-Medici
sympathies, while the *David* was likely
seen as a symbol of Florence's status
as an independent republic. It's mind-
boggling to think about the *David*
and the *Mona Lisa* being created at the
same time, just a short walk from each
other. Truth is often stranger than
fiction.

Bellina is a fictional character, which
makes it possible for her to navigate
everything from Lisa's bedchamber
to the visitor's corridor at Santissima
Annunziata to the powder keg of secret
Florentine meeting spots during the rise
of Girolamo Savonarola. Stefano, Dolce,
and Bardo—also fictional—helped
shape my depiction of a city ripped apart
by the emotional allegiances that must
have severed friends and families during
this tumultuous chapter in Florentine
history. As a novelist, I have long wanted
to explore the mind of someone who
threw a treasured possession onto the
Bonfire of the Vanities in February 1497.
Poor, tormented Bellina turned out to
be the perfect victim.

The World War II sections also
portray fictional characters—Anne,
Corrado, Étienne, Marcel, and Kiki—
intermingling with those inspired
by real life—characters like Lucie,
Jacqueline, André, René, and Monsieur
Schommer. An archival photograph of

an unnamed gray-haired Louvre guard
with a spunky expression, a wonderful
handlebar mustache, and his hand on
the secret crate with three red dots was
my inspiration for Pierre.

My spark of inspiration for Anne's
character came from a single line in a
1944 BBC broadcast: "*La* Victoire du
Samothrace *fait du vélo.*" ("The *Victory
of Samothrace* is riding a bicycle.")
BBC announcers broadcast coded
radio messages like these so the French
Resistance would know their secret
messages had landed in the hands of
the Allies. I wondered who this *Victory
of Samothrace* might be—perhaps a brave
yet unassuming-looking person riding
a bicycle, carrying critical information
about the Louvre's hidden depots.
The character of an unlikely heroine—
a symbol of victory just like the ancient
winged sculpture itself—sprang forth
in my imagination. Suddenly, there was
Anne, riding her rusty bike down a
wooded path.

The true story of the Louvre staff
and their ever-shifting chess game
of treasures is surely one of the most
amazing adventures of World War II.
Gerri Chanel's nonfiction book on the
subject, *Saving Mona Lisa,* is an excellent
read and a testament to the power of
individual leadership in a time of crisis.
With a level of formality, polish, and
high diplomatic skill that only a 1940s
French museum head could pull off,
the Louvre's director, Jacques Jaujard,
managed to stall, delay, excuse, and ▶

bureaucratize things just long enough to hold off the Nazis and allow his museum's masterpieces to return home unscathed.

Meanwhile, in the countryside, Jaujard's staff—many of them women of exceptional courage—protected thousands of priceless, irreplaceable masterpieces with their own lives. Lucie Mazauric scrambled the inventories at Chambord under the Germans' noses. Christiane Desroches-Noblecourt, curator of antiquities, was one of the few staff members with a German *ausweis* pass, which allowed her to pass resistance groups' messages in and out of Occupied France. Thanks to the Louvre staff, who put the safety of these works ahead of their own needs, these masterpieces returned to the museum. Those of us in the ensuing generations benefit from their acts of bravery in the face of what must have seemed like one impossible situation after another.

French resistance groups gained steam after the fall of 1942, when the Vichy government's forced-work program, the Service du Travail Obligatoire, recruited young men to fill labor shortages in Germany. Many thousands of young people fled into the woods, organizing into paramilitary groups with networks across France and beyond. The Louvre staff's collaboration with these resistance groups played an important role in the return of these masterpieces to Paris. Many Louvre depot directors, including Lucie Mazauric's husband, André Chamson, were closely involved with cells of *maquis* during their time in southern France. Museum guards—many of whom were World War I veterans—and other depot workers helped funnel cash, ammunition, weapons, and information to and from the *maquis*. Jeanne Boitel, a French actress and resistance leader with the code name Mozart, met Jacques Jaujard during the course of her resistance activities and married him after the war. She inspired Chopin, the *maquis* leader in this story.

When the *Mona Lisa* returned to the Louvre after nearly six years of hiding in her specially designed crate, enthusiastic crowds lined up outside the museum to welcome her. Louvre curators hung the portrait in a special gallery on the museum's ground floor so they could funnel in the eager museumgoers.

Today, in addition to braving the crushing crowds surrounding the Florentine lady inside her bulletproof vitrine at the Louvre, you can visit many other sites that play a role in this story. In Florence, Lisa and Francesco's house still stands, in a much-altered state, at 23 via della Stufa. A short walk away is the monastery of Santissima Annunziata and its wonderful square, the cathedral, the Piazza della Signoria, and the via Por Santa Maria leading to the banks ▶

of the Arno. You can still buy handcrafted
scents and beauty concoctions from
the apothecary at Santa Maria Novella.
Traveling north to Milan, you can view
Leonardo's famous *Last Supper* in the
refectory of Santa Maria delle Grazie,
as well as visit the Castello Sforzesco
where Leonardo spent more than a
decade working for Ludovico Sforza
before returning home to Florence.

Across the Alps, you can admire
Leonardo's double-helix staircase at
the Château de Chambord. About an
hour's drive to the southwest stands
the lovely little Château du Clos Lucé
in Amboise where Leonardo da Vinci
took his last breath. Loc-Dieu, the
medieval abbey church that once held
thousands of the Louvre treasures,
stands like a bastion in the peaceful
countryside. At Montauban, the Musée
Ingres operates as an important regional
art museum along the river Tarn.
The Château de Montal is also open
to visitors as a historical monument.

The Stolen Lady is the most research-
intensive novel I've ever undertaken
(the *Mona Lisa,* Leonardo da Vinci, *and*
World War II? What was I thinking?).
When I look back through the centuries
at these artistic achievements and the
courage of so many individuals, I feel
incapable of doing their stories justice
inside a single book. All the same,
I hope to have brought to life in these
pages something of the incredible
and important adventure of a single

portrait, one that stands as a symbol of the highest aspirations of human creativity.

For more historical background, videos, images, research, lists of further reading, and resources related to World War II art theft and this book, as well as access to my online seminar on the Secrets of the Mona Lisa, visit lauramorelli.com/lady. ∿

In Lucie's Words

Whenever I start a historical novel, I always begin with primary sources. Nothing compares with traversing the past alongside a person who lived in the time period and experienced things firsthand. One of the best primary research sources for *The Stolen Lady* is a memoir written by the Louvre archivist Lucie Mazauric, whose fictionalized alter ego plays an important role in this novel.

Lucie's husband, André Chamson, was an acclaimed curator and Nobel Prize–nominated novelist. During their time hiding the Louvre treasures, André reportedly hid some handwritten pages in a hollow tree at Montauban. But it was Lucie's own words—her hopes and fears as a Louvre specialist, her worries as a wife and mother—that captured my imagination.

Lucie's memoir about the Louvre staff's flight from Paris—a work both fascinating and immeasurably valuable—was published in 1978 as *Le Louvre en Voyage*. Thanks to Éditions Plon for permission to share this excerpt with you. The translation from the original French to English is my own.

From Chambord to Loc-Dieu

We had with us Isabella d'Este, *the beautiful drawing in the Louvre attributed to Leonardo da Vinci (which is perhaps not by Leonardo da Vinci and which is perhaps not a portrait of Isabella, but which is, certainly, a wonderful* masterpiece). It shows a beautiful young woman in profile. Her lovely hair is styled with headbands and she wears a bodice with a low neckline and wide sleeves in striped fabric. Like the Mona Lisa, she had her own personal case. It was a small crate. Because of its size, they did not store the drawing in a truck so as not to put it at risk, but it was entrusted to the best driver of the convoy (that was Madame d'Eugny, not me), with instructions not to leave it day or night. In our overnight camps, this drawing remained between our beds like the sword between Tristan and Isolde . . .

Our truck convoy was impressive. The heavy packages containing the rolled-up paintings worried us a lot. In the event of a breakdown, their unloading would have been very difficult, but we had three escort vehicles and even a tow truck, which was a great safety . . .

The gathering took place on the lawn in front of [Chambord] castle. All those who were not leaving came to say goodbye to us. They both pitied and envied us. We were heading toward a very different destiny, and we did not know when and how we would meet again. In our turn, with our precious baggage, we entered the moving river, teeming with people, which rolled rumbling toward the south.

The hardest part was the start, the Chambord-Valençay stage. There were vehicles all over the place. The terrible traffic on the roads hampered our progress, and on ascent toward Valençay, I had the misfortune to catch my bumper on my friend Madame Delaroche-Vernet's ▶

vehicle. *We would never have gotten out of it—and we would have ended up being crushed by the flood of cars, which their drivers steered like sleepwalkers, without seeing the obstacles—if not for a strong guy who unhooked us and cut short our gratitude by saying: "We are already pissed off, so what would we do if, on top of that, we didn't do ourselves this favor?" This kindness helped us endure the rest. In civilian cars, soldiers crowded with other soldiers and civilians, a confusion that seemed quite natural. Children were piled onto army trucks. And in this mess, we had to admit that our panic was more palpable than sadness. German planes constantly flew over the roads. If they had wanted, this exodus could have been carnage.*

In Valençay, the first night, we were accommodated as best we could. The castle was full, housing a large number of works of art, many museum officials, and refugees. Our sleep was not peaceful. In the dark room assigned to us, a strong bombardment woke us with a start. It was the first we heard so close by. Fortunately, it did not touch the castle. Early the next morning, we hit the road. There was no question of delaying, as the advance of the Germans was continuing rapidly . . .

Loc-Dieu

At Loc-Dieu, we thought we were at the edge of the world, safe from all threats. The management wanted us to quickly give them a complete inventory of the three

thousand paintings gathered around us.
At the moment, the cases were all sealed
and it was already a difficult operation.
I remember a morning when Suzanne
Kahn [a Louvre curator] and I, wishing to
count the boxes in each row, had to start
the work over several times, climbing the
stacks, without ever finding the same
number, so many boxes were piled up
and tangled together. Opening a crate
was an adventure! Most of them,
compartmentalized inside, contained
a large number of paintings of different
sizes. They were crammed with fiber
and paper pads that needed to be saved
and which, when unpacked, formed a
huge clutter and posed a fire hazard. We
could then reseal the boxes that had been
checked and refill them carefully. In this
way, we moved very slowly. All our records
agreed with the original lists, and that
foretold the success of this operation.
But the work would take a long time
to achieve, and we were aggrieved that
we could not say immediately to Paris:
"Everything is here, so don't worry," which
would have allowed management to say
that our evacuation was complete, was
performed in perfect order, and that no
one had to interfere.

During this time, life was getting
organized as best it could. Miraculously,
one of the last couriers from Blois brought
me a blessed interzone "gray card," with
which I could circulate without misleading
the gendarmes. It arrived just in time. In
addition to helping with the inventories, I
was responsible for shopping for our meals.
Every day, in my car, I went down with ▶

In Lucie's Words *(continued)*

another lady to do our collective shopping in Villefranche-de-Rouergue. The inhabitants of Villefranche were of a kindly, reserved character, half mountain people, half people of the plains. Relations with them were easy, especially for me, who found in this country some of the features of my native Cévennes. Refueling was not yet disrupted. As a precaution, we bought yards of sausages that we dried in our medieval rooms, where they made very surreal garlands. Butter was already scarce, and we replaced it for breakfast with Cantal cheese—excellent, by the way—but eventually we grew tired of eating it. Just seeing it, we were full. I'm not sure how I handled my job as a kind of boarding school supplier, but I flourished in my world somehow and learned a lot. As at Chambord, any work was good for me, whether making menus, bookkeeping, cards, typing, inventory work, etc.

Large family groups marked our time at Loc-Dieu. As soon as we were together, my husband and I, we made the decision to go get our little girl. She was in the Cévennes, with her grandmother, in the small mountain farm that my mother had managed to buy for us at the beginning of 1940 with the modest royalties of the last book my husband wrote during the first months of the war. No question of going to Cévennes by rail. It would have taken eight days. No way to use our own car for lack of gasoline. No question of using the gas at the depot, which was reserved for the safety of the works. We had to make do with the few buses that were still running, making a detour via Rodez *and Millau. On all the roads that started from Rodez, we met bands of soldiers who circulated on foot, in all directions, without leaders, walking toward who knows what encampments, in a state of disorder and indescribable filth. It was not a pretty sight . . .*

Loc-Dieu to Chambord

Italy having entered the war on June 10, 1940, under dubious conditions, as one knows, we had every reason to fear they would take advantage of the situation and put their own claims back on the table. We had to be able to answer for the works in our possession, and the documents that authenticated our property were in Chambord, in the museum archives. I was therefore asked to go to Chambord to take all necessary measures for the conservation of these documents. We even thought I might bring them across the demarcation line, because we feared the Germans might seal our archives, as they had done for other archives, in order to make them inaccessible in case we needed them.

So I received my orders for Chambord. I still have them. The purpose of this mission was to be kept secret. It was July 22, 1940. France was still embroiled in the disorder of armistice, and the roads were uncertain. My daughter and my husband were worried that I would be lost so soon after finding me and were anxious for me to take a long drive alone in the car with such poor driving experience. André was not yet demobilized and could not ▸

accompany me in uniform until the end of the trip. But it was decided that he would come with me to the limits of the occupied zone and wait for my return to the Château de Valençay, still occupied by the museums. My little girl was entrusted to our friends at Loc-Dieu . . .

We set off together on the road to Saint-Aignan, the dividing line between the two zones on the edge of the Cher. Then I continued the journey alone. It was the first time I had seen these places since the defeat. I was terribly moved. I had asked the soldiers at the line how the Germans at the post would behave toward the French. They told me it depended on the arrival of beer during the day. This shipment must have been normal that day because they let me pass without difficulty. They were neither gracious nor the opposite; they looked carefully at my papers, without comment. I liked that just fine. But I felt a new humiliation when I realized I needed a German stamp to travel within the country of Ronsard and François and I could not hold back my tears when I got back to my car after the check. This was especially true when I saw, on the edge of a ditch, a smashed French tank called the Vercingetorix. It was absurd, but it made my cup overflow. I mourned at the same time the defeat of Gaul and that of France: I felt in full Déroulède [Paul Déroulède, the French nationalist poet]. I was ashamed, but I could not help it. I owe the truth to say that the German soldiers watched me cry without anger, with a kind of pity that hardly consoled me.

In Chambord, I found my old "Schommer friends," who welcomed me warmly and sheltered me at the château. This time, there was no question of staying at Hotel Le Meur. The Germans occupied it. The old guards' canteen facing the Henry II wing was also used by German soldiers, who sang in chorus while marching. The sound of their boots was awful, regulated like an unforgiving mechanism, but the songs were beautiful, I must admit. Well rhymed; too well rhymed. Yet they were so unusual that I find them in the background in all my nightmares of these dark years. The Schommers told me what had happened since our departure from Chambord, the last moments of the exodus, the madness, the hysteria, the fear, the diseases, the wounded, the castle closed like a fortress for security, the arrival at a great spectacle of the German officers, the first reports, the return to Paris . . . For my part, I told them the details of our voyage and our installation at Loc-Dieu.

But we had to get to work. I found the documents I needed quickly, thanks to my files. They formed a fairly large mass of original pieces. Some large folio inventories were part of it. What to do? If I took them, they couldn't fail to attract the attention of occupants as they passed through the area. They were in danger of being confiscated, which would have been catastrophic because they were unique documents. I took it upon myself, despite the orders I had received, to leave them at Chambord and to copy the passages that concerned only the captures during the Revolution. ▶

In Lucie's Words *(continued)*

I spent two days and two nights without sleep, working tirelessly. I was thinking of my husband who was waiting for me in Valençay, of my daughter who was waiting for me in Loc-Dieu, and that gave me wings. All this work resulted in a very handy scribble that I could decipher on my own, that I could easily fit into my suitcases, that would not attract attention, and that I could easily record at Loc-Dieu. Then I dispersed all the original documents thus recopied in the many archive boxes that remained in Chambord. I took careful note of where I put them . . . One would never go looking for them there. Only a specialist working several months in a row could have reconstructed these dislocated files and seized them. So I left completely reassured about the mission. I was able to execute for Hautecoeur a small alphabetical file of works taken from Italy that would indicate exactly for each of them the origin of our possession and the treaty or the agreement that confirmed it, whenever possible. This I did as soon as I arrived in Loc-Dieu. Then I left the "Schommers" and Chambord once again, just before the rules for crossing the area became more severe, and crossed the demarcation line without incident.

Montauban

Each day, storage got easier. All our paintings, the greatest masterpieces of the Louvre, except the very large-format works left in Sourches, were now within reach, organized by period, numbered, humbly posed without frame one against another, following a principle so simple that it did not take more than one or two minutes to reach them, wherever they were. The Mona Lisa had a place of her own in the charming, tiny office that René Huyghé had set up in the corner tower of the museum. From time to time, we opened her double box to see if she was doing well. It was a very tired painting, and in order to see all the details, it had to be presented against a white background. Many times I have taken off my white coat and put it under the panel to facilitate this examination. Despite her dilapidated condition, she seemed quite solid—she was more worn out than sick—and if one had the wisdom not to try to restore it (there was no question of doing this), it could last the years without the wear marks on it becoming more pronounced. We looked at her closely, as a doctor scrutinizes a face and analyzes the smallest clues, signs of some secret illness.

After the landing in North Africa in November 1942, the Germans invaded the unoccupied zone. One morning at dawn, the prefect Martin warned Huyghé and my husband of the imminent arrival of the Germans . . . The next day, the French were gone and the Germans were there. They were quietly taking possession of the city. They also seized all the food reserves, which they had no need—sugar, pasta, coffee, chocolate—which had been stored in the barracks in anticipation of hard times and which should have been, before their arrival, distributed to the undernourished population. We had ▶

In Lucie's Words *(continued)*

lost everything, even our false freedom. Bondage was everywhere. In addition to personal and national worries, there were professional anxieties. They ended up making us forget all other concerns. All day long, from the windows of the Musée Ingres, we watched the German troops parade without stopping on the bridge of the Tarn. Certainly, the Anglo-Americans were warned clandestinely of our presence on this bridgehead, but the slightest bomb thrown without order risked provoking a catastrophe. We had, I repeat, in a small space, 3,500 paintings, among them the most beautiful in the world. It was an atrocious day, one of the darkest in the war, lived in a sense of utter helplessness.

In this misfortune, I remember a small fact that particularly hurt me. On a bridge over the Tarn, I saw a group of Germans, mounted in a tank, crossing the river. They were cheerful, noisy, in good health, happy with their group, delighted to discover this rose-colored town on the banks of its great river. They thought more of taking pictures, like tourists, than fighting like warriors and it was a concert of "so schon, sher schon" [sic]. It was truly the triumphal entry into a beautiful conquered country, the quiet occupation of the landscape, and this all-natural takeover was more humiliating than a hard-lost battle, their cameras more evil than their submachine guns.

The next afternoon, we made a decision. We could not think of moving from the depot as long as the Germans were in the area, but we could immediately put ourselves in a position to move when the time was right. First, we could start crating the smallest, most delicate paintings that took the longest to wrap, and take the boxes down to the cellar. The sixteenth-century portraits, the Clouets, the Fouquets, were carefully put away, and we had a very busy afternoon. Once again, we saw the calming value of our work. We would dive into our files, we would look at the masterpieces, we would put them away, and at the same time our personal anxiety diminished.

La Treyne

From the start of our stay in La Treyne, my husband established close contacts with the maquis *in the region, who, alongside Jewish persecution and the institution of the STO [Service du Travail Obligatoire], were gaining more importance. He saw them regularly, and his visits discreetly increased. The wild landscape of Les Causses made for an excellent refuge, and the few large farms there were more than enough to supply these groups. Little by little, above the local chiefs, a sort of general staff was emerging, including our friend Charles Hilsum, who was just coming out of Vichy prisons. Allied airdrops were beginning to supply weapons in fairly large quantities to the FTP [Francs-Tireurs et Partisans, an armed resistance organization]. We often found containers in the woods.*

My husband soon led a double life. Head of depot at La Treyne, he became Commandant Lauter when he went up to the maquis. *While most of his friends* ▶

In Lucie's Words (*continued*)

had taken pseudonyms drawn from names of mountains or regions very close to ours (he could have been called Aigoual, like the mountain that had enchanted his childhood), André had chosen the name of the small river of Lauter, which separates France from Germany, the river on the banks of which he was often found during the winter of 1939–1940. Such a choice seemed natural to him and almost necessary, because it emphasized the liberation of Alsace, and until the liberation of Alsace, there was no total liberation for France.

While awaiting this liberation, he was studying fire plans and ambushes, or helping to refuel the maquis staff.

The contact between André and the maquis was most often provided by a person who shared her life between Souillac and Les Causses. I was always a little annoyed when I noticed that in order to talk to André, she was waiting for me to leave the room. I thought I was being treated like a child. I now know that the precaution was wise and that it was better that few people knew the secrets and the places of refuge of the resistance fighters. ∾

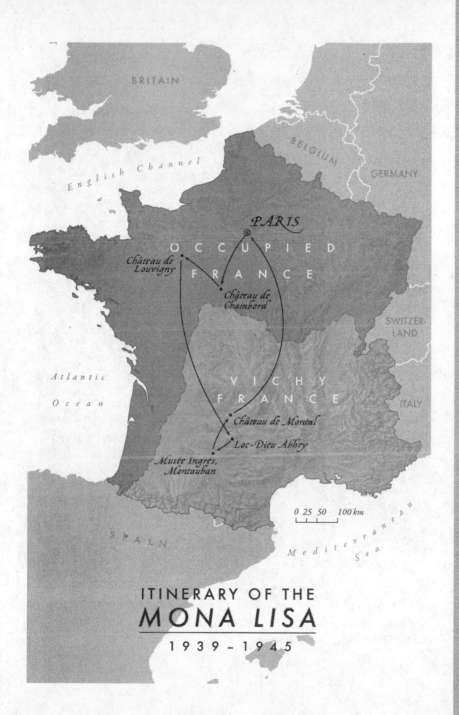

BRITAIN

English Channel

BELGIUM

GERMANY

PARIS

OCCUPIED

Château de
Louvigny

FRANCE

Château de
Chambord

Atlantic

Ocean

SWITZER-
LAND

VICHY

FRANCE

ITALY

Château de Montal

Loc-Dieu Abbey

Musée Ingres,
Montauban

0 25 50 100 km

SPAIN

Mediterranean

Sea

ITINERARY OF THE
MONA LISA
1939-1945

German soldier on guard at Chambord castle, 1940. © *bpk Bildagentur/ Hanns Hubmann (1910–1996)/Art Resource, NY*

Return of the masterpieces to the Louvre after the war, 1945. © *Pierre Jahan (1909–2003)/Roger-Viollet*

Opening the specially made crate protecting the *Mona Lisa*. © *Pierre Jahan (1909–2003)/Roger-Viollet*

The *Winged Victory of Samothrace* descends the Louvre's Daru staircase on wooden runners. © *Ministère de la Culture—Médiathèque du Patrimoine/ Noël Le Boyer (1883–1967)/dist. RMN/Art Resource, NY*

The *Mona Lisa*'s secret wooden crate with the three red dots, indicating a work of inestimable value. © *Pierre Jahan (1909–2003)/ Roger-Viollet*

Reading Group Guide

1. Leonardo da Vinci's portrait of the *Mona Lisa* stands at the center of this story. Before reading *The Stolen Lady,* what preconceptions did you have about this portrait? How has your appreciation of this painting changed since reading this story? What do you think is special about this portrait, and why do you think it's so famous?

2. Anne begins with the belief that she's "just a typist," but she ends the story by playing a critical role in the fate of the Louvre's works of art. At what point does Anne make a shift toward a more active role in saving the Louvre's works of art? What other choices do you think she might have had? What choice do you think *you* would make in a similar situation?

3. Throughout the novel, Bellina walks a thin line between protecting her mistress and putting the family at risk. How do you think Bellina navigated the narrow set of choices a servant woman might have had in Renaissance Florence? How might things have turned out differently for her if her indiscretions had been discovered?

4. Bellina wrestles with how luxurious material goods might be considered sinful or a force for good. Can you think of other examples in our contemporary society where people must weigh a similar question?

5. How have Bellina's, Lisa's, and Anne's upbringings prepared them—or not—for the trials and tribulations they face in this story?

6. Leonardo da Vinci spent much of his professional life striving to be a great inventor and engineer, while history remembers him first and foremost as a painter. Why do you think this is? Do you think he would be surprised to learn that his *Mona Lisa* is the most famous painting in the world?

7. Why do you think Bellina decides to hide Lisa's portrait? What does she risk? Would you have done the same? Why or why not?

8. How do the themes of hiding and secrets weave throughout the story? What are each of the main characters—Anne, Bellina, Leonardo, and Lisa—hiding from others? What are they hiding from themselves? ▶

9. How much freedom do Bellina and Anne have to make choices about their own futures? What are the constraints on their choices, and how do they navigate these barriers given the circumstances of the times in which they lived?

10. What parallels did you draw between characters in Renaissance Florence and those in World War II France?

11. In the Renaissance story line, the French are the invaders, while in the World War II story line, the French themselves are invaded. In the midst of war and political turmoil, what is the role of art? How does art retain its value when so many human lives are on the line?

12. In this story, what is "stolen" and who is the thief? ∾

Discover great authors, exclusive offers, and more at hc.com.